Ans	_____	M.L.	
ASH	_____	MLW	_____
Bev	_____	Mt.Pl	_____
C.C.	_____	NLM	_____
C.P.	_____	Ott	_____
Dick	_____	PC	_____
DRZ	_____	PH	_____
ECH	_____	P.P.	_____
ECS	_____	Pion.P.	_____
Gar	_____	Q.A.	_____
GRM	_____	Riv	_____
GSP	_____	RPP	_____
G.V.	_____	Ross	_____
Har	_____	S.C.	_____
JPCP	_____	St.A.	_____
KEN	_____	St.J	_____
K.L.	_____	St.Joa	_____
K.M.	_____	St.M.	_____
L.H.	_____	Sgt	_____
LO	_____	T.H.	_____
Lyn	_____	TLLO	_____
L.V.	_____	T.M.	_____
McC	_____	T.T.	_____
McG	_____	Ven	_____
McQ	_____	Vets	_____
MIL	_____	VP	_____
		Wat	_____
Mackay 3/10		Wed	_____
_____		WIL	_____
_____		W.L.	_____
_____			
_____		_____	
_____		_____	
_____		_____	

MURDER IN THE LATIN QUARTER

Murder in the Latin Quarter

Cara Black

THORNDIKE
CHIVERS

This Large Print edition is published by Thorndike Press, Waterville, Maine, USA and by BBC Audiobooks Ltd, Bath, England.

Thorndike Press, a part of Gale, Cengage Learning.

Copyright © 2009 by Cara Black.

The moral right of the author has been asserted.

An Aimée Leduc Investigation Series.

LIBRARY OF CONGRESS CATALOGING-IN-PUBLICATION DATA

Black, Cara, 1951–
 Murder in the Latin Quarter / by Cara Black.
   p. cm. — (Thorndike Press large print mystery)
 ISBN-13: 978-1-4104-1746-6 (alk. paper)
 ISBN-10: 1-4104-1746-8 (alk. paper)
 1. Leduc, Aimee (Fictitious character)—Fiction. 2. Women
private investigators—France—Paris—Fiction. 3. Quartier latin
(Paris, France)—Fiction. 4. Paris (France)—Fiction. 5. Sisters—
Fiction. 6. Large type books. I. Title.
 PS3552.L297M799 2009b
 813'.54—dc22   2009011979

BRITISH LIBRARY CATALOGUING-IN-PUBLICATION DATA AVAILABLE

Published in 2009 in the U.S. by arrangement with Writer's House LLC.
Published in 2010 in the U.K. by arrangement with the author.

U.K. Hardcover: 978 1 408 45666 8 (Chivers Large Print)
U.K. Softcover: 978 1 408 45667 5 (Camden Large Print)

Printed in the United States of America
1 2 3 4 5 6 7 13 12 11 10 09

To the memory of
Colonel Henri Rol-Tanguy
and all the ghosts.

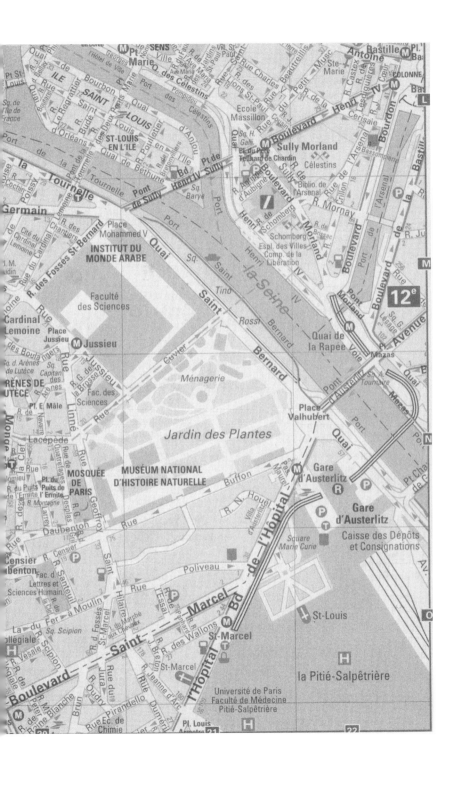

". . . this life is a perpetual chequer-work of good and evil, pleasure and pain. When in possession of what we desire, we are only so much the nearer losing it; and when at a distance from it, we live in expectation of enjoying it again."

— MADAME DE SÉVIGNÉ

Paris, September 1997, Monday Afternoon
Aimée Leduc's fingers paused on the keyboard of her laptop as she felt a sudden unease but it vanished as quickly as the mist that curled up under the Pont Neuf. At least, she thought, thanks to the cleaning lady, the chandelier gleamed, the aroma of beeswax polish hovered, and Leduc Detective's office shone. For once. It should impress her high-powered client, the Private Banque Morel's administrator, who was due in ten minutes.

Aimée checked for lint on her Dior jacket, a flea-market find. She heard a footstep and looked up expectantly.

A woman in her late thirties stood in the doorway to the office. She was a tall, light-complected mulatto, wearing a denim skirt and clutching oversize sunglasses in her hand. She stepped inside, her gaze taking in the nineteenth-century high ceilings and carved moldings as well as the array of computers.

"This place isn't what I expected," said the woman in lilting French. She had an accent Aimée didn't recognize.

"Maybe you're in the wrong place, Mademoiselle," Aimée said, irritated. "Our firm handles computer security only." She ran her chipped red fingernails over the Rolodex for the card of a female private detective in the Paris region.

"Non." The woman waved the card away. She's persistent, Aimée thought. And for a brief moment, as the breeze fluttered through the open window and a siren whined outside on rue du Louvre, Aimée sensed that she was being subjected to a curious scrutiny. It was as if this woman was measuring and found her, like the office, wanting.

Aimée glanced at her Tintin watch impatiently. "As I told you —" Aimée's cell phone beeped. "Excuse me," she said and dug in her bag, found it, and listened to the message. The client she expected was in a taxi . . . minutes away.

"The owner of this establishment knew my mother," the woman said. Her accent was now more pronounced.

Even after all this time, former clients

called expecting to find him, Aimée thought sadly. "You're referring to my father, Jean-Claude Leduc," she said. "But he passed away several years ago." She used a euphemism instead of graphically describing his death during a routine surveillance in the Place Vendôme from an exploding bomb.

"Passed away?" The woman blinked. "And you're his daughter?"

Aimée nodded. "We've put the old case files in storage. *Désolée.*"

"But you don't understand." The woman tilted her head to the side, gauging something, ignoring Aimée's words. Her fingers picked at the strap of her straw bag.

"Understand? Mademoiselle, I am waiting for a client who is due any moment." She checked her phone again. "Make an appointment, and then I'll see what I can do for you."

"That's him, *non?*" The woman pointed to the photo behind Aimée's desk. It was of her father caught in time: younger, his tie loose, grinning. The one Aimée kept to remind her of what he'd looked like alive, not the way she'd last seen him, charred limbs on the morgue's stainless-steel table all that remained after the explosion.

"My father —"

"*Our* father," the woman interrupted. "I'm

your sister, Aimée."

The phone fell from Aimée's hand.

"But I don't have a sister."

"It took time to find this place, to make sure," the woman said. Her voice quavered, her confidence evaporating. "And to summon the courage to come here. I need to talk with you."

Aimée steadied herself. "There's some misunderstanding, Mademoiselle. You're . . ."

"Mireille *Leduc.*"

Stunned, Aimée looked for some resemblance in the almond-shaped eyes, the honey color of the woman's skin, the shape of her mouth: that full pout of the lips, those white teeth. Could her father have had another child?

"You have proof? I'm sorry, but you walk in here and claim you're my sister," Aimée said. "How do I know you're . . . that what you claim is true?"

"You're shocked," said Mireille, her voice urgent. "Me too. I had no idea until three weeks ago. During the *coup d'état,* I had to leave Haiti. I only found out. . . ."

"Haiti?" Aimée shook her head. "Papa never went to Haiti."

"Your father and my mother had a relationship in Paris, before you were born,"

14

the woman said. "I can show you photos."

Aimée felt the air being sucked out of her lungs. Glints of afternoon light refracted from the prisms of the chandelier into myriad dancing lights. It was as if she'd been hit by a shockwave; words froze in her throat.

The wire cage elevator whined up to the office landing and rumbled to a halt. Her client had arrived to tell her the verdict. Would Morel, a prestigous private bank, extend Leduc Detective's data security contract?

"I never knew my father," said Mireille. Her mouth pursed. "Was it a one night stand or a *grand amour* . . . who knows?"

"That's not like Papa. He wouldn't have fathered a child and just —"

"Mademoiselle Leduc?" A smiling middle-aged woman in a navy pantsuit knocked on the frosted glass panel of the open door. "Am I disturbing you?"

"Of course not, Madame Delmas, please come in." Aimée forced a smile, stuck her trembling hand in her pocket, and gestured to a Louis Quinze chair with her other. "The data analysis report's ready."

Perspiration dampened Aimée's collar. "Why don't you start reading the report while I see my visitor out, Madame?"

15

Mireille paused next to Aimée on the scuffed wood of the landing, a vulnerable look on her face. "*Maman* went back to Haiti. I don't know if he knew she was pregnant."

A cough came from inside Aimée's office. One didn't keep a client like Madame Delmas waiting.

The woman calling herself Mireille Leduc gripped Aimée's hand hard. Hers was as hot as fire. A thin red string encircled her wrist. "*Mesamey,*" she said.

"I don't understand," Aimée said, her voice low.

"*Mesamey* is the *Kreyòl* word . . . I don't know how you say it in French. I've only been here a week. Would you say *surprised?*"

Aimée felt a frisson course through her. "But what do you want?" she asked.

"Please, I lost my papers. I didn't know who else to ask."

"Papers . . . you mean you're illegal?"

Mireille nodded. "But I can prove we're sisters. I am in some trouble. I thought my father could help. This man who's been helping me gave me a file, and. . . ."

Madame Delmas's chair scraped on the floor, a fax machine whirred, and the office phone rang.

"I'll wait for you in the corner café,"

Mireille said. "You'll meet me, Aimée?"

What else could she do? Aimée nodded. Her eyes followed Mireille down the dim spiral staircase until the last glimpse of her curly hair disappeared. She could still feel the heat of Mireille's hand on hers. Then she realized she didn't know her address or even how to reach her.

Time to get to the bottom of this, Aimée thought, emerging from her building into the warm air of the rue du Louvre. The limestone building façades, with their wrought iron balconies and pots of geraniums, shimmered in the late-afternoon sun. Aimée's heels clicked over the uneven pavement as she passed the newspaper kiosk plastered with posters proclaiming "New leads in Princess Di's death." September 1997, two weeks after Princess Di's accident in Pont de l'Alma, and the media wouldn't quit. *Nom de Dieu,* she thought, why couldn't the paparazzi let the poor woman rest in peace?

A group of laughing schoolchildren raced by, joking about their recent vacations. September was time for *la rentrée,* the return to work and school, when the city emerged from the summer doldrums like a dog shaking its wet fur.

Aimée hurried into the corner café, searching for Mireille. Only a few tables by the window were occupied: two financial types in business suits huddled in conversation, an old couple with their dog arguing over an article in *Le Soir,* and the locksmith in his overalls, his heavy-lidded eyes semiclosed, at the counter.

No Mireille.

Suspicion mingled with disappointment. The slim thread of hope that Mireille might really be her sister began to fray. She'd always wanted a sibling, and for a moment she'd hoped it was true. Yet how naïve to credit a stranger who walked into her office, promised proof, and vanished.

Grow up! she told herself. She had to grow up. And she repressed the longing she'd always felt for family, any family.

"*Bonsoir,* Zazie," she said to the young girl with red hair and a splash of freckles who smiled at her from behind the counter she was stocking with Orangina bottles. "Has a woman asked for me? Curly hair, light caramel-colored skin, wearing a denim skirt?"

"*Un moment,* Aimée." Zazie helped out in the café after school while her mother tallied accounts and her father took deliveries. Frugal and close-knit, in true Auvergnat fashion, the whole family worked together.

"So was she here, Zazie?"

Zazie shrugged. "Better ask *Maman,* she'll be back in a minute."

Maybe Mireille had stepped out for a moment but would return. Aimée tapped the toe of her high-heeled shoe on the tile floor, which was littered with sugar wrappers and cigarette butts. She wanted proof of the truth of the woman's claim. If Mireille was working a scam, expecting money, she'd be disappointed, Aimée thought, as she considered Leduc Detective's finances.

"Your usual, Aimée?" Zazie asked.

"Make it a double." Aimée hiked her bag up on her shoulder and nodded to the locksmith next to her, who was nursing a beer. The faint stain of twilight tinged the trees and traffic leading to the Pont Neuf. She scanned the outdoor pavement: only anonymous passersby and Maurice, the one-armed veteran news vendor, selling newspapers at the kiosk.

"So you're working tonight, Aimée?"

There was a click and bubble of steam as the dark liquid dripped into a demitasse cup. Tacked on the wall were children's stick-figure crayon drawings.

"I've got a new client." Aimée twisted the blond highlighted strands and wisps of her

19

shag-styled hair behind her ears. Part of her new look, responsible for a big check to the stylist at the coiffeuse.

She scanned the café again, looking through the windows to the shadowy street. Still no Mireille. Her impatience mounted.

"Try to remember, Zazie. Was there a woman with sunglasses, big ones? A tall woman with light brown curly hair?"

Zazie lifted the demitasse of espresso onto a small white saucer. "Lots of people come in here." She hefted a thick textbook onto the counter. "I've got a geography test tomorrow."

Aimée unwrapped a sugar cube, stirred her coffee with the little spoon and wished she had a cigarette to go with it. Too bad she'd quit. Second time this month.

Zazie chewed her pencil, then leaned forward as if confiding a secret. "Aimée," she said, "I may have a case for you."

"Really?" Aimée smiled.

"*Oui.* Listen, this boy, Paul, sits in front of me in geography."

Aimée nodded, noticing the hint of mascara on Zazie's lashes. Zazie must be twelve or thirteen now. "You like him, Zazie?"

Zazie blushed. "Paul's father went out to buy cigarettes and never came home."

A child's cry came from somewhere in the

café's kitchen.

"His father left one day, Aimée. Just like that!"

Aimée averted her eyes. Like her own American mother, a seventies radical. A mother who hadn't been home when eight-year-old Aimée returned from school that rainy March afternoon. Just a note telling her to stay at the next-door neighbors'. And an empty armoire.

"Paul thinks his father is a secret agent who had to go on a mission."

More likely a deadbeat dad who skipped out.

"Could you find Paul's father, Aimée?"

"That's the *flics*' job, Zazie," she said. "Paul's mother should talk to them."

Through the café's window Aimée saw a flash of denim. But this woman was blonde. Not Mireille.

"Paul won't go to school. He's waiting for his father. . . ." Zazie paused, wide-eyed. "I saw his mother at the market, crying. You're a detective. Can't you find him, Aimée?"

Aimée sighed, seeking an excuse. The sharp ache she herself felt, a knife-edged pain — wanting to know what had happened to her own mother — never stopped.

Zazie pushed another espresso toward her. "Paul's got an allowance; he can pay you.

Please, Aimée," she pleaded.

"No promises, Zazie. It depends on whether my friend still works at the Commissariat."

She pulled out a black lipstick tube, swiped Chanel Red across her lips and blotted them with a café napkin. Again, Aimée scanned the people walking by on the pavement. Still no Mireille.

She heard another cry, more piercing this time, followed by the shattering of plates.

A moment later, Virginie, Zazie's mother appeared, hefting a baby on her on an ample hip. Smears of honey glistened on the baby's cheek.

"Do you remember a woman who came in here looking for me, Virginie?"

Aimée repeated her description.

Virginie brushed a wisp of hair from her forehead. "Last time I'll serve her!" Virginie's eyebrows shot up in disapproval. "She didn't say a word, just pointed her finger."

Aimée kept her mouth shut.

"Like she's too good to talk with the likes of me, like I'm the hired help," Virginie said.

"Pointed to what, Virginie?"

Virginie reached for a café napkin wedged between the pastis and Dubonnet bottles on the shelf in front of the beveled mirror.

"She left this for you." Virginie's mouth

puckered in a moue of distaste.

"You mean *that* lady, *Maman?*" Zazie said, her eyes wide. "The one in the raincoat? She ran away."

Aimée leaned over the counter. Sometimes she got more sense out of Zazie than from her harried mother.

"What happened, Zazie?"

"The motorcycle pulled up." Zazie gestured out the window to a small alley. "She looked scared. Then she ducked behind the counter. I saw her bend down."

"Like she was hiding?"

"Then she ran away. Out the back door away from the motorcycle." Zazie shook her head. "I didn't know she'd been waiting for you, Aimée."

The napkin was marked with a damp brown circular coffee stain. She turned it over and saw her name written on it. She unfolded the napkin and read the scribbled words "Loge B. 2A5C, 61 rue Buffon." The Latin Quarter.

"Aimée?" Zazie asked, tugging her sleeve. "Do you know her?"

"Not as well as I'm going to, Zazie." She palmed a ten-franc note into Zazie's hand. "Big sisters have it tough. Treat yourself to an Orangina."

Aimée turned the ignition key of her faded pink Vespa scooter. She stepped on the kick-start pedal, popped into first gear, and edged the Vespa into the traffic crawling past the Louvre's Cour Carrée and into a cloud of diesel exhaust from the Number 74 bus. She wished she'd worn jeans instead of the Dior pencil skirt and heels.

She drove by pet shops and *bouquinistes,* the secondhand book stalls on the banks of the Seine. On her left, Notre Dame's gray shrouded, scaffolding-wrapped hulk was in the midst of a seemingly eternal cleaning. As she crossed the Petit Pont to Saint Michel, the Seine beneath flowed khaki-green flecked with copper in the last rays of the sun.

On the Left Bank she bypassed tree-lined Boulevard Saint Michel heading up rue Saint Jacques, a part of the ancient pilgrim-age route to Compostela in Spain. She turned left past the Sorbonne, where from the Middle Ages until the nineteenth cen-tury classes had been taught in Latin. The streets narrowed in the Latin Quarter, one of the oldest of Paris, home to churches, Roman ruins, universities, the *Grandes*

Ecoles, book stores, and, now, research facilities. It was still an intellectual center. The cobbled passages were traversed by students spilling out of small bars tucked into medieval two-story timbered buildings. Strains of remix from the DJ *du mode* wafted in the warm air, along with the fumes from the cigarettes everyone smoked.

By the time she had woven her scooter through the warren of streets below Montagne Sainte-Geneviève, darkness had descended. Her knuckles ached from squeezing the brake levers on the steep inclines. All the way here, she had wondered who Mireille had run from and why she'd left an address on a napkin for her.

Aimée located 61, rue Buffon, opposite the nineteenth-century Natural History Museum, which stood in the leafy gardens of the Jardin des Plantes. Number 61 was a worm-holed wooden gate in a crumbling stone wall plastered with old, curling advertisements posted despite the faded DEFENSE D'AFFICHER warning. A small weathered plaque said OSTEOLOGIQUE ANATOMIE COMPARÉE. It was the comparative anatomy research facility. She pulled out the napkin and entered 2A5C on the digicode keypad.

Her feet crunched on gravel as she stepped inside a double-deep courtyard leading to a glass-roofed, wood-and-brick, vine-covered building. Shadows deepened. Quiet reigned, apart from the dense chirping of distant crickets.

To the right, an old turreted gatehouse loomed over the stone wall. Cracked steps overgrown with lilac bushes led inside. A faded sign read Loge B. Vacant by the look of it, but there was light glowing from an open window.

A strange place to meet.

She mounted the gatehouse stairs and reached a dim landing on which there were two doors. One stood open, and light shone from within. Then Mireille was expecting her.

"Excusez-moi," she called out and knocked. "Mireille?" A breeze scented by wild lilac floated from the open window. She stepped over a newspaper crumpled on the hexagonal brick-colored tiles. The place felt unlived-in, like a storeroom.

"Mireille?" she called again.

In the room ahead, she saw a stool standing upside-down, metal file cabinets tipped against the wall, a large mahogany desk overturned by the window. Trashed, and signs of a struggle.

The hair rose on the back of her neck.

She reached for the stool leg to wield as a

weapon. The breeze ruffled a paper on the wall, a small dog-eared black-and-white photo that had been partially taped over a crack. It showed a night scene at an outdoor café. A young man sat next to a woman in a sleeveless dress; the table was littered with glasses. Part of the photo had been torn off. Something about one face looked familiar. She stared at the young man in the rattan chair, smiling, raising his glass to the dark-skinned woman next to him. Aimée looked closer. Could that be her father? That crooked smile, the thin mustache he'd shaved off when he left the police force. A younger version of her Papa. She lifted the photo carefully. On the back, in faint pencil, was written "Brasserie Balzar," a well-known brasserie near the Sorbonne.

Her pulse raced.

Taped beside it she saw another much-thumbed black-and-white photo. A smiling woman held a baby in her arms; in the background were waving palm trees and a sugarcane field. The same woman from the café photo. She turned it over. "Edwige and Mireille" was written in pencil.

A torn photo of her father with this woman. Was it proof that she had a sister? She felt a pain in her gut. The walls slanted, the light dimmed. The world as she knew it shifted.

Why hadn't her father told her?

And where was Mireille?

The lilac scent of the breeze mingled with a tangy metallic odor. She rose, still gripping the stool by the leg, and edged past a wooden crate. Something glinted in the shadows behind the desk. It took a moment before she made out a design on the brick-colored tiles. A white powdery circle. She reached down to touch it, and her fingertips came back coated with rough granules.

A circle of salt.

The smell was stronger now. Sweet lilac mingling with the cloying metallic odor of blood. She peered behind the overturned desk and saw a slumped figure. *Non,* not Mireille!

A man lay against the wall behind the desk. His dark, slack-jawed face shone dully in the light, his half-opened eyes revealed dilated pupils, his black bristly hair was matted with leaves. A deep-red blossom stained the gristle that had been his ear; tufts of skin had been peeled away from his temple.

She gasped in horror and stepped back, clutching the photos with shaking hands.

A vacant gatehouse, this body, a photo of her father . . . but no Mireille.

She had to get out of here.

But she forced herself to look again. The body was that of a large man, an African or Caribbean man. He wore leather shoes, handmade by the look of them. His bloodied tailored shirt had an intact white sleeve with a gold cufflink at the wrist. He had on pin-striped blue trousers. . . . Not a homeless type.

Who would cut off his ear, peel away the skin of his forehead, and leave behind a circle of salt?

A siren wailed. She jumped. Time to leave. She stuffed the photos into her jacket pocket. She wanted to search the papers on the floor, but from the courtyard below she heard the rustling of bushes and the snapping of twigs. Was the killer lying in wait outside?

A patrol car's orange-red light flashed from the landing windows illuminating the hallway like a wash of blood. Brakes squealed to a halt outside. She couldn't afford to be caught with a corpse.

From the landing window, she saw two *flic* cars blocking the rue Buffon gate. And her parked scooter. She couldn't go out the front door and risk meeting the *flics* face to face, nor could she hide in the bushes of the compound if the killer was waiting there.

Footsteps sounded on the stairway. The

beam of a flashlight skittered over the broken tiles of the hall floor.

She stuck her foot out the landing window, pulled herself through, scraping her hip, and levered herself to the top of the stone wall, an uneven crumbling ledge of broken glass, pigeon droppings, and twigs. It was, she saw, a good twenty feet above the pavement.

She hunched down, edging away from the gate and the *flic* cars below, creeping toward a tree branch. She almost lost her balance. By the time she reached the branch, yards away, she knew she was going to have to jump. Her knees couldn't take it any longer.

She inhaled, grabbed the branch, and lowered herself. Damned pencil skirt! She heard a rip as her legs dangled in the air. She dropped and landed in a half-crouch. But although her hands were skinned, at least she was all in one piece. On all fours, she crept around the empty *flic* cars. Static and squawking noises erupted from their radios. She had to hurry. She pulled the scooter from its stand, gripped the handlebars, and walked in the shadows of the wall toward the next block. Then she swung her leg over and switched on the ignition. Her fishnet stockings were in shreds; her ripped skirt flapped open high up her thigh.

Who was the dead man?

Behind her, a car engine started. Bright headlights appeared in the scooter's rear-view mirror. The car's gears ground as it accelerated.

She revved ahead. And so did the car.

Monday Night

A knock sounded on the high-ceilinged gilt-edged salon door of the Haitian Trade Delegation. "Madame Obin?" said the attaché. "I'm leaving."

Léonie Obin paused, fingering her worn rosary. A phone rang somewhere in the suite of offices.

"Give me a moment," she called. She breathed "Amen," pressing her lips to the statue of Saint George, whom she also knew as Ogoun. She brushed ashes from the *honte,* the mimosa herb for reducing pride, into a tin, then tied a remaining grass stalk into a knot to ward off bad luck.

Léonie tucked her juju, her amulet, under the silk scarf draping her neck. She was fifty-five years old, thin, light-skinned, with planed cheekbones and distinctive topaz-colored eyes. She was a *mélange,* a *"bouquet garni,"* like most of the fair-complected *mixte* who composed the elite ruling families of Haiti.

Léonie heard muffled laughter and a

31

murmur of conversation. Guests still lingered from the reception that had begun three hours ago. Why hadn't they left? Lateness would jeopardize her meeting with Edouard.

She smoothed down her carefully coiffed hair and hurried out. No one was waiting on the Aubusson carpet in the mirrored hallway to delay her with conversation. Then the front doorbell buzzed, and she jumped. Edouard, finally, more than an hour late? Please, Holy Mary and Ogoun, she thought, guide my way, bless my undertaking.

"Edouard?" At first she didn't recognize him in the dim hallway. His hair had been dyed a light brown and he was in shadow as he leaned against the carved door. Then he stepped forward and she saw his unmistakable grin.

"Took you a moment, eh?" he said with a familiar shrug of those broad shoulders. He wore a three-piece suit with a tailored blue shirt, presenting himself as a successful businessman. A new disguise. Two years had passed since she'd last seen him. She needed something from him and prayed he'd cooperate.

"You still have your goons watching the place, I see," he said. "As usual."

"You're paranoid, Edouard," she replied.

"More like careful." He sniffed, his gaze sweeping over her. "And you're up to your old tricks, too. Offering to Ogoun."

She venerated a tapestry of saints, spirits, and deities, typical of the island. The mix of Christian and West African spirits was woven into the fabric of everyday Haitian life. Léonie had grown up believing that the more deities you prayed to, the better. Ten years in Paris hadn't altered that.

"Your call surprised me, Léonie. You've changed since I last saw you. You're so much thinner," he observed.

Her bones hurt. The "weakness," she had the weakness. No one called it an epidemic. Before it prevented her, she had work to do.

"Quick," she said, ignoring his comment. "There are people here. Come into my office."

Once inside, Edouard stood under the wavering light of the chandelier, a relic of the room's former use as a dining room. If he suspected that Léonie was ill, he didn't pursue it.

"After avoiding me for so long, what changed your mind, Léonie?" he asked.

"Edouard, I'm your aunt, for God's sake," she said. "Address me with respect. We need to talk."

"I think you want something from me."

She knew he saw a disapproving old woman. She had always presented an obstacle to him. "What do you mean?" Léonie took a deep breath.

"I know you have access to all the bank accounts," he said.

"I merely handle the trade delegation agreements, you know that," she said.

Edouard's eyebrow raised. "Not according to people we've questioned." Like a dog scenting a fox, he never gave up. "You handle a lot more, Léonie."

She waved an arm dismissively. "Years ago, maybe I did. But Duvalier's money's gone. *Pfft* . . . spent. That's why you need to stop this bank account inquiry."

Edouard stiffened. "We have testimony and documentary evidence."

"Think of the future, Edouard," she told him. "Think of the programs for Haiti, the projects awaiting funding —"

"And forget the massacres that took place and the daily shootings in the street that continue?" Edouard interrupted. "Listen to you, Léonie, you sound more colonial than the plantation owners did. You love looking more *blanche* than your sheets, acting cultured . . . but you should realize you've never fit in here. And you never will. To them, you're black."

Stung, she averted her eyes, concentrating on the lozenge-patterned wood floor, the intricately inlaid blond and ebony strips of wood.

"We know Duvalier's attempting to access the accounts." He paused, running a tan finger over the mahogany surface of her desk. "We will block his access, freeze the accounts. That money belongs to the Haitian people."

She shook her head. "Don't you ever learn, Edouard? Why do you look for danger?"

"You can't protect me, not that you ever did. The price on my head keeps going up." He grinned. "Haven't you heard?"

"It's not something to boast about, Edouard. Who do you think helped you —" She bit the words back. She had protected him in the past and paid for it in more ways than one. And would shield him now, if he'd furnish her with Benoît's file. She ached to reveal the file's importance to him. Could she make amends before it was too late?

"Haiti needs this World Bank loan, Edouard," she began.

"World Bank loan?" He snorted in disgust. "We come from a country with no infrastructure, no delivery system except for the bribes that go straight into the pockets of officials and developers." Edouard grasped her wrist. "You're living in the clouds, *Tante* Léonie. The last project funded was abandoned a year ago. Benoît's research —"

"He approached you, didn't he?" she interrupted. "He must share his findings with us so we can straighten matters out. You wouldn't want to jeopardize funding agreements. Right now his research complicates matters and brings up irrelevant questions."

"Brings up questions?" His grip turned to iron. He shoved her against her desk, overturning the bowl of freesias. Water dribbled down to the floor.

Léonie winced.

"I'm sorry." A brief flicker of shame crossed his face.

She'd use his guilt. Coax him a little and he'd acquiesce.

"You're Benoît's friend. It will be simple for you," she said.

"But Benoît's an academic," Edouard said. "I don't see why his research matters."

"And he doesn't understand the implications either," Léonie said. "It's muddled, but I'll sort out the situation. Just get me his file."

"What file?" Edouard's expression hardened.

Stupid, she'd never meant to be so direct. None of this had gone as she'd planned. She was losing her tenuous hold on him.

"Everything that backs up the Trade Delegation analysis helps, Edouard," she said.

"Now I see," Edouard said. "That's why you called. You want arguments to outweigh the risk factors of continued political stalement, lack of political commitment to reform, and weak institutional capacity."

"That's textbook talk, Edouard."

"Actually, it's from the conclusions of the last International Monetary Fund report on Haiti," Edouard said. "The elite evade taxes and skim off aid money as usual. But those funds are drying up, eh? If you haven't gotten Benoît's report, there's a reason. So you're desperate."

"It's not true, Edouard."

"Don't tell me, *Tante* Léonie. I know you still funnel funds from Lichtenstein front companies through the Swiss bank accounts. But Benoît's embarrassing you, *non?*"

Stricken, she shook her head, but she looked away.

"So I'm right," he said, a sad note in his voice. "I hoped I was wrong."

Two men appeared behind him. They

were dark-skinned and wore black clothing and tennis shoes.

"Who —" she began.

"Never mind," he interrupted.

And then she remembered she hadn't heard the front door click shut when he came in. Her lips quivered in fear. He'd planned this all along.

Edouard opened the drawers of her desk, rooting through the papers and dossiers. Fear coursed down her spine. Nothing was going as it should. Instead of listening to her, he'd taken control. But he wouldn't find the bank accounts.

He paused and stared around her office. "It's all a song-and-dance, Léonie. You want Benoît's file, and for all I know you would go so far as to steal it. But you'd counted on using me to get it."

"*Non,* Edouard. Why can't you understand that what's in this file puts everything at risk?"

"Lies. Like always."

She held her breath. He steered her toward a framed oil painting, reached up and lifted it off the wall. Edouard pointed to the circular steel safe that had been hidden behind the picture.

"Open it," Edouard said.

"Only the *chargé d'affaires* knows the

combination," she said.

She prayed to Ogoun, clutching the knotted straw.

One of the men pulled out a drill from a duffel bag and headed to the safe.

"Stop him, Edouard."

"No wonder my uncle left you," he said.

Little did he know that his uncle had left only after he'd infected her with the "weakness." Edouard remained the ungrateful, spoiled child who'd run off to join the rebels, putting his family at the mercy of the Duvaliers. The lies she'd had to tell, the corruption she'd been forced to cover up, to survive. Edouard hadn't changed.

He stood close to her now. So close, she could smell his faint citrus scent. Then his hands rested on her trembling shoulders. He lifted her chin, staring into her eyes. "Still shielding a black *houngan,* an evil dictator, even when he's in exile." He shook his head. "You're living on blood money."

As if she'd had a choice. But it wasn't like that now. It was *worse.*

"In Port-au-Prince, you closed your eyes with rest of the elite," he said. "You're all the same, barricading yourselves in your villas to avoid the sight of blood running in the gutters from the maimed limbs hacked off by machetes. You tried to blind me too, but I can see reality."

"Edouard, pursuing the Duvalier bank investigation will stall the loans the Haitian people need so desperately."

"Is that really what scares you, Léonie?"

He'd ruin their chance of obtaining a World Bank loan. Rather than procuring Benoît's file, she'd aroused Edouard's suspicions.

But she had to keep trying. "Benoît's report is exactly what the Bank officials would use as an excuse to cut —"

He reached under her scarf and, in a quick movement, caught her *grigri,* the juju amulet, and yanked it free. A sad smile crossed his face. "Some things never change, Léonie." He tossed the amulet to one of the men, who caught it and held it to the light. Inside, there was a slip of paper. The man read out the series of numbers written on it, the combination to the safe.

She struggled to speak, but only muffled sounds came out. Her heart thumped in her chest. The grass stalk fell from her pocket onto the floor. She heard a metallic click as the safe door opened. And then a tightness gripped her chest like a vise clamping her lungs shut.

Monday Night

Aimée gunned her scooter down rue Buffon, feeling every pothole. The car following her gained speed. Too late, she noticed the traffic light and a truck crossing the intersection, headed right at her, horn blaring.

She panicked. To escape, she'd driven the wrong way down the narrow one-way street. There was no way out.

She squeezed the brake levers and, at the last minute, swerved left through the open Jardin des Plantes gate and into the botanical gardens. The scooter's wheels spit gravel and lost traction. She heard the grinding of a hydraulic digger working inside as it shuddered to a halt, and she saw halogen beams trained on upturned earth and lawn.

"*Attention!* The garden's closed. You can't come in here," yelled a GDF — *Gaz de France* — worker in a hard hat. An emergency GDF repair vehicle stood parked on the lawn. "There's a ruptured gas line."

She looked back. The driver following her had pulled onto the pavement. The car's doors slammed shut. Her heart raced. They were after her.

"Stop!" The hard hat ran after her. "It's dangerous."

She ignored him and sped over the gravel path under manicured plane trees, eerie in the moonlight, heading for the fountain. Shouts came from behind her. Lights bobbed over the plane tree branches.

She panicked. The gardens were locked at night. She'd have to find some way out.

Veering to the right, she passed the spouting fountain, the old glass-roofed hothouse, and headed across the garden to the back gates. Roars and cries came from somewhere ahead as she drove down a path. Branches scraped her legs. Musky animal smells assailed her. The zoo . . . of course; it had been founded to house the animal menagerie from Versailles. She skirted the zoo fence, riding by the reptile gallery, careening through dark maze-like paths, hearing the screeching of the ostriches. Somehow she had to find another exit, a way out. Then a scream of alarm sounded from the monkey house.

Her weak bobbing headlight illuminated the tail of a huge beast: the concrete dinosaur of a children's climbing structure. Shouts came from the distance. It would only be minutes until security, alerted by the alarms, appeared.

She gunned by the Paléontologie et d'Anatomie Comparée offices, desperately looking for a way out. Then saw a passageway between the buildings and the

42

crumbling storehouses. She downshifted into the passageway and stopped. As she wiped her damp forehead, she faced a bolted wooden gate. Trapped.

On her left were the lighted windows of the caretaker's lodge. She saw a man inside, sitting at a desk, leaning back on his chair. Last year's calendar showed a blonde, topless on white sand. No video monitors were visible. But a control console above him displayed alarm lights blinking red.

Bunches of keys hung from hooks on the wall. He held a wine bottle, his eyes closed, his head swaying to and fro. No wonder, she thought, noticing the CD player. He was wearing headphones.

She cut the engine, leaned the Vespa against the wall, and opened one of the lodge's water-stained double doors. The place reeked of wine. Sawdust sprinkled the floor. She had no idea which of the keys opened the gate. And any minute now he'd notice the blinking alarm lights. She reached for the nearest bunch of keys and stole away, carrying a ring of large greasy old-fashioned keys. Her hands trembled as she tried several in the old-fashioned brass lock in the dark. None fit.

She turned to the lock in the smaller door. One of the keys went in. She turned it, but

43

nothing happened.

Panting now, she shoved and jiggled the key. Then she heard the mechanism tumble. A ray of light fell at a slant onto the packed earth. The guard had come out to investigate.

She looked up and saw his leering face, his eyes glazed and unfocused. He was a tall stocky gorilla of a man. The alarm from the zoo shrieked.

"I did it again!" She smacked her forehead and forced a smile. "Silly me. Sorry to bother you."

"Did what?" His footsteps crunched across the gravel, unsteadily. "Hold on."

"Trust me to set the alarm off. I'll just —"

"Why the hurry, *chérie?*"

With final desperate urgency, she used her knee to shove the door open.

He grabbed her scooter. "Not so fast. I've never seen you before. What are you doing here?"

"I'm new. This exit's so much closer to where I work," she said, making it up as she went along.

"New? Since when?"

"You weren't on duty that night." She said the first thing that came to mind. "When's your shift finished?"

"Eh?"

"Don't pretend." She licked her lips and jerked her thumb toward the mineralogy building. "I work late and I've watched you."

His eyes narrowed. "What are you doing with those keys?"

"The keys were in the door." She licked her lips again. "Such a good-looking *mec.* Why don't we have a drink? You could come to my place after work."

His hand relaxed. Confusion and interest battled for supremacy.

"You look like my type," she added.

His chest puffed out. "Think so? There's only one way to find out." He edged closer.

She kicked him in the knee.

"Salope!" He stumbled against the wall, clutching his leg.

She wrested the scooter from him and with her other hand turned on the ignition. She stepped on the pedal. The engine rumbled to life. She revved into first and shot over the cobblestoned street, grazing a parked truck's bumper. A car alarm blared and she took off.

She heard the man's shouts. He half-ran, half-limped after her. An apartment window creaked open. "I'm trying to sleep," yelled a man, shaking his fist.

The scooter's engine sputtered. Sirens sounded behind her. A late-night bus crossed the road and she veered behind it, then shot ahead onto the pavement abreast of the bus. She kept pace, hoping no pedestrians would appear, then turned with the bus onto Pont de Sully.

The Seine gurgled below, dark and sluggish; the plane trees lining the bank filigreed the pavement with shadows. The dark hulk of Place Bayre on Ile St. Louis loomed on the right, the park's horse chestnut trees nodding in the breeze. And then more sirens sounded. Flashing lights peppered the stone-walled quai.

She braked, took a sharp left onto the sidewalk of rue Saint Louis-en-l'isle, cut the engine, and coasted under the stone portico of Hotel de Bretonvilliers, a seventeenth-century *hôtel particulier* in the midst of renovation. Shaking, she shoved the Vespa between the dumpster and the crumbling stone wall and ran.

Tuesday Morning

In Aimée's dream, it was the freezing December after her mother left them. Papa was working at home, his piles of paperwork on the kitchen table. Her ninth birthday approached, and deep snow resembling glistening sugar carpeted the Jardin du Luxembourg.

"Get my mitten, Aimée," came a plaintive child's voice.

Icicles sparkled like shiny teeth from the garden's gold-spike-topped gate. A blue mitten lay in the snow; the chill air reddened the little girl's honey-colored cheeks.

The girl had Mireille's face.

"Help your sister, Aimée," her Papa was saying. But it was so cold, so wet. She wanted to take her Papa's hand, leave behind this demanding stranger with the runny nose. Go away. As she reached out, the mitten turned into a dark severed ear. Blood droplets spattered the pristine snow.

Aimée blinked awake on cold smooth sheets; she must have kicked her duvet onto the floor. A miasma of guilt engulfed her. She reached for the duvet and for Miles Davis, her bichon frisé, a bundle of fur asleep near her pillow. His little breaths warmed her arm. Pale apricot rays of dawn glowed through her window.

Since Mireille had walked into her life, asking for help, Aimée had discovered a corpse and been chased. Assailed by doubt, she wondered again if Mireille really was her sister. Or if she'd been set up.

She rubbed her eyes, unable to clear the images of the man's severed ear and that circle of salt from her mind. At her laptop on the bedside table, the screen blinked with an e-mail from her partner, René, marked urgent. "Aimée, can you meet the contractor at the office? Aérospatiale's interested in our proposal . . . I'm at La Défense meetings all day."

Bon, she had to get to the office early. Would she find Mireille waiting with an explanation? Some scenario that would make this nightmare disappear?

Not likely.

In the kitchen she made coffee, then scooped the horsemeat from the butcher's waxed paper into Miles Davis's chipped Limoges bowl.

"Breakfast, Furball."

In the night, it had rained. Clear drops glistened on the window. Lingering pearly puffs of clouds hovered over the blue-gray rooftops across the Seine. She opened the window and inhaled the rain-freshened air suffused with the dense foliage smell from the trees lining the quai below.

And then she saw them. Two men sat in the front seat of a dented Peugeot parked in front of her building. Acrid puffs of cigarette smoke drifted from the car's open window. Her fingers tensed on the cup handle. She stepped back, afraid they might be watching her apartment.

Flics used dented Peugeots for stakeouts. But it was after 6 A.M., the time when *flics* had the legal right to come to her door and question her.

One of the men emerged from the car. He wore a brown leather bomber jacket and sunglasses. He flicked a cigarette butt onto the quai and leaned on the stone wall. Alarms rang in her head. He'd broken the first rule of police surveillance: never make your presence known.

If they weren't *flics,* she wondered who they might be. Her mind returned to the previous night and the car that had followed her. Nervous, she ran to her room, opened her armoire, and grabbed the first thing at hand, a dry cleaner's plastic bag containing a vintage black Lanvin dress, her denim jacket, and black patent leather heels.

She stuck the laptop in her bag and locked her front door. As she ran down the building's worn marble steps, she swiped Chanel Red across her lips, then hurried over the black-and-white diamond-shaped foyer tiles. She wanted to avoid Madame Cachou, her inquisitive concierge.

Instead of leaving by the front doors, Aimée passed through the old carriage house to the rear courtyard. She walked over damp magnolia leaves into the next courtyard and exited via a smaller door cut into the main one. Now she stood on crowded rue Saint Louis-en-l'isle among parents taking their children to the *école maternelle* around the corner. She saw a taxi and, instead of dealing with her scooter, waved it down.

In the taxi she took advantage of the moment and went to work on her face, taming a rogue eyebrow, outlining her eyes with kohl. A few blocks later she turned to look through the rear window. The dented Peugeot was two cars behind.

"Try the less direct route," she told the taxi driver, a small man wearing a rain cap.

"What do you have in mind, Mademoiselle?"

She thrust fifty francs over the top of the front seat. "Get creative."

A half hour later, after the taxi had circled the block twice, Aimée reached her office. She stared out the window of Leduc Detective. Below, on rue du Louvre, the usual snarl of traffic crawled and horns blared, punctuated by the ringing of bicycle bells.

No dented Peugeot in sight.

But no Mireille waiting for her with an explanation.

Instead she'd found Cloutier, the contractor, gesturing to her from the rear of the office. She shoved down her worry, tried to clear her mind and focus on the work at hand.

Cloutier, a large-boned Breton with a wide brow and thick mustache, looked like he'd be more at home at sea than in the cluttered interiors of buildings. He had a nice array of crowbars and steel hammers which would be handy for protection, in case. But he didn't know that.

"*Désolé,* Mademoiselle, the truck-driver strike held up my supplies," he told Aimée. He took a notepad from the pocket in his overalls. "I took measurements according to the specifications of your partner, Monsieur Friant, and ordered the lumber and structural braces."

Aimée scanned the blueprint Cloutier spread over the top of the fax machine. An opening in the adjoining wall, a partition to be erected. A straightforward job to merge the next-door office with Leduc Detective. Nothing could be more simple, she thought.

"So, when can you start?" Aimée asked.

Cloutier grinned, rocking back on his workboot heels. "My supplier guaranteed delivery tomorrow morning. We'll start early."

The radiator groaned, emitting heat. In

typical fashion, as René often pointed out, it functioned full bore in warm weather while giving out only dribbles in the bone-chilling days of December. Once construction started, the office would be a mess; she'd work at home. But if Mireille showed up and didn't find her . . . she'd have to figure that out.

After Cloutier left, she stared at the papers on her desk. Again she repressed unease; after all, the taxi had lost the Peugeot. Work faced her: surveillance to monitor, client calls to follow up, and bills to pay. A business to run.

But those men obviously knew where she lived. Would they know the location of her office?

Needing information, she punched in the number for Morbier, her godfather and a Police Commissaire. She heard a series of clicks, then a low buzz. She'd called on his direct line at the Commissariat.

"Group R," answered a disembodied voice.

She didn't like this. Morbier worked one day a week in Group R at the Brigade Criminelle. He'd never explained what he did there.

"Commissaire Morbier?"

"Unavailable. You have a message?"

She hung up before the system could trace the call. At least she hoped the tracer still needed fifteen seconds. Not smart, considering that she'd fled a murder scene. Talking to Morbier person to person was one thing, leaving a message that could raise questions another.

She debated calling her father's former police colleague, Nenert, in the robbery detail. Nenert liked to talk over a glass of wine; after several he grew voluble and disregarded regulations and confidentiality. If he didn't know an answer, he'd find out.

"Nenert's retired," said a woman's voice, too pert for this time of the morning. "What's this regarding?"

She thought quickly. "A robbery on rue Buffon," she said, "but this morning someone said a murder had occurred. . . ."

"You have information, Mademoiselle?"

"The murder alarmed me, I live nearby," she said. "Who — ?"

"The Brigade Criminelle handles homicide."

She knew that. And no one in the Brigade would reveal a word.

She hung up and scanned this morning's *Le Parisien*. The continuing investigation into Diana's death filled most of the front section, along with the annual article warning mushroom hunters taking to the forests this season to beware of the poisonous varieties. The sidebar listed the past ten years' statistics as to deaths due to poisoned mushrooms, proving that few paid attention.

She locked the office door, sat down to work, and slipped off her heels. Every time the phone rang, she'd answer at the first ring, anticipating Mireille's call. She looked up from her desk whenever she heard footsteps on the landing and went to check outside. It never was Mireille.

After an hour, her client calls all returned and several monitoring systems reviewed on René's terminal, she pulled out her checkbook. Leduc Detective barely broke even, in part due to clients who paid them for their service, like other independent firms, last. But this month, at least, they were not in the red. And if René's meeting at La Défense netted a contract. . . .

A sense of hollowness pervaded her. Mireille had been scared. So scared, according to Zazie, that she'd *run* out of the café. What if Mireille had discovered the man's body and run away before Aimée arrived?

She wouldn't learn about Mireille's connection to the murder by sitting here. Or uncover the victim's identity. Time mattered in an investigation her father always said. Witnesses forgot, leads grew stale. She glanced at her watch, shouldered her bag, and locked the office door.

In the bright daylight, Osteologique Anatomie Comparée at Number 61 appeared even more dilapidated than it had last night. Cracks fissured the crumbling soot-stained wall, weeds sprouted in the gravel of the courtyard. This ungentrified slice of the *quartier* opposite the Jardin des Plantes consisted of a maze of passages leading to eighteenth-century buildings.

Beyond the building's open portal, blue-uniformed *flics* stood in the courtyard. Yellow crime-scene tape fluttered in the warm air.

It brought back the image of the man's bloodied temple, his matted hair and severed ear. That circle of salt on the wooden floor. She shuddered.

She saw no place from which to observe without calling attention to herself. She leaned down, as if to wipe something off her shoe. From the corner of her eye she saw a figure in a doorway a few meters away. A man pressed numbered buttons on the digicode keypad. Several minutes passed. There was no answering buzz. He stood, unmoving. He was watching the gatehouse.

An older man, wearing a guard's blue work coat and smoking a cigarette, shuffled through the gate. He headed up the street, flicked his cigarette into the gutter, and entered a café. If he worked at the gatehouse, he would know something. She waited a few minutes before following him into the café. But, inside, she saw no one except the café owner behind the counter. The scent of fresh-pulped oranges came from the juicer, the gurgling steamer frothed milk; where had the old guard disappeared to?

She edged past the round marble-topped tables in the rear and saw him. He stood playing a fifties-style pinball machine.

She smiled. *"Bonjour,* you're the caretaker on rue Buffon, *non?"*

"And if I am?"

"You look thirsty," she said. "What about a drink?"

"Women offer me a lot of things, but not that." His sentence dangled in the air, suggestively. He was in his early seventies, she figured, had a thatch of white hair and wore thick black-framed bifocals. After a long look, he returned his gaze to the pinball machine.

"There's always a first time."

"Non, merci."

Her attempt at charm evidently didn't work with the senior set.

"You're a reporter, eh?" he asked.

Aimée shook her head.

"What do you want?"

"Besides peace on earth, Monsieur? Just to know the last time you saw the victim."

"Victim?" He shook his head, his eyes never leaving the pinball game.

"The man murdered last night in the gatehouse."

"Professeur Benoît? Why not say so?"

Now she had a name.

The GAME OVER sign blinked. He shot her an irritated look, his pupils like black balls magnified by the thick lenses. "You're not an investigator. Not dressed like that!"

Not only ornery, but a fashion critic too.

"Who are you, Mademoiselle?"

"Special investigations, Monsieur. We don't wear uniforms, if you know what I mean." She pulled out her father's police ID with her name on it. The card she kept for special occasions.

His eyes widened behind the thick lenses. Then he leaned forward. "Aaah. Special branch. . . . Like in that Jean Gabin film?"

Jean Gabin hadn't made a film in twenty years.

"That's all I can say." She put her finger to the side of her nose, indicating secrecy, a gesture she'd seen an old Corsican mobster perform. "I'd like to ask a few questions. First, if you'd run down what happened yesterday for me and then keep your ears open . . . I'll mention you in my report."

"Report?" He shook his head in alarm. Fear fluttered behind those magnifying lenses. "Then round me up, like the *Boches* did?"

Mon Dieu, he's still living World War II, she thought. She'd said the wrong thing. She put her hand on his arm. "Not even for a commendation? I'd really appreciate your help."

He sputtered. "That's different. I am a patriot. At seventeen, I served on the Maginot Line. Got the medal to prove it."

The impregnable Maginot line. The Germans had panzered around the end of it in record time.

"When did you last see Professeur Benoît?"

"*Quelle misère.* After it was too late." The old man shrugged, exhaling.

"I mean alive, Monsieur."

His brow furrowed in thought. "Let's see. The delivery came . . . maybe at four o'clock."

"See, you're helpful already." She smiled. "Monsieur . . . ?"

"Darquin. But I told the *flics* all this already."

"Of course, Monsieur. I'm just rechecking." She thought hard. The *flics* had questioned him, so she needed to elicit some detail, something they might have missed, a question they might not have asked. "Was that before or after you saw the young woman, tall, a mulatto with curly hair, wearing a denim skirt?"

"Who?"

She tried a hunch. "The woman working for Professeur Benoît upstairs in the gatehouse. Perhaps you noticed her before?"

"By mulatto, you mean . . . ?"

"Half Haitian, half French. She has light caramel-colored skin and speaks with a slight accent." She added, "Like the professor."

A beeping noise sounded in his pocket. "Time for my pills."

He shuffled to the counter. Why would the research lab employ a geriatric case, well beyond retirement age, she wondered. Frustrated, she followed him and ordered a Vittel from the sloe-eyed café owner. The moisture-beaded bottle of mineral water and glass with a lemon twist arrived on the zinc counter with a slap. Aimée set down five francs.

"That's right," he said, taking several yellow pills from a container. "Now it's coming back to me."

Her ears perked up. "You remember her?"

"Professeur Benoît acted as if it was very hush-hush, you know, when he left the packet."

"A packet? Large, heavy, or like a regular envelope?"

"A padded envelope. The woman picked it up later."

Excited, Aimée leaned forward. "The woman? Her name?"

"He'd written her name on the front of the envelope. Mireille."

It was her!

Darquin exhaled slowly. "I never saw her again."

She thought of the timing. At her office, Mireille had mentioned a file and that she was in trouble.

"So that was at about 4 P.M.?"

"My memory's a sieve . . . it might have been later."

Darquin took another pill, a green one, and swallowed it. Did he have a memory problem?

"Would you say it was closer to 5 P.M.?"

60

"I am half dead. With all the commotion, I couldn't sleep. At least the *flics* took them to the station."

"Who?"

"Wouldn't surprise me if they were suspects," he said, uncapping a bottle of water that he'd taken from his pocket.

A skinflint, too tight to buy a drink in the café. He had needles in his pocket, as the saying went. Bringing one's own drink to a café was just not done. The patron whistled in disgust and emptied some half-full glasses into the sink.

"I caught the couple in *flagrante delicto,* I think they call it. That's why I called the *flics.* Seems they were married, but to other people. The way they rut like cats in the bushes at night. . . ."

Confused, she thought about what he'd said and hadn't said. He seemed more outraged by this couple than by a murder. "Let me clarify this. You saw a couple in the bushes, and . . . ?"

"They woke me up." He took a swig of water, set the empty bottle down, and muttered to himself.

Then it dawned on her. Darquin had called the *flics* due to the amorous couple, not the murder.

"And what time was this?" Aimée asked.

61

"Late. I don't know."

Two men in plumbers' blue overalls, wrenches and pipes hanging from their pockets, entered the café arguing over last night's motocross matches. Aimée moved farther down the counter.

"Monsieur, didn't you notice that the gatehouse room was lit up?"

"The *flics* did," he said. "They found him, the poor man. What's the *quartier* coming to? I was born here, lived at Number 12 behind the lab my whole life. But the area's changed."

She had to get him back to the point.

"You can ask until you run out of air; I don't know any more," he said. "You're more direct, much heavier-handed than the other *flics*."

She'd better watch her step. He needed coaxing.

"But Monsieur Darquin, I tried for the light touch. Conversational, breezy."

"Sure. Breezy like the wind that blows the horns off a bull."

She hadn't heard that saying since she'd worn knee socks drinking hot chocolate in her *grand-mère's* kitchen.

"My nephew suffered an attack of acute appendicitis yesterday. I filled in for him," Darquin said. "And look what happened on my shift!"

In other words, quit badgering him. But what if he knew more? She checked her phone for messages. None.

"Help me to understand, Monsieur," she said. She smiled, sipping her sparkling water. "Let's start at, say. . . ." She thought back to the time at which Mireille had run out of Zazie's café. "Seven P.M. What do you remember? Did you see the woman again?"

"I've answered enough questions," he said. He pulled a pocket watch on a chain from inside his blue work coat. "Time to sort the mail."

"Please, just to help my inquiries, one more thing, Monsieur. Did you notice if this woman, Mireille, went into the gatehouse? Did she leave carrying the envelope?"

"The Professeur was very specific. Like all the ENS. 'It is only for her,' he said. I didn't see which way she went."

Aimée choked on the water she was swallowing. "Did Professeur Benoît teach at ENS?"

"Like most of them here."

ENS was the Ecole Normale Supérieure. A *Grande Ecole,* one of the country's prestigious and highly elitist state schools. Very selective. She stifled her excitement and handed him her card. "*Merci,* Monsieur Darquin. Please call me if you see her or if you should remember something else. Don't forget about that commendation you'll receive."

Darquin shuffled out the open café door. Pigeons cooed in the lilac bushes overhanging the laboratory wall. The same wall she had jumped from last night.

Despite the old man's gruffness, he'd provided information: a Professeur Benoît of the ENS had left an envelope for Mireille. As to why he'd been murdered surrounded by a circle of salt on the floor, or Mireille's connection to him and to the crime, she remained in the dark. But if Darquin had relayed the same information to the *flics,* she realized they would be searching for Mireille too.

Again, Aimée pulled out her cell phone to check her messages. None. She left fifty-centimes on the worn zinc counter for a tip and turned.

"I think we should talk," a man said, blocking her way.

He was thirtyish, lean and square-jawed, his carved cheekbones highlighting a cinnamon complexion. Yannick Noah, move over, she thought, but better-looking. He wore dark glasses and a tailored black jacket over jeans, and he exuded a citrus scent. A mix of rumpled chic and bad boy. On closer inspection, she realized he was wearing the same jacket as the man she'd noticed earlier in the doorway on rue Buffon.

A frisson of fear rippled her down her spine.

"Do I know you?" she said.

"Not as well as you could, but. . . ." His words trailed off. Suggestive. He took off his glasses. Amber eyes. He gestured to the small marble-topped table overlooking the street. "We can change that. Please, sit down."

Self-assured. And cocky. She couldn't place his accent. But she knew his type. The kind one should kick out of bed, but didn't.

"Sorry," she said, trying to sidestep him, "not interested."

"You run a good game," he said. Feet planted, he stood unmoving. "Got the old man going just as you wanted."

Aimée froze.

"As if it's second nature, or you've been doing this for a while."

Busy with Darquin, she'd missed his arrival and he'd eavesdropped. Denial would be useless. He seemed more polished than the usual RG — *Rensignements Generaux* — operative. The security branch tapped

65

phones and surveilled foreigners; its members could be blunt.

She'd bluff it out. Still, she wished she'd had time to touch up her mascara. "What's it to you?" Aimée asked.

"The Special Investigation unit left an hour ago," he said.

He was too damned observant.

"You want to do this standing up, or should we — ?" he began.

"In your dreams." Time to get out of here. Now. "I don't talk to the RG."

"Me?" His tone changed. "Benoît was more than my friend," he said. "We shared the same saint's day."

His tawny complexion . . . she realized . . . he was part Haitian, light-complected like Mireille. But a common saint's day meant they shared a bond. To some it was as deep a bond as the fraternal one.

"My grandparents came from his village." Sadness and anger mixed in his light brown-yellow eyes. "I'm no *flic.* My name is Edouard."

Yet she couldn't trust him. He could say anything; how would she be able to tell if it was true?

She sat, and so did he.

The owner appeared with her half-filled glass, setting it down on the marble-topped table. *"Merci,"* she said. "But why talk to me?" she asked the stranger.

"It's personal." He set down a folded issue of *Le Figaro* and ran a hand through his hair. "Benoît's murder didn't even merit a short column on the back page. But the speculation about Princess Di's Mercedes hitting the thirteenth pillar in the tunnel occupies pages."

"So?"

"*She* knows who murdered Benoît," Edouard said.

Was he fishing? Trying to get her to confirm Benoît's death?

"Who does?" She'd feign ignorance and see what he knew.

"The woman you're looking for. Mireille," he said. "I need to speak with her."

With effort, Aimée kept her hand steady. Get in line, she almost said.

"How do you know that Mireille has that information?"

"Makes sense, doesn't it?" he said. "And no one can find her. She's disappeared."

"I don't know who you are or why you're interested."

"Edouard Brasseur. Import/export, lucrative and boring." He set a high-end cell phone down on the table, switched the ringer to low. "I haven't asked why *you're* looking for her."

True. He hadn't. And she had no intention of telling him.

"Edouard, convince me that you don't know where she is." She sipped the fizzing water.

A fly buzzed, trapped between the window panes.

He ran his fingers through his hair but said nothing.

She shrugged and gathered up her bag, ready to leave.

He caught her arm. His hand was warm as he held on to her. "Wait. Why do you think I know where she is?"

"If you were close to Benoît, you wouldn't be here." She paused waiting for his comeback, a protest, but he remained quiet. Pensive.

Finally, he spoke. "They say the past is a foreign country." He shook his head. "I hadn't seen Azacca Benoît in a year or so. He was part of the past. But recently he telephoned me out of the blue. If only I'd met him."

"He wanted to meet you?" she said. "When?"

"I came to Paris from Brussels on business. Maybe he'd be alive today if we'd met on Sunday," he said. "Benoît mentioned that he needed proof. Then he said he couldn't talk, asked that we meet later that night, said he'd call back . . . mentioned 'Mireille.' That's it."

"Sounds vague to me," she said. She didn't buy it.

"How can I say this?" Edouard looked up, searching for words. "I had a feeling that he was waiting for something."

"You would know the places Haitians congregate, and his contacts, wouldn't you?"

"His contacts? I'm a stranger in Paris."

He sounded as clueless as she felt. She was conscious of his hand, still resting on her arm.

His eyes caught hers. And bored into them with laser-like intensity.

"I can't figure you out," he said.

Ditto, she almost replied. She wondered about him. His change from cocky, to sad, then to vulnerable had been rapid. But the vulnerable quality seemed real. And appealing, she admitted to herself. She sensed he would be trouble. Those eyes, the way he filled out his jacket. His citrus scent reminded her of Yves, her dead fiancé. Stop! She had to stop this.

"Your big eyes get in the way," he said to her. His voice softened. "A nice way."

Warnings rang in her head. Don't get involved with this one, a little voice in her head cautioned. She twisted Yves's Turkish puzzle ring, which she still wore on her third finger.

"Don't even try," she said.

"Nothing comes for free, I know." He shrugged. "Why should you help me, even if you could?"

"Something like that," she said.

"Benoît's work meant everything to him," he said. "He would have been killed because of it."

"You sound sure," Aimée said.

"This Mireille must know about it," he said. "For some reason, he trusted her."

True. He'd entrusted her with an envelope. Aimée figured the envelope contained the file Mireille had mentioned.

"We can help each other." He leaned forward, his face close to hers. "What's your interest in this?"

Even if she didn't quite trust him, he didn't seem to be working for the cops. And if he located Mireille, she wanted to know. She decided to use business as the pretext for her involvement.

"I'm a private detective," she told him.

A guarded look appeared on his face. "Employed by who?"

"That's private information."

Ringing startled her. It wasn't the phone on the table. Edouard reached inside his jacket. His hand came back cupping a different cell phone.

"Excusez-moi," he said, turning toward the open window facing the street. He spoke in what sounded like Flammand, a Belgian dialect.

Something had fluttered from his pocket onto the floor. Aimée stretched the toe of her shoe out to cover it, then inched it back toward her.

"Here's my number." His phone call over, he handed her a card.

She searched her bag, pretending to look for hers. "I'm all out, no paper . . . wait." She reached down to the floor and scooped up what had fallen from his pocket and a sugar wrapper.

Grabbing her kohl eye pencil, she wrote her number on the sugar wrapper.

The lilac overhanging the rue Buffon wall shuddered in a sudden gust, releasing that familiar cloying scent. What else did Edouard know? What should she reveal? To get, one had to give.

"If Benoît's murder involved his work, as you seem to think," she said, "why attempt to give him a facelift?"

Edouard sat very still. Only a muscle twitched in his jaw. "What do you mean?"

"The skin had been peeled from his temple and his ear had been severed," she said. "And he lay within a circle of salt. Symbolic, *non*? But of what?"

The lines around Edouard's mouth creased in pain. "I don't know."

"Call me when you do." She placed the sugar wrapper with her number on the table and walked out.

After a few blocks, she stopped and leaned against a stone wall to catch her breath. Her pulse raced. Edouard wanted Benoît's killer, she needed to find Mireille, and she hoped they weren't after the same person.

Tuesday Afternoon

"Porcellus, Mademoiselle," said the Ecole Normale Supérieure administrator.

Latin for pig. Aimée remembered that much. But what did that have to do with Professeur Benoît?

Looking up from the university directory, the administrator squinted at Aimée through thick glasses. "Professeur Azacca Benoît is . . . was a world authority on pigs. Renowned."

"Of course," she said, blinking back her surprise. Her gaze went to the glass door open to the Ecole Normale Supérieur's courtyard: manicured hedges, gravel paths, and busts of the learned adorned what had once been an old convent enclosing a spacious garden. The Ecole Normale Supérieur, like many of the *Grandes Ecoles,* was housed in an ancient edifice in the Latin Quarter. Yet for all the school's prestige, she thought, the building could use a paint job. The walls had faded to a burnt brown-yellow; it looked run-down.

"I assume he was on the faculty," she said.

"The Centre Nationale de Recherche Scientifique sponsored Professeur Benoît's research. He did his lab work in the Collections Osteologiques Anatomie Comparée," he said. "As a visiting lecturer, he conducted one seminar a term."

She'd just come from there! "You're sure? A seminar on pigs?"

"We were eagerly awaiting completion of his statistical survey with respect to the comparative anatomy of small hoofed animals in the twentieth century."

Talk about obscure!

"Was his seminar well attended?" she couldn't help but ask.

"The *flic* asked that, too," she was told.

The administrator shut the thick directory.

Laughter erupted in the courtyard corner where several students had gathered. Belted Levi's, short hair, clean white shirts: typical *normaliens,* anything but normal. And very unlike the tousled intellectual Sorbonne type. "Just a *tapir!*" one was saying; "they never let you forget it."

Tapir meant tutor in *normalien* argot. She'd worked with a *tapir* once, sweating out a physics course. Many *normaliens* became politicians, like Pompidou, or scientists, such as Pasteur, or philosophers, like Sartre.

"I'd like to speak with someone who worked with him."

"We've cancelled his seminar. Professeur Rady, the department head, is out today."

Before memories dimmed, conversations and details were forgotten, she had to find out more about Benoît. "Here's my card; please ask him to call me."

The man leaned forward to take it. "Academia's cut-throat, but one never thinks. . . ." he confided.

Aimée paused in mid-step. "Cut-throat?"

"You know, publish or perish." Behind his thick glasses, his eyes were shuttered. "The competition is intense. However, in the professor's category, that was not a consideration."

"I don't understand."

"As I said, Professeur Benoît was renowned in his field. He delivered papers, wrote definitive books, consulted on economic programs. He was beyond that kind of competition." The phone panel lit up and he reached to answer it. "If you'll excuse me. . . ."

"What about the professor's lab? Can I get a name of someone he worked with?"

"I'm sorry. That's all the information I can give you."

Over the Ecole Normale Supérieur's portal in gold letters was the date of the Revolutionary government's founding of the school, 9 Brumaire, année 11.* Once it had admitted every applicant, all citizens being equal. But not now. Outside, in the hot street, Aimée fanned herself. Pockets of air were hemmed in by thick-walled buildings lining quiet narrow streets threading the *quartier.* A lone child's voice drifted from an open upstairs window, followed by the clicking of a metronome and the notes of a violin scale.

Resolute, she quickened her pace. Several streets later she found herself on rue Mouffetard, which was thronged with milling

*November 10, 1802.

shoppers. Once this had been an old Roman road, the artery leading to Italy. Now it was a steep market street lined with two- and three-story slanting buildings, holding wall-to-wall people drawn by the shops and vegetable stalls.

"Peaches, Languedoc peaches," shouted a hawker. "Last of the season."

Mounds of green-seamed melons and moisture-beaded nectarines were arranged in the fruit stall, protected under an awning from the afternoon sun. It was reminiscent of the Marseilles market, she thought, though lacking the sharp fishwives' calls and lapping turquoise waters of the Mediterranean behind them. The ripe sweetness of the last fruits of summer filled the air.

An old man with a dog bumped into her. *"Excusez-moi,"* he said. He smiled, with all the time in the world.

The *flics* would have left Benoît's laboratory by now. She'd have to hurry to get there before the building closed.

She edged forward. Rue Mouffetard was filled with tourists in the afternoon. There were enough of them to make it difficult to move.

She thought that she'd like to show Mireille this *quartier.* On Sundays, she and her grandfather used to cross the Seine to climb the hill of *la Mouffe,* as he called it. They would catch a film at the postage-stamp-sized theater nestled between the shops. Afterward, he'd buy a roasted chicken from the corner *charcuterie* where the Mouffe crossed rue l'Arbalète.

"Why must we always come here for a chicken? It's such a long walk, *Grand-père,*" she'd asked, pouting. "I've bought *poulet rôti* from him for thirty-five years," he'd said, "why should I change now?"

Nearby Place de la Contrescarpe glinted in the sun; the cafés were full, the fountain gurgling. Bright paint, rattan chairs, looked picturesque. Yet the *clochards philosophes* from her childhood were missing. They were the soul of Place de la Contrescarpe, about whom Jacques Brel had sung. Ten years ago, the *clochards* had still congregated to spout philosophy or recite a poem for a drink. Not any more; the *flics* had run them off.

It's too sanitized now, she thought, remembering the grime that had lent the area character. The old Paris. Yet along with the tourists, the *commerçants,* the students, the old women who'd rented the same apartment for fifty years, the professors and *intellos* with the leather patches on their corduroy jackets frayed to look *à la mode,* still lived here.

No time for memories now. The fear in Mireille's face, the urgency in her voice kept coming back to her.

But apart from luring her to a murder scene, Mireille had made no further contact. Aimée needed more than old photographs before she accepted Mireille as her sister. And she needed to get inside the lab to question the staff, to find out more about Mireille and her relationship to Benoît.

Ten minutes later, Aimée buzzed the bell at the tall door of the Osteologique Anatomie Comparée. Behind her lay the gatehouse, sealed off with yellow crime-scene tape. The door creaked open to reveal a man wearing a stained white lab coat. His bulbous red-veined nose caught the light. A drinker.

"*Oui?*"

And by his frown, none too happy at the interruption.

"*Bonjour.* May I speak with the director?"

He eyed her black dress and denim jacket before asking, "Concerning?"

Beyond him stood a dark wood-paneled vestibule housing glass cabinets. Skeletons of small animals stood on dusty shelves, their ivory-colored bones illuminated by shafts of light from the overhead skylight. Jules Verne would have felt right at home, she thought.

Before she could answer, there was the sound of a crash.

"Make an appointment, Mam'zelle," the man said. His words were clipped, the sign of *un vrai gamin parisien*.

She saw her chance to question the staff slipping away. The door was about to close in her face.

"How unprofessional of me, Monsieur," she said, rooting through her bag. She found a torn envelope, the first thing at hand, and forced a smile. "My fault for not explaining sooner. Professeur Rady at Ecole Normale Supérieure sent me."

The man's eyes narrowed. "I don't know what you're referring to. . . ."

"But you do know Professeur Rady, of course?" She kept talking, improvising as she went along.

His eyes flickered in recognition. Of course he did. His self-importance irritated her.

"Check with him," Aimée suggested. It was a good thing Professeur Rady was out of the office. "Perhaps the director could spare me a few minutes? I'm sure, given the circumstances, he'd understand. . . ."

"We're a research facility. The director's not here," he said. "Arrange a visit through the University."

"Professeur Rady suggested I come to scout the location," she said, widening her smile. "Informally, of course."

She kept talking. He hadn't thrown her out yet.

"We're filming a documentary for Arte," she said, hoping to impress him with the arts-and-intellectuals *téle* film channel. "So I need to check your facilities."

"As I said, you need an appointment." His mouth hardened. Was he hiding something?

"Before we know if we can shoot here," she said, determined, "I need to assess the utilities. Minor technical details. I had a short break en route to my next shoot . . . so I'd appreciate your assistance. I'm sure your director will understand."

"Understand?"

"Monsieur, I'm squeezing this in. We're filming a three-million-franc documentary highlighting ENS, the programs, and the world renowned . . . surely. . . ."

"The receptionist returns in an hour. Come back then."

Didn't everyone want to be filmed?

"Tant pis!" The sound of a man's voice, and wood creaking, then another crash. "Show her in, Fabrice, before I rupture myself again!"

The irritating Fabrice opened the door wider, revealing a sweating man in a long white coat. "Film people!" the new man panted. "*Alors,* you run by a different clock. But I'm sorry, we have no one to show you around."

"*Pas de problème.* You won't know I'm here."

Now she had her foot in the door. She'd chat up a lab technician, and, if she was lucky, get a lead to Benoît's puzzling murder and a link to Mireille.

"Give me fifteen minutes." She smiled, glancing at an old fusebox with porcelain knobs hanging on the wall. She made a note with her kohl eye pencil on the envelope.

Fine powder-like dust settled on the wooden floor. Bone dust, she wondered?

The sweating man stuck his hand out. "I'm Lamartine, anatomy cataloguer."

She shook it and saw that her hand was now smudged with dirt.

"We've got this crate to load."

"I'd like to see the research lab," she said. "To check the amount of light available, and the outlets."

"Go through the gallery, then turn right. If you need help, come back and ask me."

She nodded, slipping past a tight-lipped Fabrice and by a deep old-fashioned sink with a backsplash of cracked blue tile.

The spiral staircase in the gallery, a soaring elongated room, led to a high walkway ringing the space that provided access to ceiling-high wooden drawers upon drawers. Each drawer had a metal slot in which appeared yellowed inscriptions in Latin in fading black script with dates from the nineteenth century. Bleached animal skulls bearing horns lined the upper wainscoting. The air was musty; it was a library of bones.

She kept going, her steps raising fine dust.

In the next gallery, she saw small animal skeletons on long worktables covered with brown paper. There were scalpel-like instruments laid out next to them, but no technicians.

She turned the knob of an adjoining door to find gleaming stainless-steel counters and metal ducts venting to the ceiling. A modern "state of the art" lab, in contrast to the rest of the place.

Whirring sounds came from an autoclave on the counter. A larger, more industrial version of the sterilizer used in the rue du Faubourg Saint-Honoré manicure salon she visited — considering her chipped red nails, not often enough.

A man in a blue work apron leaned over a microscope.

"Pardonnez-moi," she said, taking a chance. She didn't have much time. "Didn't Professeur Benoît work here?"

"Aaah, the pigs. You want to see the pigs, *non?"* The man straightened up from the lab table.

What was it with these pigs? Would he show her a pen filled with snorting hogs?

"Of course, but. . . ."

"Here." The man gestured to the microscope. "You're late, Mademoiselle. But I'm glad we can grab a few minutes so I can show you."

She bit her lip. Late? Who did he take her for?

"Monsieur?"

"Assistant Professeur Huby. We spoke on the phone. Benoît was right," he said. "Amazing. The article's already been accepted for publication in the October *Anatomy Journal.* So you won't be able to steal our thunder for the science department journal. That's why I agreed to speak with you."

He thought she had come from the ENS science department. If she didn't go along with his mistake, she'd lose an opportunity. But how could she keep up this pretense? How long before the real person with an appointment appeared?

"After your call, I thought it better you see for yourself," he said, his brow raised, gesturing to the microscope. "Benoît was on the verge of a breakthrough in his work on Haitian pigs."

She played along. She took a breath and put her eye to the eyepiece. Through the microscope, she saw a pinkish-brown series of swirls with yellowish dots like nuclei in the center. A black line divided this half of the slide from a similar scene. A breakthrough? The slides told her nothing.

She looked up. She recalled the words Martine, her journalist friend, would use.

"Can you describe this to me in your own words?" Aimée said. "I'd like to hear it from you. First reactions . . . you know, for a sidebar giving the background."

"Benoît sampled two different species of pigs," he said. "As you can see, he discovered the same epidemiology."

Huby ran his hands through his long brown hair.

"To you, that proves . . . ?"

"Not only to me, Mademoiselle, but to the scientific community. His slides show porcine liver tissue containing residues of heavy metals in quantities sufficient to damage the central nervous system."

Her one year in med school hadn't covered

epidemiology.

Huby continued: "He used GFAA — graphite furnace atomic absorption — spectometry, the most sensitive spectroscopic technique for measuring concentrations of metals in aqueous and solid samples."

Huby gestured to an off-white machine resembling a microwave, hooked up to a computer on the corner counter.

She didn't know what any of that meant, except that it didn't sound good. "Of course," she nodded.

"But I knew you'd get a better sense of his findings from viewing the actual tissue samples."

There must be some mistake, Aimée thought. Was the corpse she'd found last night the same man as this pig professor? Had the old security guard Darquin mistaken the name?

"For the journal, I need a different angle," she said. "Describe the professor for me."

"Eh?"

"His physical traits, how he worked, his schedule, his students."

"See for yourself. Look at my copy." Huby placed a thin journal titled *Ecole Normale Supérieure Laboratoire News* by the microscope.

She glanced at the cover. PROPERTY OF

ASSISTANT PROFESSEUR HUBY was stamped on it.

Then his eyes narrowed. "But you know all this. I faxed you the article yesterday."

She thought fast. "That is so, but I'm writing several different articles right now. Would you mind refreshing my memory?"

A photo on the cover showed several figures at a banquet table raising wine glasses. All men. All *white* men. Not the victim she'd discovered last night.

No wonder this didn't make sense. The *flics* had identified the wrong man. Never mind the professor. How did this involve Mireille?

Any moment now, the real journalist would appear. She'd have to get out of here fast. But Huby had flipped the pages open and was pointing to another photo above an article.

"There's Professeur Benoît in happier times. Such a loss. I'm determined to continue the professor's work."

To her dismay, Aimée recognized the man wearing a laboratory coat, squinting in the sun as he stood behind the skeletons of what appeared to be pigs. A large man, handsome and dark-complected. The man she'd found in the gatehouse with his ear severed.

"That's why I consented to talk with you."

A sad expression appeared on his face. "It's only right that the scientific community knows."

She suppressed a shudder. "Any chance you could point me to his assistant? I believe her name's Mireille?"

"But *I* assisted Professeur Benoît."

"What about a half-Haitian woman? Didn't she type up his notes and keep his records?"

"*Désolé.* If she did . . . there was a young woman. . . ." He stared at Aimée.

"My height?"

"Like you," he said, his words slower, "but a mulatto."

"Where?"

He shrugged.

"Did you see her yesterday?"

"*Entre nous.*" He leaned forward. "The professor let her stay in the gatehouse storage room. That's all I know. After all his research, all his trials, now when he's poised on the brink of announcing a discovery . . . it's a terrible loss."

"So *you* assisted Professeur Benoît," she said, trying to put this together. "Were you his research partner?"

"His part-time assistant. And I felt privileged to help, let me tell you," he said. "But we've spoken about this."

She stiffened, remembering the administrator mentioning "cut-throat" competition and the words "publish or perish." All of a sudden, the possibility of an academic murder loomed.

"Would this discovery put him in danger?"

Huby blinked. "What? This is an academic treatise. What danger could publication here pose for the professor?"

Did Huby's ambitions extend to claiming equal credit for Benoît's findings, Aimée wondered.

"Granted, but Professeur Benoît was murdered."

Huby's jaw dropped. "Murdered? But I thought, an accident. . . ."

"No accident, Monsieur. Murder." She watched him. "Didn't you know? Didn't the police interview you this morning?"

"They told us. . . ." Realization dawned in his eyes. "You're not from the school. . . ."

"Where were you this morning, Assistant Professeur Huby?"

"This morning? Why, at the dentist. I'd lost a filling." His eyes narrowed in suspicion. "But why all these questions? Who are you?"

"Aimée Leduc, private detective," she said. "I'm sorry. I should have told you the truth. I'm looking for a woman called

Mireille."

"Assistant Professeur Huby?" A smiling, petite woman wearing red-framed glasses stood at the lab door. "Elise Cadet, from the science department. Sorry I'm late." She strode into the lab and glanced around the room. "Fantastic lab facilities. Mind showing me around?"

Aimée realized she could learn no more now. She leaned close to Huby. "Can you meet me later?"

"I've got to give an interview to a real journalist."

"Here's my card." She put it in his hand. "It's vital. Please."

The microscope with its tiny brightly lit slide sat on the counter. But what could she do with a slide? "I'll take this journal with me, if you don't mind?" she told Huby. And then she felt a whoosh of air as he strode away to meet the real journalist.

Leaving by the back door, she followed the crumbling outer steps into a small rear courtyard. In front of her stood a two-story atelier, its glass roof half-covered by fallen leaves. The atelier's tall windows revealed a spine of bones hanging from the ceiling. An elephant or dinosaur? She didn't know. But she did recognize the crossbeams framing the structure. Azacca Benoît had stood here with his pig skeletons in the journal photo.

So far, according to Darquin, a secretive Benoît had left Mireille an envelope. The timing was right for Mireille to have had the envelope with her when she appeared at Aimée's office. Huby had revealed that Benoît had made a discovery regarding pigs, and also that he'd let Mireille stay, on the quiet, in the gatehouse where Aimée had found his body.

She had to learn more.

The atelier was cool. Lab coats hung on a rack next to a box of disposble white net mouth masks. She donned a mask and took a lab coat embroidered with the word TECH-NICIAN. She expected more state-of-the-art equipment, but found another nineteenth-century gallery filled with skeletal specimens on tables. Boxes, boxes everywhere. Where to begin?

She heard grunting, the sounds of card-board sliding, and saw a cardboard box moving across the floor.

"Excusez-moi," she said. "Someone there?"

No answer.

She edged past the skull of a rhinoceros and saw a small blonde woman heaving a large box onto a table.

"Madame?"

Still no answer. Talk about unhelpful staff!

And rude.

The woman looked up, her face flushed. *"Un moment."* She took a flesh-colored plug attached to a wire from her lab coat pocket.

She removed her face mask and adjusted the plug in her right ear. "May I help you?"

Hard of hearing? Or totally deaf. Not from old age: the woman was fairly young and attractive.

"Professeur Benoît worked here, *non?*" Aimée said, pronouncing the words with care.

"I read lips, too. Face me and you can talk at normal speed."

Abashed, Aimée paused. She pulled the mask away from her mouth. "I'm sorry, and I can see you're busy, Madame."

"Wait a minute, it's a new hearing aid. I'll adjust the volume."

Aimée waited while she fiddled with a knob.

"Madame, I'm looking for Professeur Benoît's work area." She displayed the page of the journal with Benoît's photo.

"I've never seen you before." The woman cocked her head. "Where do you work?"

Aimée thought fast. "Physical sciences division at ENS. Dr. Rady, the department head, sent me over. It's urgent."

"Urgent? Why?"

"All I know is that instead of cancelling Professeur Benoît's seminar, Dr. Rady contacted a substitute," Aimée said. "But Dr. Rady needs the notes of the professor's lab findings. I guess he figures this will help the person who's taking over the seminar."

"No one told me."

She'd keep the story vague. There was no way she could come up with details if this woman persisted. She had to hurry before the woman got more suspicious and checked.

Aimée shrugged. "They just recruited me. It's not my job, I assist in the lab." She shook her head. "Kind of strange. And it's so abrupt, but Dr. Rady stressed its urgency." She paused looking at the woman, questioning her with her eyes. "Has something happened?"

"You don't know?" The name tag on her lab coat read "DR. SEVERAT."

"Dr. Severat, I'm just a gofer. If you could help me, I need to get the files to Dr. Rady as soon as possible."

"But the professor's dead."

Aimée could have sworn the women's eyes welled with tears. For a moment, she sensed her relationship with Benoît had been more personal than collegial.

"I'm so sorry, I had no idea."

92

"The police poked around and took his things."

Merde . . . the *flics* had beaten her to it.

Dr. Severat wiped the corner of her eye. "The professor assembled specimens here. Like that one." She dusted her hands on her lab coat and pointed to a pig skeleton. "He examined bones, as well as tissue and organ specimens."

"Did you work with him?"

"Me? I'm in paleontology research; 'in the next barn,' as we say."

"But I can't go back empty-handed," Aimée pleaded. "I don't know what to do."

Dr. Severat looked at her watch. "*Zut!* The university van's arriving any minute to pick this up. I wish I could help you, but I've got to move this box next door." She expelled a breath of air.

"Two can do more than one," Aimée said. "Let me help."

"You're sure?"

She'd get more information if she stuck with this woman. "Glad to."

By the time they'd lugged the box across the gravel path, a sheen of perspiration dampened her brow. "This feels like it contains rocks."

"Actually, it's paleolithic-era volcanic stone embedded with shells and early marine fossils," said Dr. Severat.

Aimée felt new respect for scientific staff who had to lug their own prehistoric samples.

"I know your work's important," Aimée said, wondering how to turn the conversation back to Benoît.

"All scientists regard their work as important, as vital to society." A look of amusement flitted across her features. "Here we investigate fossils, bones, to find out what happened thousands, millions of years ago," she said. "This helps us discover things like how continents were formed and why the Ice Age ended, and shows prehistoric links to contemporary species. But Professeur Benoît's work was different. It was directly related to the present day. He lived for his work. It was all that mattered to him. It consumed him." She gave a shrug. "But in the grand scheme of life, well, I don't know."

How did pigs matter, Aimée wanted to ask. How could research into pig anatomy "consume" a scientist?

"You know, he came from Haiti, a poor country," Dr. Severat said.

The poorest, Aimée thought. And she remembered Edouard saying the same thing.

"He tried to make a difference." Dr. Severat's face clouded. "And now. . . ."

The waiting van backed up with a beeping sound.

Dr. Severat paused in the shade, took the clipboard from the truck driver, and signed.

"Dr. Severat, one more thing, if you don't mind?" Aimée said.

Dr. Severat adjusted the small knob behind her ear. "Sorry. That's better."

"I have a name. Mireille. Does that sound familiar? His assistant, perhaps? Anything you know would help me."

Dr. Severat gave a brittle laugh. "That one, an assistant?"

Aimée's ears perked up. "I'm not sure, but. . . ."

"A hanger-on."

Aimée detected jealousy in her voice.

"He felt responsible for people from his country; he was sorry for them. She had no papers and, like so many, she took advantage of him."

"In what way?"

"I don't know exactly. Any way she could."

"Since Dr. Rady wrote her name down, I should try and find her." Aimée hoped that sounded plausible.

"Good luck. She disappeared after the fight."

"Fight?" Aimée hoped the shock didn't

95

show in her voice.

"I've told you what I know." Dr. Severat stuck her pen back in her lab coat pocket.

"I know it's not your problem, but my job's on the line. I'm only on probation. I mean, after. . . ." She searched for what to say, how to engage this woman woman's sympathy and enlist her aid. "My boyfriend kicked me out. But I stopped drinking, got in a program. Started a new life. I need to prove to Dr. Rady that I can do the job. I'll do menial things, anything he asks me."

The chirp of birds came from the bushes.

"He sent me here for Dr. Benoît's notes. Dr. Severat, I'm just running to try and stay in place."

And those were the truest words she'd spoken so far.

No answer. She didn't know what else to do.

"I'm sorry," Aimée said. "You're busy."

Aimée turned to leave.

"That Mireille can't help you," Dr. Severat said. She stepped forward. "The *flics* questioned me. I'll tell you what I told them." Her eyes flashed now. "She's a little schemer. They had a heated discussion. Right there." She pointed back to the lab they'd come from. "But they spoke . . . some patois, *Kreyòl,* I think. I didn't understand,

I couldn't read their lips. But they were arguing, I could tell that much from their body language."

So Mireille had argued with the professor. And later, Aimée had discovered his body in the storeroom where, according to Huby, he'd let Mireille stay. It didn't look good.

"That's not much use to you, I know. But you helped me. And well, we should help each other when we can, right?" For a moment, humanity shone in her eyes. "Professeur Benoît's locker's in that lab where we met. The *flics* left after they questioned me. Far as I know, his papers will still be there."

Guilt flooded Aimée at having misled this kind woman.

"*Merci,*" she said. "I am very grateful to you."

She made her way over the gravel and back to the anatomy building. After searching, she found a small room containing wooden lockers and a file cabinet. She looked around.

Each locker bore a name. The third said PROF AB. At last! But it was locked.

She took the Swiss Army knife from her bag, inserted the tip, and jiggled it. On the second try, it opened. She heard footsteps crunching the gravel. There was no time to go through the contents, so she scooped everything into her bag. Including a lab coat.

Voices came from the courtyard. Her heart sank.

She closed the locker and waited behind the door. The footsteps came closer. Two people were in conversation. She heard them enter the laboratory. They were right outside the door.

"Professeur Benoît worked in here, Mademoiselle Cadet. . . ." Huby's voice droned.

Frantic, she looked around the small room. No other door. No way out.

A high oval window emitted slants of light. Too high to reach, unless. . . .

She stepped on the chair next to the lockers, hitched up her dress, reached her arms and elbows over the locker's top edge, and hoisted herself up. Her knee banged against it as she struggled to lift her body. Once on top, she half-crouched, lifted the old brass latch, and edged through the cobwebbed window opening. Her second window egress in two days.

"Pardonnez-moi," Huby said. "I heard something fall in the back room. Let me check."

Aimée dove through the window, praying no rocks were below. Airborne, she stuck out her hands and let herself fall. She toppled onto thorny branches and came up with a mouthful of dirt, cobwebs streaking her hair. Her bag strap was skewed around her shoulders. Birds scattered, fluttering in alarm.

A shout came from the window.

She staggered to her feet and ran like hell.

Tuesday Noon

Léonie Obin struggled against her dream, fighting the rhythm of beating drums despite the sticky spilled cane-sugar liquor coating her hands. She tried to turn away from the beads hanging from the skeletal neck of Baron Samedi, his black top hat bobbing in the dance of death. Inviting her, *non,* insisting that she join him. So easy, yes, now to follow him. Succumb, and take the black-beaded necklace he offered her. Like wisps of smoke, the dream faded. A white light spread inside her throbbing head. Léonie shuddered. Bone-numbing tiredness weighed her down.

She opened her eyes and found her feet tucked under a blanket as she lay on the brocaded divan. She'd collapsed again. Someone had taken pity on her and. . . . Then last night came back to her.

Edouard, those men, and then it all grew dim. The weakness took over. Her thoughts clouded . . . the image she sought kept slipping away.

Each day, her illness worsened. The clinic doctor said her memory would be the last to go, once her brain was involved. Agitated, she stared at the painting. The frame was askew. The safe . . . more came back to her . . . she remembered. Fear clutched her as she recalled those black-hooded men and Edouard ransacking the safe. Stealing the bank account records.

Maria Madonna and Ogoun help me.

She must have spoken aloud. Someone stood by her side; a vague outline of a head came into view. She tried to focus.

"Madame Léonie, you work too much."

A clucking sound. "Second morning this week I find you sleeping here. Are you all right?" Now there was concern in the voice. Marie's voice. Marie was the cleaning lady. Her short brown hair and wrinkled face became clear as well as the scarred furrows of flesh that descended from under her ear down her neck. She was a burn victim. Marie's scars put others off. But Léonie had felt the energy, the purity in her heart. Ogoun felt it too.

A wave of lucidity washed over her. Familiar things appeared; her desk, her jacket draped over a chair. It was as if she'd returned to the land of the living. And for a purpose.

By the time Marie brought a tray with lemon tea, the haziness in her brain had subsided. Léonie held the Sèvres cup handle, and not a drop spilled into the saucer.

"Madame Léonie, I came early to clean up from last night," said Marie. "But you're so pale, let me help you."

The Madonna, St. George on his rearing horse, spear in hand, and Ogoun, the warrior, had let her come back. The warrior. Let her come back for a reason. Now it grew clear. Even if Edouard knew the system, legal roadblocks would stall his bank account search. She'd make sure of that.

But in her clumsiness she'd alerted Edouard to the existence of Benoît's research file. Her fault. She had to reach Benoît before Edouard did.

"Marie, my medicaments, in the drawer, please."

Her strength ebbed and flowed like a sluggish river. She'd take her time . . . time she didn't have, as her body rebelled. She injected the anti-viral cocktail, swallowed the black paste pellets from the healer, leaned back and tried to take deep breaths. Let her body absorb them, let these things battle inside her and hope they won. The effects of the potent mix lasted a day, two days at most.

She slept. This time restfully, without dreams or visitations.

By mid-afternoon, she'd managed to change into the dress she kept in the closet and apply rouge to hide her pallor. She folded the one bank statement they hadn't discovered, next to her will, in her handbag.

She reached for the hated cane. Another sign of weakness. The knob was a carved goat bone, in the shape of a leering mouth. It was her only remnant of Edouard's uncle, besides the illness he'd given her.

Fatigue hit her again. But she couldn't succumb. Wouldn't. As a young woman in Port-au-Prince, she'd started down this trail of lies and now it had grown out of proportion. She had nothing to lose, but Edouard did.

"Call a taxi for me, Marie, if you'd be so kind."

She'd take care of this; she should have done it years ago. Her legs buckled and she gripped the cane.

Her juju . . . she felt for it around her neck. Gone. Edouard had taken it.

"Madame?" Marie smiled, her work-worn hands folding her apron. "I'm glad you feel better; it's good you go out. And how nice you look."

She needed her juju. What if Edouard had tossed it away?

"Marie, I think I dropped something on the floor."

Marie bent down, embarrassing Léonie for a moment . . . a French woman on her hands and knees for her. "You mean your earring?"

"It's like a sachet, Marie. A small pouch."

"*Non,* Madame, nothing. I don't see it."

"*Désolée,* Marie. . . ."

"For what, Madame Léonie?" Marie stood. "You gave me this job. No one else would hire me. The staff don't treat you right, Madame. Of course, that's not for me to say."

"We promised not to go through this again, Marie."

She nodded, her face now a mask. "Nothing on the floor, Madame."

The taxi waited. But she couldn't go without her juju.

She looked at the clock. She had to go now before the place closed.

"Madame, I hear something; there's a call on your cell phone."

Léonie took the phone from Marie and hit the button.

"They found Benoît," the voice said without preamble.

"Then you've got the information."

"He was murdered. The file is gone."

Shock flooded over her.

"It's up to you to find it," the voice continued.

The phone fell from Léonie's hands and clattered on the parquet floor.

Darkness descended . . . *non,* not now. She breathed, forcing the air into her lungs. If she didn't go now, it would be too late.

Tuesday Afternoon

Aimée entered Piano Vache, a student dive down the hill from Place Sainte Geneviève on the narrow rue Laplace. The place was dark; the corners smelled of beer. Despite the outside heat, the stone walls kept the interior chilled. Like a cavern, she thought, the blackened sixteenth-century stone walls unchanged, a favored haunt of students for centuries. And hers, too, in her Sorbonne days when she'd spent hours drinking and debating philosophy, trying to sound intellectual like everyone else. Always aware that in the *quartier* they followed in the footsteps of Descartes, Verlaine, and Camus.

Furnished with flea-market tables and mismatched chairs, the place had a homey feel. Here she could clean up, examine what she'd found, and still reach the database center in time.

In the lull before the aperitif hour, the bar was deserted except for Vincent, who was setting up bottles in rows behind the bar. A good place to sift through the contents of Benoît's locker undisturbed.

"Long time, Aimée," Vincent said. Tanned, muscular, in his thirties, all in black except for the silver belt buckle that caught a gleam of light. He hadn't changed.

He ran an appreciative glance over her. "Rough and tumble, *comme toujours.*" He hadn't forgotten. A few years ago, their one-night stand had extended for a week. Until she'd found out that he was married. Very married, with a pregnant wife.

"Here for a drink, a chat, or both?" He winked. "*Le strychnine?* The usual?"

Why not? On second thought, though, she changed her mind. She needed a clear head.

"Without the strychnine," she said.

He bypassed the absinthe bottle, reached out and knocked the grounds from the metal espresso filter. The machine grumbled to life.

She passed through the stone arch to the cavernous back room and took a seat at a table by the upright piano, below the stuffed cow sticking out of the wall. Beneath them, in the ancient vaulted caves, existed the remains of a torture chamber with rusted iron instruments on the walls, at least according to Sorbonne lore. She'd never explored to find out for herself. On weekends, DJ's spun here and bands played for a hefty cover charge. Chalk it up to the ambience.

A minute later, Vincent set a demitasse of espresso on the wooden table gouged with initials, and a small shot glass of milky absinthe beside it.

"On me. In case you change your mind."

She'd almost changed her mind about *him* once. "How's your wife?"

"Finished law school. And left me. Now I have the kid." He pulled out his wallet and flashed the photo of a pink-cheeked toddler.

"*Trés belle,* Vincent."

"Like you, Aimée." He grinned. "My life's different now."

She nodded. "Right, you're a single dad. And your life's not your own."

Like her own father.

"It's funny, but I kind of like it this way." Fatherhood became him. He gestured to the seat beside her. "Feel like some conversation to go with that?"

She felt tempted. After all, the only male in her life right now had a wet nose and short legs, and needed a grooming appointment.

"Only if you're a world-renowned expert on pig anatomy."

She smiled and dumped the contents of her bag on the table next to the demitasse.

"I knew I'd picked the wrong profession," he said, taking the hint.

At least he had someone who waited at home for him . . . albeit with colic or wet diapers.

"The place heats up in an hour or two. But you know that. Take your time." He strode back to the counter.

Alone, she sipped the espresso. If laced with too much absinthe, it became lethal. It had been outlawed for years; she'd always wondered how the owner obtained the illegal liqueur.

She stared at the few assorted items relating to Azacca Benoît among her Le Clerc compact, kohl eye pencil, daytimer, and broken shells from the Marseilles beach. Not much. Then she got to work.

The loose papers, a notebook, graphs, and charts she put in one pile. The lab coat, folded, in another. A plastic bag with a moldy uneaten piece of something in another.

Touching these things gave her a strange feeling. Stolen. A corpse's things. A man sprawled lifeless under the gatehouse window, so far a cipher except for his status as a world authority on pigs, and for Dr. Severat's words . . . consumed by his work, passionate, dedicated. She'd found a window onto this man; now she needed to open it, discover his connection to Mireille, and what had put her in danger.

Or what had led her to murder him.

She found the item that had fallen from Edouard's pocket: a postage-stamp-sized pouch of straw-colored burlap. She sniffed it. It gave off a sage and cinnamon smell. Affixed to it was a red cloth string, similar to the red string she'd observed tied around Mireille's wrist. Some kind of Haitian amulet?

She'd watched her father once at his desk in the Commissariat, touching a hairbrush, a tattered holy card, a small bottle of Arpège with faded gold letters on the label. "Why do you look in ladies' purses, Papa?" she'd asked. He'd shrugged; the banal residue of a life was spread over the green blotter on his desk. "It's to get the feel, the least I can do," he'd said. Later, she realized he was attempting to discover a person, a sense of them. To accord the victim some respect.

She opened the notebook and flipped the pages. A pencil-scrawled list, left-handed by the slant, named common chemicals like sulphuric acid, lead, and mercury. She could tell that much. Like a shopping list. And lab requisition slips for these chemicals were tucked into the next page. There was no explanation, no notes to help her.

A waste. And now she'd have to figure out how to return it.

In Benoît's lab coat pocket she found a rolled-up *Pariscope,* the weekly entertainment guide published on Wednesdays. Thumbing through it, she found a page folded back with a red line circling a listing for a baroque music concert at the Roman baths in the Musée Cluny at 5 P.M. the previous night, Monday. Just prior to Benoît's murder: she'd found his body close to half past eight at the laboratory gatehouse.

But at least it told her — *non,* she thought: it gave rise to the supposition — that a man *immersed* in research had nevertheless attended a baroque music concert at the Cluny. A baroque music aficionado?

She took out her cell phone, checked the

listing, and reached the Musée Cluny office a moment later.

"*Bonjour,* I'm inquiring about the evening baroque music concerts."

"*Désolée,* they've just ended for the season," said a high-pitched voice. "We always end mid-September when the weather starts to change."

"But I missed last night's concert. . . ."

"A shame, Mademoiselle. The last of the season."

"Of course it was open to the public?"

"*Bien sûr.* Sold out."

That told her nothing. She thought hard. Perhaps they still had a list. "Do you have a record of the reservations?"

"I doubt that's still in our computer."

She thought fast. "I'd like to know if my friend bought me a ticket. I need to repay him if he did."

"But you could ask him, Mademoiselle."

Too late for that. "Do you mind checking?"

"Hold on, please."

A few clicks. A small sigh. "The system's down, Mademoiselle. I'm sorry."

System down? It figured. National museums like the Cluny operated through the Ministry computer system, which was slow, ponderous, and outdated. If René ever got

110

his fingers on it, he'd fix it in a moment. He loved a challenge. He had once threatened to enter the Louvre site, streamline the catalogue and database section up to the fifth century . . . and give the seventy-year-old staff members heart attacks.

"But you do have a printout of reservations?"

"We're about to close."

A typical *fonctionaire* answer. Employed by the government to push papers in return for salary, stellar benefits, and secure jobs for life. The joke went: "Work? Of course I don't work: I'm a *fonctionaire.*"

"This list. . . ."

Voices erupted in the background. "Mademoiselle, I'm sorry, but. . . ." More voices. "I can't help you. Apart from the usual organizations who reserve. . . ."

Organizations. She hadn't thought of that.

"That's it! He'd have done it through them. Tell me again the names of those organizations."

"But I didn't tell you yet."

Of course she hadn't. But Aimée had to get this *fonctionaire* to spill. "He just changed jobs, but he. . . ."

"Apart from Charité Saint Vincent de Paul and Hydrolis, who reserve seats for guests and contributors, as usual, I can't help you."

111

But she had. A long shot, but it gave her a place to start. Benoît could have reserved through either of them. It would be a tedious job, but if she located his name she might find a connection to whoever had provided him with a ticket.

Then again, he might have just shown up and bought a ticket on his own. Alone? Somehow she didn't think so. . . .

Charité Saint Vincent de Paul said no Azacca Benoît was on their guest list, and the Hydrolis receptionist informed her in a curt voice that she'd need to check with Human Resources. She'd have Human Resources get back to Aimée tomorrow at the earliest. Ten minutes on the phone, and Aimée had struck out at both places.

Too bad her laptop was still in her office. Otherwise, she could have hacked in to check their records. But they might not have kept the data, since the season had ended.

She stared at the absinthe. Tempted, imagining the licorice taste, the kick like a knock on the head. But she had to focus. She took a last sip of the now-cold espresso, set her cup down, and then realized she'd left a moisture ring on the notebook cover. Lifting it up and wiping it with her jacket sleeve, she noticed indentations . . . marks, *non* . . . writing . . . she ran her fingers over

112

it . . . then grabbed the eyeliner pencil from her bag, angled the kohl tip, and rubbed it over the cover. Numbers showed in white where the kohl didn't penetrate. 01 . . . a phone number? Paris land lines began 01 . . . followed by the eight digits of a Paris phone number.

Stemming her excitement, she transcribed the phone number to the back of the envelope. Something? Or nothing. She had to think, to figure her approach.

First she hit INFORMATION on her cell phone.

"Reverse Directory, please."

"The number?"

"01 43 90 76 82," she said.

Pause. The shot glass of absinthe caught the light slanting in from the open door. A murmur of voices, the slap of an exchanged high-five, and Vincent's laughter came from the bar.

"Osteologique Anatomée Comparée, 61 rue Buffon, Mademoiselle."

"Merci."

The lab where Benoît worked. Odd that he'd written it down. A reminder to himself? she wondered.

She tried the number. A tired much-played recording came on. "You've reached the central lab directory. If you know the extension you want, enter it now. For the office directory, press 2." She pressed 2, found Assistant Professeur Huby's number, and entered it. Instead of Huby himself, his voicemail came on. Before the short recording cut off, she left a message asking him to call her.

She glanced at her Tintin watch. Ten minutes to get to the bank's database center. She slid Benoît's belongings back into her bag, left the absinthe, and slapped some francs down on the counter on her way out.

Vincent's good-bye trailed her as she stepped out onto rue Laplace, a twelfth-century street lined with stone and timbered medieval buildings. Already she felt a change in the air taking the edge off the heat. Slight, but a harbinger of fall and of curling leaves on the cobbles.

René Friant, Aimée's partner, all four feet of him, stretched up to reach the data disks on the shelf. A handsome dwarf with a trimmed goatee, wearing a silk shirt with suspenders holding up eggshell-white linen trousers, he reached up standing on the tiptoes of his handmade shoes. Despite the fact that he had a black belt in karate, his short arms and legs made even the simplest tasks a challenge. But she'd never heard him complain.

She kissed him on both cheeks. She couldn't read the look that clouded his green eyes. She hesitated. He hated being helped. "Everything go smoothly at your La Défense meetings, René?"

"You're half an hour late, Aimée," he said, looking her up and down. He pulled over a chair, hiked himself up, and stepped on the seat.

"Traffic, René, *désolée*." She ran her fingers through her hair. They came back sticky with cobwebs and leaves. She'd been so absorbed, she'd forgotten to clean up.

"And hens have teeth, Aimée."

"Look, René. . . ."

He held up his pudgy hand.

"Save it. I've got another meeting at La Défense. Tomorrow. They love meetings, these bureaucrats." He scratched his neck. "Did Madame Delmas give us the green light?"

Aimée stepped over the cables running to the bank of computer screens and slipped off her black patent heels. The cold concrete floor sent a welcome shiver up the soles of her tired feet. She set her bag, brimming with reports, on the floor.

"Bright green. 'Keep going,' she said, and

115

she complimented you on a 'thorough data analysis.' "

René grinned.

"Before you rub your hands in glee, René," she said, glancing at the numbers on one of the screens and clicking open a file, "check this out. She offered a suggestion."

René tugged his goatee, scanning the comments written in the data analysis report's margin. "She's sharp. Makes sense, the way she's suggested, to back up the data this way."

"Glad you agree, partner," she said. "What system report needs running?"

"Done. Just back up these disks and we're set for tomorrow."

"Bravo, René," she said.

On top of his form, too. He relished this private bank job and the prestige that tunneling into a bank system gave him among his hacker students. She couldn't understand it; some hacker thing.

She slid in the disks. They were sitting in a windowless concrete bunker, the private bank's data center. Banque Morel, several kilometers away on the Right Bank, owned this rundown anonymous eighteenth-century building near the Val de Grâce church, a huge edifice built by Queen Anne after twenty-three years of sterility to celebrate the birth of her son, Louis the Sun King. The adjoining abbey, closed at the Revolution, had become a military hospital.

The data center's headquarters, two levels down, were part of the old Roman remains honeycombing the Latin Quarter. Now retrofitted with reinforced concrete and a ganglion of fiber optic cables, the tunnels supposedly had once led underground to an ancient Roman road. No one would suspect that the bank's data center was located here. The pumping heart of operations contained the private information of the world's wealthy individuals and corporations.

The first disk backed up, she slid in the next, producing a slow whirr. She kept on target, ignoring the itch to check her cell phone for messages from Huby or Mireille. It would have been useless; there was no reception down here.

"Want to tell me about this?" René stood next to her, holding up the small black-and-white photo of Mireille.

Her hand shot out. "*Merci.* Must have fallen out of my bag."

Irritation crossed his face. "I thought we agreed. . . ."

"Whatever do you mean, René?" She lowered her eyes to the screen, clicked commands on the keyboard.

"You promised. No missing persons. No other cases, period."

First Zazie and now René.

"Who said —"

"I'd like to believe you." René counted on his fingers. "Let's see: I've heard that seven times — *non,* last year on rue de Paradis you said it too. That makes eight."

Her lip quivered. She wished the photo hadn't fallen out.

"With Yves dead, murdered, did you expect me to forget investigating?"

He leaned forward, his green eyes blazing. "We've just snared this contract that will lead to bigger and better things. We've signed the lease to expand our office next door. Saj's going permanent part-time to service our growing client list. Why does my gut churn, thinking you'd put our progress at risk?"

She blinked. Swallowed. René was working overtime and more to build the business. She really wasn't taking on her fair share of the workload.

"René, I won't let anything interfere with my work."

And right away remembered the pile she'd left on her desk.

"So the way you ran in here, distracted, chewing your thumb and looking like you'd fallen out of the dustbin, signifies you're on top of it?"

The whirring stopped and she inserted the next disk. She stilled her tapping toe, slid her feet back into her shoes. She tried to ignore the claustrophobic ten-foot-thick concrete walls, the fluorescent lighting, the constant hum of air ventilation.

"We're solvent for once, building the agency," René said. "Getting more work than we can handle, yet something makes me think you're going backward." He grabbed the file, thumbed the pages. Then paused. *"Bon."* René tented his short fingers. "Your jacket's full of cobwebs, mascara's trailing down your cheeks." He shrugged. "I get it now. A tumble in the hay . . . another bad boy."

Foolish to think she could hide this from him. "René, I think . . . I have a sister." She took a breath. "I first met her yesterday."

"What?" His eyes widened.

"She appeared just as Madame Delmas arrived for our appointment. So we could only talk for a second."

He blinked. As the words left her mouth, they sounded weak, even to her. She went on. "Supposedly, my father had a daughter. She's half-Haitian."

Aimée rarely talked about her father. Or

119

his death in the Place Vendôme explosion while he was carrying out a contract surveillance for the Ministry. The surveillance had not only killed him, it had discredited him.

"But you never told me, Aimée."

"How could I? It's news to me. I didn't know until yesterday afternoon," she said. "Look on the back of the photo."

René turned it over. "There's a date . . . looks like 1964. Call me a skeptic," he said, shaking his head, "but that's during Papa Doc Duvalier's regime of terror in Haiti. Do you think it's worth the paper it's printed on?"

She sat up. "What do you mean?"

"The whole island was in undeclared civil war. The government was so corrupt that it bankrupted its own health ministry and took sanitation funds to finance the presidential palace. They had no running water to drink, much less to wash the blood from the streets."

"Since when do you know so much about Haiti?"

"From Loussant, my student at the hacktaviste academy, an escaped Haitian exile." René smoothed down his tie. "Tonton macoutes butchered his family. He lost his leg."

"Tonton macoutes?" Aimée asked.

"Papa Doc's paramilitary."

Aimée thought back to the tilt of Mireille's chin, the vague familiarity, the movement of her hands.

"You're saying what, René?"

"This woman claims Monsieur Leduc was her father?" He paced back and forth in front of the banks of terminals. "Eh, why not? She's done her homework, learned your background. Under the Code Napoleon, she'd be entitled to half of everything. Half your inheritance. Have you thought about that? Your apartment, the business. We'd be ruined."

"She's shown me no proof, René," she said. "As a matter of fact, she never showed up again."

"*Et voilà,* she tried a scam," said René, the beginning of relief in his voice. "Scammers work quickly so their marks don't have time to think. Any interference and they move on to the next mark."

René stopped mid-step and stared at her. "What's wrong?"

Aimée's hands were trembling. "It didn't end there, René. She's a murder suspect now." Aimée didn't need her degree in criminology to know the *flics* would go after Mireille once they'd questioned Darquin and Dr. Severat.

René's mouth dropped open.

121

"Sit down, René."

And she told him about it from the beginning.

Worry creased René's face. He rubbed his forehead.

"Stay out of it, Aimée. This Mireille's running a scam. The murder doesn't involve you," René said, his voice quiet. "Furthermore, your father's name, Jean-Claude, is not an unusual one. There's more than one Leduc in the phone book."

"That's crossed my mind too," she said. René was right: Mireille had lured her to the murder scene and disappeared.

The disks whirred, stopped. She hit EJECT.

"And your father never told you about her, right?"

She shrugged. "Maybe he didn't know."

"A woman walks into the office claiming she's your half sister. . . . You don't really believe this story, do you?"

Put that way. . . .

"Logic would dictate —" Aimée began.

René interrupted her with a shake of his head. "You've got that look on your face. A look that says otherwise."

"I mean . . . I don't know. I need to learn more."

"What does this Mireille want? Money?"

"I've told you all I know," Aimée said.

"She looked scared, mentioned a file. Then I found a man, a Professeur Benoît, dead." She hesitated, then spoke. "Someone saw her arguing with him."

"Who?"

"A woman, Dr. Severat, noticed Mireille arguing with the professor yesterday afternoon, before he was murdered."

"So she claims she's your sister; lures you to an address to take the fall for a murder; and, of course, she's never contacted you, you've never seen her again."

"I know all the arguments, René. I've gone over them again and again in my head. It looks simple, but it's not." Torn, she didn't know how to explain it. Couldn't find the words for this feeling in her heart. "René, put yourself in my place. A woman claims she's your sister. She's about to show you some proof, but men chase her for some reason; she's involved in a murder. The facts don't *seem* to add up, but they could. What would you think?"

"Depends on her height, Aimée."

Exasperated, she reached for her bag.

"You can't be sure until she shows you more proof than this, Aimée."

"Did I say I was?"

He seemed on edge, touchy tonight. The cold air in the climate-controlled cavern did nothing to improve his mood.

"Leave it alone, Aimée."

As if she could.

Guilt stirred her. "I had Papa, a childhood, food on the table." She stared at René. "But maybe she didn't. I need to know."

"You're reading too much into this, Aimée."

He meant she *wanted* to believe. Maybe a big part of her did. But she had to see proof.

The job finished, Aimée and René emerged onto the shadowy street. The bushes of the hedgerow rustled. And a lone starling flew up in alarm, batting its wings and scattering fallen leaves on the windshield of René's vintage Citroën DS.

Even if she'd lost the men who watched her apartment, she was wary, on the alert. She scanned the street for a dented Peugeot. But the only vehicle, a parked butcher's truck, appeared empty.

"Where's your scooter?" René asked.

She needed to recover it from behind the dumpster near her apartment.

"Sparkplug problems. Mind giving me a ride?"

The Pantheon's dome, half-illuminated like

a lunar landscape, rose ghostlike over the buildings. The fingernail of a crescent moon hung over the chimneypots riding the rooftops.

Aimée glanced at her cell phone. No messages from Mireille or even Darquin.

René shot her a look. "How's the contractor working out?"

"There's a glitch already. But it's under control."

She hated complying with building codes, following regulations, getting a new loan and other headaches. But René had insisted that they needed to expand. And he was right.

"Stay on top of it. That's where your mind needs to be, Aimée."

"True, René." But a supposed half-sister entering her life and then disappearing, followed by a murder, made it hard to focus.

René turned down the radio. His voice had changed. "I know these students who're working on a computer marketing venue, a new concept. An *incubateur* they call it, like those startups in Silicon Valley." René pronounced it Zeleekon Vallée, his eyes gleaming. "One's got his Papa's money, another's a techie, and the third's a marketing genius. We could get in on the ground floor, Aimée. You know, help them set up, work on the platform."

Of course this excited him. He loved new challenges.

"It's the coming thing. No one's done it before. It's the future, Aimée."

Maybe he was right. But marketing and selling ideas, concepts built on air with the expectation of profits overnight — or so the dot.com hype went — made her wary.

"Let's talk tomorrow," she said.

Reaching Ile St. Louis, she pointed to narrow rue Saint Louis-en-l'isle. "I'll get off here."

"But your apartment's a block away."

"I don't want to take a chance with those *mecs* who followed me," she said. "Besides, my scooter's parked here."

"If you're nervous, stay at my place, Aimée," René said.

René inhabited a small studio filled floor-to-ceiling with computers, printers, and scanners. She'd have more room curling up on his Citroën's leather rear seat, with his police scanner to keep her company.

"*Non, merci,* René," she said, shutting the car door. "*A demain,* until tomorrow."

He drove off through the long shadows of horse-chestnut trees. A church bell pealed, echoing in the night. Nervous, she checked the street. Only the glow from a few lighted windows, the trickle of water in the gutter. She hitched her bag onto her shoulder and found her scooter. She tried the ignition. Dead. The engine didn't even turn over.

She cursed, pushing the scooter over the cobblestones, vowing next time to replace the old spark plug sooner. Old and tempermental, the scooter sat in the courtyard carriage house more often that not.

Instead of rounding Quai d'Anjou to her apartment entrance, she used the rear door as she had this morning. Perspiring and out of breath, she shoved the scooter and lifted it over the threshold. She fumbled for her keys.

"Don't turn around." A voice that could have been female or male.

Aimée's spine stiffened. A current of air floated over her legs as the door clicked shut behind her.

She grasped the Swiss Army knife in her bag, flexed her fingers. As soon as she reached the overhanging pear tree branches, she'd. . . .

"Keep going, Aimée."

That voice. The lilt in those words.

"Mireille?" She spun and almost lost her grip on the scooter handlebars.

She saw a different Mireille, her composure of yesterday afternoon gone. She was young-looking, yet she had to be older than Aimée. Mireille's large eyes batted in fear. She wore her hair pulled back in a disheveled knot.

"A man followed me in the Metro," she said, her voice quivering. "I'm scared."

A surge of protectiveness filled Aimée despite her suspicions. "We can't talk here." She pushed the scooter onto its kickstand, then took Mireille's arm. Light from a tall window facing the courtyard glowed. "Upstairs," she said and led Mireille up the worn marble stairs illuminated by a circular glass lantern to the black-and-white tiled landing and her door.

Mireille took in the tall double doors carved with rosettes and chestnut leaves. "You live here?" she asked.

Aimée pulled her inside and bolted the door. Miles Davis emitted a slow growl and sniffed Mireille's ankles. He scooted off, his tail between his legs. She guided Mireille over the creaking parquet hall floor to the kitchen window. Pinpricks of light dotted the Seine. The plane trees, dark blots between the street lamps, lined the stone wall. There was no one standing on the quai.

Still no guarantee. They could be watching from a dark car.

"Were you followed here, Mireille?"

"I ran." Her voice cracked. "I waited for you around the corner for an hour. I don't think I was followed."

It paid to play it safe, keep the lights off and use the rooms in the back wing, whose windows couldn't be observed from the street. Aimée opened the double doors of the salon, a high-ceilinged room filled with musty air she rarely used. It held a directoire desk, matching chairs, and her grandfather's finds from Drouot auctions. Aimée picked up the box of wooden matches and lit the half-burnt candles still in the candlesticks.

"It's like a museum," Mireille said, glancing at the shadows on the *trompe-l'oeil* muralled ceilings.

"Grandfather. . . ." Aimée hesitated: it felt awkward saying this. ". . . bought this place cheap after the war. His seventeenth-century bargain, with archaic plumbing and nonexistent heating."

Mireille paced by the window overlooking the interior courtyard and stared out, clutching her hemp bag. "They're hunting me like a dog. I shouldn't have come here. . . ."

Not here five minutes, and already she wanted to leave.

"First you're going to answer my questions," Aimée said. "Why did you set me up, Mireille?"

Mireille's shoulders tensed. "Set you up?"

"You're running a scam —"

"I don't understand," Mireille interrupted.

"I found Azacca Benoît's body. His ear was cut off. You lured me to rue Buffon to take the blame for his murder."

Mireille made a sign of the cross, then raised the gold cross she wore from her neck to her lips. She rubbed the thin red thread knotted at intervals around her wrist. "You're serious . . . *mon Dieu.* I didn't know."

"You were seen arguing with him, the *flics* suspect you . . . and you don't know?"

"Forgive me for endangering you." Mireille's lip quivered. "I just bring trouble. Bad juju." She rolled down the waistband of her skirt, revealing a red-pink spiral on her honey-colored hip. "The sign. I'm marked."

"That's just a birthmark," Aimée said.

"Ogoun marks his warriors."

"Ogoun?"

"That's what my Auntie said. Ogoun's the defender, the warrior deity. You call him Saint George the dragon slayer."

Aimée pointed to the cross around

Mireille's neck. "But. . . ."

"I'm Christian, like everyone in Haiti, *bien sûr.*" Her brow creased. "But where I come from. . . ." She paused. "The spirits, the offerings to deities, our beliefs are all woven together. Like a patchwork. The African gods aren't separate. I grew up with these beliefs; they're part of our culture."

Candle wax dripped down the tarnished silver candlesticks in a slow trail of drops.

"That explains nothing," Aimée said. "Look, you walk into the office, claim you're my sister, tell me you have proof and want to meet. Then you bolt from the café, leaving an address on the napkin. I find a dead man, a professor of animal anatomy, there. But you want me to believe you didn't try to frame me for his murder?"

Mireille crossed herself again. "I didn't know where else to meet you." Her chin trembled.

"You sent me to the gatehouse and I found his body. What's your connection to Professeur Benoît? What do you want of me, Mireille?"

"I had the professor's address. He came from my Auntie's village. I was desperate and I begged him to help me. Bound by our ways, he let me stay in the gatehouse so they wouldn't find me."

"So *who* wouldn't find you?"

"The men who stole my papers," she said. "Benoît offered to help me get a temporary permit and a real job."

Not according to Dr. Severat's story. She'd said Mireille was a hanger-on taking advantage of Benoît's kindness, exploiting a village tie.

"A staff person overheard you arguing with him in the laboratory."

Mireille looked away, her gaze resting on the frayed edge of the Aubusson rug.

"Do you deny arguing with him?" No answer. "The *flics* believed her. You're a suspect, Mireille."

"A suspect?" Her eyelids batted in fear. "I don't understand this. *Who* told the *flics* this?"

Aimée remembered that brief flicker in Dr. Severat's eyes. Did it come down to jealousy?

"You didn't answer my question, Mireille," she said. "But we've got the whole night to find the truth."

"You always pay, *non?* Nothing's free." There was bitterness in Mireille's voice. She collapsed on the Louis Quinze *fauteuil.* Her fingers raked over the frayed upholstery seat. "Professeur Benoît's a generous man . . . was. Bit of a womanizer, but. . . ."

She shrugged. "Nothing unusual. When I said no, I'd find somewhere else to stay, well, he got mad. That woman must have overheard."

"When was this?"

Mireille bit her fingernail. "Sunday, I think. But later Benoît apologized to me," Mireille said. "He told me he'd gotten too involved with this woman. She'd pressured him to move in with her. But he had so much on his mind . . . he worked all the time. I'd see the lights on in the lab. Then on Monday he asked me to keep a file for him."

That caught Aimée's attention.

"You mean the file he left for you with the guard?"

She nodded. "It would be just until he came back, he said."

"Came back from where?"

"An appointment? I don't know." Tears welled in her eyes. "He seemed nervous. Jumpy. He told me he trusted only me."

"Trusted you, over any of the laboratory staff?"

"I don't know why, I don't understand anything they do there," she said. "He said I owed him a favor, that I should do what he asked and keep my mouth shut."

"I don't understand why you didn't come

to find my father earlier."

A look of shame crossed Mireille's face. "Call it pride, but I wasn't going to look him up until I got settled and had a job. It was easier to seek help from a village connection. But Professeur Benoît never came back yesterday," she said, her voice rising. "Then this man followed me from the laundromat on rue Buffon and lurked across the street. When I was in the café waiting for you, I saw him again and ran."

"What did he look like?"

"Dark glasses, big, filled out his leather jacket." Aimée remembered the man on the quai, the Peugeot? Same man? "He had a motorcycle." Mireille shivered and put her hands over her face. Her hair came loose, curly strands escaping down her neck. She looked up and took a breath. "He chased me. I took the wrong Metro train and got lost. By the time I made it back to rue Buffon to meet you, the place was crawling with *flics*. I knew I couldn't go inside."

"Why didn't you tell them this and explain?"

"Me, with no papers? I thought the *flics* had come to arrest me and deport me."

"Mireille, a lawyer can help you claim asylum," she said. "I know someone. . . ."

"Do you know how many Haitians petition for asylum, how many are waiting? The quotas won't even cover *last* year's appeals."

Aimée had had no idea.

She held out the old photo of her father, the one of Mireille as an infant with her mother. "Can you explain these photos?"

Candlelight flickered over Mireille's expression. *"Tim tim.* You want me to explain? *Tim tim."*

"I don't understand," Aimée said.

"We say *tim tim* to indicate a riddle. Like, what goes in white and comes out mulatto. If you give up, you say *bwa seche."*

"Bwa seche?"

"Bread. A mulatto's like toast."

"How do you know my father is yours too?" Aimée asked. "I need more than this."

"I never knew him. All I had were the photos, that card. . . ."

"What card?" Aimée remembered René's words. A third-world country, the poorest in the world . . . Mireille suddenly appearing. . . .

"These photos don't prove he's your father."

The torn photo taken at the Brasserie Balzar with her father smiling, Mireille's mother sitting next to him in a sleeveless dress . . . a typical scene in the Latin Quarter. They could have been students.

135

Her father would have been a recent police recruit at that time. Who were the other people with them? Who was Mireille's mother gazing at? Who was missing from this photo?

"They look happy," Mireille said. "A group of acquaintances, friends . . . see those glasses? There were others. The photo's torn off."

Aimée sat down next to Mireille. "Why did you come to the office of Leduc Detective?"

Mireille took a small leather-bound journal from her bag, opened it, and handed Aimée a postcard. On the front was a yellowed map of Haiti, titled "The Pearl of the Antilles." The other side, dated May 1964, bore a message: "Jean-Claude — all my letters have been returned. They took the farm, I need help. There's no one else to ask . . . we're in hiding . . . my baby's five years old." The inscription ended with a blotted ink smudge, as if tears had fallen and smeared the surface.

The card was addressed to Jean-Claude Leduc in care of Leduc Detective, rue du Louvre, Paris. But it hadn't been signed or sent.

"My Auntie gave me this before I left," Mireille said. "My mother had burned everything else. My Auntie assumed this was addressed to my father. She said it was all they ever found."

Was this true?

"My mother never told me his name. I was seven years old when we had to hide in the countryside," Mireille said. "We were always moving around. One day these big men wearing sunglasses and machine guns took *Maman*. The tonton macoutes. They shot her by the water pump."

"Why?"

"Her face . . . I can't forget what they did to her face. . . ." Tears dripped down Mireille's cheeks. Her voice was faint. "*Maman* called me her *princesse*. She said that's what he'd called her."

Ma princesse. The words struck Aimée like a blow.

"He? You mean. . . ."

"My unknown father."

"That's what Papa called me too," Aimée said. "But why did the tonton macoutes —"

"Kill *Maman?*" Mireille interrupted. "For consorting with a Frenchman? Or maybe because Duvalier had woken up on the wrong side of the bed that morning. One never knew. With all the massacres, what did one more murder matter?"

"But it mattered to you." Aimée leaned

forward. "I'm sorry."

"My grandmother hated my mother." Mireille wiped her eyes. "As for me, well, it seems having a mulatto bastard grandchild didn't earn her points with her fancy neighbors in Pietonville."

Aimée didn't know what to say. She stared at this woman who she hadn't known existed two days ago, searching for a resemblance. There could be something. Perhaps the green eyes flecked with brown were shaped like her father's.

"I didn't grow up in a place like this." Mireille gestured around her. "Or have what you had."

Aimée felt a pang of guilt. But then René's words about an inheritance reared up in her mind. Did Mireille want money?

"My mother kept writing letters, but he never replied," Mireille continued.

That was so unlike the Papa she knew. Candlelight flickered; the smell of burning wax lingered in the air. Aimée wondered if she should dig out photo albums with snapshots of her father and show them to Mireille.

"Her letters must have gone astray, Mireille," Aimée said. "Maybe he didn't know about you." That had to be it. "Papa was a good man. I miss him. It's sad you

138

didn't know him, Mireille."

"*Maman's* family didn't want to know me," Mireille continued, her jaw set, as if Aimée hadn't spoken. "To live, I cut sugar cane. I slept in the fields."

"But you were a child."

"Oh, I wasn't the only one." Mireille shook her head. "When I got taller, I could work in the factory. But an aunt found me. I got lucky; she took me in. She confirmed that my Papa was French but said I had to keep quiet about it. These things were dangerous. Auntie scraped up money for me to attend the *lycée.* I got a scholarship to the *collège* in Gonaives."

How differently their lives had turned out, Aimée thought. She felt a deep connection to Mireille. She'd been an only child and now, suddenly, it felt as if a vacuum in her existence had been filled. But could she be sure Mireille's story was true?

"I trained as an accountant and worked in the Banque National office in Port-au-Prince. But, in the last coup, everything crumbled. I had to leave."

"And now?"

"With no papers?" Mireille shrugged. "No one like me got an exit visa from Haiti."

"I don't understand. Why would an exit visa matter?"

Mireille blinked in surprise. "Educated people can't leave unless they have connections and money to grease palms with. Otherwise there would be a mass exodus, and only poor cane-cutters would be left."

Aimée stared at her. "Yet you made it here."

"People Auntie trusted smuggled me across the border to the Dominican Republic. For a price. Then I sailed to Guadeloupe."

"Guadeloupe's a department of France," Aimée said. "You could have gotten papers there —"

"With what?" Mireille interrupted. "All my money went to the man who'd made the arrangements to get me to France. Fifty of us spent weeks at sea, hidden in the cargo hold. At the port in Calais they jammed us into huge lorries. The drivers stopped on the outskirts of Paris." Mireille closed her eyes and took a breath. "They demanded we work off the 'surcharge' for all the unexpected bribes they'd had to pay. Liars."

"You mean they were human traffickers?"

"Traffickers? I don't know this word. The drivers saw a chance to make money from us. Their cut, they said."

"Frenchmen?"

"African blacks, muscle men, who spoke

140

French." She nodded. "I remember their gold chains, bad breath, their drinking. They laughed and refused to give us back our papers."

"What papers?"

"My ID card from Haiti. That's all I had. They intended to sell us to pimps or to sweatshops. But I got away."

Mireille paused. "At least I thought I'd gotten away. They threatened to cut our throats if we tried to escape. To set an example, they said. If they catch me, they'll kill me."

Now she had all the pieces of the puzzle, Aimée thought, but she didn't know how to connect them. It still didn't make sense. Moments passed, marked by the drip of candle wax.

"When you appeared at my office, I was surprised," Aimée said. "Forgive me, I should have been more. . . ."

"Like a sister?" Mireille's voice sounded almost childlike now. She stared at her feet. "I assumed you knew about me."

Nonplussed, Aimée shook her head. Whatever she said seemed wrong. And then she brightened. "We'll get to know each other."

Bonding, wasn't that the word? It might take time, but they'd find things in common. She tried to think what those could be. Her parched throat cried out for water, but she didn't want to go get it, not just now. She hesitated, afraid to believe, desperately wanting to.

She hunted in the rack under the ebony-inlaid mother-of-pearl end table. She found a bottle of St. Emilion, blew the dust off, found a corkscrew in the drawer and two mismatched Baccarat wine glasses.

"Here." She filled a glass and handed it to Mireille, who clenched her fist around the stem.

Aimée swirled the dense St. Emilion, sipped, then set her half-empty glass down. She had to ask. "You don't really think its the traffickers, do you? You think you're being chased for Professeur Benoît's file."

Mireille nodded. "I did what Professeur Benoît asked me to do."

"What's inside the envelope?"

"I do not know." She crossed herself, then opened her bag. "You'll know what to do with it."

"First, you must explain to the *flics* how you came by the envelope. They're looking for you. Talk to them and clear things up."

Mireille shook her head, twisting the hemp bag's strap in her fingers. "You don't understand."

"Understand?" Aimée took Mireille's

other hand. "Try me. Mireille, I'll help you get the file to the right person. But you're a murder suspect. You need to speak with the *flics*."

"I never meant . . . but to understand. . . ." Mireille hesitated. "Growing up like this, you can't imagine. . . ."

A flicker of doubt crossed Aimée's mind. She leaned forward. "Did Benoît threaten you, Mireille?"

"What?"

"Did he hold the promise of a job over your head, demanding that you sleep with him?"

Mireille would not meet her eyes.

"Or did he attack you? You defended yourself, of course, you never meant to hurt him, but you hit him too hard."

"Me?"

"If this was self-defense and you were scared and ran away, explain it to the *flics* —"

Loud knocking on the front door interrupted her.

Mireille bolted from the chair, terror in her eyes. "He's here . . . he found me."

"Who?"

Mireille backed up against the wall. "The killer's here . . . he's found me . . . don't you understand?"

The knocking continued, loud and insistent.

"I didn't kill the professor. He helped me. They want the file . . . you have to believe me, Aimée."

Aimée couldn't take the chance of handing over her own sister . . . or any woman . . . to a killer.

The knocking had become pounding. And somehow, Aimée realized she believed Mireille.

"Help me, *mon Dieu.* Look at my hands. I didn't cut his ear off. How could I? My left arm is almost useless. The tendons were severed in the sugarcane factory. I still can write, but I have no strength in it."

No wonder she'd held the glass that way.

Panicked, Aimée looked around the room. She remembered a small niche in the wall, the hidey-hole used to conceal priests during the Revolution. As a little girl, she'd hidden there playing hide-and-seek. Maybe Mireille would fit.

She ran her fingers over the wood panels. Felt the smooth wood, the ridges. Then her index finger caught the well-worn wooden knob. She grabbed it and turned. The small panel half-opened to a space built in the paneling. A crawlspace, dark and smelling of dust.

"Hide in here, Mireille."

"In there? But it's too —"

"Quick, there's no time. Trust me." Aimée brushed the cobwebs away, gestured, and helped Mireille inside. "Just until I get rid of him."

She closed the panel, heard it click, and prayed Mireille had enough air to breathe. Aimée's cell phone vibrated in her pocket.

Who would be calling at this time of night?

She took her unlicensed Beretta from the hall *secretaire* drawer. On her tiptoes she stared out the door peephole. Darkness.

She stepped back, hit ANSWER on her cell phone.

"Open the door, Leduc," Morbier's voice said. "I'm waiting."

What was Morbier, her godfather, a Commissaire, doing here? Shocked, she almost dropped the phone.

"I didn't see you through the peephole."

"Try again."

On her tiptoes, she looked again and saw Morbier's face shadowed in the dim light. Alone.

She unbolted the door, a bad feeling in her bones.

"Kind of late for a visit, Morbier," she said, letting him in.

"Do you always greet guests with that,

145

Leduc?" He gestured to the Beretta. "Mind putting it down?"

She set the safety and stuck the gun in the drawer. "No offense, Morbier. Just a precaution."

Morbier was more than usually rumpled: his brown tie hung loose, his shirtsleeves were rolled up, and his corduroy jacket with patched sleeves hung over one shoulder. His thick hair was now more salt than pepper at the temples, the circles under his drooping eyes more pronounced. He bent and petted Miles Davis, whose tail wagged nonstop.

"Miles has gained a little weight," Morbier said. "He needs exercise."

"You dropped in to tell me that?"

She figured Morbier's men had trailed Mireille. Either he knew she was here and was playing ignorant, or he'd dropped in to sniff around.

"Didn't you call me today, Leduc?"

"Me?" Just her luck that she hadn't managed to hang up before the system traced her call. "My phone's acting funny, the call list —"

"Going to offer me a drink, Leduc?" he interrupted.

He wanted to visit. But with Mireille in the cramped airless hidey-hole, she knew she had to get rid of him.

146

"Why didn't you call earlier, Morbier? I've got an early meeting in the morning," she said.

"Me too." He stood, feet planted, unmoving. His shoulders drooped; his complexion had an unhealthy sallow tone. "A Brigade Criminelle meeting concerning you."

"I don't understand." She kept her tone casual.

"I'm thirsty, Leduc."

She wasn't going to be able to get rid of him.

"Meet me in the kitchen," she said.

Miles Davis trailed Morbier down the hall, sniffing his trouser cuffs. She ducked into the salon. Now, if she could reassure Mireille that Morbier's visit was the perfect opportunity to relate what had happened, to shed some light on Benoît's murder . . . that circle of salt . . . Aimée turned the knob.

The hidey-hole was dark.

"Mireille?"

Empty, except for the dead, stale air inside. She felt in the worn dust-filled grooves, groping within. Her hands encountered nothing but cobwebs.

"Need help, Leduc?" She heard Morbier's footsteps in the hallway.

"No. I'm coming."

She grabbed another bottle of wine and glasses, began to run, then stopped and returned for the corkscrew. She felt a current of warm air now and noticed the window, open to the courtyard. The night breeze made the candle flame flicker. The only remnant of Mireille was her wooden comb, left behind on the chair where she'd sat.

Her heart sank. Mireille had fled, too afraid Aimée would betray her. By airing her suspicions and accusations, she'd scared her off. The opportunity to learn who was following Mireille or what Benoît's "file" signified was gone.

In the kitchen, Morbier stood silhouetted before the window, the light from a passing *bateau mouche* framing his hair like a halo. A long, low toot and the barge disappeared under Pont de Sully, leaving white wavelets in its wake.

"What's the occasion, Morbier?" Aimée asked.

"Besides the moon in Scorpio?" He gestured to the web of clouds obscuring the tip of a sliver of a moon.

She set the bottle down and dusted it off. She worked the corkscrew, wondering what the Brigade Criminelle wanted with her.

"Aaah, St. Emilion. Nineteen sixty-eight,

an excellent year even though Sorbonne protestors shut down the *quartier*," Morbier said without skipping a beat. "But to hear those Sixty-eighters talk now, it was the highlight of their lives. Everything's gone downhill ever since."

He stared at the label. "I should come more often, Leduc, if you've got this lying around."

"That would make a change," she said. "The last time you were here was for Papa's wake."

He stared at the sediment in his glass. "So it was. I'm sorry, Leduc."

He'd never apologized to her in his life. Or spoken of the past. What had come over him?

"Confession time, Morbier?" The words came out in that accusing petulant little-girl tone before she could stop them. Part of her wanted to open up, to confide in him. But the time had passed when she could rely on him as she had years ago.

"Not me. Your turn, Leduc."

Morbier set a Polaroid photo by his glass. In lurid color, it showed Azacca Benoît with matted hair, the skin at his hairline flayed. This time his eyes had been closed.

Her stomach churned.

"Do you recognize him, Leduc?"

"Should I?" She kept her voice calm with effort.

"They ran your Vespa registration through the system. It was parked in front of the place where he was murdered, on rue Buffon. And don't tell me your scooter was stolen."

She put the bottle down before she dropped it. "Sarcasm's not becoming, Morbier."

"Want to tell me about it, Leduc?"

"You suspect *me?*"

"If I did, Leduc, we'd be having this conversation at the Prefecture. We found a witness, but I can always use. . . ."

"*Bon,* then you wasted a trip here."

"Did I say witness?" He shook his head. "Wishful thinking."

She paused in her twisting of the corkscrew.

"Now I see I've caught your attention, Leduc. The *flics* discovered a married couple — married to other people, that is — in the bushes, as well as a doddering caretaker. Their evidence amounts to zip."

"You're a Divisional Commissaire now, Morbier," she said. "A big promotion. Too important to pursue an investigation in person, I would have thought."

She poured the wine into his glass.

"Right." Morbier sniffed and took a sip. "I shuffle more papers now. The piles get bigger."

"Why are you working this investigation, then?"

"I'm not," he said. A vein pulsed in his temple. "Leduc, the responding *flic* knew your father." Morbier shrugged. "He recognized your name and alerted me. You know, it's like a family. On the Force, we do favors for each other when one of us gets involved."

Us. Once a *flic,* always a *flic.* One never got away from it. The ranks closed. They protected their own from outsiders. Even after the false accusations against her father, she was still included.

"Should I regard this as a favor, Morbier?"

"Take it any way you want, Leduc. The other suspects are chatting with a hardass at the Brigade Criminelle," Morbier told her. "The one who investigated your father's case."

"Papa was acquitted, you know that, Morbier." That verdict had come much later. But the stink of corruption surrounding her father's career had driven him to leave the Force.

Morbier set his wine glass down so hard that red droplets sprayed the counter. "I asked why your scooter was parked on rue Buffon, then disappeared after the discovery of this man's body!"

She detected more than anger in Morbier, a veteran who kept his emotions in check. Frustration, fatigue, or something else. She could see no way out but to talk.

She reached for a towel, wiped the counter, and set down the napkin from the café on its surface.

"That's why."

He turned it over with nicotine-stained fingers. "So? I'm waiting, Leduc."

"A woman called on me at the office yesterday. She said she was my sister."

"Oh? Her name?"

"Mireille Leduc." She took a deep breath. How could she quickly construct an edited version of Mireille's tale? "I went to meet her in the corner café as we agreed, but she'd left. The owner said she'd run out; someone was chasing her. She'd left this address and two photos for me. I rode to the address, but after I saw the *flics* on rue Buffon, I left. That's all I know."

Morbier watched her, saying nothing.

"Did you know I might have a sister, Morbier?"

"Leduc, nothing your mother did would surprise me."

Her mother? Shocked, she'd never thought of that.

"No, she says she's Papa's daughter," she told him. "She was born in Haiti."

"In Haiti?" He shook his head. "There's a lot of water between here and Haiti. An ocean."

Aimée hesitated. A pigeon strutting on the balcony ledge outside her window cooed. She twisted her fingers. "Did Papa ever speak of her mother, a woman named Edwige . . . a baby?"

"You're the only one he talked about, Leduc. His *princesse.*"

Aimée bit her lip. Was he trying to protect her?

"Look at these." She showed Morbier the photos. The half-smile of the woman glinted in the sun, her wrist raised against the light. Her other arm held the baby. Aimée set the much-thumbed black-and-white photo of her father and the woman at the café on the counter. "Do you recognize her?"

He sipped the wine. "It's torn. But that's Brasserie Balzar." He turned it over. "Must be 1958. We were walking a beat together then, up in Montmartre."

"How can you tell, Morbier?"

"Miss France. See?" He pointed to the placard in the Balzar window. "Auger . . .

you can see that part. Claudine Auger was Miss France in 1958. Amazing, eh, the things you remember." He shrugged, his thoughts somewhere else, in another time. "We pinned up her photo at the Commissariat. Your father had friends at the Sorbonne and hung out there."

She stared at her father's face. The warmth in his eyes made her heart ache. It ached for his loss.

"So this woman says she's your sister," Morbier summarized, "doesn't show at the café, leaves the photos and an address for you. And you fall for it?"

She added, "Her mother had Leduc Detective's address."

Morbier pulled out a pack of unfiltered Gauloises from his pocket, reached for the kitchen matches by her Aga stove, and flicked the match.

"It was a ritualistic murder." In typical fashion, he had steered the conversation in another direction. Like a prizefighter, a feint to the left, then a quick jab to the gut. "Symbolic, Leduc."

"Symbolic of what?"

"Think about it. A deserted place at night," Morbier said. "A circle of salt surrounded him, like some vodou rite. Mirielle could help us with our inquiries, if she wasn't trying to frame you."

Vodou? Did it add up: the signs of a struggle, his missing ear, the circle of salt? If only she'd had time to ask Mireille what it meant.

"*Non,* Morbier you think his murder is tied to Papa somehow. Otherwise you wouldn't have come here. And whatever that means, you're not telling me."

Morbier let out a deep breath. "And why would I think that? Like I said, the *flics* noted your scooter plates."

"You and Papa were partners. Why didn't Papa confide in you? Or me?"

"Maybe because you're his only daughter," Morbier said. He took a drag, expelled the smoke, and checked his phone. His thick brows knit. "Why do you think she's your sister?"

"I don't know that she's not."

He pointed to the Polaroid of Benoît. "You really don't recognize him?"

She shook her head. She was clueless, but sure Morbier knew more than he was letting on. "Don't tell me you haven't ID'd him by now."

"Azacca Benoît, resident of Haiti, according to his International Driving License. Visiting lecturer at Ecole Normale Supérieure, researcher, consultant to the

155

World Bank."

The World Bank. She'd learned something new. "So he's the *créme de la créme?*"

Morbier's cell phone rang. He stubbed out his cigarette in the sink. *"Oui?"* He listened, then flicked it closed. "We've got a lead to that Fiat Uno seen speeding away from the Pont de l'Alma tunnel!" But he sounded spent. The bags under his eyes were more pronounced than usual. A day's growth of whiskers shadowed his cheeks.

"Immigration's interested in this Mireille," he said. "Next time she contacts you, alert me."

"So you can turn her over to Immigration?" She wanted to bite her tongue. "What put them on her trail? Why do they think she's illegal?"

"Leduc, *charette de guillotine's* not my department." He used the nickname for immigration raids in old vans, ending with airport deportation. One-way tickets to their country of origin, often guaranteeing the immigrant involved a short life. Like the guillotine.

Morbier set his half-full glass on the tiled counter. At his feet, Miles Davis yawned, then licked his tail.

The blue light from a barge illumined Morbier's expressionless face. His hollow look made her skin crawl. She saw the cold detachment of a professional who dealt with murder, rape, and violence. The ugly side of life was a daily occurrence for him. His mind was always cataloging, filing the bits and pieces that came his way for future use.

"A former colleague works in Immigration," he said slowly. "If she's innocent, I could help Mireille sort this out."

That was the deal. But his look unnerved her. He might use her as bait for Mireille.

The muffled peal of a church bell drifted from l'eglise Saint-Louis.

"You always wanted a sister, eh, Leduc?" Morbier was saying. "I remember you played with dolls, pretending. . . ." He shrugged. "You gave tea parties, like all little girls do."

Right at this table. Every day after school, waiting for her father.

"What aren't you telling me, Morbier?" she said. "Some pressure from above, is that it? Or your health?"

A lost look crossed his face. Despite his distant, gruff façade, Morbier remained a tenuous anchor to her old life. To her father. Now he seemed to be drifting away from her.

He coughed, checked his cell phone again, then glanced out the window. A *flic* car with a flashing orange-red light waited on the quai.

"Damned Fiat Uno!" He shook his head. "Thanks for the wine. Superb, Leduc."

And just like that, he left. She ran after him.

At the half-open door he paused, his face in shadow. "Next time Mireille makes contact, I expect you to inform me. As usual, Leduc, I've stuck my neck out for you."

"I don't understand."

"The Brigade's focused on this Fiat Uno hunt. But it's a matter of a day or two at most."

"Until they find it?"

"Until they haul you in. There's a limit to how long I can keep them off."

Her shoulders tightened. "Why?"

"Every time I try to help, you throw the past in my face. Can't you move on? Find a good man and, for once, keep him? Make babies?" He shrugged his shoulders. "I promised your father I'd watch out for you. But there's only so much I can do if you aid and abet a homicide suspect."

"Why didn't you tell me that Mireille's a suspect instead of giving me this song-and-dance? But what if someone framed her? Have you thought of that?" Now *her* anger took over. "No wonder they're watching me."

"Watching you? You're paranoid, Leduc."

"Weren't your men sitting in a car on the *quai* this morning?" She pointed outside the window. Now there was only Morbier's vehicle with the telltale light on top.

Morbier shook his head. "Not from our division, nor from the Brigade. Their plate's full with the Princess Diana investigation. The world's watching, as they never tire of telling us. Top priority."

Merde. If the *mecs* who had trailed her weren't from Morbier's division or the Brigade, who were they?

She watched his car drive off down the quai. Morbier knew how to play her. Dangle a carrot to get her to turn in Mireille. But, in his own way, he also tried to protect her.

She was sure Mireille hadn't killed her professor, her protector, much less carved off Benoît's ear or peeled his skin back with her weak hand.

Aimée grabbed Miles Davis's leash from the coat rack, wrapped a scarf around her shoulders, and ran down the stairs.

"Mireille?" She called. No answer. She let Miles Davis water the trees, then searched the rubbish bins, behind the pear tree, even the carriage house and the walkway to the

159

next street. No sign of life. A chill breeze nipped her arms. Coldness settled over her as she realized that Mireille was long gone.

Wednesday Noon

Loud drilling sounds and the screeching of metal on metal by the pipefitter drowned out the voice on the other end of Aimée's office phone. There was no way she could work here, with Cloutier and his crew hammering and drilling.

"Un moment, s'il vous plaît," she said to the caller.

She grabbed her bag, the phone crooked between her neck and shoulder, waved good-bye to Cloutier and pointed to her cell phone. He nodded, mumbling something, his mouth full of nails. In case Mireille made contact, she'd told him how to reach her.

All morning, her mind had been occupied with Morbier's allegations of the previous night. She realized that if she didn't point the *flics* at Benoît's killer, she'd end up at the Brigade Criminelle herself. A tall order, but now she had no choice.

She closed Leduc Detective's door and set her bag down. In the relative silence of the dim landing, Aimée could finally hear her caller. "Sorry; please repeat that," she

160

said to the Hydrolis Human Resources secretary on the other end.

"Our director, Monsieur Jérôme Castaing, purchases concert tickets at the Cluny Museum for the organizations he supports," she said. "To express appreciation."

The woman had returned her call. Progress, she thought. If a ticket to Monday's baroque music concert had been given to Azacca Benoît, he had been at Cluny just before his murder.

"I'd like to make an appointment to see Monsieur Castaing today."

"Would this concern the foundation? Monsieur Castaing's very involved with human rights in Haiti, but his time is fully booked."

Haiti. Her ears perked up. "If he could give me ten minutes?"

"I'm sorry, his calendar's full. Next week?"

"But I can be at your office . . ." She looked at the address in the Latin Quarter she'd jotted on her checkbook. ". . . in fifteen minutes."

"Mademoiselle, I've told you his schedule's full."

She had to persist.

"This is important. Since he attended the concert with Professeur Benoît, he'd want to know what I have to tell him. What time does he go to lunch?"

"Monsieur Castaing has already gone to lunch."

"Can you leave him a message to call me?"

"Bien sûr," she said.

Aimée gave her number. "And what time could I expect a call — that is, when will he return?"

"I can't promise you that he'll call right away."

"I understand. But I'll want to keep my phone on . . . so if you could give me a range?"

Phones rang in the background. "He returns close to two . . . but then he's busy all afternoon."

"Merci." Aimée ran down the spiral staircase. It was 1:45. Taking no chance that she might be followed, she left through the back door.

The taxi dropped her in front of the bistro across from the Musée Cluny. On this warm September afternoon, waiters in black vests and long white aprons hovered over patrons at the outdoor tables. The murmur of conversation and clinking of cutlery could be heard over the distant hum of traffic on Boulevard Saint Germain. Hydrolis's office building, a balconied five-story sandstone affair, stood at the corner of rue de Cluny above a publisher displaying thrillers in wraparound windows.

Aimée hurried along the butterscotch stone walls of the looming twelfth-century Cluny Museum. The crenellated stone wall, like filed teeth, reminded her of a fortress. Once a medieval abbey, the place reeked of age. The Dark Ages.

She followed a group of schoolchildren into Square Paul Painlevé, a small garden crossed by gravel paths lined with benches, enclosed by bushes and trees. The ironwork fence gave the square a sense of separation from bustling Boulevard Saint Michel a block away and the Sorbonne across the street. She sat on a bench in the shade of linden trees. A quiet oasis, and a perfect vantage point from which to view Hydrolis's entrance at 1, place Paul Painlevé.

Most company directors took extended lunches. She figured Castaing would be no exception. Fifteen minutes later, two men left the bistro and walked up rue de Cluny, suit jackets over their arms, one a thin scarecrow of a man, the other broad-shouldered and stocky. They were deep in conversation and paused at the door to the Hydrolis building as the thin man put on his jacket.

"Monsieur Castaing?"

The thin man turned around. *"Oui?"*

His cheeks were flushed, presumably from wine he had consumed at lunch. Confident, now that she'd found him, she edged closer, smiled, and said, "If I could just speak with you regarding the Musée Cluny baroque music concert on Monday?"

His mouth pursed and he looked irritated. "My secretary informed me." He jabbed his finger in the Musée Cluny's direction. "Don't tell me you people have more problems with next year's reservations."

"Monsieur, it's concerning Professeur Benoît."

He turned. "Go ahead, André. I'll catch up with you in a moment." He nodded at her. "Let's talk over there." They crossed together, between a parked van and a Renault, to the gates of Square Paul Painlevé. They passed through and halted near the fence. Behind them, on rue des Ecoles, stood the bronze statue of the philosopher Michel de Montaigne. Touching the toe of Montaigne's bronze foot was thought to bring good luck; it had been rubbed shiny.

"Merci, Monsieur Castaing. You're busy, so I'll just take a moment of your time." She handed him her card with the inscription *detective privé.*

"A private detective?"

Laughter rippled through the garden. Small children tossed breadcrumbs at a waiting pigeon.

"I'm sorry, Monsieur," she said. "My instructions, well, I've been hired to document Professeur Benoît's movements on Monday."

"You seem to think this involves me," he said. "What's this about?"

Didn't he know of Benoît's death? Was he asking questions to gain time? She was afraid he'd bolt any minute.

"Can you confirm that you both attended the baroque music concert on Monday night at Musée Cluny?"

"There's some mistake," he said. "Mademoiselle, those seats go to our clients and the associations I support."

"But did Professeur Benoît attend the concert?"

"How would I know?" Castaing replied. He made motions like he was about to leave. "I have meetings all afternoon, and I don't appreciate this interruption."

"According to the ticket reservation list, he attended the concert," she said, taking a guess. She had to start somewhere and hoped Castaing would point her in the right direction. "A few hours later, he was found murdered."

"Murdered? But this morning we were informed that there had been an accident."

She saw fear in the small eyes behind his heavy horn-rimmed glasses.

"This is hard to believe," Castaing continued. "I'm shocked. A distinguished professor, a world authority, this makes no sense."

"Monsieur, the concert might have been the last place he was seen before his murder."

"*Alors,* Mademoiselle. Every year, I purchase a bloc of seats to donate. That's all I know."

She'd gotten nowhere. His fingers played with his jacket buttons.

"Were you acquainted with Professeur Benoît?"

He removed his glasses, blew at the dust on the lenses, then fitted them back on his face. "We'd met a few times at social functions."

"Your help's vital. Please, did he seem nervous or on edge the last time you saw him?"

Castaing's brow wrinkled in thought. "Not that I can remember. I'd like to help you, but it's been weeks since the reception at which we spoke."

A dead end. And she'd had high hopes

this would lead somewhere. But she did sense that Castaing was nervous.

She was at a loss as to how to proceed. She hadn't had time to prepare. But she couldn't give up. "In what capacity did your firm deal with Professeur Benoît?"

"We have so many consultants, I'd have to check," he said. "Call me this afternoon."

"Just to clarify, Monsieur." She pulled out a bank receipt, found a pencil. "So I don't bother you with needless questions. Was the professor consulting with respect to your projects in Haiti?" That sounded vague. She remembered Morbier's words. "Regarding the World Bank?"

"Mademoiselle," he said, his voice firm now, "I want to help, but I'm twenty minutes late."

"And these projects with the World Bank . . . ?"

"We employ more than fifty consultants to assist with our World Bank RFP's."

RFP's: Requests for Proposals. She and René knew them well. RFP's were required for outsource contracts. She filed that away in her head for later.

Castaing turned and unlatched the park's metal gate. The peeling metal fence looked in need of another coat of dark green paint.

"Monsieur Castaing, forgive me, but I'm

investigating a murder. Anything you can tell me would help."

He paused in thought. "Have you checked with Father Privert's foundation?"

She shook her head. She didn't recall the name from the Musée Cluny concert list.

"Talk to the priest. We provide him with tickets to support his foundation. His latest project is a wonderful free food program for Haitian children that we contribute to. Father Privert runs a shelter on rue Amyot for Caribbean immigrants."

Her ears perked up. Mireille might have gone there.

"Now if you'll excuse me, Mademoiselle?" Castaing closed the gate.

An immigrants' shelter, run by a priest, would be a safe place to hide. She headed out of the park. Her phone trilled in her pocket.

"Mademoiselle Leduc?" said a high voice. "Madame Ornano with the Musée Cluny. You had questions about the baroque music concert?"

Finally! But the sooner she reached Father Privert's shelter, the better. "*Oui.* Madame, may I call you back this afternoon? Say —"

"Impossible! I'm leaving in twenty minutes. For a month."

Should she race to the Privert shelter or follow this new lead?

"I'll be there in two minutes, Madame." She hung up, glanced around, saw no one looking, and rubbed Montaigne's foot. At this point, she needed all the luck she could get.

"We use volunteer ticket-takers and ushers for our baroque music concert series," said the smiling Madame Ornano in the Musée Cluny office. "The program runs itself. I'm very proud of it."

"Runs itself, Madame?"

Madame Ornano stuffed her TGV train tickets into her briefcase, closing it with a snap.

"I delegate, Mademoiselle." She leaned forward, took the silk scarf from her desk, wrapping it around her neck with a flourish. "That's the secret. Delegate. I sign the checks, that's all."

In other words, she'd be no help to Aimée. She'd wasted her time when every minute counted.

"Villiers, the cellist, stepped in to seat patrons on Monday," she said. "He even helped us put the chairs away after our event. Not above his station. He talks to everyone. So popular, and the patrons love him. The baroque quartet . . . ahh, the music they make, soaring to the vaulted rooftops in the old Roman baths, the ancient baroque music . . . it's as if we'd been taken back in time."

With the plague, rats pawing raw sewage in the narrow lanes, high infant mortality, bathing unheard of, and autocratic monarchs? No, thank you, Aimée thought.

Madame Ornano clasped her hands to her chest, hummed, and then in a well-trained voice burst into song.

Startled, Aimée realized she'd have to get her back on track. A man had been murdered, and this romantic interlude of Madame Ornano's was no help. Maybe the cellist would prove more useful.

"Such a wonderful voice, Madame," Aimée said. "But we're both pressed for time. I'm planning a birthday party and I want to hire him."

"Do you have a . . . a sizable budget, Mademoiselle?" she asked. Madame Ornano's frugal calculating side showed. "He's a soloist, a member of the Conservatoire. Of course, the Ministry of Culture underwrites our concerts."

Aimée wouldn't hold her breath for the day she could afford to hire this cellist.

"But my friend, the baron . . ." Aimée

paused for effect. ". . . *adores* baroque music."

Aimée quickened her step past the gray stone of the Sorbonne, weaving through the students choking the pavement, hurrying up the hill to the Pantheon. Hope soared that she'd find Mireille. En route to Father Privert's shelter, she punched in the phone number of the cellist, Villiers, from the card Madame Ornano had given her. In view of Madame Ornano's further rambling discourse about volunteers, Villiers was the person to start with. He or another quartet member might remember Benoît and whether anyone had accompanied him. Villiers might prove observant. She hated this tedious pursuit of details, but following up as to details had netted Jérôme Castaing and through him the name of the shelter where Mireille might be hiding.

A strain of Bach played on Villiers's answering machine, followed by the breathy words "I'm on tour in Lyon this week. Leave a message, s'il vous plaît." She hoped he checked his messages.

She summed up what she knew: Azacca Benoît, a world authority on pigs, visiting lecturer at one of the *Grands Ecoles* and consultant for the World Bank as well as for

Castaing's firm, with a fondness for the ladies, had entrusted Mireille with some important papers. He might have attended a baroque music concert, if that was the "appointment" Mireille had mentioned. According to her, he had never returned from that appointment. He had then been murdered, not three hours later.

Aimée hiked along the curving street, which followed the old Roman road. She feared she'd arrive too late to find Mireille or any trace of her.

This slice of the Latin Quarter felt run down. It was mainly inhabited by students, distinct from the gentrified tourist haunts a few blocks over. A genteel class of landlord, made up of widows or women of a certain age, rented students rooms in their overlarge apartments, or let out sixth-floor *chambres à bonne* — maid's rooms under the eaves — to them.

Next to an old wooden storefront nestled amid tilting sixteenth-century buildings she found the sign for Shelter Caribe, almost covered in strands of ivy. She pressed the worn bell, heard a click, and pushed open the little door inset in a massive arched green double door. An arrow and small hand-lettered sign pointed to a damp cobbled courtyard in the rear of a shabby *hôtel particulier,* a mansion that had seen better days. On the right, vaulted stone arches bearded with lichen reminded her of the cloister which, no doubt, it had been in the Middle Ages.

The whole *quartier* had been filled with churches, convents, and priories until the end of the Revolution in 1799. Incensed with the Church's power, the rebels had razed what they could. Twelve churches remained. Twelve too many, her grandfather would complain.

She climbed the wide stairs, grooved in the middle from centuries of footsteps, and followed a winding hall's leaning walls and crooked angles, leading down to three steps. This was a makeshift arrangement of buildings that had been cobbled together over time.

On the second floor, she rapped on a tarnished brass knocker. A moment later, the door opened to air redolent with the scent of coconut. She was in a hall with blue-green wall hangings picturing the sea, carved wooden figures, and simple, flat paintings of black figures working in sugarcane fields. A Haiti-Democracy political poster hung on one wall.

Expectantly, she stepped inside.

"Bonjour," said a deep male voice.

Her eyes adjusted to the light. A middle-aged man wearing black, his shirt topped by a white clerical collar, greeted her. He had pink cheeks and thin brown graying hair. One of his blue eyes was filmed by the milky haze of a cataract.

"*Désolé,* Mademoiselle, the room has been taken."

She took a guess. "Father Privert?"

"Guilty." He gave a little smile and turned. "Josephe, please find that hostel referral list."

"No need, Father. Jérôme Castaing of Hydrolis referred me to you." That wonderful smell permeating the air, a blend of coconut and fish, made her stomach growl. She'd only had a brioche today.

"Monsieur Castaing? *Mais oui,* our benefactor. I'm happy to help you."

"That's so kind, Father," she said. "But I'd like to see Mireille Leduc."

"The name's not familiar."

Her heart sank.

He took a magnifying glass from his shirt pocket and consulted a thick register. When he looked up, his milky eye unfocused, he shook his head. "No one here by that name. I am sorry."

She fingered the leather strap of her bag. Did he offer sanctuary to illegals and was therefore fearful of revealing information? Instead of taking it slowly in order to win his confidence, she'd barged right ahead: her bad habit, as René often pointed out.

"Father!" a voice called from down the hall.

"One moment, please." He disappeared, walking quickly.

Disappointed, she entered a small sitting room but saw no one else to ask. Her shoulders ached with fatigue. And she still knew no more of Mireille's whereabouts.

"In here, Mademoiselle," he called. She found Father Privert at the copier in a small alcove office.

"I checked our records, but I'm afraid I can't help you," he said.

Had he consulted with whoever had called him and decided to get rid of her? Disappointed, she wondered if he was hiding information. She looked around and noticed a bulletin board on the wall.

Photos showed hollow-cheeked children, hair a light straw color from malnutrition, eating from a garbage can behind a fish stall in an open-air market. A street scene showed sewage from a latrine running down the middle of the road. Women at a rusted water spigot were shouldering water cans beside shacks made of cardboard and flattened metal peanut-oil gallons. Fat crows sur-rounding a tin labeled POWDERED MILK US-AID clustered near a crying barefoot child. Above the photos was a quote from Mother Teresa: "Cité Soleil's not the poorest place in Haiti, it's the poorest place in the world."

She took fifty francs from her wallet and stuffed the bill into a collection box labeled FOR CITÉ SOLEIL'S HUNGRY CHILDREN.

"Father," she said, "you do relief work in Haiti?"

"I try." His shoulders sagged. "The gov-ernment denied me reentry, you know," he said. "Well, of course you don't. I do what I can, but they think God's work is too politi-cal."

"God's work . . . you mean feeding chil-dren is considered political?"

"Father Privert's too dangerous," a woman said. She stood in the doorway, a blonde in khaki pants. Her angular face was almost pretty, but it lacked expression. "After his prison sentence, they are even more afraid of him."

Aimée blinked. "They put priests in prison?" It sounded like the Inquisition. Then she wanted to bite her tongue. How naïve she must sound.

"L'Ardeville," she said, as if Aimée would understand. "Amnesty International paid attention, exerted pressure to obtain his release. For once!"

"Josephe!" Father Privert smiled sadly. "Monsieur Castaing referred this young woman to us. She's looking for . . . I'm sorry, who's the person you're looking for?"

"Mireille Leduc." Aimée hesitated. Compared to hunger and prison abuse, her quest paled in significance. But Mireille's life was at stake. "Mireille's tall; she has caramel-colored skin and curly light-brown hair. Have you seen her recently?"

"The residence is full," Josephe said. "Father hasn't been able to take on any new residents for the last two months."

"Mireille's half-Haitian. I thought she'd come here." Aimée swallowed hard. "She's my sister, although I met her for the first time on Monday."

And when she said it, she almost believed it.

Josephe and Father Privert stared at her. From outside the window overlooking the courtyard came the banging of a metal trash can, then a cat's cry.

"Mireille has no papers. I don't know who else to ask," Aimée said. Desperate, she tried another angle. "It's not my business if you provide sanctuary to *sans-papiers,* but Mireille's in trouble, on the run. I want to

177

help her."

"Of course," said Father Privert, "but I don't know how. Our last Haitian student is now doing graduate work in the States."

She paused, unsure whether to reveal more about Mireille's trouble; but if you couldn't trust a priest. . . . About Josephe, she wasn't as sure. But this information could tip the balance in favor of persuading them to help.

She took a chance. "This concerns the ENS professor murdered Monday," she said. The aroma of wild lilac and the metallic smell of blood came back to her. Her hands shook, and she hid them in her pockets.

"Not Professeur Benoît?" Father Privert made the sign of the cross. "We're organizing a memorial. But I don't see the connection."

"The *flics* suspect Mireille," she said. "I'm terrified for her."

"Nom de Dieu!" Josephe and Father Privert exchanged a look. "You're sure?"

"I wish I weren't," she said. "Professeur Benoît helped Mireille, letting her stay at the lab. The guard heard some noises, and I think he saw something."

Darquin, the guard, knew more than he'd told; he had to. Maybe he didn't recognize the importance of what he'd seen.

"You mean he could clear her?" Josephe said.

"Mireille didn't kill Professeur Benoît, that's all I know," Aimée said. "The professor might have mentioned your shelter. Mireille's afraid. As a child, she saw the tonton macoutes murder her mother, and she's never gotten over her terror."

She searched their shocked faces, hoping that if they indeed were hiding Mireille, they'd trust her.

Josephe shook her head. "I don't understand. Professeur Benoît's a famous scientist. Who would kill him?" She fingered the fringe on her vest, paused, and glanced at Father Privert, who'd folded his hands in prayer.

Father Privert nodded. "*Oui*, a distinguished man, a role model for Haitians. Born in a ravaged farming village, one of twenty children, he was the only one who went to school," he said. "He studied and worked hard to make his people's life better. He's . . . *was* . . . a world-renowned researcher, a . . . such a waste. May God have mercy on his soul."

She hadn't known all that. Had she judged him too harshly . . . or had Mireille lied? She didn't know what to think. But the

179

truth in Mireille's voice came back to her.

Josephe took the priest's arm. "The Lord gives and He takes away, Father."

Aimée sensed they knew something. She had to keep probing, find the link, a connection. Something.

"Didn't he have a ticket to the Cluny baroque music concert, a ticket that Monsieur Castaing had provided to your organization?"

Josephe nodded, her face blank. "I left his ticket at the museum, as usual, for him to pick up. Monsieur Castaing's so thoughtful."

That placed Benoît at the Cluny. As she'd suspected. What if he'd met his murderer there?

"Not three hours after the concert, his body was discovered at the laboratory."

Josephe clapped a hand over her mouth.

Father Privert laid his arm on Aimée's. His good eye centered on hers. "I understand your concern," he said. "But the best tribute to Benoît consists of continuing my work feeding children. A sad commentary, you may say. We never forget that Toussaint l'Overture led the Haitian slave rebellion that overthrew colonialism and made Haiti the first independent country in the Americas. Ironic, too, as Benoît never tired of not-

180

ing that Napoleon, who admired l'Overture's ideals and had his body interred in the Pantheon, exacted the reparations Haiti still pays to France, even today, which cripple the economy."

A mixture of hope and sadness painted his features. "President Aristide blazed a new trail. His successor, Préval, is working to eradicate poverty, unemployment, torture, and arbitrary arrests. The country's changing. My foundation feeds our future, children, the one thing Haiti's rich in. Our benefactors make that possible."

"Father Privert's work is vital." Josephe took over, as if used to handling requests for the priest's time and energy. She handed Aimée a brochure printed in *Kreyòl* and French. "I volunteer to help manage this shelter so Father can devote himself to his work," she said. "But we depend on generous help from Monsieur Castaing. So does our voter-initiative group in Haiti, which focuses on political solutions."

In other words, they were busy. But Aimée wasn't going to leave until she'd gained *something*.

"In what ways does Monsieur Castaing support your work?"

Josephe's eyes brightened. "He understands Father's mission and makes our outreach possible. Not only does he support both groups financially, he raises funds. We'd be nowhere without Monsieur Castaing."

"Polluted water's killing more Haitian children than hunger," said Father Privert. "We're educating mothers to cook only with water from the new pipelines."

Father Privert switched on the copy machine, which rumbled to life.

"But they're wary of Monsieur Castaing's sewage-treatment plant," Josephe said.

"Why?"

"Superstition. Oh, that's changing." Josephe smiled. "Opportunists charge a fortune to bring water from the hills in water trucks, then gouge these poor people. But Hydrolis offers them free water, so they will learn to use piped water."

Father Privert leaned down, stacked a pile of copies, and fed more sheets of paper into the machine. The machine spit out copies in a steady rhythm. "Father?" Josephe shrugged. "He's deaf in one ear from being tortured," she explained to Aimée.

Aimée shuddered. But persevered. "Please understand, I respect your work," she said. "And why you might feel reluctant to speak. But if you know where Mireille's hiding —"

"I'll ask around," Josephe interrupted.

"But people disappear."

The finality in Josephe's voice raised the hair on Aimée's arms.

"Father's optimistic; his faith guides him," Josephe said. "The people who live in Port-au-Prince get electricity for one hour a day, if they're lucky, and running water for a few hours daily. Human rights abuses in the system have changed little since the Duvalier days. The violence. . . ." She shrugged.

"You mean the tonton macoutes?" Aimée said.

The phone rang.

Josephe said, "Change comes from the grassroots level."

The copier emitted a printed page that read: "More myths by those who claim to help Haiti . . . their lies endanger aid. Under the guise of party reform, Edouard Brasseur, former rebel against Duvalier, makes false accusations of corruption."

The name Edouard Brasseur caught her eye. But he'd told her he worked in import/export.

"Josephe," said Father Privert, picking up a sheet of paper, "I told you we must only write about feeding children and working to provide clean water for Cité Soleil, not about factional infighting. These inflammatory, divisive articles. . . ."

"We're exposing the truth," Josephe said. "You agreed. Remember, Father?"

Aimée wondered: was Josephe a radical? She wished she'd been able to speak to Father Privert in private. She distrusted Josephe now.

Josephe's eyes flashed as she continued: "Remember that radio interview, and the lies he fed them?"

"Enough, Josephe. Edouard supported us before."

Aimée asked, "You're in contact with this man, Father?"

"My dear, no one knows how to reach him. The government has put a price on his head."

But Aimée had just talked to him in the café on rue Buffon. "Yet he gives radio interviews?"

"He lives in the shadows, Mademoiselle. That's all I know."

Yet he'd come out of the shadows to question her, even given her his card. Didn't smell right, as her father would have said.

"We've got a deadline," Josephe said with finality.

"Thank you for your time." Aimée put her card in Father Privert's hand. "Just in case you see Mireille."

■ ■ ■ ■

Aimée crossed the courtyard, which was bathed in afternoon shadows. The crisp scent of laundry wafted by her. With a quick step, she avoided dripping water from the newly laundered shirts hanging from the balcony above.

If Father Privert and Josephe harbored illegals and provided them with sanctuary, she reasoned that they'd never open up to her, putting the foundation and their work at risk by doing so. But now she knew that Benoît had attended the Cluny concert hours before his murder.

Hunger gnawed at her. She found an empty table at the nearest outdoor café and ordered. It was time to use a connection, to call Martine, her best friend since the *lycée*. Martine worked part-time at *Le Figaro* on the editorial side, doing investigative journalism, as well as consulting on book projects for a Left Bank publisher. She tried Martine's flat overlooking Bois de Boulogne, shared with Gilles, her well-off aristo boyfriend and his children. No answer, so she called Martine's cell phone.

"*Allo?*" Martine's voice wavered.

Aimée heard the pop of a cork in the

background. Laughter.

"Martine?"

"I'm in a meeting, Aimée," Martine said.

"Sounds well lubricated."

"Welcome to publishing. You wouldn't believe the expense accounts for these meetings, and for book launches," she said. "The stories I could tell you about Bernard-Henri Lévy's editor. . . ."

"I'm more interested in the story behind Edouard Brasseur's interview on RTL."

"Hold on. Who?"

"Edouard Brasseur," Aimée repeated. "How'd RTL get an interview with a former rebel who's wanted by his government?"

"The Haitian? Rumor is that he approached the producer," Martine said. "Something relating to a high-profile researcher who was murdered Monday night. He insisted on giving a statement, refuting the allegations being made."

Aimée caught her breath. "Allegations against Azacca Benoît, the ENS professor?"

"But didn't they find photos . . . with boys . . . ?"

Aimée sat up. "You're kidding."

"Kidding? Look at today's *Choc.*"

A scandal tabloid.

"*You* read *Choc*?" Aimée asked, surprised.

"Everyone does, even if no one admits it."

"The man was a womanizer, Martine. . . ."

"*C'est ça.* I'm wrong, I confused him with Catherine Deneuve's gardener."

"Benoît also consulted for a firm, Hydrolis, on World Bank proposals," Aimée said. "Know anything about them?"

"The World Bank?" Martine laughed. "Take a number. There's a long line."

"Eh?"

"I mean the World Bank's under fire, left, right, and center," she said. "A consultant, tainted by the same brush? That's what you're thinking?" Martine didn't wait for an answer. "But what's it to you?"

"My sister . . . well, I'm not —"

"Sister?" Martine interrupted. "And you're letting it out now, Aimée? All these years . . . you never told me?"

Hurt layered Martine's voice.

"Like I knew, Martine? Call me confused and bewildered. She appeared in my office just this Monday, claiming she's my sister from —"

"Your wild mother?" Martine interrupted. "Well, that makes sense, given that she changed names like she changed countries. Who knows how many half-siblings you have?"

Aimée caught her breath. Morbier had jumped to a similar conclusion. A chill crept over her heart as she thought of her mother starting a new life without her. Ridiculous. She didn't even know if her mother was alive. What could she do about it, anyway?

"*Non,* Martine, a half-sister from Papa."

"Your *father?*"

Loud voices, then a squeal of laughter in the background.

"Hold on . . . the top model who wrote her life story has just arrived. And they call that literature!" Martine snorted. "Still, it makes for a change from the usual navel-contemplating literary types. But it's the busiest time of the year, Aimée. I'm jammed with the *Rentrée de Litérature* . . . seven hundred books published this month. Tell me who'll read even half of them!"

Martine paused and exhaled. "What's Edouard Brasseur's connection to this half-sister?"

"That's what I want to find out. Please, Martine."

"You mean she's really your sister?"

"I think so. But it's worse: she's a suspect in Benoît's murder."

"*Merde,* Aimée . . . your family. . . ."

More laughter.

"I'll sniff around," Martine said. "Meet me tomorrow at the hammam. Got to go." And she hung up.

The waitress set down a *tartine,* a long crusty baguette filled with cheese, cornichons on the side, and an espresso.

"Merci."

At least the afternoon's temperature had fallen by a few degrees. As she sunk her teeth into the sandwich, Aimée noticed a message on her phone, from an unknown number.

She leaned forward on the small marble-topped table to hear the message. Someone clearing his throat, then a small cough and a whisper, difficult to identify. "Listen, it's about Benoît." Familiar, but definitely not Mireille. "That commendation. Well, when he came back . . . maybe it won't matter."

It was Darquin, the guard. About time. "I never saw that Mireille again, but . . . *non,* it's better to tell you in person. If you get this message, meet me at 5 P.M. I'll be at the mass at the Eglise Saint-Étienne-du-Mont."

Darquin had remembered something. Perhaps it might clear Mireille. Aimée grabbed the *tartine,* left the espresso and a twenty-franc bill, and ran for the bus.

Wednesday Late Afternoon

"Madame? May I help you?" asked the corner flower-seller whose station was

189

across from the Pantheon.

Léonie smiled. "That bunch, please," she said, pointing at the blue delphiniums. Perfect for a church offering.

Her cell phone rang. It was Ponsot, her former chauffeur, now a rent-a-guard. She used him from time to time for little jobs, like delivering messages and carrying out surveillances. But he wasn't even good at that.

"A problem, Ponsot?" Léonie said, glancing across the cobblestoned street. She scanned Saint-Étienne-du-Mont's Gothic and Renaissance soot-stained façade. This was the church that housed the relics of Saint Geneviève, the patron saint of Paris.

"He's late. Not my fault," Ponsot said. "He's an old man."

She had beaten a path straight here after Ponsot's first call. Rushed over. She summoned her strength. Control . . . she had to get control. After last night's fruitless effort, she'd gotten this link from her contact: the guard at the lab where Benoît had been murdered.

"According to you, Darquin will attend the five o'clock mass here."

"He's cheap, too, wouldn't pay for a drink at the bar. Blamed it on his constipation."

Léonie didn't need scatological comments

from Ponsot. She didn't pay him for that.

"Not ten minutes ago, he used the public phone," Ponsot said. "He called a woman, acting like he's some kind of secret agent, and left her a cryptic message."

Why didn't you press him, get more information? she wanted to say. It was what she paid him to do. But when so much depended on something, she'd learned you had to do it yourself.

"Merci." She paid the flower-seller and took the fragrant blue delphiniums in her arms.

"Cryptic message?" she repeated.

"I overheard him say Benoît's name," he said.

At least Ponsot was good for something.

Then she saw him. An old man, in a dark blue suit too large for his shrunken frame, standing at the corner near the bus stop, by the church. Cars and buses raced around the Pantheon, leaving a trail of diesel exhaust. Classes over, teenage students from the *Lycée Henri Quatre* opposite, carrying books and wearing backpacks, spilled over the pavement on rue Clovis.

A young crowd. The old stood out. Like she did.

"Thick white hair, black-framed glasses?"

"That's him," Ponsot said. "Lost his wife last year."

191

She edged across the pavement toward the white-striped pedestrian crossing. Only narrow, cobbled rue Montagne Sainte Geneviève lay between them.

She'd planned to find a pew near him and strike up a conversation after mass. To enlist his aid with her offering of flowers to the Virgin. Old widowed gentlemen loved to appear gallant at no cost to themselves. She'd lead him into a conversation about his job, ask where he worked, slowly guide him, and then pump him about Benoît. Find out what he'd seen in the hope of eliciting information that would lead her to the file. Nothing difficult, if she did it right.

She had to hurry, before the woman he'd contacted might appear.

Laughter and shouts from students filled the afternoon air.

"Monsieur —" the rest was lost in the ambient noise. Darquin looked up and turned, as if he recognized someone calling him. She saw a medal on his lapel, a war veteran who wouldn't let anyone forget it.

The Number 89 bus hurtled past, blocking her view. Followed by a Renault. She heard the screech of brakes, then a loud thump, and didn't see Darquin any more. But she heard raised voices, shouts . . . a scream. Students were pointing.

"I'm a doctor. Make way . . . clear some space! *Nom de Dieu* . . . the old man's under the wheels. . . ."

The crowd parted. The flower-seller hurried into the street, raising her hand to stop traffic. And then Léonie saw blood pooling between the cobblestones' cracks. Darquin's body was half under the Renault.

Léonie dropped the delphiniums, backing away. No one paid attention. And no one paid attention as she melted back into the crowd.

Wednesday Late Afternoon

Aimée jumped off the bus across from the neo-classical columns of the Pantheon, the final resting place of the great: Voltaire, Rousseau, Émile Zola, Victor Hugo, André Malraux, and Resistance leader Jean Moulin. Among them, as well, Marie Curie, the first woman whose own accomplishments earned her a place, albeit sixty years after her death, alongside France's most eminent men.

Aimée stuck her half-eaten *tartine* in her bag. Five P.M., and she had to hurry to meet Darquin. But further on, a crowd blocked her way, staring and pointing. What was going on?

Paramedics were loading a stretcher into

193

the ambulance parked at the curb. She gasped when she saw Darquin's chalk-white face before they pulled the sheet over it. Too late.

"What happened?" she asked the teenage girl next to her, horror-stricken.

"The old man fell. Terrible," she was told.

"You mean just like that?" Aimée asked. "In front of the car?"

The pimple-faced boy next to her shook his head. "One minute he stood there, then he was going forward, his arms out."

His arms out? A natural reaction to break a fall. Especially if he'd been pushed.

"Did he look confused, afraid?"

The boy shrugged. "He smiled."

"Smiled?"

"I thought he . . . well, he reminded me of my grandfather." The boy shifted his backpack, turned to the girl. "Come on, Sophie, we have to go."

She couldn't let them leave.

"How did he remind you of your grandfather?"

"He wore a military medal like my grandfather, who always talks about the war." This boy was more alert than the average teenager. "So he seemed happy, and he smiled."

She thought for a moment. "Like he'd just met someone?"

"I guess so. He turned around and I almost bumped into him. *Oui,* he spoke to someone . . . then . . . I don't know."

An accident? She didn't think so. Hadn't he left her a message concerning Benoît? The poor old man had wanted the commendation after all.

She replayed Darquin's voicemail, searching for a hint of the meaning behind his words. Nothing. Whatever he'd wanted to tell her had gone with him.

A smile, a flash of recognition . . . Darquin knew the person who'd pushed him in front of the car.

"Did you see the person he'd met?"

"Look, I only noticed the old man because I almost bumped into him."

The boy and the girl left before she could suggest they talk to the *flics.* What could she do? What *should* she do?

She glanced around. It could be anyone . . . no, not *anyone* . . . someone from the laboratory or his neighborhood. The *flics* had arrived and were directing traffic; the crowd melted away. She saw no one over twenty-five.

Get out of here, said a little voice in her head. Now! Darquin had been killed only minutes before the time he'd set their meeting for.

She edged among the bystanders lingering on the pavement. The ambulance blocked the street. Then she saw the library doorway, a place to hide.

Keeping pace with the students, she ducked into the entrance of the Bibliothèque Sainte-Geneviève and pulled out her library card. Access was restricted to students, scholars, and researchers. Some security, at least.

Upstairs, she entered the Salle de Lecture Labrouste, the vast reading room whose vaulted barrel-like ceiling was supported by pierced leaf-patterned cast-iron arches. It always reminded her of a cross between a train station and a covered market hall. And once it had been her home away from home, during med school and later the Sorbonne.

The *bibliothèque* hadn't changed: seven hundred and fifteen seats, small globe lamps interspersed among the long tables, rubber book-trolley wheels squeaking over the wood floor, the turning of pages, hushed whispers, and the smell of the sun hitting old polished wood.

She took a place that provided a view of the reading room entrance but not much cover. She squeezed her eyes shut, but it didn't erase the vision of Darquin's chalk-white face, the blood in the cobblestone cracks. Sick at heart, she knew Darquin had been pushed to prevent him from meeting her.

But regret wouldn't help Darquin now. She'd use the hour remaining before Banque Morel's data system update to find answers, the answers Darquin now could never tell her.

Aimée located the fifth arrondissement business directory and found the Hydrolis company's history and description. Founded in the 1960s, she read, by Brice Castaing. Sorbonne-educated, a geographer, his land-survey work for UN relief in Haiti had led him to develop Hydrolis, now an international firm specializing in water-treatment facilities and sewage plants. Hydrolis had grown and now counted four Caribbean countries among its clients. It was now managed by a board of directors, and his son Jèrôme was its CEO. Not much she didn't know already.

With the help of a librarian assistant in periodicals, a twenty-something long-haired *mec* who gave her the eye, she requested the *Journal de L'eau* from the past five years and the recent *Journals de Culture Haitian*. Also *Lancet,* the British medical journal; she hoped her English wasn't so rusty that she would be unable to understand the article on pigs.

In the marble-tiled restroom, she called Cloutier. He answered on the fifth ring; sawing and hammering noises were in the background. He'd removed an office wall, from what she could understand, and had several hours' more work to do. There had been no message from Mireille. No use going to the office tomorrow, she thought, where she wouldn't be able to hear herself think.

The stack of journals arrived, and she went to work. She skimmed the *Journal d'Eaux*'s table of contents for the past few years. In the March 1995 issue, she found an article on water sewage treatment plants in Third World countries, focusing on the Caribbean.

Her eyes began to glaze over. She could use an espresso.

She skipped over the tables and percentages of chlorine used, the facility maintenance reports, the statistics as to the flora and fauna of areas surrounding sewage-treatment plants. Hydrolis was cited as an example; it had led the way in building the water infrastructure in the Dominican Republic and Haiti. Hydrolis's 1996 proposal for expansion of their treatment plant outside Port-au-Prince appeared to be under consideration for World Bank funding. An addendum to the article noted that, due to the unstable political climate, foreign investment projects in conjunction with the World Bank were on hold.

She copied that down. And wondered why Benoît, a world authority on pigs, had been consulted about Hydrolis's water-treatment proposals. She had to search further. At the documents desk, she requested information on World Bank funding for projects in Haiti. The long-haired *mec* winked at her. "Those documents come from the basement. Sorry, you missed the last request time by half an hour."

"You mean . . . ?"

"First thing tomorrow."

She'd have to come back. Unless Martine already had the skinny tomorrow.

"The coffee machine still downstairs?"

"I'd love to join you, but I'm on shift. It's on the lower level."

She put four francs in the espresso machine. A thick spurt of brown liquid dripped into the plastic cup. The same watered-down taste, but it was full of caffeine. She tossed it away after a few sips. Poor Darquin, she thought, if only she knew what he'd wanted to tell her. She felt even less safe than before.

Her horoscope in the latest *Elle* advised her to take out life insurance. She'd never even made out a will. Who would her apartment go to . . . Miles Davis? René? Or would the law award it to Mireille?

Back upstairs at the long wooden table, now more wide awake, she checked the *Journals de Culture Haitian* for historical articles and those on vodou. To understand the meaning of that circle of salt, Benoît's severed ear and peeled skin. . . . The article that caught her eye concerned black vodou.

Black vodou rituals, not practiced in modern times, came from old practices in Benin and the Cameroons, in Africa. They involved the severing of extremities. The leader, the *Grandissime,* tortured victims, preferably young ones, and drank their blood, which was thought to give a certain potency to him.

That could put another spin on Benoît's murder, a gruesome one, as Morbier had suggested. But she doubted that the murderer had killed Benoît to drink his blood.

In an article about the 1758 colonial laws governing Haitian sugarcane harvesting, she found an interesting and revealing quote: "The cane was rushed to have its sweet sap crushed from it between rollers. If a black slave happened to get a limb caught in these rollers through excessive haste or exhaustion, it was simply hacked off with a machete and the wound cauterised with a torch rather than production being slowed."

Aimée read further: "It was legal for any White to take anything from a black or mulatto he thought better quality than what he owned himself — be it a piece of furniture, a horse or the coat off his back — and if that black ignored this, *his ear was chopped off.*"

Significant? But this had taken place under colonial rule long ago. After twenty minutes, she sat back disappointed. Circles of salt were used in vodou for purification, a cleansing rite. Nothing linked salt to execution or death: quite the opposite.

It didn't add up.

She thumbed through the *Lancet,* the British medical journal. A real egghead's delight, full of technical studies.

In the third issue, she located an article on swine fever and the importation to Haiti of a white pig species. In essence, it blamed U.S. imperialism for the replacement of the native species of small black pigs. The *Lancet* entry listed an article in the UK *Guardian* from a year earlier as a source.

Pressed for time, she hurried, but it took

ten more minutes before she located the *Guardian* on microfiche. What she saw in the Letters to the Editor section made her sit up. The letter, dated 2 April 1996, had been written by Professeur Azacca Benoît.

Dear Editor,

To give historical context to your article on African swine fever, I bring to your attention the fact that the disease entered the Dominican Republic and soon spread down the Artibonite River and over the border into Haiti. The epidemic swiftly killed one third of Haiti's pigs. But, by late 1981, it seemed to have run its course. The U.S. was taking no chances, however. It funded a program to slaughter every pig in Haiti.

To the peasants producing most of Haiti's food, the program was devastating. Their small black Haitian pigs, which largely fended for themselves, were so critical to their economy that the same word was used for "pig" and "bank." People hid their pigs in holes and caves, but President Duvalier's tonton macoutes rooted the animals out and shot them. Even quarantined herds were exterminated. This decimated the peasants' economy.

The U.S. Agency for International Development (USAID) argued that the slaughter should be seen less as a problem than an opportunity. By replacing the small black pigs with large white ones from the U.S., Haiti could become a pork exporter and a lucky new participant in the modern world agricultural economy.

The new pigs grew fast, but needed as much pampering as the Duvaliers. While the peasants lived in bamboo shacks and ate only the food they grew for themselves, the white pigs needed concrete houses, showers, and imported food and medicine. Water resources were prioritized for pig-breeding, which became the preserve of big business, leaving the peasants with nothing. It is no exaggeration to say that the demise of the *Kreyòl* pig sped the demise of Baby Doc.

President Aristide's new government began to import black pigs from other islands and distribute them to the peasants. As a result, when Aristide was overthrown, the new military leaders declared that the black pigs were communist pigs, whose owners should be rounded up as subversives. The white pigs, by contrast, were capitalist pigs and a source of national pride. By the time Aristide returned, in 1994, the peasant economy had been strangled, and much of the peasants' land had been bought up by companies growing coffee or flowers for export to America. The water systems were now prioritized for foreign export agriculture.

Respectfully,
Professeur Azacca Benoît,
Ecole Normale Supérieur, Paris

Benoît's own words. She wondered if, a year and a half later, this letter was connected to his current research. Huby would know. He'd shown her the pig-tissue slide. She called the lab, got the recording, and hit Huby's extension. Voicemail again, and he still hadn't returned her previous call. She left another message.

She checked the time. If she didn't hurry, she'd be late. Outside, in the bustling square fronting the Pantheon, the pavement cafés were filled with students. The only evidence that Darquin had died there was the street cleaners, with their plastic brooms, watering the cobbles and sweeping his blood into the gutter.

"Digging to China again?" Aimée asked Delair, the Banque Morel security guard at the reception desk. She gestured to a hole in the floor surrounded by orange plastic netting, a grill-like fence, and danger signs.

Delair shrugged. "Pipes burst three floors down. Nice mess in the remnants of the Roman cistern. Again."

It made her spine prickle. She hated the enclosed claustrophobic feel of the database center below, knowing that tons of rock, sandstone, and concrete were suspended above her. And she wondered if siting the bank's database center underground had been such a good idea. No doubt a web of tunnels, quarries, and old German bunkers honeycombed the earth beneath their feet.

"Like rats, those cataphiles," said Delair, ex-army by the look of him: short *en brosse* hair and straining biceps under his blue shirt. He punched the newspaper he held, whose headline was "Diana autopsy results inquiry," then pointed to a small article: "Party disrupted in tunnels under the Arènes de Lutèce," the Roman arena.

"My former unit would make *pâté* of them. *Zut alors,* these underground *flics* treat these types like playground kids, slapping their wrists."

"Most of the cataphiles are students or office workers getting their weekend thrills partying," Aimée said. "Harmless enough."

Delair shook his head. "Not only dangerous," he said, frowning, "but full of undesirables, hiding. . . ."

"That's an urban myth, Delair," she said, signing in on the log.

"Myth? Before the bank installed the steel fence, they rousted out a nest of illegals camping in the adjoining Roman cistern." He gestured to a printed EVACUATION/EMERGENCY diagram of the building on the wall highlighting the exits and placement of fire extinguishers. "There. Right next to where you work. Walled up now, of course."

She'd never realized. "But how do they find these places?"

"They come out of the sewers at night, like the rats they are, take night jobs from people who need to work. Filch and steal, too."

She'd attended parties in the catacombs; all-night benders put on by third-year med students. Could Mireille have gone underground *literally?* She'd need a contact, an *entrée* into that world. Negotiating the kilometers of tunnels, passages, and quarries required knowledge. No easy feat. The cataphiles knew of entrances and passages the authorities had no clue about. They could always burrow their way one tunnel ahead of the authorities.

Right now she had security systems to run here. She didn't relish seeing the expression on René's face when she arrived late. Again.

Delair waved her through the metal gate. She went down three flights of stairs, held her badge up to a reader, and the steel doors of Morel's database center opened.

"René?" she called. But she heard only the low whirr of running computers and the humming ventilation system. She saw a note in René's slanted script — to check on a glitch in the virus program — taped to the first terminal screen. Surprised, she set her bag down. So unlike René.

Bien sûr, he'd set up the network monitoring system, and at this point she could run the security program in her sleep. Yet she remembered René's more than usual irritation at this "wild goose chase" over Mireille. Had he thought she'd gone too far? But she knew she hadn't even touched the surface.

René's accusations came back to her: getting sidetracked, his fear that she'd neglect the business.

She remembered his large green eyes wide with excitement over that startup: "the coming thing," he'd called it. She'd brushed his suggestion off with a quick "later" and had seen the slump of his shoulders.

But data security systems waited for no one. She did a few neck rolls and got to work.

Two hours later, systems monitored and virus scans complete, she debated calling René. She felt hesitant to interfere or interrupt some powwow with this startup client. He thrived on exploring new challenges. She'd agreed to expand their work and hire Saj. Why, they'd signed the contract with the contractor this week! Leduc Detective had broken even for once.

Yet the thought that he might find working for a startup more appealing stuck in her mind, wouldn't go away. A nervous dread vibrated through her. René, the cautious and conservative one, never jumped without thought.

She used the land line and dialed René's number. No answer.

Wednesday Night

René stumbled on the cobbles, cursing the dark street once known as rue des Malefies, the street of witches in the Latin Quarter. His hip ached, had for days, and, despite his misgivings, he'd sought a *rebouteux,* a bone-fixer. A healer with the "gift" who selected her clientele. Similar healers went by many names: *rebouteux* or *panseux* or

magnetiseurs, and thousands of them practiced in France.

In pain and desperation he'd come here,
to this dark hole, this practitioner of a
nebulous craft, despite all scientific or
analytic knowledge. And he'd sooner die
than let Aimée know.

He knew of the laying on of hands and
the incantations, the ancient mix of Latin
and *patois,* handed down from one *rebouteux* to the next. Sorcery, some called it, in
his village bordering the château where he'd
grown up. He'd witnessed both healings and
those beyond healing. Along with the kids
from the village, he'd mocked the old ways,
for once feeling part of the group . . . but
when seven-year-olds knocked on his door
for him to come out to play, he'd shrunk
back. He'd been eighteen, preparing for university.

But old wives' tales, as his mother said,
were based on something.

At the address for the healer stood a small
produce shop with a torn awning. A mistake,
he thought, and checked again. No mistake.
What healer practiced out of a rundown
grocery?

René hesitated, the whole idea now seem-
ing like superstitious nonsense. His fibula,
the outer bone in his lower leg, had grown

faster than his shin. The doctors had advised straightening and lengthening his legs, a torturous procedure utilizing the braces he'd suffered in childhood, now looming again. It was what he wanted to avoid.

He'd come this far, left the work for Aimée. He'd ask across the street at Bar Mimile, a crumbling stone-and-plaster affair with windows none too clean. In the window he could just make out a board displaying a *bière* special written in white chalk.

"Eh, Monsieur?" An olive-skinned man with thick black eyebrows wiped the counter at the level of René's head.

A narrow room, cigarette smoke spiraling from an ashtray, high stools. In this kind of place, one ordered a drink before pumping for information.

"Un bière," he said. "Stella, *à la pression."*

The man slapped a cardboard coaster on the zinc counter. He reached for the Stella Artois beer pull.

René looked around. No tables. A sixties decor: brown wood veneer, faded turquoise walls, a framed autographed photo of a young Françoise Hardy with her guitar. The still-reclusive singer had to be in her sixties now.

A young man in tight jeans sat in the

corner talking on a cell phone. A cigarette dangled from the corner of his mouth.

"And how will I reach the glass?" René asked.

"How you usually do, I imagine." The man set down the tall glass of golden beer topped by white foam. He came around the counter, flipping the towel over his shoulder, and pulled out a stool. René imagined the difficult climb to mount the rungs.

The man took the beer and coaster and set them on the stool's red leather seat. "Peanuts?" he asked.

"Non, merci."

"I'm Mimile," the man said, an expectant look in his eye.

René reached into his pocket, figuring he wanted payment.

"You don't remember me, do you?"

René blinked. Nothing about Mimile looked familiar: thirties, slight paunch, brown wavy hair long behind the ears, a Mediteranean complexion. To most people, all dwarves, like all Asians, looked alike. He couldn't count the times people "recognized" him.

"Désolé," he said, wondering how to phrase his question about the healer.

"Funny," Mimile said. "Since your girlfriend killed my cousin Déde."

Surprise banished René's pain. Fear took its place. "Déde . . . who?"

"Belleville Déde," he said. "On the water tower. I saw you at the inquest."

Now he remembered. Wary, he stepped back. "You mean my partner?" He didn't wait for an answer. "Déde kidnapped her and held her at gunpoint at the Belleville reservoir. She acted in self-defense. If you remember, the court exonerated her."

Mimile's expression hadn't changed.

"Guess if you have a problem with that, here's your money," René said.

Not the best time to defend himself. Of all the bars in the Latin Quarter, he'd picked this one to walk into. His hip ached; pains were shooting down his leg. But he prepared for a fight by centering the force in his *chi.* He winced. He'd never get to the first defensive position. Times like this, his black belt counted for nothing. Retreat, he realized, was the best option, and he eyed the door.

"Finish your drink," Mimile said. "Blood counts for something, eh, but Déde was a bad seed my mother never tired of saying. A two-bit player."

René's shoulders relaxed a centimeter. "Sorry, Mimile."

"Belleville breeds them, eh?"

René didn't know, but he nodded.

"Not like here. Like now, anyway." Mimile pulled out a cigarette, lighting it with a flick of his lighter. "Just thirty years ago. . . ." He took a drag, gestured out the window. "People attended church and were afraid to turn the corner because of the gypsies, afraid of the evil eye. Whole gypsy families lived in one room in the rundown hotels."

René took a sip. Mimile evidently liked to talk.

"Eh, once I knew everyone on the street; a preserve of poets and students, shopkeepers, workers, bar owners like me, professors from the *Grands Ecoles.* Some working girls." Mimile winked. "Even the old alchemist in his nineties who lived upstairs."

Mimile swiped down the counter with a towel and shrugged.

"That's until Mitterand moved a few blocks away and made the neighborhood fashionable. And too expensive."

Shadows lengthened in the street. René downed his beer, wishing it had given him more courage than he felt.

"Not many of us left now," Mimile said. He shook his head in disgust. "Full of tourists, too."

"I heard there's a healer nearby," René said.

"Aaah, you buy into that?"

René gripped his beer glass. "What have you heard?"

"A strange one. *Maman* avoided her, some story from the war. Others call her a sorcerer."

"And you?"

"A bag of hot air. You're looking for her, right?" He pointed. "Across the street in the produce shop."

René set ten francs down, but Mimile waved it away. "On me."

"I'd feel better if you'd take it . . . Déde and all," René said, unsure if that had come out the right way. But then what did one say?

"Sooner or later Déde had to face the accordion, that's what my *maman* said, the big one in the sky."

"Still, like you said, family. . . ." René stumbled for words.

"How do you think we pay the mortgage on this place, eh? Déde's insurance money. *Zut!* I thought you were sniffing around, you know, checking up on us."

"Not me, Mimile."

Out on the street, René paused in front of the torn awning. A light glowed inside. "*Et alors,* now or never," said a man beckoning from inside the produce shop. "I'm closing up, *petit.*"

René ignored the taunt, biting back the comeback on the tip of his tongue. He wished he could ignore the searing ache in his hip. If he swallowed more painkillers, he'd still ache tomorrow. And he'd never know until he gave the healer a shot.

In the shop's interior, the man gestured to the back room, hung his blue work coat on a nail, and disappeared.

René winced with pain as he edged himself up onto the work bench. His short legs dangled, his only company crates of red and white-tipped radishes, a bin with assorted plastic price signs, several crossword-puzzle magazines, pages folded back and puzzles filled out, and a two-burner cooktop stained with grease. A bright red fire extinguisher hung on the cracked wall. Incongruous, he thought, here in the dank supply room with its permeating smell of yesterday's leeks.

What kind of healer practiced in a place like this? he wondered for the tenth time. Aimée would call him silly, prod him to have the surgery. But she didn't know how slim were the chances of the operation succeeding nor how high the odds that he'd have a setback. She didn't know a lot of things, including the way he felt about her. But he repressed that.

An old man mounted the stairs, a cap tilted on his head, his eyes rheumy red.

"What's going on?" René asked.

The man took in René's stature. He jerked his thumb. "You're next."

Without a word, René descended from the bench, trying to keep his leg straight, trying to compensate for the flaming ache in his hip, the straining in his calves. But the minute his foot contacted the hard earth floor, pain shot to his hip and up his back.

He wanted to brush the dirt off his linen trousers, but he couldn't bend to reach it. Never had he let himself appear dirty, nor would he wear the children's clothes that fit him: the shirts with trucks on them, the shoes with lights. He'd vowed with his first paycheck that he'd wear custom-made garments from then on. And he'd starve before he changed that.

He gripped the railing, biting his lip, determined not to cry out. He felt the impact of each step, all ten of them.

By the light of a flickering lantern René saw a figure in a chair in the cellar under the shop. The lantern emitted a kerosene smell and cast a harsh light. The wooden wheel of a barrow, a remnant of produce-sellers who had once filled the streets, leaned against the damp vaulted stone wall.

He wanted to turn around, leave. But he couldn't face the trek up those stairs again quite yet.

He saw a woman in her sixties, a porcelain-white face lined by wrinkles, gray steel wool hair, a blue apron over her floral print dress . . . she could be anyone's grandmother or a produce-shop owner, both of which she was.

Or a charlatan as well preying on the desperate and afflicted? Like him.

"Madame Suchard?"

"You're the last one tonight," she said, adding in her deep Parisian accent, "I sense your reluctance."

The dampness emanating through the cellar increased the pain in his hip. A barred window in the thick wall above revealed the legs of passersby on the street.

"It's not what I thought, Madame."

"You expected walnut furniture and deep bookshelves? Whether I can help you remains to be seen." She shrugged thin shoulders. "But it's your choice."

In other words, put up or shut up. What did he have to lose?

She indicated that he should take off his jacket and remain standing. "Now, tell me."

He did, describing the shooting pain flaming from the arches of his feet up his back, the debilitating ache with no respite.

"Any surgery?"

He shook his head. "Never."

"Come here." She motioned him forward, put her gnarled hands out and laid them on his hip. She closed her eyes. And for a moment in the wavering light, with her sunken eyes and her prominent cheekbones, she resembled a corpse. He repressed a shudder.

She kept her hands on him, her body utterly still.

"Inflammation." After a few minutes, she said, "Turn."

He turned and winced. She put her hands on the small of his back. He felt nothing but the hard earth floor beneath his feet. Then, a lifting. A curious coolness. As if the heat had been drawn up and away, like smoke. He stood there he didn't know how long, aware of the kerosene fumes, of an occasional thump overhead.

The pain had subsided. He could straighten up. There was only a small dull throb in his calves. Whatever she'd done had worked.

"Madame?"

She slumped in the chair, her lids half-lowered, her breaths shallow.

"What do I owe you?"

No response.

"What's wrong, Madame?" he asked, worried.

Her lids fluttered open. "It takes a lot out of me," she said. "There's still hip inflammation. Take salt baths. Return in two days."

Spent, she waved away the francs he thrust in her hand.

"No money."

"Please, it seems only fair," he said, not wanting to owe her. Or anyone.

"It's the power working through me. But you must not speak of this."

Why not? he wondered. Did she hook the afflicted, only later to run a scam and demand their savings?

"If you do, I'll know," she said. "This doesn't work for everyone."

"If I can't pay . . . what can I do?"

"Aah, that part. . . ." She nodded. "The time will come. You'll know."

The old woman's enigmatic words echoed in René's head. And then he dismissed them to concentrate on this curious cool sensation and the alleviation of his pain.

Blocks away, he unlocked his car, parked on Impasse Maubert, the short passage infamous for the townhouse where Saint Croixe and his lover, the Marquise de Brinvilliers, notorious poisoners in the seventeenth century, had concocted potions before the guillotine took the Marquise's head.

He checked his phone. A message from Aimée. And then he took the paper from his pocket. The fax that Loussant, his Haitian student, had sent him. Should he tell her?

Wednesday Night

"Finished with your paper?" Aimée asked as she signed out at Delair's desk.

He nodded, hunched over *Voici,* a weekly scandal glossy with photos of Princess Diana. She took *Le Soir,* dated that evening, scanning the article on cataphiles partying at the Arènes de Lutèce. The last line of the article caught her attention. "Several Haitian *sans papiers* caught at the scene were linked to the recent flood of illegals transported here by human traffickers."

What if Mireille and the illegals she'd been smuggled into the country with had been caught? Only one way to find out. She called Lucien, her friend from Ecole de Médicine, now a resident at Hôpital Val de Grâce and a zealous cataphile.

"Emergency. Lucien Lelong," said a crisp voice.

"Caffeinated and on duty, right, Lucien?" she said.

"You know it, Aimée. Straight through until 6 A.M."

A summons could come for him at any moment. She cut to the chase. "Know anything about the Arènes de Lutèce bust? The article indicated they caught Haitians, illegals —"

"Most got away," he interrupted. "Hold on a minute. . . ."

She waved goodbye to Delair and walked into the dark street. A feeling of unease overcame her. She paused under a plane tree, her senses alert for watchers in a car. Or movement. There was just the distant rumble of the Metro underground, a clear night sky with a star-frothed Milky Way, a few parked cars. No dented Peugeot.

"Got away, Lucien? What do you mean?"

"We restore those tunnels; it's a labor of love, let me tell you," he said. "The Haitians were helping out; they kept watch," he said. "My friend said the *flics* bungled the bust and didn't seal off all the tunnels. Thank God for small favors."

"Any chance you saw a Haitian woman by the name of Mireille?"

"No women at all that I remember. But I haven't gone below since last week," he said. "They work us like mules here. Sleep and work, that's what I do."

"And soon your *maman* will have 'her son the doctor,' " she said.

"If I survive that long."

She heard moaning in the background. "Need to go," Lucien said, "my patient needs a morphine-drip adjustment."

Another shot in the dark that had gone nowhere, she thought, disappointed.

"The Haitians crawled right back, according to my friend," Lucien said. "Some of them camp under the Roman bleachers."

She heard the opening and closing of what sounded like metal cabinets in the background. "*Les pauvres,* they're desperate," Lucien said. "A shame these people must hide or be hunted down."

Desperate and on the run. Like Mireille. An idea came to her. Her father always said if something speaks to you, check it out.

"Lucien, I want to go down there. Can you take me?"

"I'm on shift, then sleeping, Aimée."

"It's important, Lucien."

"It's *always* important with you, Aimée."

"You owe me, remember?"

Her casual background check on his

222

mother's new boyfriend had revealed that the charming and distinguished white-haired Hungarian "comte" was in fact a failed insurance salesman from Belgrade.

"How can I forget? You never let me." The moaning was louder now. "Look, a car crash patient's not feeling too good."

"And you're the king of multitasking, Lucien." She imagined him right now injecting the morphine and adjusting the drip. "If the *flics* didn't close all the tunnels, where can I get down? Come on, you must know."

Sirens wailed in the distance. "SAMU's arriving, Aimée."

"Quick, Lucien, please."

"By the hollow under the bleachers on the northern side. At least it was open last week. There's a sewer opening in the recess to the left."

"*Merci,* Lucien."

"But first you have to get in; the arena's locked at night."

She knew Lucien, an ardent cataphile, had connections. All the cataphiles knew each other, shared quarry and tunnel maps, even made copies of keys to the parks. "And the park's gate key would be . . . ?"

Lucien sighed. "Under the ivy, the fake rock by the lilac bush on the left side of the gate on rue des Arènes. Where we always keep it."

"Call me when you're off duty, Lucien." She hung up.

The first-century Gallo-Roman arena stood just a few blocks away. Ten minutes if she hurried. Her phone rang.

"Sorry I didn't make it, Aimée," said René, apologetic. "Something came up. But you handled it, right?"

Aimée sensed his uncertainty. Her shoulders tightened. "No problem. I ran Morel's programs. We're set for tomorrow."

"We should talk."

Dread filled her as she thought of the start-up that had excited him. Leaves scuttled under her feet, the wind swirling them around her ankles. If René left, she would feel adrift, too.

She had to salvage their relationship. She couldn't lose René. But right now she had somewhere to go.

"OK," she said. "My mind's been occupied, you're right, René. But no reason we can't figure this out."

"Figure out what?" René asked.

Her bad feeling mounted. He obviously wanted to tell her in person.

"You're on your scooter, right?" he asked. "So come and meet me."

"Not now, René."

"Where are you?"

"Near the Arènes de Lutèce."

"This time of night?" he said. "But it's closed."

"Not for me. The *flics* rousted some Haitians in the tunnels —"

"And you think Mireille's involved," he interrupted, exasperated, "don't you?"

"I won't know until I check it out."

"Not alone, Aimée."

"Got to go."

Bad news could wait. She hoped she wouldn't find any ahead of her.

Rue des Arènes, a winding street with a small Metro exit identified by a thirties Metro sign, glimmered in the haze of streetlights. At the Arènes de Lutèce's main gate, behind the green bars, she found the rock in the lilac bush with the key taped to it. She looked behind her and saw only dark bow-windowed buildings, a pointed Gothic turret nestled among the rooftops, and a stray cat slinking over the cobblestones.

Gripping the key, she unlocked the padlock. A car pulled up and she ducked. No cover. And not fast enough.

The headlights illumined her foot. A car door slammed. Footsteps crunched leaves.

She held her breath as the figure paused, half in shadow, then stepped toward the gate with a rolling gait, a slight limp.

"Over here, René," she whispered, her relief battling with concern.

He stood, hands on his hips, shaking his head. "You're not going through with this."

"Shhh." She cracked the gate open.

"Good thing I came here."

"Why?"

"Remember Loussant, my student?" René said, "He's worried, something to do with a Haitian human rights campaign involving Edouard Brasseur. He faxed me this."

Edouard Brasseur, Benoît's childhood friend, the elusive former rebel, former ally of Father Privert. Why lie to her about his "import/export" business?

"I thought you should see this, Aimée," René said.

She was at a loss for words. "*Merci,* René." She dusted her hands off, taking the fax from René and reading it.

"It's only a message that he'll make contact and send me an article," she said, disappointed. "Nothing else."

"Loussant doesn't have a phone, Aimée." René paused. "He works in Lyon now, but he always says if work were good for you, the rich would leave none for the poor. And he's careful."

Careful of what, she wondered. No time to worry about that now. She slid inside the gate. "Time's wasting. See you tomorrow."

"You're not serious, Aimée," René said. "You can't think you'll find Mireille."

Or, for that matter, that Mireille would trust her. But she might find someone who knew her.

"The guard at the lab wanted to give me some information, but he was pushed under a car before he could. Mireille's a homicide suspect. I'm considered her accomplice, René. I have to find her." She stared through the bars of the gate, then at him. "You look tired."

"And you never change," he said. "Pig-headed. Stubborn."

The trees rustled. A squirrel scurried over the grass, leaving a trail of dew glistening in the moonlight. No time to argue.

"See you tomorrow, René."

"I'm coming with you."

And with that, he slid inside the narrow opening, closed the gate, and started following her.

"René, if something comes down. . . ."

"I'm a black belt, remember?"

"Things okay, René?"

"Never better," he said.

She kept her observation of his limp to herself. Though she was loath to admit it, she was glad of his company.

Together they walked into the remains of the first-century Gallo-Roman amphitheater. The rooftops of rue Monge were silhouetted like dark stairsteps against the sky. Dampness radiated from the park that surrounded the arena on three sides. The excavation of the grounds in the nineteenth century during the building of a tramway, had revealed the old arena. The sunken field had once served as a cemetery. Like every part of Paris, history was layered upon history. Victor Hugo had led a campaign to save the ruins from demolition. Now limestone bleachers ascended the side of the sunken arena where gladiators had fought.

An opening showed between the bleachers, dark and forlorn, one section being reconstructed under scaffolding. The feeling of desolation was heightened by old plastic bags and trash clumped against the construction shed and the wire fence, blown there by the wind and then coated with dust.

Each step they took echoed eerily from the other side of the arena.

"The Romans had acoustical engineering down pat," René said. "But their entertainment leaves something to be desired."

He pointed to the ground-level green-tinged bars that had functioned as gates for openings in the stone. "Animal cages. Think of hungry lions, waiting for a meal."

Overhead light beams made yellow pools on the dirt floor near a shed labeled DCD CONSTRUCTION. It was dark and padlocked. The cyclone fence surrounding the site seemed to sway in the wind.

When she went closer to it, the fence proved easy to push aside.

"This doesn't seem like a good idea, Aimée," René cautioned.

But she stepped through and continued on until she reached a dank vaulted arcade.

"I don't like this," René persisted, catching his breath.

She didn't either. Where was the opening Lucien had mentioned? The curving arches disappeared into the darkness. An eerie glint, then a swath of light appeared as the Tour Eiffel's hourly beacon swept the distant treetops.

"Let's go," René said, his voice echoing. "No one's around."

Gravel crunched under Aimée's heels. "If someone came through here. . . ."

She shone her penlight ahead. The yellow beam illuminated chipped stone stained by moisture. Scratching noises came from somewhere. Inside the recess under the old bleachers, plaster scraped beneath her heels. She stopped. A damp draft wafted the scent of mildew to them. Candles on the floor flickered.

In the sputtering light, she saw a figure just ahead of them.

"Who are . . . ?" Her words died.

A body hung suspended in a web of crisscrossing ropes between two sculpted stone burls that flanked a coved arch. Its arms were outstretched, wrists tied with rope. Like a fly caught in a cobweb. Long curly hair. A woman!

"God help her," René gasped.

Her heart reeled. "Mireille?"

In the wavering candlelight she saw a painted face, made-up eyes, dark red mouth. Frozen features. A wig. A cruel caricature of Mireille. A string of black beads and a bottle of rum on the floor. Some vodou rite to torture Mireille?

She gasped with relief. "It's a mannequin, René."

From the recesses of her mind, she dredged up a memory. The elite forces case training video enactment. A supposed victim was shown, tied up like bait on a hook, as well as the ensuing slaughter when a rescue was attempted.

"René!" She whispered. "Stop!"

"What?"

"A setup. It could be booby-trapped . . . a bomb."

The sound of crunching gravel came from near the arch. Someone was there. A small red dot shone for a moment, the unmistakable infrared dot of a night-vision high-powered rifle. Did vodou rituals involve high-powered rifles?

Then there was a rustling in the corner. The dim candlelight revealed an approaching figure, the bulk of a big man.

"Get down." She pushed René back against the wall, where they crouched.

Not much time. A minute or two at most until he reached them. She took René's hands, stared into his face, and whispered, "Listen and do what I say." She scooped up gravel from the ground, putting it in his hand. "See that red light coming from behind the column? It's a rifle scope. I'd guess we surprised those *mecs* and they're wondering who we are."

The rot of mildew and old stone odors grew stronger.

René gripped her fingers, his face almost touching hers. "You mean they expected Mireille to show up here? But why?"

"For God's sake, this place was in tonight's paper," she said. "Whoever's after Mireille knows she's superstitious and believes in these things. What else makes sense? But where's the encampment?"

The rest of her words were drowned out in sharp clucking, scrabbling noises, and a whacking sound that echoed. And a chicken ran across the packed-earth floor in front of them.

Aimée's yellow light beam caught it. A headless chicken, its severed neck spurting blood, staggered in a drunken circle of death before it fell, out of view.

Bile rose in Aimée's stomach. She pulled the Swiss Army knife from her bag. "Toss the gravel over there, René," she said, indicating a wall in the opposite direction.

"Who's . . . ?" A low voice echoed off the stone behind her. *"Aimée?"*

She turned to see Mireille at the end of the tunnel.

"*You're* here?" Mireille's voice wavered.

"And you?"

"The traffickers promised me my papers," Mireille interrupted

They'd set a trap to lure Mireille inside, to shoot her. She had to warn her . . . stop her.

"*Non,* run! It's a trap!" Aimée shouted. "Get out, Mireille!"

The crack of rifle shots filled Aimée's ears. Bullets peppered the limestone. Then there was darkness. She heard retreating footsteps. "Halt! Security!" came a loud voice. And a figure in a blue uniform carrying a bobbing flashlight appeared.

Aimée ran down the tunnel past the dead chicken. Zigzagging, she made it halfway to the arch and then dove onto dank foliage and dirt.

No Mireille.

Wednesday Night

Léonie threaded her way across the crowded Institut Oceanographique's evening reception, looking for Jérôme Castaing. He'd requested that they meet here at the "Water Initiative Programs in the Third World" reception. Léonie finally caught a glimpse of Castaing among the well-dressed crowd.

Chatting under the crystal chandelier, well-preserved wives in cocktail dresses, whose husbands worked for nongovernmental organizations, drank aperitifs. Ministry *fonctionaires* in red ties clustered with aid-organization officials, engrossed in their conversations. Expensive perfume competed with the odor of Sterno from the hot platters of hors d'oeuvres. How could she and Jérôme talk here?

Jérôme bowed out of the group around him and edged toward the Institut's lobby. Léonie followed suit, nodding to officials of the International Monetary Fund, until she found her path blocked by a waiter bearing a tray of small *foie gras*-coated toast squares.

Léonie felt his gaze before she looked up to see Royet, a World Bank official. Trim, fortyish, with prematurely white hair, he was watching her. Disconcerted, she smiled. Royet raised his aperitif glass as if in salute and returned her smile.

"We have to stop meeting like this, Madame Léonie." Royet winked before kissing her on both cheeks. "My wife will become jealous." He had a fondness for World Bank female interns, so he enjoyed a well-deserved reputation as a *roué,* which he played to the hilt. His wife put up with his indiscretions, maintaining "an eighteenth-century outlook," he liked to say.

"There's a way around our problems, *non?*" Royet said to Léonie. He kept a wide smile on his face as he leaned closer to whisper in her ear, "I think you know what I mean."

She wished she did. Royet's job consisted of ironing out creases in the World Bank's image. Her hands went to her neck for her juju, but it was no longer there.

"It's . . . how could we put it?" She searched for a noncommittal phrase that trade delegations and NGO's used all the time. "Under consideration."

"Stronger than consideration, I hope," he said, his smile forced. Royet stepped back. "You're ravishing, as always, Madame Léonie," he said, his voice louder. He handed her a glass from the tray of a passing waiter. "A toast to your health."

Little did he know. But she did feel better tonight, strength flowing through her, apart from the unsteadiness in her legs that meant she needed to rely on the damn cane. She was strong enough to deal with Castaing.

"We need to talk," Royet said. "Tomorrow?"

She nodded, accepted the drink, and clinked her glass against Royet's. She exchanged small talk with an earnest IMF statistician until she could excuse herself.

Out in the foyer, Jérôme paced on the creamy marble floor.

"Let me help you, Madame Léonie." Jérôme held open the wire-cage elevator door.

The elevator, a red-velvet-lined gold grilled cell from the last century, waited. In it they would be secure from being overheard, she supposed.

But she was wrong. Jérôme put his finger over his mouth as the elevator creaked upward. She leaned on her cane for support, hating to appear weak in front of him.

The elevator shuddered to a halt. And then they entered another chandelier-lit hall. A couple stood entwined near the marble columns. Jérôme opened a double door and suddenly they were standing inside the balcony of a grand amphitheater used for lectures. Ornate turn-of-the-century plaster friezes framed a ceiling of leaded-glass panels. A whaling-boat mural took up the back wall. Rows of wooden benches descended like waves toward the stage.

Jérôme shut the door and peered over the balcony. All the seats were empty.

"Nice of you to show up, Léonie. Give me the file."

"When you speak, I hear the cold, demanding voice of your father," said Léonie.

Jérôme blinked, then recovered. "That's rich, considering how well you did off him."

"But Jérôme, you're not an embittered old man like he was," she said. "What's your excuse?"

"Papa?" Jérôme's mouth pursed in disgust. "You wanted him to forgive and forget the fact that the tonton macoutes blinded him in one eye?"

"And he's taken it out on us ever since," Léonie said. Any information she'd been prepared to give him was no longer going to be available.

"Quit taking a high moral stance." Jérôme took off his black-framed glasses and wiped them with a handkerchief. Then he replaced the glasses, adjusting them behind his ears, each action taken with studied deliberation. "Just give me the file."

Business as usual, like his father.

"I need more time, Jérôme."

"Time is what we don't have. Delivery problems, Léonie?" he said. "Unusual for you. I assumed you'd have this under control."

No need for him to remind her. But more underlay his words. She wished she knew what it was.

"Of course I do, but what's the hurry?" Léonie said.

A door opened; footsteps sounded. The couple from the foyer peered in. "Excuse us," they said. They beat a quick retreat.

"Hurry? With Benoît's death, the entire proposal's in jeopardy," said Jérôme in a matter-of-fact tone.

He'd avoided the word "murder." She leaned heavily on her cane, a sinking feeling in her stomach. Darquin, the guard, had died before she could talk to him. She shook her head. "Then we all stand to lose. . . ." She let her words trail off and sagged against the burled-wood paneled wall.

But Jérôme didn't look worried. Or at least he hid fear well.

"Stall the committee, Jérôme," she told him. "Throw a wrench into the procedures. I don't know how, but do whatever you usually do. Refer to deterioration of the physical evidence . . . it's a scientific report, they'll understand that. Diminish its importance."

"Not this time, Léonie." He gave a tight smile.

"Has something else happened, Jérôme?"

"Certain information's disappeared."

A surprise. She hated surprises like she hated snakes. If only this weakness wasn't hampering her. She should have planned for the worst, had a backup scheme.

"What information?"

"From our company laboratory in Port-au-Prince," Jérôme said.

Jérôme's fiefdom. He talked about control, but he couldn't even grease the proper palms in his own firm! The mandatory bribe to security, the ministry, the military . . . the list went on. It wasn't only the price of doing business; it was the *only* way the country worked these days. The only way the electricity functioned, the grain market opened, the water flowed. As the saying went, "A little that's bad makes a lot of good happen." Didn't he understand? His father had. Remarkably well for a *blanc* — and a Frenchman.

"Run damage control," she said. "It's Haiti, it's your own firm. No one knows about your loss on this end."

"But Benoît's contact had already shipped samples here," he said. "There was a leak."

This put a new slant on everything.

"You're implicated, Léonie. So it's in your interest to locate those samples, as well as Benoît's report," Jérôme said, his small eyes behind his designer frames scrutinizing her like a lab specimen.

"Me?" Perspiration beaded her upper lip. More important things were weighing her down. "*Non,* Jérôme. Edouard suspects." She took a breath, summoned her strength, and fixed her gaze on Jérôme. "He broke into my safe."

Jérôme's mouth tightened. She had his attention now.

"This complicates things," he said.

More than he knew.

"Edouard's bent on exposing corruption.

239

He's a political idealist. He stole the bank statements. Now I'm up against the wall."

"A shame that he got involved," Jérôme said. "Idealists shouldn't play politics; they should play with themselves."

Jérôme was cunning, like his father. He'd have his antennae out; he wouldn't rely only on her. Breathe, she told herself. She had to breathe, and think.

"Find the samples and this file, Léonie. I'll handle your idealist," he told her.

For a horrible moment, she wondered if he'd taken care of Benoît.

"We all have secrets, Léonie," Jérôme said. "Especially you. Once you were Duvalier's favorite."

"Old news, Jérôme. No one cares these days," she said.

He shrugged. "Things could get sticky for you."

She saw her ten years of work in the trade delegation doomed. Her projects: aid for microbusinesses, small-farmer initiatives, the infant-toddler milk program . . . all vital, all jeopardized now. Her body ached.

Her interest was Haiti; but foremost with Jérôme, like his father, was his company.

Now she realized that under Jérôme's veneer of calm, he was scared. The contents of Benoît's report — and now these samples

— must endanger his company.

"Explain to me what makes these samples so important," she said. "What did Benoît plan on doing with them?"

"He'd demand a bigger payoff, Léonie. Which you people do so well."

He lied. She knew it in her bones. He still hadn't given her a real explanation.

"That's all you need to know," Jérôme said.

So it was simple: *she* had to find Benoît's samples *and* his file. Find out what Castaing feared and use it herself. She couldn't count on Castaing to help Haiti.

"Then I have no other choice," she said. "Will you honor your commitment to the ongoing projects?"

The vein in Jérôme's neck pulsed. "The meeting is the day after tomorrow. If you don't get the samples and file to me before then, Léonie, there's nothing to negotiate. No projects. If I go down, the whole trade delegation goes with me," Jérôme said. "You'll no longer be able to act as a front for Duvalier's bank accounts."

As if Edouard hadn't taken care of that already. But she couldn't let Jérôme stall the pending aid projects. With the last breath in her body, if necessary, she'd see it through. But she'd let him think he held the cards.

"Consider it done, Jérôme," she said.

"Done? Only when it's all in my hands, Léonie." He opened the door. "I'll leave after you."

Leaning on her cane, she walked out. Opening the elevator's accordion grill door, she reached inside and pushed the ground-floor button. But instead of entering, Léonie just closed the gate. As the elevator descended, she stood behind the column, where the couple had stood earlier.

Jérôme emerged a moment later. He noted the lit elevator button, scanned the hall, and pulled out his cell phone. Only his polished black shoes beating a tattoo on the marble floor broke the silence.

"Ah, cherie," he said, his voice softened. "I miss you. We'll meet later." Then there was something she couldn't catch.

He punched in another number on his cell phone. "Tell me good news," he said.

A pause.

"Imbecile!" he barked. "Keep looking for her. Don't stop until you find her. *Comprends?"*

Wednesday Night
Aimée crawled under the Roman bleachers on her hands and knees, her fishnet stock-

ings catching in the twigs and dirt. Dim light from the sputtering candles cast a yellow glow in the arcade. She felt the hard, rounded leather toe of a man's shoe.

Her heart pounded. René? Dead? Please, God, no.

"I took out the guard by mistake, Aimée." René's voice sounded strained.

A click, and then René's face appeared in the beam of her penlight. Beyond René she made out a stocky body sprawled on the floor and heard loud moans as a man struggled to come to.

Big mistake.

"Are you all right, René?"

She reached out to René. Her palms came back sticky and wet. Blood. And then her beam showed a trail of blood droplets on the stone.

"You've been shot, René!" She blamed herself for letting him come. What the hell had she been thinking? "Where are you hurt?"

"We have to get out of here," René said.

She leaned down, placing her arm around his shoulder, trying to control the shaking of her hands. Crawling, shielded by the walls, they reached the hole in the fence and got to their feet. There was no sign of the shooters.

René stumbled. She grabbed his shoulder. "We can make it, René. Just a bit farther."

She hoped she was right.

Aimée stared across the open-air arena. Spotlights focused on the dirt where old men played *petanque* on warm days. The soft cooing of pigeons reverberated off the limestone. Nodding plane tree branches shifted in the wind, the only movement in the otherwise deserted arena. It was a long way to the car.

René wavered and almost lost his balance again. Then she shone her flashlight on an embossed metal manhole cover. Ajar. Most were cemented down, but not this one. That's how the shooters must have escaped. Gone to ground after the security guard appeared and Mireille vanished.

She couldn't envision René managing the steep steps in his current condition. And moving him, injured, was the worst thing to do. Light flicked on in the construction shed. A siren wailed.

Now they had no choice.

She bent down. "Get on my back, René."

"Aimée, I can do this."

"You're losing blood, René."

The siren sounded closer now. "You're not going to carry me!"

"Like there's a choice? Climb on, René."

She felt his weight settle against her back, his hands clasp her shoulders, and she stood.

"Hold on!"

René let out an involuntary gasp.

Panting, she made her feet move, compensating for René's weight with each step. And she felt every cigarette she'd ever smoked. Now lights flooded the Roman arena behind them.

René tensed on her back. She heard his labored breathing. She prayed they could reach the car before the *flics* intercepted them.

At the gravel path she kept to the tree shadows, staggering but moving as fast as she could. The narrow street ahead lay in shadow. By the time she'd relocked the gate and reached René's Citroën, she was exhausted.

She gunned the engine and tore down the narrow street without headlights. René's face was plastered against the window, the rays of the streetlights they passed flickering over him.

A sick feeling filled her. Mireille had disappeared, and René was wounded, seemingly in bad shape.

"Pull over here," René said, the color drained from his face.

"Try to hold on," Aimée said. She clutched the steering wheel, downshifting with her other white-knuckled hand. "Just a few more minutes to the hospital. My friend Lucien works in Emergency."

"For what? Questions, a police report?"

The last thing she wanted. But René was hurt.

She fumed, wishing the light they were stopped at would turn green.

"No reports!" René said. "No surgery!"

But right now he was losing blood. "Where were you shot?"

"I need a few stitches, that's all. . . ."

"René, you don't know that." She ground into first, accelerating toward Boulevard Saint Germain.

"Jumping to conclusions as always, Aimée. The place was a trash heap. I just cut myself on glass from a broken bottle. Look."

He lifted his arm. She saw a glint of glass in a deep slash. There was only an ooze of blood. "You were in medical school. Can't you fix this?" he asked.

Her jaw dropped. "Me?"

"Forget the hospital. I'm not going."

Was he trying to do her a favor, knowing the *flics* would question her about Mireille?

"René, you know I dropped out of Ecole de Médicine . . . you need real medical attention at a hospital."

"First carrying me, and now insisting on a hospital. . . . No way."

She'd humiliated him, as he saw it. But what else could she have done? Or was there more behind his refusal? He'd always avoided hospitals, fearing surgeons who wanted to put him under the knife to try surgical intervention to cure his hip dysplasia.

"René, I don't have instruments. And I certainly don't have the knowledge," she said. "And when was your last tetanus shot?"

She saw the determined set to his mouth.

"But I know someone who can help," she finally offered.

"I thought so," René said, a groan escaping his lips. "Hurry up."

Aimée's stomach churned. She gritted her teeth and forced herself to watch. At the wooden table in the pantry, Professeur Zarek's brow was furrowed in concentration, her bifocals reflecting the penlight Aimée held while she probed in René's chest with tweezers. In the adjoining white-tiled kitchen, a kettle boiled on the stove, steaming up the back windows facing the Ecole de Médicine. Through the dining-room double doors came children's squeals and low adult voices.

Only eight o'clock, but it felt like midnight.

"Voilà," said Professeur Zarek. "The culprit." A triangular brown glass shard emerged. "Hmm . . . from a Belgian lambic beer, *framboise* flavored," she said, reading the still-attached label.

René winced. "Nice to know."

Professeur Zarek shrugged. "You're fortunate it missed the artery. And if you'd moved much more, you would have bled like a stuck pig." She grinned. "Sorry for the medical jargon."

The last stitch sewed, Professeur Zarek pulled off her surgical gloves, revealing the faint number tattooed on the inside of her arm. She smoothed a stray hair into her white bun and glanced back toward the kitchen.

"You're still practicing, Professeur?" Aimée asked. She must be past retirement age, Aimée thought, despite her unlined face, taut skin, and petite figure, not much taller than René. Professeur Zarek was part of the wartime generation: no meat, dairy if they were lucky, and then the camps. At medical school, the rumor went, Professeur Zarek's hair had turned white at seventeen, in the Lodz ghetto.

"I'm called in for consults at the dissection lab," she said. "A young boy had fallen through a skylight, the shard pierced . . . well, he wasn't so lucky."

René swallowed hard. Aimée met his gaze, then Professeur Zarek's.

"More than lucky," she said. "If the shard had lodged just a centimeter to the left . . . and. . . ."

Aimée's knees weakened, thinking what could have happened to René.

"I don't want to know the story, Aimée." Professeur Zarek raised her hand. Then she reached for a crystal decanter on the pantry shelf behind her. "This calls for something medicinal, wouldn't you say?" With a brisk air, she poured thimblefuls of liquid into small pastis glasses. "*Eau de vie* distilled in Normandy, from a patient."

The tang of blood and antiseptic mingled with the pear-liquor aroma. Aimée sank onto a kitchen chair.

The liquor took Aimée back to Professeur Zarek's office, when she had been Aimée's department adviser, and the late February afternoon on which she'd dropped out of medical school.

"Madame le Professeur, it's with respect that I must tell you. . . ." Aimée had hesitated. "I'm not cut out for this program."

"How many times have I heard that pun!" Professeur Zarek made a pained face.

Instead of the protest Aimée had expected, Professeur Zarek nodded. "Your gift lies elsewhere, Aimée."

She had felt inadequate, struggling to keep up. Squeamish at the sight of preserved organs beside her yogurt in the lab refrigerator. With that weakness, she wouldn't even have made a good *flic* like her father.

The professor shrugged. "You'll disappoint your parents' expectations. . . ."

The opposite, in fact. Her father never had understood her studying so hard and passing the scientific *baccalauréat* exam, determined to enter the field of medicine.

"Guilt's a luxury." Professeur Zarek lit a filtered Gitane with her Bic lighter and exhaled a stream of blue smoke. It lingered in the air. She gave an odd smile. "Only the living can afford it."

Aimée didn't know what to say. Rays of weak light hit the professor's desk. Treatises and medical journals were piled on shelves in the bookcases. Acrid cigarette smoke mingled with the smell of paper and old books.

"To tell the truth, I didn't think you'd last this long," Professeur Zarek told her. "The first year weeds out 84 percent. Only one out of six make it. Don't beat yourself up over this. It's not worth it."

"But I wanted to try. . . ." Try harder.

"Take it from me. Guilt doesn't change anything. Or bring anyone back." Professeur Zarek's eyes shone; deep dark pinpricks, their gaze somewhere else. In some other time. Another place.

She'd pulled a decanter and two shot glasses from her desk drawer and uncorked the crystal stopper. It had contained amber liquor smelling of pears. "From a patient. Homemade in Normandy, *eau de vie*."

She poured the clear liquid into the glasses. But then there was only the sweet smell of the liquor, not the coppery smell of blood.

"Aimée . . . Aimée?"

Startled, Aimée came back to the present. She was standing in Professeur Zarek's pantry. René was stitched up, and a birthday party was going on in the dining room.

"Your heels, Aimée. Look at the blood on your shoes."

Her mind went to the mannequin caught like a fly in a spider's web, Mireille's effigy, the shots, the headless chicken. . . .

She grabbed a paper towel. "*Désolée,* Professeur, I'll clean this up." She got down on her hands and ripped fishnet-stockinged knees to wipe the floor clean.

Professeur Zarek downed her *eau de vie.* "Now if you don't mind, Aimée, my granddaughter's birthday. . . ."

"Forgive me for taking you away," she said. "Many thanks."

"For what? An excuse to share a drink with a former student and her partner?" She paused. "Just make sure you go out the back entrance through the courtyard."

"Grand-mère!" A doe-eyed four-year-old, with chocolate cream icing like a moustache on her lip, stood at the pantry door. "I saved you a piece, *Grand-mère.*" She opened her small arms. "This big."

"So you did, *mon p'tit chou.*" Professeur Zarek leaned down to kiss her forehead. Only Aimée noticed the slight tremor in the professor's cheek. Then it was gone. With a quick movement, she rolled her sleeve down over her tattoo. "So you did."

Wind whipped up the narrow street. The pillared Ecole de Médicine loomed darkly ahead. Aimée paced on the worn cobblestones outside Professeur Zarek's building, deep in thought. "René, we disrupted a ritual."

"I'll say. Bad men with guns." René stood, his suit jacket balled up under his arm, blotting the dried blood on his shirt with a handkerchief. He sniffed. "I doubt if blood comes out. So my new Charvet shirt's ruined!"

A sharp dresser, René wore only hand-made shirts.

"Mireille talked of Ogoun, a vodou deity," she said. "But she said the traffickers promised to let her have her papers back. If they lured her by performing a vodou ritual. . . ."

"To shoot her?" René paused, his hand on the door handle. "Who knows? More to the point, the bad guys saw *you.* They heard you warn Mireille."

Her chest tightened.

"Come clean with Morbier, Aimée!" René said. "Tell him what's happened."

"That we fled from a shooting?" No use arguing with René right now. And then it hit her.

"We'll listen to the police scanner in your car." Why hadn't she thought of this before?

"To find out —"

"What the *flics* know, René," she interrupted. "If they've apprehended those *mecs.*" Or Mireille.

Inside René's car, she switched on the police radio scanner. Short phrases came over the police frequency . . . "Alpha . . . Arènes de Lutèce . . . suspects fled . . . no sign of the departing vehicle. . . . Make? Looked like Citroën DS taillights . . . no license number noted . . . not visible . . . any victim? . . . negative."

Relief mingled with disappointment. No Mireille.

René leaned forward in alarm. "The *flics* will run every Citroën DS registration in Paris through the computer." He turned the knob to lower the scanner volume. His green eyes flashed. "They'll pull me over tomorrow en route to my meeting at La Défense."

"It doesn't work like that, René," she said. "They don't have a license plate number. And checking thousands of Citroëns takes time. Princess Diana's on their mind right now. There's a manhunt on for that Fiat Uno, the one that fled the Pont d'Alma tunnel. They won't have the manpower to devote to us."

"All the more reason to explain to Morbier."

"Not after what he told me last night," she said. "The Brigade's ready to haul me in."

"Ridiculous. You're not an accessory to murder."

"The *flics* noted my scooter's license plate on rue Buffon," she said. "Mireille came to my apartment last night; right after that, Morbier 'dropped in.' I've seen men watching my place, but I don't know who they work for. I need to know how this all fits together."

"Stop trying to connect everything that's happened, Aimée." He raised his hands. "You're grasping —"

"High-powered rifles with night-vision sights and a vodou ritual, the chicken. . . ." She shook her head. "I need to understand what it means. Can you reach Loussant?"

"He doesn't have a phone. I told you."

Great. The traffickers who were going to elaborate lengths to trap Mireille might have murdered Benoît. But that made little sense unless the set up had been staged as a warning to Mireille. A complicated warning. Too complicated. And to warn her of what? Mireille had been convinced that whoever was following her was after Benoît's file.

"Go home and take care of yourself, Aimée."

Guilt washed over her. "You've suffered trauma to your chest. I'll drive you home, René, then. . . ."

René raised his eyebrow. "Then what?"

"Play it by ear." She shrugged. "Find a Haitian resto or bar where students hung out. Ask questions. Shoot arrows in the dark, see if one strikes home."

"Another wild goose chase?" René's voice lowered. "Look, you haven't heard the last from Mireille. She's desperate, she'll find you. Tomorrow there's the contractor to deal with at the office. I'm at La Défense. You have to concentrate on work."

True.

"Have you seen the office, René? It's knee-deep in plaster. You can't hear yourself think for the sound of drills."

"Work at home."

"Good idea."

Her exhausted body cried out for sleep. The twenty-four-hour kind. But if she didn't attempt to find out what lay behind this . . . she wouldn't sleep a wink anyway.

"First I'll take you home. Then I'll take a taxi."

René didn't argue, just opened the car door and slumped back against the seat.

She pulled into his underground garage on rue de la Reynie. "There's something you're not telling me, René."

In the dark garage, she felt his warm hand on hers. "You're obsessed with Mireille." He paused. "But it's been almost two years since Yves was murdered, and we never talk about it."

She twisted the copper puzzle ring on her

third finger, the ring Yves had given her the night before his murder. Yves, her fiancé for a brief night, had been an investigative journalist. She'd tried to get over his death. Did René think she was trying to avoid her grief for Yves by distracting herself with Mireille? She didn't want to talk about it.

"What's to say?"

"So, no 'bad boys' in sight?"

Edouard? Attractive, but she didn't trust him.

"Not a one, partner," she said. "For now, that's fine. I burden you enough with my nonexistent love life. You're sweet, René." She leaned across the seat and bent to kiss his cheek.

He felt rigid.

"You all right, René? Let me help you upstairs and get you settled in. I noticed you limping."

"That's all you noticed?"

She could feel the atmosphere change. She'd said the wrong thing.

"Of course not," she said. "Your idea about that startup, getting in on the ground floor, is brilliant."

"I've heard things . . . a boom," René said, "but if it's got no foundation. . . ."

Second thoughts? He'd seemed so excited the other night. She'd felt cautious, for once more careful than René, wary of the dot-.com bubble hype.

"Let's explore it," she said. "Anyway, we'll talk tomorrow."

An odd look shone in his eyes. Then he opened the door. Slammed it.

What had she done wrong now?

"René?" She ran after him to the elevator. He turned. Worry replaced the anger in his tone. "Forget this so-called sister, Aimée."

"Mirielle? I can't . . . she's . . . I think she's really my sister."

"And that proves what?"

"A family. The only one I have."

"Right. And now you're in danger, too. Don't you see?"

"I'll handle it, René."

"If you're out of commission, how can you help her? Or our business?"

"It was selfish of me to put you in danger. Forgive me."

"Like it's the first time, Aimée?" He shook his head. "Talk to Morbier. If you don't trust him, well, you know other *flics,* right?"

She nodded. But it had gone beyond that. The help she needed had to come from the other side. "You're right, René," is what she said.

■ ■ ■ ■

Were men watching her apartment? She was tired, her nerves were frayed. She didn't want to find out. She reached Madame Cachou, her concierge, on her cell phone. Despite the late hour, Madame agreed to mind Miles Davis, who loved her.

After a ten-minute walk, Aimée rounded the block onto rue du Louvre. The corner café's windows were dark. A couple holding hands were walking to the corner; otherwise the street lay deserted. No watchers in sight. A light shone from the office window below that of Leduc Detective.

She kept to the shadows. Inside her building, she mounted two flights of the narrow staircase in the dark. From the landing, she could hear the muted sound of classical radio, a France-Inter symphony concert, the real estate broker's usual choice at this time of night. The only other occupant, on the floor below her, who worked late. She took off her heels and padded upstairs barefoot. The dim single bulb barely revealed the hall's scuffed woodwork. A smell of floor wax lingered in the air.

Leduc Detective's frosted glass door was dark, the landing deserted. She clasped her

Swiss Army Knife in one hand, her office keys in the other. Silence, apart from the last strains of the Haydn concerto below.

She unlocked the door and shuddered when the bolt made a noise. Then she stuck her knife out. Fine plaster dust, visible in the light from the window, carpeted the floor. Like a moonscape, plastic sheets covered the desks and furniture.

The room was empty.

Her shoulders sagged in relief. Lathe and plaster poked from the opening cut in the wall. Cloutier's tools littered the parquet floor.

She wedged the top of the Louis Quinze chair under the door handle and stacked phone books on the seat. She'd make it difficult for anyone to break in; and if they did, she'd be ready.

From the coat rack she took her shearling suede coat, bought in the market in Istanbul. Tired, she pulled off the plastic covering the recamier, set her shoes beneath it and her knife within easy reach under the cushion. She pulled the coat over her and rolled up her jacket for a pillow.

But, too on edge to sleep, she grew aware of a thumping sound. Wide awake now, she grabbed her knife. Her gaze swept the dark outlines of her desk, the fax machine covered by plastic. No one. The chair stood firmly braced against the door.

She sniffed, finding only the smell of decay and old wood from the open wall. The hint of sewer gas. She tiptoed barefoot to the radiator as the sounds got louder. Faster. Listening, she backed up against the marble fireplace. Rue du Louvre's globed streetlights were reflected as hazy pinpoints in the tarnished beveled mirror. There was an invitation to a *vernissage,* a painter friend's gallery opening, wedged in the frame. From last summer.

She heard a muted shout, what sounded like cries, and then the rhythmic thumps ceased, followed by a woman's throaty laugh. No wonder, she thought, and she stepped back. The realtor below had a new paramour. He went through new secretaries with regularity.

She stared at her father's photo on the shelf; even in the dim light, she could make out his crooked, tired smile. It was a mask, she realized; the past and his secrets had gone with his ashes to the marble drawer in the Père Lachaise mausoleum. Why hadn't he told her she had a sister? Had he been ashamed? Or was he ignorant of Mireille's existence? She'd never know.

Weary, she turned back toward the recamier. The fax-machine light glowed like a beacon under its plastic cover. Transmission received.

She lifted the plastic and took the sheet of paper from the machine. She turned on her penlight and read it. There was no header. Only three words: WHERE IS SHE?

She grabbed a piece of paper and wrote: WHAT DO YOU WANT? WHO ARE YOU? She entered the transmission number at the top of the fax, slotted the sheet of paper into the machine, and hit SEND.

The fax machine grumbled to life, the paper fed through, and she waited. A moment later it came out.

The digital message read: "No response at this transmission number."

She ran to the window, staring onto rue du Louvre. It was deserted, apart from parked cars. The Louvre's *Cour Carré* was a faint outline in the distance. There was not even a taxi, nor a stray cat.

Whoever may have been watching her office had melted into the shadows. Or were they on their way up? Her spine stiffened.

She had to find a place that was off the radar. Not a hotel. A place where she'd be invisible: hostels, student squats, the Latin Quarter.

The sooner the better.

She threw disks and download programs, along with a pair of stockings and red-soled Louboutin heels, inside a bag. She'd emptied the armoire to protect her clothes from construction dust. But on a hanger, sheathed in the dry cleaner's plastic, she found a vintage beaded Schiaparelli jacket. For now, that would do. The old station clock read 11:45 P.M., so the Metro was still running.

She slipped on her metallic-bronze ballet slippers, shouldered the laptop and her bag. Outside on the landing, she paused and listened. Quiet, except for the scurrying of mice and the gush of a water pipe somewhere. At the ground level, she opened the cellar door and descended past the garbage bins to the cellar. She ran over the beaten-earth floor to the rear exit leading to rue Bailleul, ascended a series of stone steps, then scanned the pavement. No one.

In the moonlight, she hurried through the back streets to catch the last Metro.

The seventeenth-century carved wooden door of the Collège des Irlandais clicked open. Aimée stepped into the dark hush of a stone-flagged *porte cochère*. The college had once been an Irish seminary where Napoleon's brother spent his student days, later a military hospital during the Franco-Prussian war, and, following the Libèration in 1944, a shelter for displaced persons. Now little remained of its past except the ornate woodwork and the whispers of ·ghosts. It now functioned as the Irish Cultural Center and visiting artist's residence.

Aimée followed a flashlight beam to the woman holding it. She wore gold mules and a checked wool coat over her nightgown. A blue hairnet framed thin plucked eyebrows and a lined face that Aimée could see had been beautiful.

"Albertine? *Merci.* I feel lucky you had a room."

"You should," Albertine said and coughed. A smoker's cough. "Last one. If it weren't for your father, may he rest in peace. . . ." She made the sign of the cross. "He got me the job . . . well . . . otherwise, we'd both be on the street. This way."

Aimée followed her through the tall glass doors, up a worn stone staircase with a balustrade of sculpted iron, for several flights. Albertine showed her into a white-walled room with a high sloping ceiling containing a white bed with a metal frame. Spartan, silent, a phone jack and modern outlets. Perfect.

"Showers and facilities on the third floor. Five francs. Meals, you're on your own."

Before Aimée could thank her again, Albertine disappeared.

Aimée took the surge protector strip from her bag and plugged it in, then attached the wire to the phone jack for a dial-up Internet connection. She plugged in the mobile printer/fax and her phone to recharge it. The view from the window set into the mansard roof was of a gravel-covered U-shaped courtyard.

She kicked off her ballet slippers and collapsed onto the crisp white duvet. She inhaled the fresh laundry scent and booted up her laptop. Was she safe? For a while, maybe.

She struggled to keep her eyes open. A second fax came in, but her eyes had already closed. It read: NAUGHTY GIRL YOU CAN RUN BUT YOU CAN'T HIDE.

Thursday Afternoon

Aimée awoke to pounding on the door. She bolted upright, still dressed, her laptop on the pillow. Sunlight streamed in, warming her toes. Disoriented, she wondered where she was for a moment.

A machine roared. She heard banging on the wall. She saw the last fax still in the machine. Fear galvanized her, and she looked around for an object to defend herself with. Not even a chair or a lamp. She unplugged the surge protector and rooted in her bag. Armed with the surge protector in one hand, her Swiss Army knife in her other, she rushed to the door as the knob turned.

She'd been so tired, she'd forgotten to lock the door!

A small woman in a babushka and a blue smock walked in with her arms full.

"Housekeeping." She screamed and dropped the sheets.

"*Désolée,* I thought. . . ." Aimée put the knife down. "Forgive me, I didn't mean. . . ."

The women backed out, still screaming.

Aimée caught up to her in the hallway and held her by the arm. "Nightmares. I'm sorry."

The woman looked unsure. "But it's afternoon," she said.

Aimée checked her Tintin watch. Two P.M. She'd slept for hours.

"You're right," she said. "Let me help you with those sheets."

By the time Rena — as she insisted Aimée call her — changed the sheets Aimée hadn't slept in and, in broken French, imparted a traditional Latvian cure for nightmares — a grated ginger bath — Aimée had figured out a plan and called Martine.

Her work could wait till later.

Aimée entered the arched portal of the hamman that stood opposite the mosque. She followed a woman holding an armful of towels through the swinging double doors.

"*Le gommage?* The works?" said a disembodied voice. Aimée saw the flash of a gold chain around a woman's neck through the vapor tinged by eucalyptus. She'd arranged to meet Martine so she could get information and a change of clothes. But as Martine hadn't shown up yet, she might as well get the dirt off first.

The door behind her swung open. Voices rose over the clatter of tea cups, the rest lost as the door pinged shut.

"Loofah scrub, steam, hot soak. Seventy-five francs."

Aimée paid.

"Cabin 14."

She stripped, pulled a thick white towel around her middle, then joined the figures misted in steam in the tiled bath area. Her gaze couldn't penetrate the rising vapors.

"Next!"

Aimée felt an arm grip hers, then the hard slap of slippery marble as she was deposited on a slab. She winced as the Turkish woman's loofah raked over her body, gritting her teeth at the *gommage,* a full-body exfoliation. Strong hands lathered her back with black soap, and the loofah process was repeated. Then repeated again. She closed her eyes in the veil of steam, sweat pouring off her. Already she'd lost several layers of her skin, scrubbed raw in the soapy, warm water.

"Done." The woman grunted, her black hair matted on her forehead.

The next victim, a perspiring fiftyish matron, took her place on the Turkish woman's slab. Murmurs came from the women amidst the slaps of the masseuse and splashes of water.

"Plunge time." A girl wearing rubber flip-flops guided her through the steam over the slick floor. Aimée felt like a shriveled whale. "Take a step, then a big breath."

Sweat dripped from the corners of her eyes. She held her breath as she plunged into the blue-tiled ice-cold bath. Every pore came alive. It was like the chill of salt water in the aqua-blue depths of the sea. She emerged sputtering, breathless.

"Showoff," said Martine, who was sprawled on the slick marble step.

"Coward. You should try it." Steam emanated from Aimée's body. She grabbed a towel, wrapped it around her head like a turban, and joined Martine. She noted Martine's flushed face and furrowed brow. A bad feeling hit Aimée in the gut. Had something happened to Martine? She breathed in the steam and coughed. "What's wrong, Martine?"

"Gilles's ex-wife moved back from Buenos Aires." Martine leaned back, a towel wrapped around her middle, her hair enfolded in a turban. "She's made an offer on an apartment downstairs from us. Can you imagine?" Martine expelled a breath in disgust, not waiting for Aimée's reply. "And don't get me started on her newest craze for Scientology."

Aimée wiped her forehead. Comparing notes was their tradition in the hammam; they'd been doing so since they were fourteen. But she didn't have time for it now.

"Martine, what did you find out?"

"But you're glowing," her friend said.

Nonplussed, Aimée wiped the sweat from her eyes. Her skin felt as soft as a newborn baby's.

Martine surveyed her under moisture-beaded eyelashes. "Anyone I know?"

"Blame it on the loofah."

A shrug of Martine's red lobster-like

shoulders. "Find a bad boy. A fling will enhance your vitality, *joie de vivre.*"

"Never mind my affairs. Last night Mireille was almost shot, and she's disappeared again."

Martine's face wavered in the rising vapor. Aimée heard the masseuse's slaps and water splashing. "How do you know she's your sister?"

Aimée picked at the thick towel. "I saw her photo of Papa."

"That's it? She wants something, Aimée," Martine opined.

"Don't you have something to tell me?" Aimée asked.

Martine splashed cold water on her neck. "You won't like it, Aimée."

She didn't like this much already.

"There's something you should read," Martine said. "Let's have tea, and you can look at it then."

After showering, Aimée slipped into the tailored black agnés b. dress Martine had brought her.

"Keep it," Martine said. "Every time I quit smoking, it no longer fits."

In the hammam's tea room they sat at a brass tray table. Behind them were washed walls, turquoise and gold patterned tiles, and Moorish arched windows. A sparrow

270

flew in through the slit of a window and perched on the hanging brass lamp.

Martine bit into a crescent-shaped sugar-coated Moroccan pastry, then reached for the hookah. Aimée tried to ignore the thick tobacco smell and wished she didn't want a drag so much.

"Think of Chanel No. 5. It leaves an impression, hugs the body, yet a hint of mystery remains."

Aimée sipped from the little gold-scrolled glass of mint tea. "I suppose you mean something by that, Martine?"

"According to my connection, Professeur Azacca Benoît consulted for both the World Bank and IMF."

Aimée had known about the World Bank, but not the International Monetary Fund. "In what way?"

"There's a program of microbusiness seed grants for Haitian animal husbandry: that is, pigs, goats, chicken farms; you know, 'building an infrastructure.' " Martine set an *Economist* article dated earlier in the year on the brass tray table. "Here's the kicker. Read this."

The World Bank and International Monetary Fund (IMF) faced tough questions about their lending policies during annual meetings in Prague in early December.

Critics are asking how the IMF could allow tens of millions of dollars loaned to Russia to disappear, and why the World Bank continues to issue loans in countries where corruption is rampant. U.S. authorities are investigating allegations that IMF loans to Russia were illegally funneled through the Bank of New York as part of a US $7 billion money-laundering scandal.

France, meanwhile, is studying an internal World Bank report alleging that over 20 percent of funds for projects in Haiti had been lost to "some leakage" — that is, siphoned off by corrupt officials.

A criticism leveled against both institutions is that they are disbursing credits without appropriate loan conditions or monitoring programs to ensure that the money goes to the intended recipients.

Earlier this year, finance ministers from a group of leading industrial nations welcomed steps already taken by the IMF to foster improved accounting standards and compliance with legal codes in emerging markets.

"You're implying that Benoît's part of this corruption. How was he involved? Was he murdered in an attempt to cover up this 'leakage'?"

Martine took a drag from the hookah and expelled a plume of smoke. "Hydrolis is the largest firm dealing with Haiti. As a matter of fact, it's the only foreign firm still active during the upheavals.

"I didn't have time to check much," she continued. "But I did learn that the Hydrolis founder, Castaing Père, was an *ancien* regime type."

"I've met his son, Jérôme."

"Lucky you." Martine took another drag from the hookah. "If he's anything like his papa, he's got mistresses and mulatto children all over. The tonton macoutes gouged out the father's left eye. He made repayment in kind in several villages rumored to be harboring tonton macoutes."

An alarm rang in Aimée's head. "Benoît's ear was severed," she said.

"You see a connection?" Martine asked.

"Say Jérôme's skimming aid funds and Benoît got wind of it."

"Why chop off his ear?"

"I don't know."

"More important, Aimée, what's Mireille got to do with it?"

"Benoît trusted her with his work, a report in a file."

"Yet you've never seen it, right?" Martine lifted her eyebrows.

"Jérôme Castaing is a big contributor to Father Privert's foundation. It runs a Feed the Children program in Haiti," Aimée said. "Are you suggesting it's a front, just so he appears philanthropic? I could believe it. He left a sour taste in my mouth. Too nervous by far."

Martine expelled a stream of smoke and shook her head. "But Father Privert's regarded as a saint there."

"I didn't get anywhere with him or Josephe, the political activist who runs his shelter," Aimée said. "If they knew Mireille, they didn't let on."

"Political activists!" Martine said. "Call them bleeding-heart liberals who are taken in by the 'big talk' programs for Haiti."

She remembered the worry on Father Privert's face as Josephe was printing the newsletter.

"Find anything out about this Edouard?"

"I'm checking," said Martine. "Still, my contact says due to Benoît's consultancy, another nail has been hammered in the World Bank's credulity coffin. The World Bank provides loans for programs requiring the borrower country to use private foreign companies exclusively to manage basic systems."

"But the article I found stated that Hydrolis already operates the water sewage treatment in Port-au-Prince," Aimée said.

"Yes, but think of the rest of Haiti," Martine said. "Aristide fought the World Bank's privatization requirements, but he's been deposed. Gone. Figure it this way: if Castaing's angling to run Haiti's entire water system, he needs the World Bank. His father wanted to privatize the water system, but never could under Duvalier. Then his company moved into Santo Domingo, then expanded to other places in the Caribbean. Global capitalization and global profiteering; but it's almost impossible to prove."

Aimée thought for a moment. "Say Benoît's murder was staged as some vodou ceremony. Mireille had appeared, and Benoît helped her and trusted her. So the murderer shifted his plan to finger her for the killing. I smell a frameup, Martine."

"You don't know that, Aimée. Neither do I."

"But you're still connected to that young journalist at *Le Monde,* right? The one dying to carve his name in the investigative journalists' Hall of Fame?"

"Stop right there, Aimée. A story needs facts, corroboration." Martine signaled for the bill. "Not rumors. And rumors, albeit from well-placed sources, are all that I've heard."

Aimée had to make Martine understand.

The server appeared with a teapot. Martine waved him away.

"Last night we interrupted a mock vodou ritual aimed at Mireille. Complete with high-powered night-sensor rifles."

"I've already stuck my neck out, Aimée, and asked too many sensitive questions. No more," Martine said. And then she looked up over the cloud of hookah smoke. "What do you mean, a vodou rite with high-powered night-sensor rifles?"

"Exactly, Martine."

"Be careful, Aimée."

"Mireille has Benoît's file containing his report. And the murderer knows that."

"Maybe you suspect Castaing," Martine said. "But I doubt he'd be that stupid."

"Perhaps he's desperate. If the contents of this file jeopardize his proposal for the World Bank funds —"

"Big *if*, Aimée," Martine interrupted. She leaned forward. "Look, it's touching that you want to help Mireille."

"She's my sister, Martine."

The photos, Mireille's memories, and the card her mother had never sent seemed to substantiate her claim. Martine had several sisters, which fact Aimée envied in secret despite their continual saga of sibling rivalries that never altered their closeness.

"At least it looks like it's true . . . that's what she believes."

"And her proof?"

"Her mother wrote to Papa, there's a photo of them together. . . ."

"A half-sister who's a homicide suspect!" Martine said. "You've done all you can, Aimée. They'll implicate you next. Morbier implied as much, didn't he?"

But she couldn't simply abandon Mireille. Wouldn't.

"DNA." Martine said. "Take a simple to test to find out if she's your sister."

"What?"

Martine glanced at her cell phone. "My appointment. I've got to go." She stood up. "Get a sample of her DNA."

"Easier said than done. She's in hiding, terrified."

"Maybe you're the one who's terrified," Martine said.

Aimée bit her lip.

"*Tiens*, I didn't mean it like that." Martine put her hand on Aimée's arm. "I just want to protect you, Aimée."

Protect her? But that angle of Mireille's chin, that look . . . like her father's. Of course Mireille had to be her sister.

"It's best to know the truth, even if it hurts."

The truth. An elusive thing at best. Her father had never revealed Mireille's existence; she had a mother whose name her father had refused to mention after she'd left, as if she had never existed. Her life was entangled by the cobwebs of the unspoken past.

"If you have a sample — hair, saliva, skin — Gilles's brother can test it. He works at a private lab," Martine said.

She wanted the truth, too. And would prove it to Martine. "Wait a minute."

She remembered Mireille's hair, pulled back, with the wisps hanging over her face, her tears . . . the comb Mireille had forgotten on the armchair in the salon.

Aimée's fingers trembled as she held the tiny tea glass. Did she *really* want to know?

"He likes opera, Aimée," Martine continued.

Aimée gulped. Expensive. "You're saying, as a personal favor, he'd test a sample of our DNA. But doesn't it take weeks, more like months?"

"Season tickets."

More expensive. "You mean. . . ."

"He's the lab director, Aimée."

"So?"

"Certain VIPs use his private express services in paternity matters, a pre-litigation maneuver. Amazing, who's related to who!"

Martine put on her trench coat, a essential component of the Left Bank literati uniform. "Matter of fact, I have to drop off a christening gift. Another godchild, the fourth in his brood. Shall I arrange it?"

Aimée gulped. The hot mint tea burned her throat. "But I don't have time."

"Or you're not game?"

Aimée wiped her mouth and shouldered her secondhand Vuitton bag, trying to control the shaking in her knees.

"Where's your car?"

A simple swab taken from the inside of her mouth, the hair sample from Mireille's comb delivered to the nondescript lab, and ten minutes later Aimée stood on the street. Why didn't she feel better doing the DNA test? More sure that was doing the right thing?

She wished her emotions would calm down. Hiding in the Latin Quarter, aware of every passerby's gaze, nervous that at each corner café men could be watching for her.

She raked her fingers through her damp hair. She couldn't concentrate: impossible for her to work in that spartan room, awaiting the next threatening fax.

Despite the darkened sky, she pulled sunglasses from her bag and a crumpled silk scarf that she knotted around her neck. Huby, the assistant professor, hadn't returned her calls. Time to pay him a visit and find out why.

Aimée, wary of surveillance, entered the lab by the rear delivery entrance on rue Poliveau. Lilac thickets bordered the dirt service lane; no doubt it had been a cart path in the previous century. Midges skittered in the hedgerow. The ozone smell of rain hovered.

This was once a village, she thought, this forgotten slice of the *quartier,* long before cars, buses, and the Metro. The river Bièvre, now cemented over, ran underground. The tanneries and dyeing industry of the Gobelin tapestry works, which polluted it, were a thing of the past.

Rounding a bend, a perspiring sanitation worker in rubber boots and a lime-green jumpsuit labeled EAU DE PARIS blocked her way. "Sewers are backed up, Mademoiselle," he said. "Minor flooding. No one's allowed in."

"But I'm meeting Assistant Professeur Huby," she said.

"Maybe in a few hours you will. That's if we get the suction pump running and complete the water-quality tests."

"Water-quality tests?"

"It's required," he said. "We test the water several times a day. Especially after a flood. The staff has left."

She stepped back, frustrated. A twentyish man with a briefcase headed to a car parked near the hedgerow.

"Monsieur?" She smiled at him. "Excuse me, but I'm late for my appointment."

"I heard," he said. "But one of the labs is flooded. Why don't you reschedule?"

She tapped her heel on the packed earth, thinking fast.

"If I could reach him! But I don't know his cell phone number. Do you?"

"Huby's?" He searched for his keys in his pocket. "Didn't the office tell you?"

Huby was proving more than elusive.

"He's at the Cabinet de Curiosités."

"Cabinet de Curiosités?"

"His grandfather's shop."

So far Huby had seemed intent on avoiding her. She'd prefer to call ahead to make sure he would be there.

"Would you have his number?" she asked. "It might save me a trip."

"That's private information, Mademoiselle."

The man unlocked his car door. If he worked here, he might have known Benoît. She couldn't let this opportunity pass.

"I imagine Huby's upset," she said.

"We're using facilities at the ENS." He shrugged. "It's a minor inconvenience."

Startled for a moment, she wondered if he'd heard her. Then she realized he meant the flooding.

"I meant, considering Professeur Benoît's murder here," she said. "And that of the guard. For that matter, all of you must —"

"The guard was murdered?" The man straightened up. "I'd heard it was a traffic accident."

"Not according to Huby."

His eyes narrowed. "At today's meeting, Dr. Severat told us the guard had had an accident."

A spin put on the facts by the lab officials to downplay the incident? And then she remembered. Dr. Severat had heard Mireille and Benoît argue. She should contact Severat later.

His car door slammed; the engine turned over. Through the windshield, she noticed him grabbing his cell phone. Then the tires spit gravel, raising a cloud of dust. Nervous, hurrying to warn someone? she wondered.

She returned down the lane. A few minutes later, Information connected her to the Cabinet de Curiosités.

"*Allo,* Assistant Professor Huby, please."

"Speaking," a man said. "Who's this?"

"Aimée Leduc, the detective," she said, glancing at the address she'd noted. "Why have you avoided my calls? Not returned my messages?"

"What messages?" Huby said. "I've been trying to reach you."

"You have?"

"I copied down your number . . . must have gotten it wrong."

"But I gave you my card," she said suspiciously.

"I'm helping my grandfather, but we should talk. Later."

"What about now?"

"After you left, well . . . I thought about what you said. Asked some questions. . . ." He hesitated. "Then with Darquin's death. . . ."

He paused.

"You don't think Darquin's death was an

accident, do you?" she said. "I don't either. He had arranged to meet me, but I got there too late."

"I was thinking about Benoît's work," he said. "I didn't realize the test tubes —" She heard a crash, the tinkle of glass. "*Non, grandpère,* let me do that. Excuse me, but I have to go."

Excited now, she pulled out her pocket map. She needed to talk to him before he had second thoughts.

"What test tubes, Huby?"

"Not now," he said.

More tinkling of glass.

"Are you involved, Huby?" she said. "Academic rivalry? Maybe you're hoping to claim credit for his research?"

"Me? Benoît's a brilliant researcher. Was," he said, his voice rising. "You missed the point. What he found proved his theory."

"His theory? Did it relate to the metal deposits in the pig tissue on the slide you showed me? Is that what was in those test tubes?"

A click came over the line. "*Un moment,* I have another call," he said.

She wouldn't let him fob her off. "Look —"

"Talk to the department head. I'm not sure I should be speaking to you." Fear vibrated in his voice.

"Huby, I'm leaving the lab now," she said. "I'll be there, say, in fifteen minutes."

But he'd hung up.

Why hadn't he mentioned this before? Was academia closing ranks? And what had made him begin, then change his mind?

She hurried up the street behind the laboratory to catch the Metro at Gare d'Austerlitz. The Number 10 line went direct to Cluny La Sorbonne, the nearest station. But two full trains passed, before she managed to find space in the third. She hadn't counted on rush hour.

The burning smell of the train's brakes assailed her nostrils, the keening whine of metal on metal her ears, as the train hurtled underground. She stood wedged, sardine-like, wishing she'd taken the bus.

Once out of the Metro, she ran three blocks on crowded Boulevard Saint Germain to rue Saint Jacques before finding the shop. A teal-blue storefront bore the white letters CABINET DE CURIOSITÉS. A definite relic of the fashionable eighteenth-century craze for collecting natural phenomena. Before the advent of museums, wealthy collectors kept rooms in a château or town-house dedicated to the burgeoning sciences of anatomy, botany, and taxidermy. A six-pronged arrangement of metal rods above the door to the shop indicated these scientific branches: naturalism, taxidermy, paleontology, entymology, anatomy, and botanicals.

Bells jingled as she opened the door. She walked into a musty shop whose walls were lined with built-in glass cabinets. Deer antlers graced the walls. The lighted cabinets held yellowed human skulls, curling manuscripts, nautilus shells and fan-shaped coral, glinting minerals, and meteorite shards. Her arm brushed something feather-like, and she jumped when she saw the glassy yellow eyes of a stuffed owl on the counter.

A white-haired gnome of a man, she presumed Huby's grandfather, emerged from behind the counter, spry despite his bowed legs. An old Charles Trenet song came over the radio's nostalgia channel, a *guinguette* dancehall tune.

"So you've met Lola," he said. "She came with the shop. Forty years now and, like all women, she still keeps her age a secret."

Aimée tried to ignore the gaze of those yellow glass eyes, which seemed to follow her.

"May I interest you in something?"

"I'd like to speak with Professeur Huby, Monsieur," she said.

His smile faded. "You're the one. You should know he's already got a girlfriend."

"*Non,* Monsieur, it's concerning the lab."

The elder Monsieur Huby turned the radio volume down. "The boy's a wonder. Don't know what I'd do without his help. Your call disturbed him."

She didn't need his grandfather to defend him; she needed Huby's information.

"I'm here to clear up a misunderstanding," she said.

"That's what they call it these days?"

She didn't know what Huby had told him, but she'd make no headway denying it. Better humor him. "My fault, I know. But we need to talk and resolve this."

The old man stared at her. "Then you'll stop badgering him? Promise not to keep phoning the shop?"

Badgering . . . phone calls? "I only called him once."

"Not according to him."

She'd get nowhere arguing. She wondered whom he was referring to. Had these calls prompted Huby to clam up?

"I think it's best we discuss the situation," she said. "Please, Monsieur."

He glanced at his watch, an old brown leather-strapped Rolex. "Wait, Mademoiselle. I'll ask him if he wants to talk with you."

Five minutes later, after she'd surveyed assorted embryos in aged formeldahyde, Siberian tiger teeth, and a tall glass jar containing a coiled snake, there still was no Huby.

She tapped her fingers on the display case. So far today she'd overslept, almost attacked a cleaning lady, and found a lab flooded. And she'd come up with theories based on nothing but "rumors," according to Martine. But if Huby would clarify his remarks, the day would not be a total waste.

"Monsieur?"

Another Charles Trenet song played, this time a ballad, the lyrics describing a chance encounter, a stolen look.

She called out again. Only Charles Trenet's plaintive words and the moaning trill of an accordion answered her. She walked beyond the counter into a cardboard-carton-filled corridor illuminated by a hanging yellow bulb. More cartons and still more.

At the back, the corridor opened onto a damp mossy stone yard, one of the warren of passages honeycombing the *quartier* that had been overlooked during Baron Haussmann's renovations. The narrow passage tucked between buildings looked as if it had gone unchanged since the Middle Ages. It probably hadn't been cleaned since then either.

She heard a bell and saw a young woman on a bicycle approaching. "Sorry I'm late, Monsieur Huby," the young woman said. "What's the matter?"

The old man was huddled against the wall, pointing to some boxes. Choking sounds came from his throat. Aimée couldn't make out what he was pointing at.

"Monsieur?" Aimée stepped forward. "Are you all right?"

The young woman screamed.

Then Aimée saw a figure lying out-stretched on top of the cartons. Huby's wide-eyed gaze stared unseeing, a piece of lace curtain clutched in his hands. Two floors up, a torn curtain fluttered from an open window. Aimée saw a line of blood trailing from Huby's mouth onto the cobblestones.

She gasped.

"You!" the old man pointed at her.

"What do you mean?"

"You threatened him . . . you made him . . . !" Tears streamed down the old man's face.

Aimée retreated. "No, I said nothing . . .

someone. . . ."

"You'll answer for this."

She bumped into boxes and found herself sprawled on the stone floor and heard another scream.

"Stop her!"

Panicked, she pulled herself up, made her feet move, and ran.

Thursday Afternoon

Léonie slid a franc into the *tronc,* the metal donation box, and lit a candle before the Virgin Mary. Under her breath she recited a prayer to Maitresse Delai, the deity who walked with the spirits. Today was Maitresse Delai's feast day. It was good juju to honor her.

A few minutes later, outside the medieval Saint Medard church, Léonie paused as the sky darkened over Place Monge. Charcoal clouds were threatening; the air held a wet smell. Thirteenth-century Saint Medard still felt like a village church, she thought, and the surrounding square was a gathering place for the *quartier.* Old men played chess on a makeshift table. On nearby rue Mouffetard, two women, string shopping bags full of leeks at their feet, discussed the price of eggs. A student hunched over a thick textbook on his lap.

Her cell phone trilled a Kompa rhythm. Kompa, the Haitian blending of Afro-Cuban and calypso music, reminded her of her youth, when a man encircled a woman's waist with his arm for dancing. Now the young people flew all over, never touching each other.

Kompa brought her back to the humid evenings, outdoor galas in the hills. The lights of Port-au-Prince below were strung like diamonds, wild jasmine scents were borne on the sea breeze, the dancers' skirts swirled among the feathered coconut palm leaves. The laughter, couples ducking into the shadows, the fire torches, Edouard's uncle, the man she'd loved, his arms enfolding her. She was lost in memories until the phone trilled again.

"Madame Léonie," said Royet, the World Bank official. "Remember? We need to talk."

She didn't recall giving Royet her number. Royet kept all the players' secrets: the developers, the corporations, the government officials to pay off. The usual.

"I'd like that," she said. Her spine prickled. News of the inquiries she'd made today had traveled fast. One must never look eager with a player like Royet, she counseled herself. "But I'm afraid, Monsieur Royet, my schedule's tight. . . ." She paused.

"Mine too," he said. "But it's important. Can we meet in ten minutes at the Ecole Polytechnique garden?"

The clock tower chimed the hour. If the spirits were willing, Royet would give her information concerning Benoît's file.

"Of course, Monsieur Royet," she said.

A taxi deposited her at the former Ecole Polytechnique, where top students, referred to as *Les X,* were educated. Now the school itself had moved outside Paris, but *Les X*'s route to the ministries and to government positions hadn't changed. Their diplomas guaranteed them a place in the upper echelon. Like in Haiti, like anywhere, she thought, the upper crust presented a united front.

Now the imposing white stone buildings housed le Ministère de l'Enseignement Superieur et Recherche. Massive carved green doors opened to a garden with a reflecting pool, pockmarked stone benches and cone-shaped topiary shrubs.

Royet, leaning against a pitted stone pillar, looked up from a slim novel with a smile on his face. Reading glasses perched on his nose. With his white hair, he reminded her more of a Renaissance merchant-prince than a World Bank official.

"So many books, Léonie, so little time."

Royet put the novel in his pocket.

As if they were here to talk about literature!

He pecked her cheeks, lingering close to her ear. "The loan-funding meeting's tomorrow. A scandal now is unwelcome, Léonie."

"Or any time, Royet," she said.

"A detective's been asking questions. A woman whose name is Aimée Leduc."

She'd expected him to give her information about the whereabouts of Benoît's file, not this woman. Another unknown.

Again, she sensed Royet, like Jérôme, hiding something from her.

And in the dense, moisture-charged air, she felt a rocking, like in a boat at sea. Like the fishing scows docked in Port-au-Prince harbor, bobbing in the current, the silver schools of fish darting among the low-lying prows in the clear blue water . . . like it had been. When flower petals floated daily on the fringed white curled waves in the ceremonies for Agwe, patron of the sea.

But no more. Now sewage drained into the port, the coral was bleached brittle and dead, the fishermen had decamped to the north or were begging on the dirt roads. Her vision changed to the dark maroon veil of clouds threatening from the mountains, before Papa Doc Duvalier took power. The time when the water springs dried up, the livestock died, the farmers sold their land to feed their families.

Ogoun brought this vision to her. She shivered with the same fear she'd felt then.

An evil wind rose and marked her. Carried by these men and the forces they represented. This was her last chance.

"I'm sure we have an interest in common," she said. Her voice seemed to belong to someone else, someone taking her over, guiding her. "To attain maximum results, I welcome your expertise, Royet. As a precaution, of course, I need to know everything you know."

Royet's features remained a mask. Thunder cracked overhead. In a moment, the sky would open up.

"Royet, I assume you want me to furnish you with the information in Benoît's file," she said. "But first I need to know Hydrolis's stake in the project from you. I mean, apart from the usual."

"You mean, what does Jérôme Castaing stand to lose?" Royet smiled. "I thought you'd never ask, Léonie."

Thursday Evening
Aimée ran up the winding street in the pelting rain. Blocks away from the Cabinet de

Curiositiés, she noticed an open grocery and ducked inside. Shaking and wet, her heart thumping, she joined the line to purchase an umbrella.

Huby's last words played over again in her mind: he hadn't gotten her messages, he wanted to meet, then his nervous manner as he put off their meeting. She remembered his grandfather's words about badgering, and phone calls. Perhaps Huby hadn't leaped from that window, he'd been pushed!

"Ten francs, Mademoiselle," said the smiling woman at the register.

"Merci." Aimée paid, took the umbrella, and went back into the street.

Now she'd never know what had changed Huby's mind. Or how Benoît's work was involved. But, then again, Dr. Severat might know.

Shielding herself from the rain with the umbrella, she reached the Ecole Normale Supérieure five minutes later. She shook the umbrella and stepped inside.

"Where do you think you're going?" said an evening guard in the lobby of the laboratory wing.

"*Bonsoir,* Monsieur. The lab on rue Buffon's flooded. I believe Dr. Severat's working here."

He snapped his fingers. "Your ID?"

She flashed her Sorbonne student ID card, covering the date with her thumb.

"Not so fast." He stared at it. "Your card has expired. It's not even from the ENS."

She slapped her forehead. "Silly me, my other one's —"

"At home?" said the guard. "Then you'll have to go get it, won't you?"

Several people in white lab coats were conferring near the chipped pillars. She noticed a woman among them, the only one: Dr. Severat, standing deep in conversation, holding a briefcase. Her hair was wet; a wet raincoat hung over her arm, dripping onto the floor.

"But there's Dr. Severat," Aimée said. "I have to speak to her."

"Regulations forbid entry without a proper ID," he said, crossing his arms over his stocky chest.

The group was walking away.

"Dr. Severat," Aimée called out.

No response. And then Aimée remembered Severat was hard of hearing.

"I'm afraid you'll need to leave, Mademoiselle."

"Dr. Severat!" she called out again, more loudly.

One of the men tugged Dr. Severat's arm and pointed to Aimée.

Aimée waved her arm. A moment later, Dr. Severat approached, her eyebrows raised.

"Sorry that she's bothered you, Doctor," the guard said, gripping Aimée's arm. "I'll escort her out."

Aimée hoped Dr. Severat would recognize her.

"*Non,* Pascal," Dr. Severat said. "She's with Dr. Rady's department. It's all right."

The guard released Aimée's arm and let her pass.

"I'm en route to a department meeting," Dr. Severat said. "I've already helped you all I could, Mademoiselle."

At least she'd remembered her. Had word of Huby's death reached the department yet?

"Then you know?"

"Know what? Listen, I'm sorry, but —"

"Benoît's assistant, Huby, promised to furnish me with some of the results of his work," Aimée interupted. "Some samples to give to the next professor. But they told me he's dead. What's happened?"

Dr. Severart stared at the group of waiting men. Then back at Aimée. "No wonder they've called an emergency meeting! I have to go."

"I'm in trouble if I don't get those

samples."

"*You,* Mademoiselle?" Dr. Severat adjusted the flesh-colored knob in her ear and leaned forward. "What about *us?* Who's next?"

Aimée pushed the salad on her plate around with a fork. She was in a cheap student canteen, one of many in the *quartier.* Garlic aromas and steam rose from the hot platters amid the clatter of trays and conversation. She sat at the long crowded refectory table, a *pichet* of rosé and a half-finished *plat du jour* in front of her, trying to make sense of what had happened.

Three days ago, Mireille, claiming to be her sister, had appeared at her office door, asking for help. She'd discovered the ENS professor who'd sheltered Mireille, murdered. The lab guard had been pushed in front of a car near the Pantheon. And now the professor's part-time assistant was dead. An academic scandal? But with Benoît's connection to Hydrolis, Castaing's firm, and the rumors Martine had passed on about the World Bank and privatization, she doubted that it was as contained as that.

"*Alors,* going to answer it?" A pockmark-faced student jerked his thumb at her cell phone resting by her plate. Lost in thought, she hadn't heard it ringing.

"*Oui?*"

"We've been getting strange faxes, Aimée," René said.

"I know."

"Then you want to explain them?" René said.

She couldn't stop marshaling her thoughts. Did the person who had murdered Benoît assume that Mireille was his accomplice? Her mind went back to her conversation in the lab with Huby. He had known that Mireille was staying in the gatehouse.

"Aimée, are you there?" René asked angrily. "Don't pretend you can't hear me. Is this some kind of kinky hide-and-seek?"

She snapped to attention. "What?"

"The last fax says 'If you want to see her again look in the quarry under Hôpital Val de Grâce.' "

The hair on the back of her neck rose. The traffickers must be holding Mireille in the quarry under the military hospital, a popular cataphile haunt.

"How long ago did you get this message, René?"

"You mean you don't know? Aren't you working at home?"

Her mobile fax machine was in the room

at the Collège des Irlandais.

"Please, René, check the time."

"Where are you?"

She pushed her plate away and grabbed her bag. "I've just finished dinner."

"The fax came an hour ago."

Already an hour had passed!

"What's going on, Aimée?"

No time to give a long explanation. "Later, René."

"But we've got a report due —"

"I'm on it." Still holding the phone to her ear, she raced up the canteen steps and searched for a taxi on rue Lhommond.

"Let me come by and we'll go over it together."

She couldn't involve him any more. He'd already been injured because of her.

A taxi's blue light signaled that it was free. She raised her arm to hail it. "I'll call you later, René." She clicked off before he could protest and jumped into the back seat.

"Hôpital Val de Grâce, emergency entrance," she said.

"In a hurry, eh?" said the taxi driver.

"You could say that."

Her Beretta was sitting in her hall drawer. All she had with her was her Swiss Army knife. And a plan.

"Fifty francs if we get there in under ten

minutes."

The taxi driver thrust the meter handle upright. "Hold on."

Aimée pushed open the Emergency Wing swinging door of Hôpital Val de Grâce and found herself in an institutional green-tiled corridor, smelling of antiseptic under fluorescent lights. She hated these places.

An orderly rushed past, pushing a gurney to the ambulance bay. Nurses scurried by, opening plastic curtains to reveal a moaning patient. An ordered chaos reigned.

"Lucien?"

Lucien looked up from the chart he was filling out in the emergency room near the triage station. His blond curls, round cheeks, and athletic build had earned him the nickname "Cherub" in her anatomy class. He stuck a pen in the shirt lapel of his blue scrubs. "Believe it or not, there's a method to our madness."

She'd phoned Lucien from the taxi, and he'd agreed to take her down to the quarry at the end of his shift. But he didn't look prepared for the quarries. A sinking feeling engulfed her.

"Ready?"

"Sorry, they pulled me for the next shift." Lucien shrugged. "Ambulances routed us the overflow casualties from a twenty-car pileup on the *periphérique.* A mess. And they're coming in any minute."

More than an hour had passed since the fax. She'd have to forget her plan; now she had no help. No backup. She'd have to do this herself.

"Where's the entrance, Lucien?"

Lucien shook his head; his curls bobbed. "It's not safe without a guide or proper equipment. The tunnels run on for kilometers, there are dead-ends, sinkholes, cave-ins —"

"Just tell me, Lucien."

"What's your rush? I'm off tomorrow. We'll go then. You need a guide."

"Too late. I can do this alone."

"You're impatient, as always, Aimée," Lucien said. "What's this woman to you, anyway?"

"No time to explain."

His brow creased. "She's one of the illegals, right?"

"Trust me, Lucien. Just point me to the tunnel entrance and the quarries."

Lucien eyed her outfit. "Dressed like that? No chance. If you got lost, there's no telling how long you'd wander without water or food. Forget it, Aimée."

"Someone tried to shoot her last night,"

Aimée said. "They're holding her down there. And she's my sister."

He dropped his pen.

Aimée bent and picked it up.

"You never told me. . . ."

"I didn't know." She rubbed her forehead. "I just discovered it myself. Long story. Please, Lucien. Don't you have some kind of map?"

He averted his eyes. Of *course* he had a map.

"But, Aimée, even with a map. . . ." He rocked on his feet. "If the hospital administration knew, I'd get in trouble. They're tightening security."

"But we used to go to parties in the catacombs after class, remember? People go down there all the time to party. I'll follow your map."

It couldn't be that tough! At least, she hoped not.

"Can't you help me, Lucien?"

Lucien glanced around the tiled hall.

"I shouldn't do this." Lucien leaned forward and pulled out a prescription pad. "The entrance to the tunnel underneath the hospital's vacant wing is here." He drew a diagram on the prescription pad. Made an X. "It's the quickest way. The tunnel leads to the limestone quarry. Don't tell anyone or let anyone see you. Here's my map." He pulled out a much-folded paper. "Stay on the marked routes. And don't lose this."

A maze of X's and zigzagging lines confronted Aimée.

"Write messages on the walls along the way." He pressed something cylindrical into her hand. A stick of chalk. "Always preface it with 'Gorgo,' then your message."

"But why?"

"That's my cataphile moniker. Otherwise it will be erased. There are codes of behavior, you know," Lucien said, grabbing a clipboard. "By the way, my friend heard of some illegals near the lake."

"A lake?"

"Feeding the reservoir. If you hit the Medici aqueduct, you've gone too far. Keep alert for the IGC."

"Who?"

"IGC, the *cataflics*. They're clamping down now, after some newspaper article made them a laughingstock. If you're caught, it means a night in the Prefecture."

Maybe she could use that to her advantage. She could point the *cataflics* to the traffickers and help Mireille escape while they were occupied with the cops. She didn't know how, exactly, but she'd figure it out on the way. She squared her shoulders.

"Just remember, any operational exit is marked by an orange day-glow circle."

"You mean I can't get out back here?"

"Not if you get lost, or if the *cataflics* show up."

An orderly tugged at Lucien's sleeve. "Doctor, a bleeder in three!"

Lucien said "Got to go." He gestured to her outfit. "But you need boots, overalls. . . ."

And here she was, wearing a beaded Schiaparelli jacket! "Can I grab some scrubs?"

Lucien pointed to a sign: SURGERY DRESSING ROOM. He paused, leaned forward, and whispered, "Be careful."

Aimée kept to the shadows in the weed-choked courtyard of the vacant wing. The light of a fingernail of a moon was reflected by tall jagged broken glass windows. She inserted the long iron key into the door's old-fashioned lock, left it under the mat, and entered the abandoned operating theater.

A rusted metal gurney stood to one side. Medical charts of skeletal systems curled from the walls. She was in a rotunda-like space with a circular balcony. This was the old military teaching-hospital section. She remembered hearing of secret surgeries performed here to save Mitterand's life. They hadn't worked. She shivered. If the ghost of the Socialist president, the darling of the rich leftists, hovered, she wanted no part of it.

Behind the suction machine, lime-green graffiti covered a crumbling hole in the wall. The entrance. She felt currents of cool air tinged with the smell of limestone. As she felt her way along the wall, her hands became covered with the flaking chalky stone. Subterranean Paris was connected in a vast web of more than four hundred kilometers of tunnels, sewers, quarries, and catacombs. The perfect place to hide.

She took out her penlight. The narrow yellow beam traced walls bearing ancient graffiti. The date 1775 was carved in the limestone. She studied Lucien's map, figuring out a route through the maze of tunnels. If she veered left. . . .

A low growl, and a dog's bark made her jump almost out of her skin. She backed up, dropping the penlight. Shaking, she searched the gritty beaten earth, miraculously found it, and shone the beam ahead of her. Instead of a growling canine, the light revealed a pair of motorcycle boots. She lifted the penlight higher to see leopard-print skin-tight leggings and a face with kohled eyes wreathed by long black hair. The tight bustier didn't quite hide the hair on the man's chest.

"You have a reservation?" he asked formally.

"Do I need one?" The snarls and barks were louder now. "Call your dog off, please." Her voice trembled.

He blocked her way. "Without a reservation, you'll have to turn around —"

She said the first thing that came in her mind. "Gorgo made it. I forgot."

He took a pencil from behind his ear, checked the book in his hand. A massive mountain of a man? Woman? Had Aimée stumbled into a gender-bender affair?

"Aaah, the cataphile. No reservation required, then. Welcome."

"But your dog. . . ."

He pressed something on the wall. The barking ceased. A recording. "Precautions, you know."

She wanted to reach the lake, find Mireille. "I appreciate this, but —" Another burst of recorded barking interrupted her.

He took her arm in a firm grip. "You'll need to step inside, if you don't mind. We have unannounced vistors."

"Eh?"

"The *cataflics.*"

She had no choice. She entered and struck her head on the low ceiling. For a moment she saw stars.

"Sorry," he said. "I always forget to warn guests about that."

She rubbed her head and heard the door close behind her. She peered through the haze of cigarette smoke to see moisture dripping down vaulted stone walls in silver rivulets. The low tunnel opened into a cavern lit by a black chandelier. On the wall hung a high-tech wide screen. Bottles of Marie Brizard, the clear anise liqueur, were lined up on the shelves behind a bar carved from a rock ledge. A banner proclaimed *"Les Ux presenté le cinema." Les Ux,* the underground cataphile group, organized film fests for thrill-seeking dilettantes who attended despite the risks of "the forbidden" and the likelihood of muddy shoes.

She surveyed a crowd of student types wearing camouflage khakis. A hollow-cheeked blonde in blue velvet trousers, drink in hand, sprawled on a modern red sofa. Standing were a sprinkling of *bobo's,* the bourguoise bohemians, in designer jeans and rumpled linen jackets. A bearded middle-aged man took notes in a corner; he was a critic she recognized from the *Cahiers de Cinema.*

The blue haze of cigarette smoke hovered overhead. She bummed a drag from a flushed girl leaning against a pitted stone arch, surveying the cavern for an exit.

"I love Rimbaud's *Death,*" the girl said. A bandanna circled her head. She wore pink jeans and had a diamond stud in her nose.

Some documentary?

"Me too." Aimée nodded and exhaled a long stream of smoke. She wanted to fit in, not draw attention to herself. Yet time was running out; she had to get to Mireille. How could she get out of here?

"It's symbolic of man's struggle against darkness. The continuing despair of humans in the twentieth century. Don't you agree?"

"Exactement." Aimée handed back the cigarette. Then she stepped forward, looking for an exit.

Amazed, she stared at the cables and wires snaking up the rock wall, siphoning power from electric lines and circuits. A backup generator stood near large black speakers and a sound adjustment console, a panel with knobs, green and red lights. Self-contained and a curiously comfortable haven, she figured, until discovery when *flics* would cut the juice. Beyond lay crushed velvet draperies.

"Silence, *s'il vous plaît*. Please take a seat. Tonight's films show two aspects of life's struggle: a recovered archival version of the *Battleship Potemkin,* Eisenstein's 1925 Russian masterpiece, the seminal film of our century. Following the screening, Monsieur Loriol will lead the discussion. . . ."

She groaned. A "*film-philosophe* happening" in this medieval cave. She usually avoided these *soupçons de culture.* The voice continued. ". . . revealing the journey of Everyman, mirroring the poet Rimbaud's strife-torn life in the nineteenth century."

She consulted the map. An exit had to exist. After the lights were lowered, she edged toward the velvet draperies and opened the door behind them to enter a storeroom. Two men, their jeans caked with white plaster and faces dusted with white powder, played cards over a wooden crate. Pickaxes and shovels lay in a wheelbarrow. Candles dripped and flickered in holes pockmarking the stone. It was quiet except for the slap of cards. To the side stood a vaulted door.

"Wouldn't go that way," said one of the men, the older one, not looking up.

Aimée's hand froze on the steel handle. "Why's that?"

"The tunnel caved in," he said. "We just sealed up the entrance."

Her heart sank. Now she couldn't rely on Lucien's map.

"Then, Monsieur, how can I reach the lake?"

"Dressed like that?"

She took the green scrubs from her bag, pulled them on over her skirt and jacket. From a pile on the dirt floor, she picked up a hard hat mounted with a headlamp and threw a fifty-franc bill on the crate. "No, Monsieur, like this."

The *mec* looked up. "That's better."

"Can you show me another way?"

"You wouldn't want to end up like Philibert."

"Meaning?" She envisioned shifting earth, sinkholes, more cave-ins.

"Philibert lost his way in the quarry. But cataphiles see him all the time near the lake."

"Guess I'll see him en route."

"Philibert disappeared in 1793."

Ghosts. Where *didn't* one live with the ghosts in Paris, she almost asked.

"I'm looking for the Haitians, for a woman —"

"You're too late," he said.

Her heart stopped. "The *cataflics* took her?"

The *mec* scratched his cheek. A fine white

311

dust settled over the cards. "Only if they wear gold chains and nuggets on their ring fingers."

"Tell me who these *mecs* are."

"The scum who sell people."

The human traffickers. The ones who'd lured Mireille to the Arènes de Lutèce.

"Did you see a particular woman? She's tall, half-Haitian, curly hair, brown eyes. . . ."

"The good-looker who screamed so much that they duct-taped her mouth."

She gasped. Why hadn't he stopped them?

"Not my business," he said, as if he'd read her mind. "A bucket of plaster's no match for their brawn."

From bad to worse.

"How long ago?"

"I never saw them leave." He threw down a card.

They could still be there. She studied the map, then thrust it near his face.

"What about this tunnel? Have you noticed any cave-ins here?"

"Like I said, I mind my own business." He threw his cards down. "You wanna-be adventurers make me sick."

Anger flushed her cheeks. "A woman's being kidnapped, and you do nothing." *You spineless wonder,* but she bit that back.

"Some people like it rough," he said,

jaded. "Eh, Stanislav?"

The other man grunted.

"He's a Pole. Doesn't understand. But he understands tunnels and digging." The *mec* shook his head. "Look, all kinds come down here and play games. They get their kicks that way. Hold Black Masses, orgies."

Not in the cavern behind them, where a noted critic was attending a film fest. But she didn't doubt that those goings-on took place elsewhere in this labyrinthine maze.

"We work hard to maintain the tunnels, support the walls, keep it all safe." His mouth formed a moue of distaste. "I spend my weekends here. It's history, you know . . . why not preserve it rather than 'tag' it? No respect."

His passion took her by surprise.

"Why do you do this?"

"You really want to know?" He leaned back. "It's quiet. Peaceful. The only time I get away from. . . ." He gestured above. "Look, last time I interfered, the scum broke my arm. It's never been right since." He lifted a crooked elbow.

"You've seen these same men before?

"Two times too many."

"Then you must know how they leave, even where they go?"

"They avoid this cavern," he said. "It's

313

too busy here. Makes more sense to use the nearest exit."

"Will you show me?"

"Why not, Wonder Woman? It's your funeral." His white-caked finger touched an X on her map. "I park above, on the cul-de-sac near the Scuola Cantorum. Easier to transport my tools."

A van. They'd have to use a van or a truck to spirit struggling victims away. If she didn't hurry, they'd make an example of Mireille, and this time they'd finish what they'd tried in the Arènes and kill her.

"Did you see their van?"

"I saw an old *camionette,* like the one by the lake. You know, an old butcher's van."

"Eh?"

He shrugged. "You can't miss it. Now, if you don't mind, rentals go up by the minute." He held out a white-caked palm. She put another fifty-franc note in his hand. "*Catalampe's* included." He gestured to a beer can with a candle in it. "Leave the lamp and hat at the exit."

"One more thing." She managed a small smile, aiming for charm. "What time did you see them?"

"I told you. . . ."

"The abducted girl's my . . . my sister," she interrupted. "Mireille. And if I don't get

314

to her before. . . ." The words choked in her throat.

Compassion mixed with curiosity crossed his face.

"Family. I understand," he said. "You should have said so."

According to the diagram, she had two tunnels and what looked like a quarry bed to cross.

He looked at his watch, then gazed at the sacks of plaster. "An hour and a half hour ago."

The limestone tunnel forked; she ran to the right. Another long winding passage, humid like everywhere down here, then another fork. This time she took a left, her feet kicking up puffs of limestone dust. She heard the faint sound of dripping water in the distance. Otherwise it was quiet in this dark underground labyrinth supporting the sprawl of the city overhead.

Then came the smell of water.

She emerged in a vast cavern. Her penlight beam danced over a turquoise-blue pool, the lake. Breathtakingly still, its source an underground spring. A feeder to the nearby Medici aqueduct under the gardens of l'Observatoire, built by Henri IV and finished by his widow Marie. And for a moment she understood the cataphiles, felt the allure of the underground wonders, the peace.

Along the side ran a rough carved declivity, a water conduit, the date 1693 chiseled into the stone. Her fingers touched the cool running water. It was still in operation.

She made out the fender and rusted grill of a Citroën *camionette,* doors and windows broken, parked abutting the cavern wall. She wondered how in the world a truck had ended up here in the cavern. Inside it she saw cushions, a rug, a copy of *Paris Match,* and posters on the walls as if someone had just left.

"Allo?" Her voice echoed in the humid, still air.

She looked closer. A layer of dust littered the *camionette*'s floor. Abandoned.

Above, carved in the limestone, was a loft with windows reached by a rope ladder. She clutched the thick rope, hopeful, climbing the swaying steps and holding on for dear life.

At the top, she found a jagged opening. Small spaces bothered her, but, like an earthworm, she wiggled inside. She half-crawled, propelling herself forward with her arms, scraping her elbows and knees. Thank God for the surgeon's scrubs.

"Mireille?"

Apart from a plastic water bottle, the space was empty.

There was a rumbling, then the walls and earth below her shook. A plume of dust and pebbles rained down on her head. Limestone crumbled to powder in her hand. This hole was caving in. Her lungs filled with dust. She panicked; there was nowhere to go. If she died here, buried under tons of earth, no one would ever know.

She had to back up. But her knees trembled, dirt blocked her way. Coughing and choking, she reached out, her fingers scrabbling over rocks. Her hand came back with something ridged and soft. The headlamp's chalky beam illumined a half-buried hemp bag. She gasped, choking. She recognized Mireille's handbag.

She couldn't let fear paralzye her. She had to move. Get out.

Grit lodged in her eyes, her nose. Head down, taking small breaths, she inched her way back through falling dust and rock, trying to will down her fear. A little farther back each time. And then her feet were in the air. Suspended. And she slid, scrabbled, feeling her way, and found the hole's rim.

Easing out, she clung to the rope and worked her way down the rope ladder.

Halfway down, her grip loosened and she fell.

She landed in a semi-crouch and rolled. Nothing broken, she concluded after feeling her arms and legs. She took small breaths, then deeper ones. Coughing, she brushed herself off. With Mireille's bag inside hers, she ran past the *camionette.* No time to check the contents. The passage narrowed. Just ahead, the diagram showed an exit, the one the plasterer had indicated. If she hurried. . . .

Shuffling sounds came from ahead. She froze. The yellow flare of a match sputtered, illuminating a man's face. Lined and craggy. Philibert the ghost who wandered forever in the quarry?

Then she saw blue jumpsuits, the flash of silver badges. Not ten feet away stood two *cataflics,* the IGC who patrolled the underground.

She shut off the headlamp, blew out the candle. Edged back, trying to melt into the stone. Somehow, they hadn't seen her.

Yet.

Static came from a walkie-talkie on the belt of one of the men. "AF12 alert. Activity near the lake." He clicked a button, spoke into the walkie-talkie. "AF12 responding. Relate the coordinates."

"We've had reports of ground distur-bance," said the voice on the other end. "A cave-in north of the lake."

The *flic* next to him sighed. "Not again. Don't they ever learn?"

"Keep a lookout for a woman near the traffickers' site."

"Description?"

"She's wearing worker's headgear, hospital scrubs, tall."

Aimée's heart pounded so loudly, she thought they'd hear it.

On her right she saw faded writing in Gothic script: BUNKER LUFTWAFFE AN-NEX. A German Air Force bunker. She stepped over rusted pipes and found herself in a cubicle with a rusted-out toilet.

The *cataflic's* flashlight beam swept the ground. She stepped up onto the toilet's cracked rim, figuring if it had supported Nazi asses, it could hold hers. But the porcelain base shifted with her weight. She held still, wishing the *flics* would finish their cigarettes and move on. For support, she gripped the rusted pipes, trying not to think of what had flowed through them. An or-ange fluorescent graffitied "O" shone above her, the exit the plasterer had indicated.

Her ankle ached. She shifted position by a centimeter and slipped.

"Over there. I heard a noise."

Aimée held her breath. The wall with its rusted pipes trailed up into the darkness. . . . Would they hold her weight if she climbed them?

"Eh?" The other *flic* scanned the wall with his powerful beam. Aimée edged back on her toes once more. The yellow light reached the tip of her ballet slipper. Another few centimeters and he'd find her.

Then the beam swept away, following the crumbling wall into the next cubicle. The *cataflic* moved past her into the other chamber.

She reached and pulled herself up by the pipe. Above her, rungs disappeared into the shadows. Slime coated the metal rungs of a manhole shaft. It would be an exhausting climb, the equivalent of several flights, up to the street.

But it was a way out.

One foot balanced on the ledge; with the other, she found a foothold and hoisted herself up. She climbed straight up the narrow shaft. No time to rest. Her foot slipped and she grabbed the rungs. Metal burned her knuckles; she was dizzied when she looked down.

"Hey, there's someone up there!" a man shouted.

Then yellow flashlight beams crisscrossed below her.

"You! Stop!"

She kept going. Her calves strained, her fingers pinched, and her bag hung heavy. Each breath was labored. Perspiration ran between her shoulder blades. And then she felt a jarring crack to the top of her hard hat. She'd hit her head on the bottom of the manhole cover.

She prayed it wasn't cemented shut.

She felt for a metal ring and tugged it, levering and shoving with all her might. It moved, grating sideways. She left the hard hat and beer can on a ledge and hoisted herself over the metal lip onto the street. Then she shoved the cover back into place and found herself sitting next to a garbage can on the wet pavement, Michelin car tires passing inches from her face.

Panting from her close escape, she removed her scrubs, balled them up, and left them in a pile under a parked car.

She had to clean up. Then she'd melt into the Metro. She dusted off the Schiaparelli jacket, pulled out her compact to check for white limestone dust in her hair. A car turned into the street.

In the compact mirror's reflection she saw a trio of blue uniforms round the corner.

IGC, the *cataflics.* One spoke into a walkie-talkie.

No wonder they hadn't followed her up the shaft: they'd simply radioed for above-ground backup. Even without the scrubs, she couldn't risk being questioned now.

Her eyes darted for cover. No cafés, a darkened bistro, a shuttered locksmith. Light from streetlights pooled in the puddles. She saw no hiding places; the doorways were all flush with the pavement.

The car, a Deux Chevaux with a rattling engine, backed into a parking space. A few doors down, the IGC shone flashlights into the doorways. Aimée opened the car door to blaring reggae music and jumped into the passenger seat.

"What the . . . ?" A man with a long ponytail turned from the wheel to stare at her. Tan, lean, not hard on the eyes. Amnesty International and Che Guevara stickers littered his dashboard. This looked promising.

"Get out of my car."

"They're after me. I'm in trouble. Deep trouble."

He sneered, taking in her outfit.

"Hey, party girl, not my problem."

"Can't you drive around the block, please?"

"And lose this parking place? No way."

Tapes spilled over the torn back seat. Handwritten labels with the names of major films. Pirated illegal tapes. Worth a nice sum in the right market.

"Slumming in couture?" He jerked this thumb. "Out."

He reached for the door handle and turned. *"Merde!"* His jaw dropped. *"Cataflics!* They don't play around! Don't pull me into this."

A billyclub tapped on the passenger window.

"Let's fog up the windows," Aimée said, tugging his sleeve.

"Eh?"

She locked her lips on his surprised ones, determined not to let him come up for air, and tried to grind her hips against him — but the gearshift got in her way. Then his leather-jacketed arms were around her as she felt him respond. Kind of nice, apart from his overpowering patchouli scent.

"Monsieur!" Harder knocking on the window. Aimée opened one eye. A trio of large IGC men loomed over the tin-can hood of the Deux Chevaux. She reached with one hand and opened the driver's window.

"Désolée." She giggled. "We're a little busy. . . ."

"And your headlights are on."

The IGC man winked and tipped his cap, and they walked down the cobbled street.

Her shoulders sagged in relief.

"Where did you learn to do . . . that?"

"That? Call it the benefits of a higher education," she said. "Thank the Sorbonne."

He blinked, his ponytail undone, his hair spread over her shoulder. He took little breaths and kept his arm around her. Such nice hazel eyes.

"I haven't seen you in the *quartier.*"

"You wouldn't," she said, adjusting the rearview mirror and using her sleeve to clean up her smudged red mouth. She took off her ballet slippers, slipped on her Louboutin heels.

"But you're not just another party cataphile escaping through the sewer."

He seemed observant. Not only that, he lived here.

"Did you see an old *boucherie camionette* tonight parked over there?" She pointed to where she figured the other exit led.

"Why?"

"Say two or three hours ago?"

He shrugged. "Maybe. I don't remember."

Information would cost, she could tell. She leaned against his chest. "If you did something about that gearshift, I could help you remember."

"Could you, now?" He turned the key in the ignition, put the transmission in neutral, and set the parking brake. The engine sputtered and idled.

She twirled a strand of his hair around her fingers. "The *camionette*'s old. There's a name on it. Cha . . . something."

"Chazel." He stiffened. "Lowlifes. They harassed my neighbor, broke his car windows. He'd complained because they parked in his space." He pointed. "Right there."

Why not tell her in the first place? she wondered. She rubbed the fogged-up window with her sleeve so she could see out. It made sense, if they'd used this exit to take Mireille and the others out unseen.

"They're more than lowlifes," he said.

"What do you mean?" She stared at him. "Tell me."

He gave a half-smile, pulled her closer, tightening his grip, his hand pulling down her zipper. "Let's talk it over at my place."

Then she saw that his other hand was inside her half-open handbag, reaching for her wallet. Talk about lowlifes.

"Right here. Number 34. I'm Ricot."

"No names." She put her hand over his mouth. "It's better that way."

His eyes widened. Large light-brown eyes. She hoisted her leg and straddled him in the driver's seat, pinning him down, keeping her hand over his mouth. "You've got beautiful eyes. And of course you want to keep them."

The tip of her Swiss Army knife touched the jugular vein in his neck.

"Now get your hand off my wallet."

He did.

"And zip up my dress."

He did.

"*Bon.* I'll ask you again: how many?"

She took her hand off his mouth.

"Two Africans," he said, "big *mecs.*"

"You're observant. What about the woman?"

"Woman? I remember the *mecs* because they broke my neighbor's car windows. Drunk and ready to fight."

"And a woman?" She pressed the knife point on his bobbing Adam's apple.

"That's right. She looked sleepy, but I scarcely saw her."

Mireille. Drugged?

"But your neighbor took down their license plate number to claim insurance, *n'est-ce pas?*"

"Put the knife down."

The Deux Chevaux's engine sputtered.

Heat rose from the floor; she wished these old models had defrosters.

"As soon as you tell me."

"I wrote it down. The paper's in my pocket."

She felt around in his leather jacket pocket. Used tissues, a crumpled pack of Gitanes, a few coins, and a balled-up paper on which was scribbled what appeared a license plate number.

"This?"

He swallowed. His Adam's apple bobbed. *"Oui."*

"See, it's not hard. I knew you'd cooperate."

She kept the knife point on his neck.

He stared at her. "You know . . . it's kind of exciting like this. People say. . . ."

She felt the bulge in his pants, and in a quick movement she opened the door and got out. "But you won't say anything. I know you live at 34, rue Henri Barbusse. And you never saw me. Right, Ricot?"

Aimée stood in a telephone booth near the Jardin du Luxembourg and thumbed through the yellow pages, searching under "Boucherie." Three pages of butchers, along with horse butchers, listed by arrondissement. She tried a hunch and ran her fingernail down the 5th arrondissement listings.

Boucherie Chazel on rue Saint Victor advertised *"Boucherie, charcuterie, volaille gros — Demi-gros pour restaurants et collectivités."*

Twenty minutes later, she stood on rue Saint Victor, a street that had once abutted the old Philippe Auguste wall, below the level of the next street and connected to it by three sagging steps. Boucherie Chazel lay shuttered and dark; its dark green wooden storefront adjoined a seventeenth-century *hôtel particulier.* On the door was a sign reading "Closed until end of September due to a death in the family."

Great.

She didn't find a parked Boucherie Chazel truck there, nor on the parallel rue Pontoise, where the old pool she remembered from swimming classes was located. Nor in the side street, with the stone-blackened thirteenth-century Collège des Bernardins, a former Cistercian abbey. Nor on any more distant side streets leading to Boulevard Saint Germain.

Her adrenalin subsiding, she sat down, exhausted, on the steps and leaned against a pillar of Église Saint-Nicolas-du-Chardonnet. The church, a bastion of right-wing Catholics, still held masses in Latin and counted Le Pen among the members of its congregation. Zola had studied next door until, unable to pay his fees, he had been expelled.

Her shoulders and legs ached from the climb from the sewer. But time mattered, and she forced her mind to run through the possibilities; instead of working at the butcher's, these men might have bought the truck secondhand.

She found the phone number in the back of her address book . . . a 24/7 operation. A direct line only used by the *flics.* She punched in the number and hoped she could invent a good enough story.

"Vehicle Division, Tissot," said a tired voice. The bureau at 3, Quai de l'Horloge, around the corner from the Prefecture, kept the *cartes grisés,* cards, and records for all vehicles registered in Paris.

"Juppe, *s'il vous plaît.*"

"He's on sick leave."

Just her luck. Juppe had graduated from the police academy with her father and done them the occasional favor. She rethought her strategy.

"His sciatica again?" She made a clucking sound. "Sorry to hear that, Officer Tissot. Maybe you can run a license plate for me."

"Eh? Those requests go through division."

By the book, this Tissot.

"And in normal cases I'd use the proper channels. But . . . we've got a situation."

"Everyone has a 'situation,' " Tissot said. "We've got a backlog of requests. Priority goes to that white Fiat Uno."

The Fiat Uno "seen" speeding away from Princess Di's crash in Pont de l'Alma. The damn Fiat Uno. She thought hard. She could use that.

"Didn't I say that?" She didn't wait for his reply. "We've had a sighting."

She heard clicks in the background. What sounded like a cup clinking on a saucer. "Your priority access code?" There was a definite spark of interest in Tissot's voice.

"Do you think I wrote it down or remember?" she said. "Listen, I'm on ground patrol, our routine sweep netted a Fiat Uno."

"Give me the license plate number."

"877 LXW 75," she said reading the number Ricot had written down. Tissot wouldn't know it belonged to a truck, not a Fiat Uno, until he'd pulled the registration.

"Paris plates." Tissot sounded alert now.

"How long will it take?"

"There's a backlog," Tissot said again. More clicking in the background. "Running a registration takes a few hours."

"But I'm in the street. . . ."

"And I've got your mobile number on the screen."

Zut! Already a record of her number at the central bureau. She couldn't help that now.

"Of course you're alerting traffic —"

"An all-points bulletin," he interrupted. "Priority one for Fiat Uno sightings. Location?"

"Rue Henri Barbusse, heading toward Jardin du Luxembourg."

Within the hour, every parking garage and street in a five-kilometer radius would be scoured, the whole of Paris within four hours. She'd unleashed the powers-that-be. A scary proposition.

"Contact me with the address," she said.

"You and a few others," Tissot said.

The trick consisted in getting there first, she thought. They'd find that truck unless it was parked in a private garage. She pushed that thought down.

All she could do now was wait.

Her hand touched something. Mireille's bag. Stupid . . . in her haste, she'd forgotten all about it.

She took off her jacket, folded it inside-out, and laid it over her knees. One by one she set out the contents of Mireille's bag on the silk jacket lining. A key chain with one key, a string of red and black beads, a worn holy card showing an old-fashioned Saint George on a horse, a loose twenty-franc note. She sniffed the myrrh-smelling stick of incense. Aimée's address was written on the back of a used Metro ticket. A small leather-bound journal. No cell phone or wallet.

Not much.

In the back of the journal she found yet another black-and-white photo of her father. He wore a police uniform from the sixties, a stiff round hat and a cape over his shoulders. She remembered that cape, weighted down with regulation lead pellets to avoid flapping in the wind. His familiar grin. He was thinner and sported a moustache. A pang of longing hit her.

Her chest heaved. She couldn't even find her sister, much less save her. Sobs erupted from deep within her. Tears dampened her cheeks.

The banner in the photo's background read *Département de Géographie, Sorbonne, "Au revoir."* A farewell party. She realized the photo was torn, like the other one. Odd. On the back, just the letters JCL and BC remained from the original inscription. One of his friends at the Sorbonne whom Morbier had mentioned? Something niggled at her, some connection. But what?

She'd think about that later.

The traffickers would kill Mireille. Self-pity wouldn't help to find her. She wiped her face with her sleeve.

Her cell phone vibrated in her pocket.

Tissot was fast.

Eagerly she grabbed her pen, hit ANSWER. "*Allo?* You found it?"

She heard the clink of glasses, muffled conversation in the background, then an inhaled breath.

"Benoît's ear was severed to make it look like black vodou."

She recognized Edouard Brasseur's voice. Edouard, the elusive rebel, the one who shared the saint's birthday with Benoît.

"But black vodou's not practiced any-more, Edouard." She fingered the black and red beads on her lap. "Not since the last century."

"You've done your homework," Edouard said. "This is a ruse, to divert suspicion from the murderer." She heard him take a breath. "Throw blame on superstitious Haitians, tie it to vodou, black rituals . . . the other thing besides poverty we're famous for."

"You mean the tonton macoutes could be

responsible?"

"Or a copycat," he said. She heard anguish mixed with anger in his voice. "Tonton macoutes peel their victims' faces off to prevent their spirits from finding rest in the afterlife. You said to call you when I knew what that signified."

She sat up. The pillar poked into her spine. "You didn't know this before?"

"They want the file," he said.

She blinked. "Wait a minute. You mean the file with Benoît's report to the World Bank? Who wants it? Hydrolis?"

"Mireille knows who."

"Can you prove that?" she said.

"Who else? Benoît trusted her for some reason," Edouard said. "The old guard said as much, *non?* Mireille picked it up. . . ."

"Now he's dead. Pushed under a car."

Mireille had not had a clue as to the contents of the envelope. That much Aimée believed.

"You're sure?" he asked.

"I got there too late," she said.

What did Edouard have to do with it?

"What's with you?" He exhaled. "I'm not the bad guy."

"You could say anything. There's a price on your head."

"Tell me about it," he said. He sighed.

"My job's investigating Duvalier's financial assets hidden in Europe," he said. "But that's not the issue here. There's more. I'll share, but I need to meet Mireille. Before they get to her. Deal?"

He assumed she knew Mireille's whereabouts.

"Too late." Her voice caught.

"What do you mean?" he asked, startled.

The call-waiting signal clicked on her phone.

She couldn't lose this call.

"Mireille's been abducted."

"Where are you?" he said.

The line clicked again. The vehicle bureau, with the address she needed to find Mireille?

"I'll call you back." She hit ANSWER.

"Check your eyesight, eh?" said Tissot. "The *carte grise* and license plate you asked about are registered to Marc-Louis Chazel, residence 14 bis, rue Saint Victor. But it's a Citroën truck, not a Fiat Uno."

Aimée thought back to the shuttered butcher shop, the *hotel particulier* . . . so the owners didn't live above the shop, but behind it.

"Was the truck reported stolen?"

"Eh? That's besides the point."

"So the truck was stolen?"

"Not according to the bulletin issued two

minutes ago."

"*Merci.*"

A dead end. Or maybe not.

Think like the perp, her father always said. Look at it from their angle, reason it their way. Logic dictated that one of the traffickers worked at the butcher shop and had use of the truck. With the shop closed and the proprietors gone for a few weeks, their quarters and what looked like a courtyard in back would be empty. The *mecs* would have free rein. Big *mecs,* strong enough to break the plasterer's arm and to smash car windows. Angry, arrogant, and drunk. It had been stupid to think she could break in and take them on by herself. And then it hit her . . . she wouldn't have to.

She clicked BACK. No Edouard. She left four words on his voicemail: 14, rue Saint Victor.

She'd provoked a citywide police alert that had netted this address. Go for the gold, she thought: involve emergency services. From a public phone near Maison de la Mutualité, a thirties deco conference hall noted for leftist political party meetings and Communist rallies, she punched in 18.

"*Brigade de pompier,*" said a voice.

"Help! The smoke alarm's gone off in

Boucheries Chazel. They're away, and I smell smoke."

"*Calmez-vous,* Mademoiselle. . . ."

"14 bis, rue Saint Victor. There's smoke's coming from the warehouse in the court-yard!"

She hung up and walked, counting in her head. Forty-three seconds later, a siren wailed from the direction of the fire station at Cardinal Lemoine, a Metro stop away. Distant, but coming closer. Two minutes and fifty seconds later, a long hook-and-ladder fire truck turned the corner. Bravo: faster than the Metro.

Wind rustled the leaves. She shivered under the dappled shadows cast by the moonlight filtering through the few remaining plane trees by the old Collège de Bernardins. The dilapidated medieval stone abbey and refectory had been many things, a plaque in front of it noted: a police station, a center for lost dogs, and until recently a fire station.

From the corner near the sagging stairs she heard the screech of the fire truck's brakes. Saw the lime-green coats of the firemen at the *hôtel particulier*'s massive arched green double door, which they opened with their key. A master key to all locks was used in such situations when a whole block could

337

ignite in minutes. Matter of fact, a fireman had told her once, they *always* used the key, since it took too long to wake tenants to gain entry.

Motors rumbled. The fire truck's searchlight scanned the stone façade and grillework balconies. Motorized ladders extended into the dark sky, hoses stretched out over the cobbles connected to hydrants. A car pulled up; the occupant got out, pulled on a fire chief's helmet, and ran ahead.

If anyone could roust human traffickers and their cargo within minutes, the *pompiers* could. Aimée waited. Lights appeared in windows.

In the courtyard, she saw inhabitants assembling in assorted nightgowns. "What the hell . . . in the middle of the night?" said a woman, pulling a robe over a bustier and garters. Others demanded to know what was going on.

Aimée stepped over the hoses to enter a sandblasted limestone seventeenth century-style courtyard. She scanned the tenant list quickly. In the arcade to the left there was a small glass-roofed warehouse built into the wall of the crumbling Collège des Bernardins bearing the sign DELIVERIES BOUCHERIE CHAZEL. Several men with hatchets herded figures through a wooden door.

A hand caught her arm. "No sightseeing, Mademoiselle. Time to leave."

She turned. "I live here. There." She pointed to a dark window on the second floor. "What's going on? A fire . . . another arson attack?"

"Wait over there with the others, Mademoiselle."

She saw no traffickers. No Mireille.

"False alarm." The Fire Chief stalked from the warehouse. "Someone's going to pay for this. You've traced the call?"

Thank God she'd called from a public phone.

She couldn't hear the rest. The men were rolling up the hoses. Incensed tenants were demanding the right to return to their domiciles. Firemen moved, and then she saw the Boucheries Chazel truck.

She couldn't let them leave.

"Monsieur . . . a word." She edged close to the Fire Chief. "The butcher shop staff sleeps in the warehouse. They're disgruntled at the Chazels. . . ."

"Eh . . . where's your apartment?"

"Souchet. *Deuxième étage.* Left." Luckily, she'd glanced at the roster of tenants on her way in.

"How do you know this?"

"They threatened Monsieur Chazel. But I

don't see them here."

He hadn't moved. Desperate to get him to investigate, to find Mireille and the traffickers, she continued: "I heard them threatening to ruin his equipment. Is it arson?" She gasped, put her hand over her mouth, as if catching herself. "I don't mean to suggest . . . but flammable chemicals . . . well, it's a hazard to the building. The whole street could go up."

Small or large, every butcher shop had at least minimal slaughtering facilities. Sanitation and safety guidelines governed the procedures under strict Ministry of Health requirements. To clean saws, knives, and the cutting and skinning instruments, flammable liquids were used. And nowadays, she knew, butchers used small propane torches to burn off the fluff and small feathers that remained after a chicken was plucked. She'd seen the blue propane gas tanks when she passed the local butchers' back doors.

"Flammable? You mean attempted arson? That's a serious accusation, Mademoiselle Souchet."

"Accusation? I know what I heard. Monsieur Chazel's unwell; it shocked me. But those men —"

A scuffle erupted among figures near the

warehouse. "Chief, we found two men in the back!"

"Can you identify these men?"

If they wore gold chains and could break arms, she could.

She nodded.

The small warehouse contained the remnants of Gothic pillars, sprouting tulip-like but crumbling with age. In one room, sides of glistening marbled beef hung from hooks in an open white-tiled refrigerated locker. Chill blasts of air hit her knees. Two men, African or Caribbean, wearing assorted gold chains, stood against the clear plastic strips that hung there to keep the cold in.

"Nothing out of order, Chief. Except these *mecs* were hiding in here."

"I work here," said one. A lilt in his accent. Ivory Coast? Or another part of Africa? She couldn't tell. "Screw you," he continued. Muscular, in his twenties, angular face and jutting chin. He spit in the tiled trough running the length of the floor. Liquor was on his breath.

"He the one?"

Before Aimée could answer, the arson inspector tugged at the Chief's arm.

"Might want to call Immigration, Chief. Look at these." In his hand were passports and identity cards. Romanian, Serbian, and

Haitian, from what Aimée could make out.

"Eh? May I remind you that we're looking for evidence of arson?"

She had to move fast.

"Him and his friend." She edged forward, sniffed. "Drunk as usual."

The other man, in dirty jeans and shirt stained with red splatters, leered.

"That's blood on your shirt." She stepped closer. "Tell them where it came from."

"Who's this bitch?"

But she'd seen recognition on his face.

His arm shot out. Aimée ducked and his fist slapped into a side of beef.

"Get her out of here," the Chief ordered.

The arson inspector guided her to the front of the warehouse. She stopped at an aluminum counter under the hooks that held the saws. "They bring girls in the back," she said. "All the time. I heard screams."

"The *flics* will question these men. We searched, but there's no one else here."

And she had a sinking feeling he was right.

"We'll take your statement," he said. "Wait in the courtyard."

How long would it take before Immigration questioned the *mecs?* And how much longer before they broke and revealed Mireille's whereabouts? If they ever did.

She stood in the *hôtel particulier* courtyard, alone. The tenants had gone back to their apartments, the firemen were packing up their hoses. What good had she done?

"You just make trouble, don't you?"

Startled, she turned. A figure stood under the damp stone arcade. In the dim glow she made out a denim jacket, black jeans. She looked twice before she recognized him. Edouard, with his beard shaved off. Another persona.

"Not enough," she said.

"I can't figure you out," Edouard said.

"Don't even try."

"So you didn't find Mireille?"

She stepped closer to him. Again breathed that lime scent, the scent Yves had worn.

"Not yet."

"Do you always wear couture to false alarms?"

She shrugged. "Amazing how designer wear holds up."

"Leduc Detective computer forensics has an impressive client list." He grabbed her by the shoulders. "I've checked you out. You did criminal investigations until six years ago. I'd say searching for Mireille's out of your line."

His hands on her shoulders tightened. Suspicion and anger shone in his eyes, those odd amber eyes.

"You're working for *them,* aren't you?" he asked.

She tried to step back, to loosen his hands. "Who?"

"Admit it."

He drew her into the shadows, leaned her against the stone arch. His hands gripped hers and pulled them behind her back, tightly. Fear prickled up her spine.

"Nice expense account from the World Bank, too." He breathed hard. "Or do the Duvalierists pay you, eh? They go for style . . . just like you."

He reached into his jacket pocket. A handgun? With one arm he pinned her against the wall.

"I think Mireille's my sister," she said. "My father knew her mother in Paris long ago. She asked for my help. . . ." Her voice faltered. She panted, took a breath. "Just who the hell are you?"

He stared at her. His grip loosened. Light from a window played over his slanted cheekbones.

"Eurodad."

Was that some kind of eurocop? It sounded like a cognate of eurotrash.

"That's supposed to mean something to me?"

"Only if you're a big player. You've heard of crimes against humanity?" he asked. "Eurodad's an organization of NGO's, advocacy and rights groups, based in Brussels. The full name is the European Network on Debt and Development. I'm their legal counsel in the financial recovery field," he said. "We're attempting to freeze Baby Doc Duvalier's Swiss bank accounts."

"But Duvalier fled Haiti years ago," she said.

"And we allege that he stole the equivalent of 1.7 to 4.5 percent of the Haitian Gross Domestic Product for every year he was in power," Edouard said.

Not exactly chump change.

Her eye fell on the Boucherie Chazel truck parked to the side. She'd been stupid. It was staring her in the face.

"Sorry, I overreacted," he said, loosening his grip. "Let's try this again. I'm a good guy."

"Now's your chance to prove it, Edouard."

She took his hand, pulled him through the dark arcade, and tried the back door of the truck.

Locked.

"What the . . . ?"

"Play along with me." She put her finger

over his lips. A fireman and the Chief, their backs to them, stood in discussion at the large door that opened onto rue Saint Victor.

She tried the driver's door; also locked. Then the passenger side. The door opened. Too drunk to lock it, she thought.

She half-crouched, Edouard behind her, in the rear of the truck's small aisle. Old meat odors assailed her; butcher paper crinkled underfoot. Aluminum meat trays shone in the gleam of her penlight. She saw a figure hanging from a meat hook.

She gasped. Mireille, wrists tied with her arms above her, hung suspended from the hook. Her bare feet dangled in the air. Dried blood encrusted her swollen mouth.

Aimée rushed forward. "Quick! Get her down!"

Was she alive?

Edouard lifted Mireille from the hook and set her down on the ridged metal floor. He felt for a pulse.

"Mireille?" Aimée knelt to smooth back the hair that was matted to Mireille's face. Her skin felt cold to the touch. She rubbed Mireille's thin arms to get her circulation going.

"A weak pulse," Edouard said. "She needs a hospital. Quickly."

Aimée thought of the Fire Chief at the entrance, the ambulance. The time it would take to explain . . . and there was not a minute to spare.

"You look talented," she said. "Ever hot-wire an engine?"

"My car's out front. . . ."

"So's the fire inspector."

And then she felt bumps in the crook of Mireille's elbow, saw the purple tracks of injections. Now Mireille's short, shallow breaths alarmed her even more.

"Keep rubbing her," Aimée said.

She unlatched the truck's hood, as quietly as she could. At least the old truck had a simple engine. Was it the red or the blue wire? Which distributor cap . . . she searched her memory for the one time she'd hotwired a car during a surveillance with her father. Prayed she'd connected the right one. And shut the hood.

The engine turned over. It gave a jerk and she grabbed the door. Edouard sat behind the wheel.

"How'd you do that?" he asked.

"I figured you attach a plus to a minus."

"Hang on," Edouard said. He shifted into first and let out the clutch as she crawled to Mireille lying in the back. He gunned out of the courtyard while she rubbed Mireille's arms and legs.

The Hôpital Val de Grâce emergency entrance swarmed with ambulances and the flashing red lights of *flic* cars, the aftermath of the collisions on the *periphérique.*

Mireille couldn't wait hours for treatment, nor could she face questioning by the *flics.* She groaned and her eyelids fluttered.

"It's all right, Mireille." Aimée cradled Mireille in her lap, her jacket wrapped around her to keep her warm.

"That *flic*'s checking our license plate," Edouard said.

Tissot had put an alert out for the truck.

"Back out. Quick."

Aimée grabbed her cell phone. It was the middle of the night. Should she?

"Allo?" The phone was answered on the first ring. At least she hadn't awakened her.

"It's Aimée Leduc. Sorry to call you so late."

"No problem. Old people don't sleep much."

She heard her inhale, imagined the cigarette smoke curling over the wood desk.

"Forgive me for asking your help again, but. . . ."

"Another run-in?"

"Overdose, I think. She's illegal."

"Since when do you take in strays, Aimée?"

The truck jolted over the cobbles. The floor shook as it took a corner.

"She's my sister."

Something rustled in the background. A door shut.

"Not here. My granddaughter came down with the chicken pox. All my children are here for the week."

Mireille needed attention now. "Val de Grâce and all the nearby hospitals are full from a twenty-car accident. Traffickers pumped her full of something and she's cold, turning blue. Her breaths are shallow and infrequent. Her pulse rate's 40. What should I do?"

"Wait." Aimée heard the sound of cards flipping on a creaking old Rolodex.

"39, rue Gay Lussac. Les Soeurs de Labouré monastery. Go to the rear chapel. Look for Sister Dantec."

"But she's —"

"I'll meet you there," she said. "You know what to do, Aimée."

She did?

"Don't tell me you forgot what I taught you," said Professeur Zarek.

She ended the call.

■ ■ ■ ■

Aimée tried to recall information from her medical textbooks on overdose, possible internal injuries, appearance of blunt trauma to the head. Blunt trauma could result in concussion. To combat an overdose, get the victim on his feet and moving to prevent cardiac arrest. But this is contraindicated if internal injuries are present. It all spun in her head. Right now she had to keep Mireille's circulation going, just to keep her alive.

She shouted the address to Edouard. Felt around for butcher paper and covered Mireille with an insulating layer, lifted her arms, rubbing them, then elevated her cold bruised legs higher than her heart. Trying to make and retain her body heat.

The truck jolted to a stop.

"What's this place?" Edouard asked.

"Drive in the back, near the chapel."

A few moments later, she heard voices. Footsteps. Fear jolted her. The side door rolled back on grating hinges.

"Hurry," said a small nun in a long black habit, a silver cross on her white starched bib-like collar. The nun gathered her skirt, stepped forward and with surprising

350

strength took Mireille's legs. Aimée climbed out, holding Mireille's limp shoulders.

"The order rises in an hour."

Aimée looked around. Edouard had disappeared.

"We're cloistered nuns, Mademoiselle," said the nun, noticing her gaze. "We take the vow of partial silence."

No men allowed. No one outside the order, for that matter. Professeur Zarek had real pull, she thought.

The clinic for the cloistered nuns contained three small pristine examination rooms and a state-of-the-art operating theater.

Professeur Zarek was already there, untying the scarf around her head. She tossed her coat over a chair and opened her black bag. "I'll examine her in here."

She helped the nun lay Mireille, who had begun to moan, on the operating table.

"Don't hurt me . . . please." Mireille stirred, thrashing her arms.

"You're safe now." Aimée smoothed the wet curls from Mireille's chalky face.

Her eyes widened. "Where am I?"

"Sister Dantec, if you'll asssist?" The small nun nodded, offering the professor a green surgical robe. Professeur Zarek washed her hands at the large aluminum sink, then tied a mask over her mouth.

Sister Dantec swabbed Mireille's arm with antiseptic. The tang of alcohol hovered in the air. Then she prepared the IV and tapped the needle, her eyes never leaving Mireille's arm as she searched for a vein.

"I found one, Professeur."

She stepped back and a needle was inserted into a vein in Mireille's arm.

"We're running a line, Aimée, giving her Narcan to reverse the effects of drugs. Sister?"

"*Oui,* Professeur."

"Low blood pressure. I need D50, the dextrose cocktail."

Mireille moaned and twisted on the table.

"Can I help?" Aimée asked.

"Keep her calm, Aimée."

She leaned down and brushed the matted hair from Mireille's damp forehead. "The doctor's here, Mireille, it's all right."

Mireille grabbed Aimée's hands. Tears pooled in her eyes. "I lost everything. . . ."

Aimée winced. "Don't worry," she said. *"Calmes-toi."*

Mireille gripped Aimée's hand tighter. Tears streamed down her face. "No way to get Benoît's file. I'm just trouble, they're going to kill me. . . ."

352

"She's agitated, Professeur," said Sister Dantec. "Blood pressure dropping."

Aimée controlled her shudder. "*Non,* Mireille." She pulled Mireille's bag from hers. "See. . . ."

She held up the key, the holy cards. "When I was looking for you, I found your bag."

Recognition shone in Mireille's fluttering eyes. Her shallow breaths slowed.

"Benoît left . . . the key . . . envelope . . . the key . . . to Marie Curie's. . . ." Mireille's words trailed off. Her jaw slackened.

What did she mean?

"Intubate, Sister. She's stopped breathing." She took an instrument from the tray to slice open Mireille's trachea so a tube could be inserted.

Horrified, Aimée stepped back. "Oh my God."

"Aimée, wheel the ventilator over here," said Professeur Zarek.

Aimée stood rooted to the floor, paralyzed in fear.

"You know what to do."

Her mind blanked. She wanted to run away.

"Now, Aimée!" the professor barked. *"Now!"*

Galvanized, her mind on autopilot, Aimée

spun around to the ventilator. She scanned the controls, switched the power on, and wheeled the machine over. She took the blue plastic intubation tube, now connected to the endotracheal tube in Mireille's throat, from Professeur Zarek's hand.

"Connect the tube to the left socket," said Professeur Zarek.

That done, Aimée looked at the ventilator screen. Little lines danced across it. She watched them, mesmerized, praying each time a line moved that Mireille would live. Seconds that felt like hours passed.

"Good job, Sister Dantec," said Professeur Zarek. "You too, Aimée. See?"

Mireille lay draped by a green sheet, eyes closed, her breathing even.

"Her pulse is climbing," said Sister Dantec.

"We'll keep her on the ventilator until she breathes on her own," said Professeur Zarek. "Could be ten minutes or a few hours. I anticipate it will be sooner rather than later. We'll have to see."

"You must leave," said Sister Dantec. "The convent rises in less than an hour."

"But Mireille?"

"Do you think we haven't done this before?" Professeur Zarek laughed. "Sister Dantec loves new converts, eh, Sister?"

"All God's children. Even you, Professeur."

"Never give up on me, do you, Sister?"

Aimée stood, watching these two small women working as a team. Professionals. She felt useless. Her shoulders ached, scratches and cuts stung her knees and arms. She slipped the key into her pocket.

Professeur Zarek pulled the retractable arm of the X-ray machine over Mireille's head.

"Barring internal injuries and complications . . . I won't know for a while," said Professeur Zarek. "But she's responding well, so far."

"Will she live?" Aimée choked back a sob.

"Count on it," she said. "Your sister's strong, Aimée. Now let me get to work."

"Bien sûr." Aimée stopped in mid-step. The truck. "I'll move the truck."

"Already taken care of."

Amazing, this little nun, she thought, and imagined little gremlin nuns at work behind the scenes.

"Now, if you don't mind. . . ." Sister Dantec stared at her pointedly.

"I don't know how to thank you."

Professeur Zarek looked up with a strange expression. "It's good to feel useful again, Aimée. You've brought some excitement back into my life. Now leave it up to us. Go to bed."

The dark smudge of night hovered over the slanting rooftops and iron grillework balconies on Boulevard Saint Michel, broken only by the glow of the streetlights. The boulevard lay still, except for the thrum of the engine of a newspaper van. A man stacked newspapers in a pile in front of the kiosk, took the van's wheel, and drove away. A crow cawed from the gabled eaves above her.

Aimée rubbed her eyes. Alone. Except for the crow.

She'd taken care of the traffickers. They'd be behind bars, at least for now. She wished she felt more relieved. But she knew that whoever wanted Benoît's file would keep looking for Mireille.

The peal of a church bell made her jump. She fingered Edouard's card. She needed to find out what he knew. Her heels clicked over the pavement as she walked down the wide deserted boulevard.

Friday Early Morning
She pressed the numbers on the digicode panel at the door of Edouard's building. The door clicked open, revealing a small

courtyard. Fading moonlight polished the sloping glass roofs of ateliers nestled in the courtyard. A few stars studded the lightening sky. Nameplates of upscale architecture firms dotted the atelier doors. Tendrils of ivy snaked up the walls. She inhaled the lime tree scent and crossed the stone pavers dappled with shadows.

Peaceful, another world. This was the once-sleepy edge of the Latin Quarter where Modigliani and Kees Van Dongen had painted in cheap ateliers. Not these days. "A shame how bourgouise bohemians and trendy firms infest the *quartier*," she'd heard a longtime resident complain over the radio; "old-timers like us can't afford it any more."

She knocked on the curtained window of the middle atelier, which bore no sign. Quiet reigned, except for the steady drip of water from a metal spigot leaving a silver trail in the moonlight. There was no answer.

Tired, she ached to lie down. Even the pile of leaves looked inviting.

Still no answer to her knocks. He wasn't here. She needed to sleep. She'd call him later and discover what he hadn't yet disclosed about the World Bank.

If she could only make her feet move, she'd find a taxi. . . .

The door opened and rays of light fell on the cobbles. Edouard, his sleeves rolled up, shirt collar open, stood framed in the doorway. The steady hum of a printer came from the interior.

"Will Mireille make it?" he asked.

She nodded. "She's on a ventilator but she's responding." Her foot caught on a stray ivy vine and she stumbled.

Edouard caught her. "Doesn't look like *you* will."

He led her into the warm interior. Fax machines, humming copiers, and several computers filled the cramped atelier. Binders labeled IMF and WORLD BANK were stacked on the floor. A cinnamon aroma filled the air. Pinpricks of light from halogen lamps danced on the glass ceiling.

"We need to talk," she said.

"Drink this first." He handed her a brown hollowed-out gourd containing a milky liquid. The rounded shape of the gourd was smooth in her hands.

"What's this?"

"*Un cremase.* You need it."

She sipped a mixture of sugarcane rum, sugar, cinnamon, and coconut. It lay thick on her tongue, potent and sweet, and laced with so much alcohol, her breath could have started a fire.

"The gourd grows on the calabas tree," he said. "Where I come from, it's said a spirit lives in the calabas."

Her mouth opened. He hadn't seemed like the type to go native. "You believe in spirits? That's kind of at odds with your persona."

"For me, gourds are like an investment." He gestured to a shelf holding a collection of incised and carved tan and dark brown gourds.

And then he lifted her in his arms, carried her, and set her down on a settee. Her right heel caught and her shoe fell off.

Her arms, legs, everything felt weighted down. She struggled to stay alert. The atelier lights were like stars.

Then his face was close to hers. Long lashes fringing those amber eyes.

"You're full of surprises," he said. "Legs to forever, big eyes, and, with all that, you're clever," he said, running his fingers through her hair.

Clever? She didn't feel very smart. But she wanted him to keep talking, to keep running his hand through her hair.

"Your hair is full of bits of . . ." He looked down at a pebble in his hand. He sniffed it. "Limestone." A pensive look came over his face. "Why didn't I put it together? Mireille was in the quarry with the illegals, right?"

"You're perceptive, Eurodad." She realized she was still holding the gourd and took a long sip. And another.

Sweetness lingered in her mouth. The rum had gone straight to her head. And his lime scent reminded her of Yves, the last man in her life.

She propped herself up on her elbow, wishing she didn't look such a mess. Wishing she didn't crave the sensation of his fingers running through her hair. Wishing she wasn't attracted to him.

Down, girl, she told herself.

She pointed to the World Bank binders. "It all comes down to Benoît's report, doesn't it?"

He nodded. The light shone on his burnished cheekbones.

"And here I thought you were a bad boy."

He smiled, the first smile she'd seen. "Well, I do have a dark side."

"Liar." She couldn't believe she'd said that.

"Guess I need to prove it."

"But the World Bank —"

"Later."

His arms were around her again. Enveloping arms, his citrus scent and his warm breath in her ear, his lips trailing down her neck. She didn't want him to do this, but at the same time she hoped he wouldn't stop. How did that song go . . . "How can this be wrong when it feels so right."

And then his fingers unzipped her dress, her legs were around him. His black hair and shoulders were framed by the glass ceiling. A single morning star blinked in the apricot blush of dawn.

Friday Midday

Ringing came from far away. Aimée's head felt heavy, her brain fogged with the longing for more sleep. She spooned into the warm arms cocooning her.

The insistent ringing pierced the layers of sleep. She felt measured breaths warm on her neck. Her eyes blinked open. She heard the soft patter of rain, like cat's paws, above on the glass roof. Saw the overturned gourd, her dress and heels on the floor. Slants of light patterned the wooden floor. And she remembered where she was.

Edouard's atelier. His long legs wrapped around hers, that cleft in his cinnamon-colored chin. In his sleep, he nuzzled her neck.

More ringing. Her cell phone. Mireille . . . what if her condition had worsened? Stupid, sleeping with Edouard; stupid, wanting to nestle, feel him all around her.

She forced herself to move out of his warm arms, picked up her clothes and bag from the floor. Her phone had stopped ringing. Barefoot, she padded past computers and leaned against the fax machine, pulling on her dress, zipping it and slipping into her heels. Her eye fell on the fax tray. A sheet with the words "Benoît's World Bank proposal, meet me at Le Champo, 3 P.M. Léonie."

Léonie. World Bank. She and Edouard had never gotten that far. What hadn't Edouard told her?

Dying for an espresso, she looked around. No kitchen. She grabbed the faxes from the tray. She'd check her phone messages outside, bring coffee back from a café. It was not the time to wake him up; she'd do that later. And discover his connection to the World Bank.

An overcast pewter sky hung over the courtyard. Raindrops beaded the glass roofs, trailing in rivulets. A steady drip from the overhead gutter mingled with the scratching of a broom from the pavement outside the courtyard's open door. Aimée took cover under the glass awning in the corner. Damp vegetal smells came from the pots of geraniums and leafy hanging branches.

She put her finger to one ear to hear better and checked her messages. "Call me" from René. She'd call him later. The second from Professeur Zarek. "Good news, Aimée. Mireille's responding well. We only had to keep her on the ventilator an hour. No complications, she's stable and resting. Now I'm going to sleep."

Aimée's shoulders sagged in relief. Time for that espresso.

Loud footsteps filled the courtyard.

"What do you think you're doing, Messieurs?" said a woman's voice.

Aimée peered through the branches as what looked like an army of men in rain jackets strutted past an older woman. The concierge, by the look of her blue work smock. She brandished her broom at the leader, a man with his back to Aimée who towered over her.

"You can't barge in here like this!"

"But we can, Madame."

Aimée saw the flash of a plastic laminated card, and, as he turned, the orange armband labeled police. Panic hit the pit of her stomach.

He gestured to the men lined up outside Edouard's atelier door.

Her cell phone rang. She hit ANSWER with

shaking fingers.

"Come back to bed." Edouard's sleep-filled voice. "I miss you, we'll take up where we left off —"

"Get up! There are *flics* outside your door."

Fists pounded on his door.

A clanging sound. He must have dropped the phone.

"Did *you* bring them here?" he demanded, awake now, accusing.

"*Non.* Is there a back door, a window?"

"*Merde!*"

"Who's Léonie? How's she involved?"

"What?"

"She wants to meet you at 3 P.M. . . ."

"The *salope.* You have to stop her, understand?"

"Why?"

"Stop her before it's too late."

"But how?"

The phone went dead.

The *flic* raised his arm. "If you'll step aside, Madame, and let us do our job," he said. He gestured to the others. "Let's go."

They used a metal crowbar to crack the doorframe.

Aimée kept to the eaves, her head down, shoulders trembling. At the courtyard door she turned right, holding her bag over her head as if against the rain, shielding her face from the parked *flic* cars. She made herself walk at a normal pace, keeping abreast of a woman pushing a wheeled shopping cart. Something rubbed against her hip. She reached in her pocket. It was a key. The key from Mireille's bag. And Mireille's words came back to her . . . "Marie Curie."

What had she been thinking? Stumbling into Edouard's atelier, then his warm arms, because he had reminded her of Yves. How could she have slept with him? While the key to Benoît's file was in her hand.

Mireille had begged her to take the file but had had no time to tell her where it was. Mireille had hidden it. Locked it away.

She tried Edouard's number, got a busy signal. Right now she couldn't help him except by meeting this Léonie. Her watch read 1 P.M.

The sky opened and rain pelted the street. Every passing taxi had an OCCUPIED light. Her hair wet, rain soaking her jacket, she kept pace with the woman with the wheeled shopping cart as far as the corner. There she broke into a run.

She had to find what this key opened.

Aimée scanned the street. No *flics*. No taxis. The nearest Metro blocks away.

She pulled out her pocket map, scanning

the rain-beaded page of the fifth arrondissement. The Marie Curie Institute and Museum was only two streets over.

She didn't stop until she spied the Curie Museum's doorway. Soaked and panting, she bolted into a group of laughing schoolchildren huddled in the shelter of the doorway for protection from the rain. She helped up a small girl from the ground.

"Pardon me," she said. "Are you okay?"

The girl nodded. A tag saying "*Ecole Maternelle 2eme,* Sylvaine" was pinned to her rain jacket. "The museum's boring. It's more fun watching the rain."

Rain peppered the rising gutters, splashing up like silver needles. The teachers stood, smoking, below an overhang. Several boys played piggyback, others exchanged trading cards, the backpacks at their feet getting soaked.

Aimée took off her damp jacket. Across from the fawn-brown brick building stood the blue-and-white street sign, rue Pierre et Marie Curie. Sheets of rain fell on the Curie Institute complex. The narrow street branched toward the Pantheon and Ecole Normale Supérieure.

She leaned down. Her heels slipped and she braced herself against the wall. Her gaze locked with that of the little girl. "So,

Sylvaine, did you like the museum?"

"It smells funny."

"Funny?"

Sylvaine's ponytailed head bobbed, her eyes serious. "Lots of radioactive things there. But we couldn't see them. They're invisible. We saw old machines."

"You're on a school field trip, *non?*" Aimée asked.

"The only fun part was the 'race for radium' game we played," she said. "The old lady had discovered invisible things, but we couldn't figure out how she did it."

"Ah, you mean Marie Curie?"

"She looked like a farmer with a microscope."

A farmer for radium. Aimée tried not to smile. "But look how smart Marie was." Aimée pointed to the street sign. "She worked hard, and they named this street after her."

Sylvaine's brow furrowed in thought. "If I have to work that hard, I want the place clean."

As if Madame Curie had had the choice, Aimée thought. She'd discovered radium in an abandoned shed formerly used as a dissecting room by the School of Medicine. She'd been lucky to have been allowed to set up a lab there.

The force of the rain was dwindling. The teachers ground out their cigarettes under their shoes. "*En y va,* children. Time to go."

Aimée edged backward among the children. Had Mireille meant the Marie Curie Museum? Or the Institute? Neither made sense; Benoît had been an expert on pigs, not radiation.

But this was a place to start.

Aimée followed a hallway, emerging in the visitors' line at the desk in the dark narrow lobby where a receptionist pecked away on a computer keyboard, a phone crooked between his neck and shoulder. Steam curled from the cup of espresso by the keyboard. The bitter aroma made her want a sip.

"Next?"

Two people were ahead of her.

Aimée picked up a museum pamphlet. Photos of a simple laboratory, and of a young woman in a long black skirt poised over a microscope, were displayed. One page gave a timeline of her experiments and discoveries, her struggle with Institute Pasteur for funding and of her Nobel prizes.

On the wall was her photo, beneath the words " 'A scientist is also a child placed opposite natural phenomena which impress him like a fairy tale.' — Marie Curie, 1933."

Amazing, Aimée thought: this little woman, who against all odds had changed the course of science and of the world. And then died of cancer from exposure to the radioactive materials she'd discovered.

"The tour's filled." The man at reception looked up with a harried frown. "Next one's in an hour."

"I'd like to speak to the administrator," Aimée said.

"Concerning?"

"We have a few questions concerning the Institute's internal audit."

He took a sip of espresso from the small white demitasse cup. "We weren't told. Your people always make an appointment."

"Not these days."

"The director's in a meeting." He shook his head. "Impossible."

Directors were always in meetings. But she was determined. Mireille had said "Marie Curie." "What's the name of her assistant? I forget."

"Monsieur Carnet?"

"C'est ca." She nodded. "If you'll show me to his office?"

"He's busy."

She smiled. "I don't think I heard you right, Monsieur."

"Eh?" he said.

"I think what you meant to say is that you're happy to assist and prove helpful to our internal audit, which will affect your funding. And your job."

He set the cup down. "Your name?"

"Mademoiselle Leduc."

A few moments later, she stood in a small office.

"Mademoiselle Leduc?" A man with a white beard contrasting with his short cropped black hair extended his hands to catch and pump hers in a dry grip.

"We're not prepared, our director's at a meeting, this seems —"

"Highly irregular, I know," she interrupted with a broad smile. "But I need your help. It's confidential, of course."

The receptionist reappeared with two steaming demitasses of espresso, then bowed out.

"Please sit down."

She set her cell phone to vibrate and crossed her legs, wishing her damp dress didn't cling like skin. She plopped two cubes of brown sugar, stirred, drank, and welcomed the jolt of caffeine. As she brushed back her wet hair, she caught Edouard's scent on her wrist and the scene of the *flics* raiding his atelier flashed through her mind. Right now she couldn't think about that. The key and Mireille's words were the only things she had to go on.

And as her father always said, if you have to lie, stick to the truth as much as possible.

"To save your time, Monsieur Carnet, I'll get to the point." She leaned forward as if to share a confidence, showing him her father's police ID to which she'd forged her own name.

Monsieur Carnet's shoulders stiffened.

"Our administrator deals with such things, I'm —"

"— part of the managerial staff who, I'm sure, will prove helpful," she finished for him. "I'm investigating a homicide." She passed him the key from Mireille's bag. "Do you recognize this?"

"I don't understand."

"Monsieur Carnet, we found this on the victim."

Flustered, he dropped the key on top of a requisition order pad.

"Homicide? Murder?" He sprung from his chair like a frightened bird. "Why are you asking me?"

She wished he'd answer instead of asking questions.

"The victim was a professor at the Ecole Normale Supérieur. We're investigating possible links —"

Recognition replaced the confusion in his small eyes. "Professeur Benoît!"

She clutched the edge of the desk. Carnet had known him. Then she realized that the Ecole Normale Supérieur was right around the corner. These *Grands Ecoles* and the top researchers hung around together.

"So you knew him?"

"The canteen."

The man stared at her as if she'd understand.

"Now *I* don't understand. Can you explain?"

"They're renovating the Institute kitchen, so we eat at the ENS canteen." Monsieur Carnet sat back down. "I eat . . . ate lunch with him. The news of his death horrified me."

Excited, she leaned forward.

"Did you eat with Professeur Benoît on Monday?"

"Monday? I don't remember." Carnet blinked. "*Mais oui,* of course, the cassoulet. . . ."

Food. Funny how memories often came down to food.

"Why didn't you inform the authorities about this?"

Carnet's hands brushed over the oak

desk's smooth surface. Aimée's antennae went up.

"You let Benoît keep something here, didn't you?"

"I d-don't know what you mean."

Nervously, his hands went to his striped tie, adjusting the knot.

"You dined with him, you knew him," she said. "Did he seem different, upset that day? Of course you asked him what was troubling him, offered to help?"

Carnet bolted from his chair. "Mademoiselle, I don't see what any of this has to do with —"

"Professeur Benoît's murder? But it does, Monsieur. We think he was murdered for the papers you were hiding for him."

"Mais non!" He shook his head. "Impossible."

"You sound sure, Monsieur Carnet."

Carnet's mouth twitched. "Benoît is . . . esteemed as a researcher and scientist." Carnet glared folding his arms across his chest. "He must stay that way."

"He was murdered on Monday night," she said. "Would you prefer to accompany me to the Commissariat?" She let her words dangle. And regretted them right away. She had no authority to take him in, much less question him. But she knew someone who could. She reached for her phone, about to punch in Morbier's number.

"*Non,* please. He said it was confidential." Carnet's words were halting. "H-he said it concerned a personal matter with a woman . . . he didn't want to walk back into the classroom with . . ." Carnet averted his eyes. "Porno."

Porno? Photos of some woman in a compromising position? She didn't think so.

Benoît had given his report to Carnet for safekeeping, telling him to keep it hidden, confiding a false reason for doing so. But whoever he'd met later at the Cluny concert, she figured, had scared him. So he'd entrusted the key to Mireille, trusting no one but her, a fellow Haitian, a woman who owed him, a woman who'd understand the file's importance. Or had it been the opposite, that Benoît had counted on Mireille's *not* understanding the contents? Even safer.

"You'll keep this to yourself?"

She glanced at the time. Almost two o'clock.

"Of course, Monsieur. Please show me what this key opens," she said. "I'm in a hurry."

He led her down the corridor, past an old laboratory, Marie Curie's simple and spartan office containing bookshelves, her desk, chairs, and a fireplace.

"We decontaminated the building in the eighties," Carnet said as they navigated a warren of passages. "Otherwise, you'd never be allowed back here. Too many of our workers had high radioactive counts."

Even then? Aimée shivered.

Carnet pointed to a door bearing faded black script: RADIUM REPORTS. He opened it to reveal a small, dark wood-paneled room lined with old-fashioned lockers.

"This one." Carnet pointed to the first on the left. "You'll keep this confidential?" he asked again.

"*Oui,* Monsieur Carnet, don't worry about Professeur Benoît's reputation . . . it's strictly confidential."

Aimée put the key in the old lock. It fit. She turned the key and opened the door. Inside the dusty-smelling chamber was a padded envelope marked "Mireille."

At last!

On rue Pierre and Marie Curie, a slight drizzle bedewed the metal fence. Aimée hurried to the next street and around the corner until she found an Internet café. She took a table near the back by the terminals. Expectantly, she slit open the envelope and withdrew the contents: several folded sheets of yellow graph paper. She unfolded them. Three pages were covered with chemical formulas, tables of statistics, percentages, and more chemical formulas. No header, no names, not even Benoît's. These were lab worksheets.

She couldn't make head or tail of them. It looked like Greek to her. Crestfallen, she wondered what these formulas meant and why they'd caused a man's murder. But she knew someone who would understand and whom she trusted.

He was working today. With luck, he'd decipher these notes and tell her what they meant before 3 P.M.

Aimée handed a ten-franc piece to the kohl-eyed woman with platinum blond spiked hair at the fax machine. "I'd like to send a three-page fax."

"Cover sheet?" the woman asked with the rolling vowels of a northern, Lille, accent.

"No cover sheet. I'm in a hurry." About to hand the papers to the woman, she noticed two men standing in the rain outside the windows of the café. She hadn't seen them when she came in.

"The fax number?"

"I'll do it."

She punched in the fax number for Serge, the morgue lab pathologist, and fed in the sheets of Benoît's writing.

"Receipt?" the woman asked.

"No, thanks," Aimée said. "Don't turn your head," she continued to the woman, "but do you see two men outside in leather jackets?" She put the sheets back in her bag.

"The ones who're getting all wet?" A real Lilloise by the sound of her.

"That's right," Aimée said.

"They must like you," the woman said.

Aimée's chest tightened. "How's that?"

"One of them's pointing at you," she said.

"There's a back door here, right?" Aimée said, placing a twenty-franc note by the fax machine.

"In back next to the WC," she said.

"And you never saw me leave."

The woman pocketed the note, slipping the confirmation printout into the shredder. "I never even saw you at all."

Aimée made herself walk at a normal pace. Instead of going back to her table, she headed for the Ladies' Room. Next to it was the sign marked exit. She pushed open the door and emerged into the rain and a traffic-clogged street. She took off running, zigzagging between the cars, inhaling the fumes of the buses that had ground to a halt. She had to make the most of her few minutes' head start.

She turned the corner, dodged into the first open door, climbed up the stairs, and found herself in the imposing marble-floored entrance foyer of the Sorbonne's Faculty of Law. She stepped inside the first lecture hall she came to and stood at the back.

No one paid her the slightest attention. The students' attention was focused on a speaker at the proscenium. All heads were bent, taking notes.

She called Serge's private lab line and cupped her hand over her cell phone.

His voicemail responded. *Merde!*

"Serge, I've faxed you three sheets of paper," she whispered. "Call me to tell me what they mean, and I'll owe you for life."

She backed out, crossed the foyer, and headed for the rear exit on rue Cujas.

Cinema Champollion, dubbed "le Champo" by generations of students, curved around rue des Ecoles. A former music hall, it had showed films since the Occupation. Le Champo, started by a critic, had run on a shoestring maintained by film buffs, students, and future directors like Claude Chabrol. A Romy Schneider film retrospective was running according to old black-

and-white film posters.

Aimée scanned the minuscule foyer.

Several students and an old man stood in line, buying tickets for the afternoon matinee. No one else. She had no clue what Léonie looked like, much less how to stop her. She tried Edouard's number. Six long rings, then Edouard's phone turned off without even offering voicemail.

Why would the *flics* raid his place if he belonged to Eurodad? What had happened to him? And so far there was no word from Serge explaining what Benoît's notations meant and how they related to the World Bank.

"The film is starting, Mademoiselle," said the usher.

Aimée slid her francs over the worn counter, received a torn ticket in return, and found her way into a hundred-seat theater. She took a seat in the back row. A 1968 Pathé newsreel showed the Sorbonne protests, long-haired students throwing cobblestones, the *flics* marching in formation from the Pantheon, screaming and yelling, was on the screen.

Déjà vu.

Her mother had taken her to the Sorbonne protests to hand out banners they'd lettered with VIVE LA REVOLUTION. Aimée remembered the cold rain, tugging on her mother's sleeve, wondering what it all meant, why her mother's eyes shone. She heard her mother's voice with that American accent, saying "We're changing the world, making history here. You're part of it, Aimée!"

But what had they changed? These Sixty-eighters now paid mortgages, wore suits, worked in the government and ministries they'd vowed to tear down. And her mother? Banned from France, a former terrorist declared *persona non grata,* on the world security watchlist.

But these memories got her nowhere. The hollowness of loss never went away, but her mother had. Stop. She had to keep to the business at hand. Finding Léonie. The old man slumped in his seat; the two students cuddled entwined, ignoring the film. There were no other heads silhouetted against the screen.

The title *Phantom of Love* flashed on the screen, the film credits rolled, and the camera settled on Romy Schneider's pale face, her pouting lips and famous widely spaced eyes projecting a vulnerable waif-like quality. The haunting opening strains of a cello filled the theater.

A woman took an aisle seat a few rows

ahead of Aimée. She looked around at the red velvet seats and turned, revealing a stylish coiffure and an expectant air.

No one else had entered the theater.

Aimée left her seat and hunkered down in the aisle by the woman. In the darkened theater, Aimée couldn't see much except that the woman wore a white wool suit, Escada by the look of it, and that her complexion was too tan for the Riviera. Her hands played over the Virgin Mary medal near the pearl button of her jacket.

"Léonie?" Aimée asked.

The woman spoke under her breath, not moving her head. "I talk to principals, not messengers."

Nice attitude! But what had she expected? Edouard had called her a *salope.*

"My name is Aimée Leduc. I'm a detective." Aimée's knees hurt from crouching in the aisle. "The *flics* raided Edouard's atelier. But you know that, don't you? He wants you to stop the proposal."

Royet had warned her! Léonie's hand gripped the medal. "Raided . . . when?"

The old man a few rows up turned around, glaring. "Shhh!"

"Just a matter of time until they show up here," Aimée whispered and gripped her arm, leaned forward. "Say five minutes?"

"Who do you work for?" Léonie asked, not missing a beat.

A shiver ran through Aimée. She wondered what this woman's connections were.

"It's personal."

"Everything's personal. Especially money."

Did Léonie think she wanted to broker a deal, for a price? How could she stop Léonie when she was clueless? It felt like driving in night fog on a twisting mountain road, hairpin curves every few feet and no visibility. "My sister's been accused of Benoît's murder."

"Quiet!" The old man turned around again.

Léonie's lips pursed. "You want to clear her? Meet me in the lobby."

Aimée waited outside the quilted-leather swinging doors. Three minutes passed. Had she played it wrong? She hurried back into the theater. Only three heads were silhouetted against the screen now.

No Léonie. Gone. How could she have been so stupid?

Aimée ran toward the EXIT sign, pushed it open, and stood on rue des Ecoles. Students crowded under the café awning ahead of her. She scanned the pavement in the drizzling rain.

No taxi stand, no bus stop. No Léonie.

The rain beat harder. Every doorway held shivering wet bystanders, café entrances were filled with slim, jeaned, androgynous types and mothers with strollers. The gutters ran with water flowing down from Mont Saint-Genèvieve, named for Genèvieve, who'd defended the city against the Huns and stopped Attila.

People ran, clutching newspapers over their heads against the rain. Then she saw the white Escada jacket amid the crowd heading up rue Saint Jacques, a flash of white in the sea of black umbrellas bobbing up the hill.

The Sorbonne's open doors let out a stream of students running for shelter and halting Aimée's progress. Léonie's white jacket disappeared. Panicked, Aimée ran faster, threading her way uphill. No sign of Léonie now.

A narrow street veered to the left. She followed it past the Collège de France's soot-stained portals, her eyes misting with rain. Another street, narrower, with leaning seventeenth-century façades of blackened stone. A passage no wider than a horse cart opened on the right.

Aimée found herself in front of a closing door. She stuck her foot in the doorway, pushed it open. Léonie was fumbling with keys.

Panting, her wet shoulders heaving, she caught Léonie's hand.

"How much do you want?" Léonie asked. Money?

"I'm not for sale, unlike Benoît."

Shock painted Léonie's face. "No one bought him off."

Aimée's mind spun. That put a different slant on the article Martine had shown her. Had Benoît planned to publish his findings and been killed to prevent him?

"Why do you want Benoît's file?"

Léonie turned away. But not before Aimée saw the haggard look on her face in the light. She looked ill. She was *too* thin.

"Who else wants it besides you?" Aimée asked.

"You don't want to know," Léonie said, her words coming in short spurts. "Or you may be next."

Aimée shivered. Soaked, out of breath, her legs aching, she wanted to hit something.

"And the men outside my apartment, watching my office? They're already after me." Aimée said. "Too late."

"You sound like Edouard," Léonie said. "My nephew's the idealist in the family. He

384

had the luxury; the rest of us had to survive."

Her hands clenched. "Edouard's your nephew?"

A thin smile creased Léonie's lips. "I see he worked his charm on you. You're not the first."

Hell, she'd slept with him, contemplated doing it again. He reminded her so of Yves. And she'd been ready to tell him about the file.

His usual tactics? But he'd helped Mireille! Was Léonie telling her the truth about him?

Her eyes closed, sighing, Léonie leaned against the lighted list of building tenants. Aimée saw an envelope sticking from her bag. Léonie Obin was the name written on it.

"Foolish, foolish boy . . . Edouard hasn't changed. He still blames me for supporting Duvalier."

"And the tonton macoutes?"

Léonie staggered, clutching her cane. She caught herself and took a step toward the door.

"You're in over your head. I'm leaving."

"Not yet."

Aimée had been reading the names on the list of tenants.

"Benoît was consulting for Hydrolis on a proposed water project. Hydrolis's application is up before the World Bank funding committee," she said. "You're after his report. But why?"

Léonie shook her head. "Forget it."

Aimée pulled the envelope from the woman's handbag.

"Give that back!" Léonie demanded.

"Maybe Benoît's report presented a problem for the Haitian Trade Delegation," she said, pointing to the trade delegation address on the envelope. A mask descended over Léonie's drawn features.

"This Caribe-Invest Bureau, up on the third floor here, it's just a front, isn't it?" Aimée ventured, desperate to provoke a reaction. "What is the significance of Benoît's file to you? Who has a financial interest in finding it?"

Even though she possessed the pages of his report, they had revealed nothing to her. If only Serge would return her call and explain. But if she prodded Léonie, maybe she would reveal their importance.

"The thugs you hired to find Benoît's report ended up killing him. And still didn't find it."

"I didn't hire them. You're naïve."

"Benoît trusted my sister, an illegal, whose

aunt came from his village, rather than you. Were you the enemy?"

"You're guessing."

Aimée thought hard . . . coming up blank. . . . She pulled out the papers she'd taken from Edouard's fax machine and read them. One concerned Feed the Children. Father Privert's organization.

"Benoît's file concerns water, doesn't it?" Aimée guessed.

From the look on Léonie's face, her words had hit home.

"Father Privert believes polluted water causes more children's deaths than hunger," she said. "Hydrolis operates water-delivery systems and sewage-treatment plants. Potential projects worth millions are awaiting World Bank funding. You and the Trade Delegation must be getting a hefty cut. You hired thugs to murder Benoît before he could deliver the results of his inquiry to the World Bank. The circle of salt, slicing off Benoît's ear . . . all done to divert suspicion to the tonton macoutes."

"Salt's for purification." Léonie shook her head. "You've got it wrong."

She'd wondered about that herself. But Léonie knew more than she'd let on. "Why don't I believe you?" Aimée said.

"You're resisting the spirit," said Léonie,

her voice matter-of-fact. "The force is working through me."

What did she mean, Aimée wondered.

"Tonton macoutes peel the victim's face off," Léonie said, "to prevent the spirit from finding rest in the afterlife." Her eyes pierced Aimée's. "But you know that. I sense it. Ogoun protected Benoît. He still does."

Aimée stepped back. Mireille's words came back to her . . . her mother's face . . . she had been unable to talk about it. Had the tonton macoutes done that to her mother?

Léonie's gaze was somewhere else. Far away.

"I think I understand now," Léonie said.

"Understand what?" Aimée asked?

"Jérôme Castaing emulates his father," Léonie said. "When Duvalier, the doctor who helped cure yaws, the tropical disease ravaging Haiti, a *noirist* — dark as night — who spoke *Kreyòl,* a man of the people, came to power, he was a good man. He gave us pride."

What did this have to do with Hydrolis? Aimée shivered in the drafty vestibule.

"At first, we regarded Duvalier as a savior, like Toussaint l'Overture, the slave who freed our country from French rule. Later

Duvalier changed. But that's another story," said Léonie. "His tonton macoutes resented the French. They ambushed Castaing, a geographer surveying the countryside, and tortured him. He lost an eye, but he lived; he was luckier than most. Duvalier interceded to save him. But Castaing figured Duvalier owed him more than that. He made the whole island pay."

"Jérôme's doing the same?"

"Jérôme's in love."

What did that mean?

"He's weak," Léonie continued.

"Weak men hire others to murder," Aimée said.

"Not he. He's a shrewd businessman. He took control of his father's Port-au-Prince water plant in the eighties, and still exploits us because he owns our water. If he killed Benoît, he'd be the first one suspected. He's not that inept, nor that brave. It's someone else."

"Who?"

Léonie closed her eyes, tired from talking. She leaned on her cane, then shouldered her purse. "Leave an old woman alone."

"Look at this." Aimée pulled the photos from her bag. The black-and-white dog-eared snapshot of her father and the one of Mireille as an infant.

She took a breath. "That's my father."

"Aaah, so that's your sister," Léonie said, a knowing look in her eye. "Fruit of her mother's student days in Paris, *non? Les cocos,* we called them. After Duvalier cut student subsidies, the girls returned home. The population swelled in 1960."

"Mireille was born in 1959. See?" She turned the photo over. "She's an infant."

"*Pfft,* what does it matter?"

Some kind of mistake? The date written wrong?

Wearily, Léonie said, "My father took command of the Interior Ministry. But when Duvalier unleashed the tonton macoutes, who hated foreigners, they slaughtered the babies and their mothers. . . ."

Like Mireille's mother. But somehow Mireille had escaped.

"She's beautiful," Léonie said. "Reminds me of a woman I knew. He liked that type."

Aimée was lost. "What do you mean?"

"Castaing."

"But didn't you say. . . ."

"Castaing supervised the building of a water plant in the mid-sixties. After all, he knew the land and he proved useful to Duvalier. An unholy alliance, until Duvalier had no more use for him."

Aimée rocked back on her heels. "There's

a point to this, I assume. But your father served in a corrupt government. Like Castaing, he used Haiti."

"Sometimes the path ahead . . . well, it's not always easy to choose." She sighed. "We wanted to live."

Every time she tried to pin Léonie down, the woman drifted somewhere else.

"The motive for Benoît's murder was personal," Aimée said. "Is that what you're saying?"

Léonie stared at Aimée's bag. "Where did you get that?"

She was looking at the straw-colored burlap sachet hanging by a red string from her bag.

"This?" Aimée pulled it out. "It fell from Edouard's pocket."

Léonie's outstretched hands shook. "Please, give it to me. That's good juju." Her voice cracked. "Powerful. *My* juju."

Surprised, Aimée handed the pouch to Léonie, who kissed it and crossed herself.

"You've been sent. I understand," Léonie said. "Not the police. *You* must find the killer."

Aimée looked at her, nonplussed. Nothing she'd said so far had moved Léonie. But this bit of burlap did. "Then will you withdraw this proposal from consideration?"

"Find me Benoît's file," Léonie said, a sheen of perspiration on her brow. "Tell Edouard I need what he stole from me. All of it. I know how to help him now."

Tension knotted at the base of Aimée's spine. She wouldn't give Léonie Benoît's data without knowing its significance and why he had been killed.

"I don't get it. If Benoît's file contains information on Hydrolis, then. . . ." She hesitated, trying to piece this together.

"Now. I must have it before the meeting," said Léonie.

"Meeting?" Aimée asked.

"There's no time to explain." Léonie's hands trembled, her pallor highlighted in the eerie light cast by the illuminated tenant roster behind her.

This made even less sense to Aimée.

"No time to explain why you want Benoît's file? Or what it signifies?" Aimée said. "You're lying."

Her phone rang.

About time. She hoped it was Serge with the information she'd asked him for. But before she could answer the phone, Léonie's hands gripped hers. Ice-cold hands.

"*Non,* I am telling the truth. Trust me. The existence of Haiti is at stake."

The door opened to a blast of wind-driven rain.

Aimée was thrown against the wall. Then her head struck the worn marble step. She felt no more.

Friday Afternoon

René listened to Aimée's phone ring and ring. Why didn't she answer? She often forgot to recharge its battery. His stitches ached with a dull throb, but thanks to the old woman healer his realigned hip felt close to normal. Amazing.

He waited for Aimée's phone to shift to voicemail. She'd gone off half-cocked about a sister, wishing it to be true. Most people wanted to run away from their family. She ran headlong toward one, the way she did everything. Why couldn't she understand the danger?

"Monsieur Friant, if you're ready?" said Bertilet, the Aèrospatiale manager.

Behind Bertilet lay the glass window of his corner skyscraper office in La Défense. Bertilet sat forward, expectant in his navy double-breasted suit, red tie, and light blue shirt. Standard attire for upper-tier bureaucrats, René thought, like a uniform.

René turned off his phone.

"Of course, Monsieur Bertilet. Please refer

to the first page, our description of services."

René cleared his throat as he aligned the pages of Leduc's computer security proposal, but he knew the pitch by heart. And Leduc Detective needed this computer security contract.

"Leduc Detective uses analytical and investigative techniques to identify, collect, examine, and preserve evidence or information that is stored or encoded on computers," René said. "And, in your firm's case, to provide evidence of either a specific or general activity."

"I understand, Monsieur Friant. But in what way?" Bertilet asked.

René forced a smile. Yesterday he'd explained this to the committee, but it seemed that Monsieur Bertilet, the bureau chief, needed to hear it in person. Yet again.

"Our forensic techniques can be of value in a wide variety of situations, including simply retracing steps taken when data has been lost."

"Give me some common scenarios," Bertilet said.

"Employee Internet abuse," René said. "Unauthorized disclosure of corporate information and data. Industrial espionage. Damage assessment following an incident. Criminal fraud and deception cases."

Bertilet tapped his pen on the desk. "How do you approach a computer forensic investigation?"

"It's a detailed science," René said. "But depending on the case, we secure the subject system, make a copy of the hard drive, and identify and recover all files, including those that have been deleted from the hard drive."

René saw Bertilet's eyes begin to glaze over. He'd better cut this short.

"Throughout the investigation, we stress that a full audit log of the firm's activities will be maintained."

René paused to let this sink in. "Monsieur Bertilet, I've painted with broad strokes. Before we take a case, we must know the details, the goal you have in mind. And then we tailor our work to establish or uncover the pertinent data."

Bertilet nodded; a small sigh escaped his lips. He sat back in his swivel chair. Behind him was a panorama of highrises dotting La Défense.

"We have a data leak, Monsieur Friant," he admitted.

After three days of meetings, now it came out. But René had expected it all along. Like a dog with a bone, he wanted to sink his teeth into this. And earn a nice check.

"I know Leduc Detective can help you,

Monsieur," he said.

"Monsieur Friant, give me a few minutes. I'd like to call in a colleague to hear more details of your proposal," Bertilet said.

René smiled. "Of course, Monsieur."

At long last he felt the time was ripe. One more presentation and the contract would be Leduc's.

Relieved, he stepped into the hallway. Stainless steel, windowed, but soulless, overlooking the vista of the Paris skyline in the distance. He punched in Aimée's number.

"Why didn't you answer my calls, Aimée?"

Crackling came over the line. A scream. Scuffling.

"Aimée?" René froze.

He heard a church bell peal. Voices. ". . . truck . . . imbecile . . . on rue Lacepede. . . ."

He was cut off. He hit the REDIAL key. Busy.

René's hands trembled as he imagined the worst. An accident? Had they kidnapped her?

He was helpless. What could he do, stuck in a meeting? And then he did what he had insisted Aimée do from the beginning: he called Morbier.

Swirls of light danced and faded. The sweet acrid smell of cigar smoke drifted across Aimée's consciousness. And then Léonie's haggard face came back to her, the scream, the dull thuds, and the blow sending her across the vestibule.

What felt like cold hard stone lay beneath her. She opened her eyes and looked at the worm-eaten wood of a doorframe. And she realized she'd managed to drag herself into the staircase leading down to the cellar.

Where was Léonie? She reached for her bag. It was gone.

And with it Benoît's report!

When she leaned forward, her head reeled. Her damp clothes clung to her skin. She had to get help. She gripped the doorframe, pulled herself up, forcing herself to take deep breaths to get oxygen to her brain. Bit by bit her head cleared; the sparks of light faded from her vision. She heard low voices, the beeping sounds of a car backing up. Were they returning to torture her for information? To kill her?

She leaned against the wall as she made her way across the worn floor. The cigar-smoke smell was stronger now. She heard wood-scraping and grunting noises. Into her line of vision came the black-and-white diamond-shaped tiles of the floor and a hypodermic needle lying on it.

"Watch out for that corner. Careful!"

"What in the world?" asked a shrill voice. "A junkie's shooting up in our building!"

A woman in a floral print dress pointed to Aimée. To the side stood two men in overalls hefting a harpsichord up the broad staircase. One chewed a cigar.

"*Non,* Madame, I was attacked," Aimée said, rubbing her head. "My bag was stolen."

"Do you take me for a fool?" the woman snorted.

"Didn't you see her, a well-dressed older woman?"

"Who?"

"She wore a white suit," Aimée said. "Used a cane."

"I'm calling the *flics.*" The woman glared at her.

"She got into a car," said the man in overalls. The cigar bobbed in his mouth as he spoke. "Didn't look too happy about it either."

Aimée winced as she touched the bruise on her head, then dusted her jacket off.

Things fell into place as her mind cleared. "You mean she was forced into a car in that narrow street?"

"She was giving him hell, too," he said.

"What's this got to do with your trespassing in a private building?" said the woman.

"Anything else you remember?" Aimée asked and felt the bulge in her jacket pocket. Her phone, still there, thank God.

"Typical, eh, blocking my truck, those bourgeois who think they own the street!"

She didn't appreciate the working-class chip on his shoulder. "What kind of car?"

"Posh. Dark windows, a black Mercedes," he said.

"I'm getting the building supervisor, young woman!" The woman fumed, and her heels clattered up the stairs.

Aimée hit Morbier's number. Busy. Then saw the phone number of the last caller. It had been René. But she hadn't spoken to him. Or had the knock on her head affected her memory?

Worried, she tried René's number.

"Aimée! Are you all right?"

"I'll live. My head hurts."

"What happened, Aimée?"

"Someone whacked me and sent me flying across the vestibule, that's the last . . . *non,* I remember reaching for my phone but Léonie grabbed my hand." Her heart sank. "They took her and my bag with Benoît's file in it."

"But you did answer," he said. "I heard a

scream, noises. You worried me!"

"I did?" She must have hit the ANSWER button without realizing it. "What exactly did you hear, René?"

"Enough to make me alert Morbier," he said. "Where are you?"

"René, didn't you hear anything else?"

"What if you've got a concussion?" he said. "After the attack you suffered in the Bastille, they warned that you could lose your vision again."

That attack had resulted in her temporary blindness. She shoved that worry aside.

"Men's voices or a name . . . did you catch anything?"

"It happened so fast."

"Anything, René? Please think."

A sigh that she knew was from frustration came over the phone.

"I heard a woman's voice saying 'Leave her,' then a man's. 'Get her to Castaing,' " he said. "But I think they were interrupted. Someone else came in talking about a harpsichord."

So Castaing was directing the thugs.

And Léonie had told Castaing's thugs to leave Aimée. Now they — Castaing — had the file. This file everyone wanted. And she'd had it and lost it.

She would have to rely on Serge's take on

the contents she'd faxed over to him. At least Serge had a copy of the report.

"Do me a favor, René?"

"Now?" René said. "I've just finished the Aèrospatiale presentation. The chief's almost hooked, he's consulting with higher-ups. I may still be needed."

This couldn't wait. "So you're on a break. Can't you run a check on Hydrolis's pending contracts with the World Bank?"

"Hack around to see what I can find out?" René said, disgust edging his voice. "Why don't you leave this alone, Aimée?"

"I can't, René! Please! They stole Benoît's file."

Her phone clicked.

"No doubt that's Morbier," René said. "Tell him the story, Aimée, like you should have from the beginning."

And he hung up.

"Leduc, what's happened?" Morbier's voice was broken up by static.

"Léonie Obin, a Haitian trade delegate, has been abducted, Morbier."

Looking at her Tintin watch, she realized that less than ten minutes could have elapsed since she'd been knocked out. "From rue de Lanneau. No more than ten or fifteen minutes ago."

"Eh?" The reception wavered in and out.

401

She described the Mercedes. "I think they're headed to Jérôme Castaing's firm, Hydrolis, on Square Paul Painlevé across from the Cluny Museum."

"What. . . ." Morbier's voice cut out.

"Did you get that? Please hurry, Morbier."

"Then you're all right, Leduc?" Concern suffused his voice.

It took her off guard. Since when had Morbier worried about her?

"Besides bruises, feeling shaky, and an aching head? Sure."

"Your partner was worried. He heard screaming."

"They stole my bag. Benoît's report was inside. You've got to recover it, Morbier."

A long sigh came over the phone. "What's that got to do with Mireille?"

She shifted in her damp heels, hating to lie to him.

"They murdered Benoît for this file, Morbier," she said. "If you go right now, you can recover it and Léonie Obin —"

"So you're making good on our deal?" he interrupted.

"Deal?"

"Don't tell me you forgot, Leduc," Morbier said. "I'm ready to do my part, to inquire on Mireille's behalf to Immigration."

He still thought she'd turn in Mireille. He'd better think again.

"Listen, Morbier —"

But he'd hung up.

"You're trespassing. Get out." The woman had returned with the building guard. Meanwhile, the harpsichord movers sat on the steps, watching and smoking.

"This is a private residence. We can't have junkies nodding off here."

Aimée edged her way out. But not before she caught the movers' gaze up her legs.

She needed a Doliprane for her head and to take it easy. Guy, her eye surgeon and former lover, had warned that another knock on the head could result in permanent optic nerve damage.

"Take your filthy disgusting drugs with you!"

The woman kicked the syringe out onto the cobbles at Aimée's feet. Talk about anger. But the woman obviously knew that diseases could be borne by needles and hadn't touched it.

Aimée bent down to inspect the clear liquid of a pre-drawn dosage in the syringe. An orange plastic cap topped the needle. "Study A" and "X011" were typed on the plastic label, which also said ALDOR in tiny print. Aldor was a large pharmaceutical firm.

Was Léonie a junkie? Or had the *mecs* drugged her before kidnapping her?

Using her scarf, Aimée picked it up and, with her fingernails, peeled off the label. No way would she carry a syringe in her pocket. She wrapped the syringe in an old flyer and debated how to discard it safely. She stuck it in the nearby clear green-tinged plastic garbage bag, labeled VIGILANCE PROPRETÉ, which had been used by the City instead of bins after the 1995 bombings.

Now she had no bag, no cash, no keys, no makeup. Only wet clothes and her cell phone.

Vincent looked up from polishing glasses at the bar counter of the Piano Vache.

"Don't tell me," he said, grinning. "You've given up on pigs and porcine experts."

If only she could.

He set the glass down. "Aimée, you're shivering," he exclaimed. "And you don't look too good."

"How about a drink, Vincent?" she said. "And a little help."

Twenty minutes later, after a double espresso, a full-strength Doliprane pain reliever, a hundred-franc loan from Vincent, and a change of clothes borrowed from the evening waitress, who kept a set under the counter, Aimée stepped out into rue Laplace. The ache in her head had subsided. Her hand was cupped to her phone. If only the waitress's borrowed jeans hadn't been so tight that they cut off the circulation in her thighs.

"Serge, what do you mean your assistant shredded my fax?"

Serge, her pathologist friend at the Institut Medico Legal, cleared his throat as Aimée listened. She clutched the plastic Printemps shopping bag holding her wet clothes, wishing she didn't look like a hooker from the *banlieues.* Sequins and gold braid studded the midriff-hugging jacket; underneath that, she wore a tight hot-pink tank top, and she'd tied a paisley scarf around her hair. She'd forgone the leather belt emblazoned with *"Cherie."* At least the outfit was dry. And the men who had attacked her and knocked her out wouldn't recognize her.

"Next time, Aimée, alert me that you're faxing something," Serge said. "Don't just spring it on me. Since Diana's death, people have broken in to steal info. We shred all faxes now. It's policy."

She wanted to kick something. Shredded!

Her fault for not checking earlier. She'd counted on Serge!

"I did call! Left you a voicemail. I guess you didn't get it.

"But," she continued, "of course you read the pages before they were shredded, *non? I'm en route to the morgue; you can tell me what they mean when I get there."

"I'm sorry, Aimée," Serge said. "I need to finish some pathology findings before I pick the twins up from school. They have come down with raging ear infections."

Again? His energetic preschool boys had more illnesses than any other children she knew. But then all her friends were single.

She needed to calm down, to control her frustration. She'd get nowhere by annoying him. If Morbier didn't nab the thugs with Benoît's file at Castaing's office, she had a big fat nothing. They could have destroyed it already. And the only copy had been shredded at the morgue.

"Serge," she said, "I know you're busy. But you must have read it first. Did any of it make sense to you?"

"I'm leaving in ten minutes."

Her heart sank.

"Don't tell me you didn't read it?"

"Refresh my memory, eh? I get so many faxes," he said.

"Three pages on graph paper filled with equations," she said, "chemical formulas, statistics. No cover letter."

"Wait a minute: let me ask my assistant." Serge spoke to someone in the background.

Aimée was near the crowded bus stop on tree-lined Boulevard Saint Michel when she realized she had no change for the bus. An autumnal orange light spilled over the mansard roofs, making them glint like firebursts. Orange and red fallen leaves crackled under her feet in the lengthening shadows. The evenings were getting dark earlier now as the equinox approached.

"There were formulas for mercury and lead compounds," Serge said. "That's what my assistant remembers. He says it piqued his curiosity."

What came to mind was a World Health bulletin about toxicity in sardines in the North Sea. "Were they at toxic levels?"

"Depends on the solution," Serge said. "But add mercury and lead to almost anything, and it becomes toxic."

"Could it be due to old lead pipes, like water pipes?"

"The origin, you mean?"

She didn't know what she meant.

"Sure."

"Beats me," he said.

Great. She heard a phone ringing. "Hold on," Serge said.

"What's that, Serge?"

The Number 96 bus rolled up with brakes hissing. The crowd surged forward. And she grew aware of a hand feeling her up inside the waitress's short jacket. She slapped the hand, shooting a dirty look at the surprised offender, a middle-aged man with mouse-brown hair.

She left the bus line.

A wave of nausea rose from her stomach, then subsided. The bruise on her temple ached. She didn't need a minor concussion right now; she needed more Doliprane.

"The team's waiting, Serge," a voice said in the background.

"Got to go, Aimée," he said.

"One more thing. Does Aldor X011 mean anything to you?"

Pause. "Look, Aimée, if you're . . . you're. . . ."

He sounded nervous. And not much made Serge nervous, apart from his mother-in-law.

"I've helped you before, but . . . infection, the twins. . . . Not my field. I know a doctor who runs a good clinic."

"What's the matter, Serge?" She wished he'd just say it.

"If your client is infected, you must take precautions."

Her stomach knotted.

"What's X011, Serge?"

"Not many know about this experimental cocktail."

She doubted that Serge meant a drink.

"The woman's not my client, Serge."

He took a breath. "Good. In the studies so far, it's the only retroviral mixture that's effective in the last stages of AIDS."

Léonie's hollow cheeks, her makeup, her fatigue!

She wondered if she'd read Léonie all wrong, as Edouard had. That curious sachet, her juju. She'd wanted Aimée to find Benoît's killer, she'd told the *mecs* not to take her. Even though she was ill, she had pinned her hopes on Aimée. Tears came unbidden, dampening her eyes.

"*Merci,* Serge."

So the notes contained formulas for mercury and lead. She remembered the list from Benoît's locker, the formulas for lead and mercury checked off. The pig tissue slides had contained heavy metals. Huby had shown them to her. That tied together. If she'd been a scientist who understood this, or if Huby had returned her calls. . . . But life didn't allow for ifs, and she shouldn't think ill of the dead.

She hoped Morbier was questioning Castaing at Hydrolis's office. And if justice existed in this world, she'd find the proof she needed.

As she hurried in the dusk across rue Mouffetard, a familiar scent filled the air. Swollen, purple figs nestled in a bed of green leaves at the fruit stall. Fit to burst, like those in her grandmother's garden in the Auvergne. It took her back to the days when she picked figs among the leafy branches heavy with fruit; tasted the ripe red flesh, the tiny seeds crunching between her teeth, the clear sap dribbling down her cheek. Back to the smell of her grandmother's *tarte aux figues,* warm from the oven, her father's favorite, and how he always claimed the largest slice. The way his eyes crinkled in a grin.

How could she explain her father to Mireille? His warmth, his crooked smile? A father Mireille only knew from a frayed black-and-white photograph, faded with time. He would have cared for her, Aimée was sure now, if he'd known of her existence.

She shook the image off. She could almost taste autumn in the air, the time when the

410

aroma of chestnuts would replace that of figs. Roasting chestnuts with street-corner vendors rubbing their hands together in the chill and heating the chestnuts over low flames.

The seasons moved on. Life moved on. Why couldn't she?

She pressed Professeur Zarek's number but got only her voicemail. She was worried until she remembered that the professor might still be sleeping. She left a message.

Her phone rang.

Already? Eagerly, she hit ANSWER. *"Allo?"*

"Nice muddle you led me to, Leduc," said Morbier. "No way I can hold these *mecs,*" he continued. "There's no proof. Their chief, Jérôme Castaing, isn't here. According to his secretary, Hydrolis employs them."

"Can't you run background checks on them? Look for priors, parole violations? Figure out something to charge them with?"

"Just like that?"

"You do it all the time, Morbier," she said. "They stole my bag. A worn black leather Vuitton."

Pause.

"Afraid not, Leduc."

They'd already passed it on, or destroyed it.

"Léonie, the older woman, she's ill."

"The only woman here is the secretary. You're wasting my time, Leduc."

"Look, Morbier —"

"And for the last time."

The line buzzed. He'd hung up. Her shoulders sagged. She'd have to do this herself.

She'd reached Square Paul Painlevè. She could see the *flics'* cars on rue Sommerand, pulled up in front of the Hydrolis building. Morbier was upstairs, she was sure, in Castaing's office. Somehow she'd have to persuade him to find Léonie before he left.

Over the metal spikes of the fence, she glimpsed Jérôme Castaing in a raincoat, not in his office at all but walking arm in arm with a woman under the plane trees bordering the square. Making an abrupt turn, he and his companion changed direction. No wonder, she thought: he'd seen the *flic* cars in front of his office.

The couple hurried into the gothic entrance of the Cluny Museum.

Aimée rushed across the gravel to the square's gate, unlatched it, and crossed narrow rue du Sommerand. She ran inside the Cluny's medieval stone entrance. There was no sign of Castaing or his companion in the courtyard, nor by the sundial with its Latin inscription NIL SINE NOBIS, nor in the damp stone arcade. For a moment she felt dizzy. Her heels slipped on the slick worn pavers, and the ground went out from under her. She reached out, catching the ledge of the fifteenth-century well, and stared into its dark depths. Breathing hard, she pulled herself up. *Slow down and get a grip,* she told herself.

Castaing must have entered the museum.

At least no line of tourists and no school groups were waiting at the reception desk.

She caught her breath, steadied herself, and smiled at the ticket-taker. "I'm meeting my friends, a couple. They just came in, a tall man and a woman. Did you see where they went?"

"Toward the special exhibition in the Roman baths."

"Merci." Aimée handed her francs over and took her ticket.

Inside the museum's dimly lit vaulted corridor, humid stale air lingered. She hated the old smell of these places, the reek of porous stone, exuding long-past lives. This fifteenth-century monolith had been her history teacher's favorite field-trip destination. It displayed artifacts of medieval life, from carved fifteenth-century hair combs to sculpted sarcophagi with Latin inscriptions.

Eerie. Any moment she expected the hovering ghost of a medieval monk to appear.

She strode down a dark passage, walked past a gallery lined with weathered sculpted heads. These twenty-one kings of Judea had formed part of Notre Dame's façade until peasants had beheaded them during the Revolution. A flight of stairs led down to the remains of the adjoining Roman baths. Vaulted brown-rose brick arches rose above the baths.

So far, no sign of Jérôme Castaing and his companion.

She'd written a paper for history class on the ancient Roman thermal baths: the *frigidarium* holding cold water, the *calderium* hot, and the steam rooms. Next came the museum's celebrated fifteenth-century tapestry sequence, *Lady with the Unicorn,* depicting the five senses. Art historians still debated the meaning of the enigmatic last panel.

Few patrons lingered in the exhibit area at this late hour. Frustrated, she walked faster, wondering where Castaing could have gone.

How could he just vanish?

She retraced her steps and glanced into a low crypt-like cavity. Somewhere, water was dripping in steady plops.

"But you can explain. . . ." a woman's voice was saying. "Tell the *flics*. . . ." The voice receded.

Aimée stepped behind a pillar. She peered into the cavern and saw Jérôme Castaing standing in a niche in the vaulted stone wall.

She stiffened. Jérôme Castaing's arms were holding Josephe, the woman from Father Privert's foundation.

"Ma puce," he said, "you worry too much." His hand cupped Josephe's chin. Her face glowed.

A couple . . . they were a couple! And so different, she thought, Jérôme dapper in a trim Burberry raincoat, Josephe in khaki pants, worn sweater, mussed hair half-caught in a ponytail.

Aimée pressed against the cold stone to catch their conversation.

"Tell them the truth," Josephe was saying, her gaze intent, searching Jérôme's face. "Deny Benoît's allegations."

Allegations? What were they?

He stroked her cheek. "Aaah, my little radical. They cannot understand how Haiti works."

Jérôme pulled her closer.

"But you do," she said. "Be careful, Jérôme. Father Privert's mission is so important. . . ."

Aimée couldn't catch the rest. She tiptoed to the next pillar.

"Dried-up wells. . . ." Josephe was saying. "The empty reservoirs, the trucks selling water, gouging the people . . . nothing functions."

This was another side of Josephe, the harshness gone. Indeed, Jérôme seemed more smitten than she.

Jérôme took off his glasses to wipe them. Aimée noticed the tremor in his hands as he put them back on. Then he took Josephe's hands, kissing them. "I'll do anything. You know that. Don't worry. You leave first. I'll find a rear exit."

Aimée's thoughts sped in rapid succession; Jérôme was in love, promising Josephe he'd do anything; the water company had been founded by his father; Benoît's report referred to lead and mercury. In the water? One thing stood out: Castaing was telling Josephe lies to keep her love.

Josephe's footsteps echoed under the cavernous arches, then paused. Had she seen Aimée? Aimée squeezed deeper into the wedge between the pillar and a stone sarcophagus. But Josephe, her gaze on Jérôme, had only turned to blow him a kiss.

She waited until Josephe disappeared around the corner.

He'd pulled out his cell phone, ready to dial.

"Too late, Castaing," Aimée said. "There's a reception committee waiting at your office. A commissaire's waiting to question you."

Surprised, Jérôme stepped back.

"Who in the. . . ." Recognition dawned in his eyes. "You! Nice outfit, Detective," he said sarcastically.

"Forget the fashion critique," she said. "Not only did your *mecs* knock me out, they stole Benoît's file from my bag. I want it back."

"I don't know what you're talking about."

"You're skimming millions, lining your pockets by selling the poor Haitians polluted water," Aimée said, moving closer. "I'd say your girlfriend's out the door when she discovers what you've been doing."

"Discovers what?"

Without Benoît's report, what could she prove? She thought fast.

"For a start, falsifying proposals to the World Bank."

"You're misinformed, Detective," Castaing said.

"Leduc. My name's Leduc," she said. "Then there's corruption, bribery."

He gave a shrug. "You don't understand,

417

do you?"

"Understand?"

"It's the cost of doing business in Haiti," Castaing said, his tone matter-of-fact. "Everyone from the military, to the ministry, down to the guards at the pumps have to be paid off to keep the system running, to keep things going. The government structure has collapsed. The rich elite have their own reservoirs. Do they care? No one provides water to those people, to the poor, the destitute. No one goes to Cité Soleil except me and my company's workers."

Now it all made sense.

"And you make a fat profit by doing so, Castaing," she said.

"The alternative's a ten-mile walk through sugarcane fields for brackish water that's been used in irrigation."

"And I suppose that's your rationale for supplying toxic water full of mercury and lead," she said, her anger mounting. "Water that poisons people and animals. How can you justify that?"

"*Nom de Dieu,*" Jérôme said, shaking his head. "Do you think I knew?"

She held back her surprise. He'd as good as admitted her charges.

"Now you're pleading ignorance? That's gross negligence. Our water's tested several times a day here in Paris. It's your responsibility to replace the pipes, clean the filtration system, and make sure you deliver clean water."

"And I will," he said. "The plan's in place to renovate the water plant, replace the pipes, and renew the sewage system. It's contingent on IMF and World Bank loans. Benoît knew that."

His hands twisted; a look of anguish appeared on his face. "Don't involve Josephe," he said. "She wouldn't understand."

And for a moment she almost felt sorry for him. Jérôme Castaing had it bad.

"Heartfelt, but not good enough, Castaing. Josephe deserves the truth."

"You wouldn't do that. You can't!"

What if Jérôme had instigated Benoît's murder? She had to know. "Benoît threatened to make public his findings that your water was tainted with heavy metals. That would ruin you. You couldn't have that."

Castaing's thin lips pursed.

"Nor have Darquin, the old lab guard, give testimony as to Benoît's murder. Nor allow Huby, his assistant, to talk to me. All along, your *mecs* have followed me. You employ killers."

"You're paranoid." Jérôme emitted a brittle laugh.

"You had them add a sick touch, to make Benoît's murder resemble the tonton macoutes' work." She didn't wait for his answer. "Big mistake. Tonton macoutes do it differently."

Shock crossed Castaing's face. He stepped back. "You really think I'd murder that big lumbering ox of a scientist? Benoît, a brilliant man, the first black lecturer at Ecole Normale Supérieure! Do you know the prejudice he battled in those hallowed halls? We differed, we disagreed. But I liked him, Detective, I respected him," Castaing said. "I don't even know those men you refer to. And I'm not like my father."

Despite everything, she believed him.

"Then who killed Benoît?"

"You're the detective."

"I made copies of Benoît's report, Castaing." A lie, but it would give her leverage. He couldn't know the truth.

Instead of the fear she expected, Jérôme waved his hand in a dismissive gesture.

"And, when the World Bank aid comes through, you'll find it too expensive or drum up some other excuses to keep your old system running. You'll pocket their money too and keep selling poisoned water."

"You've got no concrete evidence against my firm," he replied.

He reached in his pocket, pulled out his wallet, and riffled through the business cards. "Let's see, I'll make a quick call to the minister. We attended the *lycée* together."

The old-boy network. A favor called in, a promise made, scratching each other's backs behind closed doors. The big players who occupied high positions in the ministries raked in profits from the Third World without ever leaving their elegant offices. What could she do?

"You forgot the tissue samples, Castaing."

"I'm afraid you're too late."

Did that mean he'd found them?

"The Paris Club's already in session," Castaing continued. "The economic meeting's under way."

He meant the World Bank and IMF representatives, dubbed by the media the "Paris Club," the group that had been mentioned in the article Martine had showed her. The men who dictated Third World economic policy, the loans given and the loans forgiven.

She couldn't give up. She'd bluff, use Martine's connection to the press.

She said, "*Libération* will jump at the chance to publish an exposé detailing your connection with the World Bank, the bribes you pay, the laundering of funds."

"What in hell do you mean?"

"Father Privert's foundation maintains the front you need for humanitarian credentials while it launders your firm's profits," she said. "Ironic, *non?* Screwing Haiti and looking good; like father, like son. Josephe's knight in armor, tarnished by corruption."

The business card shook in his hand. "Don't slander the work of the foundation. You've got it all wrong."

"You mean, keep the truth from Josephe."

"After all these years, my family's part of Haiti," he said. "Bound to it. I help Father Privert's foundation out of goodwill."

She'd had enough. "Nice try, Castaing, but you'd say anything," Aimée said.

He frowned and pulled a photo from his wallet. "That's my sister. My *Haitian* sister."

Aimée gaped at the laminated black-and-white photo. It showed a man in a tropical shirt, next to a woman holding a toddler's hand, palm trees in the background.

She stepped back. Her brain couldn't take this in. The low throb in her temple, a concussion? Everything turned upside down, her stomach wrenched.

"But I have one too," Aimée said.

"What do you mean?" Jérôme said.

She stared at the smiling man with his arm around a black woman. The sun glinted on what looked like a well and drilling equipment.

It wasn't her father.

"The woman and the baby?"

Castaing's features tightened. "His mistress, their child. My half-sister." He spit out the next words. "Both murdered by the tonton macoutes to take revenge on my father. But that's history."

She turned the snapshot over. Gasped. "Me, Edwige, and Mireille" was written in faint pencil.

Mireille couldn't have two fathers. Some kind of mistake?

It couldn't be true. She didn't want to believe that Mireille had fed her a story, lied to her.

Was there really a connection between Mireille and Jérôme?

Castaing continued. "Father never let me forget my sister. In his drunken rants, he never shut up about them. Every night, on and on, about the tonton macoutes, the loss of his eye, their death. My childhood was haunted."

Hurt layered his voice. She wondered if his father had cared for them more than his own son.

"They'd met here at Brasserie Balzar. *Et voilà* . . . satisfied?" Behind the abrasive tone, she detected embarrassment or shame in his voice.

"And, to protect them, your father told Edwige to say her daughter had been fathered by a Frenchman she'd met in Paris," she said. "So they'd think she was just another *coco*. But the tonton macoutes took them anyway."

Castaing's jaw dropped. "How did you know?"

Maybe Mireille had been lied to and believed the lie.

Her phone trilled. Professeur Zarek with a report on Mireille's condition? She didn't recognize the caller ID. She hit MUTE.

"What do you think, Detective?" Castaing said.

"Castaing, I think your sister is alive."

"What . . . risen from the dead?" He shook his head, bewildered.

"Non. . . ."

"I get it now," he said, his lips twisting in a sick smile. "Her wandering spirit, the black vodou . . . all that crap!" He grabbed the sleeve of her too-tight jacket. "Liar!"

Seething, he shoved her against the stone wall of the crypt and started up the steps.

She stumbled. Her head hit the pillar, jarring her senses. And for a moment all she could see were pinpricks of light. She hunched over, burying her head in her arms, waiting for the wave of nausea to pass.

Two minutes, five minutes, she didn't know how long it was before she could stand, the nausea gone, her vision clear.

Castaing wouldn't get far. She'd make sure Morbier saw to that.

A knot of men stood near the entrance. Castaing's reinforcements? She lowered her head, mingling with museum patrons walking up the stairs. Her heart pounding, she made it out the door. Near the turret to the right of the entrance, she stepped into a dark covered arcade. Roosting pigeons cooed on the moss-speckled water spouts. She leaned against the damp stone catching her breath. The phone vibrated in her pocket again.

"Allo?"

"Mademoiselle Leduc, it's Villiers."

"I'm sorry. Who?"

"Forgive me for responding so late, but I'm on a concert tour, in Lyon, and just checked my messages," Villiers said. "You're interested in hiring our string quartet for your party. What date do you have in mind?"

The cellist from the baroque music concert. In the background, a kettledrum crashed, a bowed instrument twanged.

"*Merci,* Monsieur Villiers." Time to marshal her thoughts and get information. Villiers could place Benoît in the Cluny and tell her if he'd had a companion. "You come recommended by Professeur Benoît."

"Who, Madamoiselle?"

"He met you at last Monday night's concert at the Cluny."

"I don't understand. From your message, I understood *you* had heard our quartet."

"The professor raved about you," she said. "You remember him, of course, a visiting professor at ENS. Dark-complected, a large Haitian man."

There was a moment of silence.

"But I never spoke with him," Villiers said.

But he did recall him from the concert. Excited now, she went on. "But you spoke to his companion, I think?"

"Companion?"

If only she could place Castaing at the concert with Benoît before his murder. "A tall, thin man with glasses."

"You've confused me with someone else, Mademoiselle." Villiers's helpful tone had evaporated. "I'm a musician, not a social director."

"But I'm sure —"

"His companion was a woman," Villiers

interrupted. "And I never spoke with her either," he said. "Now, if you don't mind, I'm needed."

Startled, she gripped the phone. "Her hair color, Monsieur?"

"You ask strange questions."

"Please, can't you remember?"

Another pause.

"Blond, I think."

Not fifteen minutes ago she'd seen Josephe's blond ponytail. Had Josephe attended the concert and lied?

"Now that you ask," Villiers continued, "I remember wondering why a deaf woman would come to a concert. It seemed sad."

Aimée gripped her phone tighter. "How's that?"

"Her hearing aid fell to the floor. People helped her look for it, but no one found it."

Blond hair, hearing aid. "You're right, there's been a mistake. *Merci.*" *She'd* made the mistake.

She left the courtyard, passing the *flics'* cars, heading toward bustling Boulevard Saint Germain, intending to hail a taxi to the rue Buffon laboratory.

A car door opened. Morbier stepped out. "Don't tell me, Leduc," he said, gesturing to her outfit. "You're working undercover as a hooker."

"How did you guess?"

She tried to ignore the looks of the patrons dining at the outdoor bistro. "Castaing just left the Cluny. You need to question him."

"It's been taken care of, Leduc."

"What do you mean?"

"He's under surveillance. See?" She turned and watched Castaing get into a waiting black Mercedes. "The minute he steps out of line —"

"With his connections, he'll wriggle out of it," she interrupted. "I guess beating people up doesn't matter."

"Now you'll have time to tell me all about it." Morbier gestured toward the inside of the car. "After you."

Morbier told the driver, "The stable."

Her heart dropped. The old-timers called the interrogation rooms in the Prefecture "the stable." She had to persuade Morbier to let her go. She had to find evidence to prove who had killed Benoît. And now she knew where to look.

"Morbier, you've got to listen. Castaing —"

"All in good time, Leduc," he interrupted.

On a narrow winding street a few blocks away, the car braked to a halt in front of a small bistro.

"You're not taking me to the Prefecture?"

"I missed lunch," he said. "And Brigade interrogations go better on a full stomach."

One didn't keep the Brigade waiting. A lie? Or the truth? With Morbier, she didn't always know. The thought of interrogation coupled with food turned her stomach.

Morbier led her inside a dark hole of a place, low-ceilinged with blackened wood beams and exposed stone walls festooned with old plow wheels. Meat hissed, roasting on a wood-burning grill, candles flickered on wood tables, a narrow staircase descended to a vaulted cavern. Medieval and dim. Morbier had told the truth when he'd called it a stable.

"Long time, Commissaire," said a man with a white scar slicing his thick black eyebrow, wearing a none-too-clean apron. *Sanglier,* wild boar, was advertised on the chalkboard behind them.

"Business good, Bébert?"

"Can't complain, Commissaire," he said, wiping his hands on a dishcloth.

The odors of rosemary and garlic mingled in the close air; too many people in too small a place. Morbier headed past the five or six tables packed with academic types in corduroy jackets, students, and a few old codgers, knife and fork in hand, bent over heaping plates. People of the *quartier.* A few knowing glances shot their way.

Morbier sat across from Aimée at the window table, then nodded at Bébert.

"We'll take the *prix-fixe* menu. And a little quiet."

"*Bien sûr,* Commissaire." She caught Bébert glancing at her tight tank top.

Feeling awkward, Aimée leaned forward. "He thinks you're my sugar daddy!"

"He's not the only one." Morbier's mouth parted in a thin smile.

She set the plastic shopping bag with her damp clothes on the stone floor.

Bébert reappeared with a bread basket and a slab of butter, then retired without a word.

She leaned forward, keeping her voice low. "Morbier, Benoît discovered that Hydrolis was supplying water in Haiti that was not merely polluted, but toxic — full of mercury and lead. That's Jérôme Castaing's firm. As a consultant, Benoît revealed this information in a report that put Hydrolis's World Bank funding at risk. He wanted to expose Hydrolis. However, the report was never delivered; he was murdered first."

Morbier tucked a white napkin in his collar, saying nothing.

"He was killed for this report," she said, "but he'd hidden it. Do you understand?"

"And?"

Now came her variation on the truth. "After you left my apartment, Mireille appeared, asking for help. Benoît had hidden the file in a locker. He entrusted her with the key and location. But the traffickers who'd smuggled her into the country were after her for money. She was terrified. Until today, I didn't know what this key unlocked. After I found Benoît's file, Castaing's thugs stole it —"

"Where's your proof?" he interrupted.

"Proof?" She parted her hair with her hands, pointing to the bruised knot on her head. "You sound like Castaing. Talk to his thugs."

"Leduc, I questioned those *mecs*. I got nothing from them."

"So hold them on suspicion of robbery."

"You got a good look at them," he said. "Can you identify them in a lineup?"

She shook her head, wincing. "They abducted Léonie Obin, and she's ill."

"Aaah, this mystery woman!"

She patted her pockets. Empty except for her phone. "Léonie Obin's a member of the Haitian Trade Delegation. She's involved somehow with a World Bank proposal for aid to Hydrolis to fund a Haitian water project. Benoît was trying to stop it."

Morbier sighed. "Must I repeat that you need proof? And homicide is the Brigade's domain, remember?"

"Is the Brigade investigating the suspicious death of Darquin, the old guard from rue Buffon who was shoved under a car across from the Pantheon?"

Morbier's eyes narrowed below his thick eyebrows.

"Darquin had arranged to meet me. He'd seen something on rue Buffon and wanted to tell me about it. And Huby, Benoît's assistant, was shoved from a window so his death would look like suicide —"

"Serious allegations, Leduc," Morbier interrupted, "concerning a traffic accident, and a suicide as well. . . ."

Even in the dense air of this crowded bistro, the meaning of his remarks penetrated her brain. "Morbier, you've been called off."

His age-spotted hand paused on the water glass he'd just reached for.

"I'm not a dog, Leduc."

"Strings were pulled from above, weren't they?" She didn't wait for an answer. "This touches the big boys. Now I get it."

"Let's just say the Ministry and the Prefecture deem the ongoing investigation into Princess Diana's death a higher priority."

"Which ministry, Morbier?"

"Does it matter?" He sipped his water. "The world's watching us handle this Diana circus, Leduc. We've got to perform, and get it right."

"And Benoît's murder's an embarrassment during the Paris Club and World Bank meetings," she said.

"Leduc, Diana conspiracy theories abound, and MI 5 is right on our heels. The pressure's intense."

The conclusion was foregone; nothing she said would matter. He'd provide no real assistance to nail Castaing. She heard that, in what he didn't say. She'd need René's help to find proof of Hydrolis's dirty practices. But first she had to talk her way out of Morbier's clutches.

She took a piece of bread, tore out the soft white center, crumbled it. The thought of eating turned her stomach.

Bébert hovered with a bottle of Bordeaux in his hand, a white towel over his arm. "Commissaire?"

Morbier sniffed the inch of wine in his glass, swirled it, took a sip, then nodded. "That's fine."

Bébert poured some into Aimée's glass.

"A santé!" Morbier clinked her glass. She took a sip, full-bodied with a hint of oak

and berries. Nice.

"By the way, Edouard Brasseur didn't seem pleased that Mireille had run away after the nuns treated her so well at the clinic."

She choked, dabbed her mouth with the napkin. "She's gone?" Panic hit her.

"Another little detail you neglected to inform me about," Morbier said. His expression hadn't changed. "Edouard's statement makes interesting reading."

"His statement?" she said. "I don't understand. The *flics* raided his atelier this morning."

"I won't ask how you know, Leduc."

No doubt Edouard had put her in his statement. The slime.

"They had to stage a show to keep Edouard's cover in place," Morbier said, taking a long sip.

Wonders never ceased. She'd never suspected *this*.

"The Brigade Criminelle cooperates with Eurodad and similar agencies," he said.

"But Eurodad's based in Brussels. It brings cases before the International Court of Justice," she said. "What's the link?"

"Not my province." Morbier tore off a piece of bread and chewed it. "Where's your alleged sister, Leduc?"

Sister? After Castaing's revelation, she was no longer sure.

"Beats me. If Mireille's not at the convent, then I don't know."

"Why withhold information?" Morbier said. "What can a half-sister who you don't even know mean to you? All you need to do is tell me where she went."

"Mireille's been framed."

"Then she can make a statement. Furnish an alibi, prove her innocence."

"I'm worried, Morbier," she said. "I don't know any longer whether to believe we're related."

Morbier nodded. His look inviting confidences was the one he used during interrogations when he was playing the good *flic*. She trusted him no farther than she could spit.

"Then what are you sticking your neck out for?" Morbier said. "Why do this?"

She couldn't answer that. But since birth, Mireille had been a victim of violence, part of the flotsam and jetsam of Haiti's unrest, inconsequential to men in power like dictators and ministers, men who never dirtied their hands with the *les petits gens,* the little people. Mireille didn't deserve it. No one did.

"Still a Socialist Party member, Morbier?"

Morbier was a dyed-in-the-wool socialist, like his parents and grandparents before him.

He nodded. "And I vote Socialist in every election."

"Didn't you quote Fanon's *Wretched of the Earth* to me when I was still wearing diapers?"

"More like knee socks, Leduc," he said. "I'm glad you remember. But don't tell me she's a victim of the system. Murder's breaking the law, no matter what the excuse."

"Then tell me how it makes sense. Mireille had relatives in Benoît's village; he helped her."

"Relationships sour."

"That's all you can say? Physically, she's not strong enough to sever his ear. She had an accident in the sugar mill. I saw the scars on her arms."

Morbier looked down at his glass. "A distinguished ENS professor and world-renowned researcher's seen arguing with an illegal immigrant," he said. "He's murdered and she disappears."

"Too simple, Morbier. Other people wanted him silenced."

"Where's the proof, Leduc?" he said. "Give me something to work with. But you

436

can't, can you?"

She threw the napkin down and stood. "Excuse me a moment, Morbier," she said, pointing to the WC, a cubicle near the bar.

"Don't get any ideas about leaving, Leduc." He pointed in turn to the car parked in the street.

She wedged herself into a closet-like Turkish toilet complete with hanging chain, hole in the floor, and walls papered by peeling seventies posters of rock groups. She punched in René's number, pulled the chain. Over the flushing, she heard his voicemail recording.

Frustrated, she left him a message mentioning the Paris Club. Then she cupped her hands at the tiny sink, splashed cold water on her face, and wished she didn't feel naked without lipstick. She pinched her pale cheeks for color.

Back at the table, she found two plates of steak *haché* and golden brown *frites.* Morbier paused, fork embedded in a morsel of rare beef dripping with red juice.

What little appetite she still had now deserted her. She picked at the white bread, molding the bits together.

"Et alors?" Morbier said. "You did that as a child, too."

"What?"

"Pulled out the white part of the baguette and sculpted little figures."

She dropped the crumbs, stared at him. "What's this lunch really about, Morbier?"

Morbier lifted his wine glass to hers. "*Salut.* It's your saint's day, Leduc. Saint Ame."

He'd remembered. She'd been named after a Benedictine monk from Grenoble who founded a monastery, became a hermit, and died in 630 A.D. Could she help it that in the hospital, her mother had stuck her finger on the calendar and saw Saint Ame, saying "Ame; that sounds like love" . . . and she could pronounce it . . . Amy.

"As your godfather, it's one of my duties, Leduc," he said. "Another is to protect you, if you let me."

"Edouard shares a saint's day with Benoît," she said. "So that's his involvement, right? It's personal to him."

"Ask him, Leduc."

The smells of grilling meat, of people crowded into the low-ceilinged room were getting to her. The murmured conversations, clink of glasses.

"Commissaire?" A hesitant blue-uniformed *flic* stood at their table. "The Brigade chief called. He needs you out in Meudon near the Observatoire."

Morbier stared with longing at his half-eaten steak. "Another sighting of that damned Fiat Uno in the suburbs?"

The *flic* nodded and turned his cap over in his hands.

Morbier set a wad of bills on the table, pulled the napkin from his collar, and wiped his chin.

"Meanwhile, they're waiting to question you, Leduc." He shrugged. "Look, I tried."

"Tried, Morbier?" she said, clenching the napkin in her fist.

"Officer, wait for me outside."

The *flic* took off to the waiting car. Beyond lay the bell tower of medieval Saint Etienne du Mont. Cloud wisps hovered in the night sky.

"My influence extends only so far. The Brigade's on my neck, Leduc. Help me out, and yourself too. Explain to them. Get Mireille to give a statement. My Immigration contact can work something out if she's innocent."

Here it came. A deal. She smelled it.

As always, he'd make her work for it.

"Don't tell me your Immigration contact's interested in helping a murder suspect with motive and opportunity who's in hiding, as you reminded me?"

"He's in line for promotion," Morbier said and shrugged. "And the ambitious type. The traffickers give his division a bad name. But if Mireille identified them and testified against them, a deal's likely."

Mireille might even agree to it.

And if she didn't play along with Morbier, she had no chance of finding the real killer. "You're right, Morbier," she said. "Mireille's desperate; she'll try to contact me. But what good will it do if I'm being held at the Prefecture? Buy me some time."

He grimaced. "You don't want much, do you?"

"We had time for this bistro," she said. "What's a few hours? Fend the Brigade off. You're going to the suburbs. What's the difference?"

"Got something up your sleeve, Leduc?"

"I won't know until I try. And I need your help." She stood and pushed her chair in, then embraced him, kissing him on both cheeks, something she hadn't done in a long time. She felt his rough cheeks, smelled the same aftershave her father had used, saw his graying hair curling behind his ears.

"Please, Morbier," she whispered in his ear. "You know she's innocent. No one will blame you if I do this. Just say we met later."

"I can't, Leduc," he said.

"But you can," she said. "You're a Divisional Commissaire now."

She felt his shoulders tighten.

"And it's my saint's day. Call it my present, Morbier."

She pulled away and saw Morbier's red face. Morbier, blushing? She heard the engine start. The *flic* had put the flashing light on the car roof.

"Morbier, I promise."

He glanced at his watch.

"Two hours, Leduc. Don't disappoint me."

The *flic* stood, wide-eyed, in the doorway. She picked up her bag.

"Looks like we've given him something to talk about, Morbier."

"All the way to Meudon, Leduc."

She quickened her step and hit the street.

A breeze kicked up on rue Toulier. She ran past the infamous Carlos the Jackal's hiding place in the seventies. Now it was just a nondescript fawn-colored building. Carlos, during routine questioning in the doorway, had shot three *flics.* And that's what had nailed him, in French eyes. No matter how grave his acts of worldwide terrorism, it was the shooting of French *flics* that had ensured him the lifetime sentence he was serving in Clairvaux.

She felt uneasy at Morbier's conversation,

the lack of his usual probing questions. Was it the wine, or his fatigue? Looking back, he'd let her go too easily.

She turned around to look for a police tail. A long-haired man, wearing a knotted scarf and stylish rumpled jacket, gesticulated to another standing in a small bookshop doorway. The Latin bookstore she'd shopped at in her Sorbonne days. The long-haired man said "Impossible. Kant and Heidegger, two divergent German philosophers. . . ."

Just two *intellos* in passionate discussion. Where else but here in the Latin Quarter, she thought.

She checked her watch. Not much time. She headed to rue Buffon.

En route, her cell phone rang. Professeur Zarek's caller ID was displayed. She winced.

"*Allo,* Professeur."

"Aimée, Sister Dantec had visitors," said Professeur Zarek.

"I heard. Where's Mireille?"

Aimée held her breath, afraid of the answer.

"Sister Dantac works her magic in many ways. Full of surprises. For now, don't worry."

"What do you mean?"

"Why, Mireille's wearing the habit, a ripe

442

convert." A child's voice sounded in the background . . . *"Grand-mère!"*

A habit. Perfect disguise. No one looked at nuns.

Aimée relaxed. "Please, tell Mireille we have to talk."

"Must go," Professeur Zarek said. Before Aimée could ask more, the professor ended the call. Another call came through; she heard René's voice.

"Aimée, I netted the Aèrospatiale contract," he announced.

She heard the pride in his voice.

"Fantastic, René!"

"Just waiting on your signature and one from the bureau chief." René paused. "But what's going on, Aimée?"

He deserved to know. And he could help her.

"Didn't you get my message? Castaing's protected by the Ministry. This World Bank funding proposal will pass."

"What's that got to do with Mireille?"

"If Mireille's the prime homicide suspect, it makes things easier for some people. I've got two hours before the Brigade questions me," she said. "That's why I asked your help to dig into Castaing's firm, Hydrolis, and its relationship with the World Bank.

Didn't you get my message about the Paris Club?"

"Two hours? Go home, work on your laptop," René said. "It's safer. *Mecs* attacked you. Next time don't count on being so lucky."

She turned into the breeze whipping down the street. "But I need the other pieces of the puzzle, René."

René cleared his throat. "Paris Club. Talk about big shots. I found out that Benoît submitted a paper to them last year. Give me a bit longer."

Excited, she walked faster now. "*Merci,* René. I knew you'd help."

"Only if you promise you'll be careful, Aimée."

"Done."

She hoped René could link Castaing's firm to the bigger players, expose Hydrolis as a provider of toxic water.

Evening shadows sculpted the crumbling walls of rue Buffon. Aimée saw two *mecs* in bomber jackets standing in a doorway, the *mecs* she'd seen outside the café. The big one jerked his thumb in her direction.

Cold fear gripped her.

She backed up, turned, and ran straight into a uniformed *flic* on patrol.

"In a hurry, Mademoiselle?"

444

Friday Evening

At her office desk, Léonie tightened the rubber strip above her elbow, swabbed her arm with alcohol, and reached in her bag for the syringe. Her hand came back with a bank statement, her wallet, checkbook, lipstick. But no retroviral ampoule.

Perspiration beaded her brow. Castaing's men! The damned thugs had shaken her, knocking her bag to the floor in the scuffle. Her medicinal injection was gone.

She heard loud, insistent knocking on her office door.

"Léonie?" A man's voice.

She steadied herself against her desk. Her supply was gone and she had no time to reach the clinic doctor. Her bones ached; chills racked her body.

"Just a moment." She found matches and with trembling hands lit the candle to Saint George. Then she turned the statue to reveal his other side, Ogoun the warrior. She bowed her head in prayer.

The door burst open.

Léonie raised her gaze and took in the *mec.* Polo, they'd called him. Polo's stocky frame filled out a leather bomber jacket. She saw his dead flat eyes. And called on Ogoun's spirit.

"I'm praying, can't you see? What's so

important that you can't wait for me to open the door?"

Polo hesitated, uneasy. One more used to following orders than thinking. "Monsieur Castaing told me to say 'The file's in the right hands.' "

So they had taken Benoît's file from the detective's bag. The woman had been about to give it to her; she'd sensed it. But now Castaing had it and would use it. Just like his father, the bastard!

"What's his hurry?" She blew out the candle. Smoke rose as she muttered a prayer.

"He's gone."

She dropped her hands. "But we were supposed to go together."

"Not according to my instructions," Polo said.

Castaing had planned all along to shut her out of the meeting. Why hadn't she anticipated this? Now she couldn't confront him, either to blackmail him or to negotiate with him.

She reached for the dossier on Castaing that Royet had messengered over. Royet, in his role in the World Bank, understood "negotiations." But it was worth nothing if she couldn't confront Castaing before the meeting began.

"*Bon. You'll* take me to the meeting then."

"Monsieur Castaing left me no such instructions, Madame."

"It seems you're unaware that he and I are doing the meeting presentation together, young man." She summoned the little strength she had in reserve. "Bring the car to the door."

"But he said —"

"Do you want to keep your job, young man?"

He looked unsure. "I need to check."

She could not permit this.

"Get me my coat, first, would you?" she said. Léonie reached into her desk drawer and palmed the keys. "It's in the closet."

"I'm not sure about this," he said, rocking back on his scuffed loafers.

"Help an old woman, won't you?" She summoned a smile, gestured to the tall door flush with the carved woodwork. "I'm cold."

Polo opened the closet. "There's just boxes in here."

"Sorry, my coat's hanging in the back," she said. "Can't you see?"

But Polo's answer was muffled by the slam of the closet door and its click as she locked him in.

Castaing figured he'd sewn it up. Not as long as she had a breath left in her body.

She grabbed her cane, touched her juju, and walked out the door.

Friday Evening

"You're sure it's those two, Mademoiselle?" The earnest blue eyes of the young uniformed *flic* assessed the men coming down the street. Then focused on the bruise on Aimée's arm.

Them or Castaing's other minions. It didn't much matter to Aimée. They'd block her access to the lab.

"They stole my bag, Officer!"

"I've radioed for backup," he said.

"But if you don't hurry, they'll get away."

One of the big-shouldered *mecs* halted on the pavement. Unsure.

"That's him!" Aimée accused.

By the time the officer had read him his rights, cuffed him, and led him to the arriving police car, she was long gone.

This time she skirted the laboratory building entrance, keeping to the shadows. Past the crumbling walls with drains and wires snaking to the roof. Through the lighted windows, she saw the dinosaur skeletons hanging from the rafters. She smelled the wild lilac scent, which had mingled with the metallic tang of Benoît's blood. The image of his sprawled body, his severed ear, played in her head. She forced herself to keep going. Gravel and fallen leaves crunched beneath her feet. She peered in the windows of the modern laboratory where Benoît and Huby had worked. A strip of fluorescent lighting shone above the cabinets. She tried Dr. Severat's number.

No answer.

The lab doorknob didn't turn. Locked. She crept around the side of the building. An orange plastic barricade stood at the rear, the only evidence of yesterday's flooding.

The laboratory van was parked with its back doors open, revealing stacked wooden crates.

"Time for a beer, eh?" a man said, grinding his cigarette out in the gravel. He shut the van doors. Footsteps crunched on the gravel, walking away. One of the double lab doors had been left ajar.

She climbed the ramp, entered the building, and found herself in a supply room with high shelves lined with chemicals and beakers. Not here, she thought, and opened the next door. Chrome and stainless-steel counters gleamed under the fluorescent lights.

She heard the discreet hum of the ventilation system and a low whirring.

She tried Huby's office door handle. Locked. Back near the built-in cabinets, she saw light under the door to a storeroom.

Inside, she saw crates and more crates against the yellowed moisture-stained plaster walls. Tools, ropes, and cords hung from a ledge. A small red light blinked from the gray intercom panel laden with dust protruding from the wall. On it, buttons were labeled: LAB 1, LAB 2, CENTRAL OFFICE. They'd remodeled the state-of-the-art lab, but not this long walk-in storeroom leading God knew where.

Her gaze rested on the legend on the box, "HYDROLIS PORT-AU-PRINCE RESEARCH SPECIMENS — KEEP COOL." A triangle with an "H," the Hydrolis logo, was stenciled in black on several of the crates. A packing slip, dated Monday, with a signature she deciphered as Benoît's, was attached to them. But inside lay styrofoam forms, packing straw, and nothing else. Empty.

A small refrigerator stood in the storeroom. She opened it and saw a specimen tray holding several sealed glass test tubes, containing brown pinkish matter in clear gelatin, labeled "PORCINE SAMPLES #6 FARM PORT-AU-PRINCE ENVIRONS" with an "H" in a small triangle in the corner. Again, the Hydrolis logo.

It was beginning to make sense. Here were the pig-tissue specimens Huby had shown her under the microscope on Tuesday. Benoît had received these tissue samples from Haiti on Monday.

What if he'd viewed these samples and analyzed them, but hadn't had time to write a proper report to corroborate his findings? Say he'd noted down his discovery of mercury and lead in the porcine tissue samples, and placed his notes in the file she'd found.

Instead of leaving them in the old lab in the adjacent building where he'd worked, Benoît had had the tubes sent here to protect them. Smart. His colleague Huby would have confirmed the toxicity in the samples, ignorant of the implication.

Saddened, she realized Benoît hadn't been smart enough. And not only he, but Huby too, had paid.

But she thought back to Huby's protestation that Benoît's murder was an accident, how he'd ducked her calls. Perhaps he *had* hoped to use Benoît's work for his own purposes. Academic rivalry, publish or perish, the vital path to a professorship and tenure?

Still, it didn't explain his death.

She made her way out of the storeroom

and to the dim, musty older gallery, ringed by a walkway halfway up the walls that gave access to wooden drawers. If only her lock-picking kit hadn't disappeared with her bag! She passed an old glass case with bone fragments labeled "Rhino pectorus, Euphrates Valley"; then she saw a screwdriver.

Back at Huby's office door, she jimmied the lock. She jiggled the screwdriver until she heard the lock tumble, held her breath, and tugged. She worked the screwdriver handle up and down with her shoulder, pushing the door, which finally gave way, ripping her jacket as she stumbled inside a dark office filled with file cabinets and a desk piled with papers.

She switched on the light and saw a file on the desk. It was stamped RESEARCH GRANT DENIED, dated Wednesday.

Had Huby counted on using Benoît's work in hopes of obtaining a research grant? Maybe the test tubes hadn't arrived in time, so his research grant had been denied. She opened the file, flipping the pages in the folder, but the subject was bovine studies and BSE, as it was in each of the next three folders she thumbed through.

It didn't connect. If Huby had had no personal interest in Benoît's discovery, he'd had no reason to murder him.

She turned off the light and closed the door. She had to take Benoît's test tubes before the staff returned.

She walked down the long corridor, made a left, and reentered the lab. Back in the storeroom, she opened the refrigerator door and slipped several tubes into her jacket pocket.

Hearing an unexpected sound, Aimée straightened up to see Dr. Severat, the anatomy research doctor, a brown-stained apron over her white lab coat.

"Nom de Dieu," Aimée gasped. "You gave me a fright!"

"But what are you doing here, Mademoiselle?"

Aimée's eyes traveled from the door to the test tubes in Dr. Severat's latex-gloved hands. Something was fishy here.

"I could ask *you* that, Dr. Severat," she said. "Don't you work in the next building?"

"Excuse me?" The woman adjusted the volume on the flesh-colored plug in her ear.

Dr. Severat's blond hair, silhouetted against the yellow storeroom light, formed a halo. Aimée noticed her frown, her flushed cheeks. An open plastic container of bleach and a few ammonia containers stood on the floor.

"I don't understand," Dr. Severat went on. "You don't work in Dr. Rady's department: I checked. Who are you?"

"Aimée Leduc. But —"

"You're snooping. Like the others."

Aimée began to perspire. The air was close and stale, and the bleach reeked.

"Why are you taking Professeur Benoît's test tubes?" Aimée asked.

Dr. Severat backed up. "You're mistaken. I'm doing control. All equipment must meet rigorous standards. We run a clean lab. Sterile."

"I thought you worked in a different department."

"Professeur Benoît's materials do not belong here," Severat said.

Protecting his work? Aimée didn't think so. Seeing the tubes in Dr. Severat's hands was adding to her uneasiness.

Aimée backed up against the wall and crab-walked her fingers up the fissures until she felt the protruding intercom. Grabbing a bit of braid hanging from her denim jacket, she pressed one of the buttons and lodged the braid to loop around it and keep it in the transmit mode. With luck, one of the workers would have returned and would overhear them.

"The Hydrolis logo on those tubes in the

refrigerator matches those from Haiti."
Aimée pointed to the triangle. But the tube
Dr. Severat held contained pinkish tissue. "I
think you're liquidating Professeur Benoît's
tissue samples, destroying the evidence."

Dr. Severat's mouth twitched.

"Like you destroyed Huby," Aimée said.
"You pushed him from the window because
he'd figured it out."

"Me? I'm a scientist."

No surprise or curiosity. And she hadn't
denied the charges.

Aimée had to keep her talking, hoping
someone would hear. Perspiration dampened her shoulder blades; the jacket clung
to her skin. Her bag with her Swiss Army
knife was gone. Her only evidence was the
tubes in her pocket.

"After you lost your hearing aid, it took
you some time to adjust to a new one, *non?*"
Aimée asked.

"This is my old one. The stupid cords get
in my. . . ." Dr. Severat stopped and stared
at Aimée. "What do you mean?"

"The cellist remembers seeing you with
Professeur Benoît at the Cluny concert on
Monday," Aimée said. "That's why I came
here. To ask you why you neglected to
inform the authorities."

"About attending a concert with my lover?

But that's my private life."

"And then you murdered him. That was not 'private.' "

"I tried to make Azacca understand," Dr. Severat said.

She blocked the lab door. Aimée's pulse raced.

"How much did Castaing pay you, Dr. Severat?"

"Pay me?" Her voice rose in surprise. "But why would he — ?"

"These tubes contain pig tissue tainted with lead and mercury, the proof that Hydrolis is supplying toxic water in Haiti," she said. "You're destroying these for Castaing. He counts on World Bank funding to keep Hydrolis running in order to continue to exploit the poorest country in the world."

"You're talking politics," Dr. Severat said coolly. "Not my metier."

"Politics?" Aimée said. Her eye caught on a double door at the rear of the long, narrow storeroom. The ammonia odor from the plastic jugs stung Aimée's nose. "What I know of politics could be wrapped around my little finger. But Benoît's evidence of lead and mercury would set off fireworks.

"As you're a scientist," she continued, "you know how much his research mattered to Benoît. Why, you told me yourself that it meant everything to him. For Haiti. A greater good, more important than —"

"Us," Severat interrupted.

The word chilled Aimée. Dr. Severat kicked the door closed behind her. The old wooden shelves rattled. The only light came from the bare hanging bulb. Shadows flickered over the fissured walls. Aimée stepped back.

The small intercom light blinked green. Weren't the workers back? Hadn't they heard? Where was the building's security?

"So you're destroying the evidence," Aimée said. She tried to keep her voice level. She had to keep this woman talking. "Like you destroyed Benoît and Huby."

"Trust you to make it sound pathetic," Dr. Severat said. "That story, how you were down and out, dependent on Dr. Rady . . . I believed it."

"Did you argue with Benoît after the concert?" Aimée prodded. "Was that it?"

"Look at me when you talk." Dr. Severat stepped under the hanging bulb. Her mouth pursed. An intermittent buzz issued from the hearing aid.

"All our plans . . . together at last, the new apartment finally, yet I meant nothing to him," she said, a catch in her voice. "He'd been seeing another woman. A woman consumed by the 'cause' they shared, he said. He was waiting for these 'important' samples; they would change everything. After the concert, he showed me his plane ticket to Haiti." A sob escaped her.

Benoît had spurned her.

"You loved him, I understand," Aimée said, moving toward the door, desperate to get out of this old storeroom. "Men! They never get it, do they? What a relationship means to us, how they get under our skin."

"And that Haitian slut, all he could talk about was how he had to help her." A look that could cut steel shone in her eyes. Her gaze rested somewhere in the distance. "She lied about me. I saw her."

"That's right, you read lips," Aimée said. "But they spoke *Kreyòl.* You couldn't understand that. Mireille didn't murder Benoît. But you told the *flics* they'd quarreled to implicate her."

"He made a pass at her. She was the one he trusted, that slut," she said, tears brimming in her eyes. "Why couldn't he trust me?"

"He hurt you."

"Azacca? Hurt me?" She shook her head, a tear trailing down her cheek. "No one ever made me feel the way he did. I didn't have to prove myself to him like I do here every day to keep my position. I thought you, of all people, would understand." She gave a short laugh. "Ten years in the lab, and I'm still under contract. Not like the others with tenure for life. Would they do that to a man?"

Aimée gestured to a wood carton. "You're trembling. Sit down."

Dr. Severat sat, still clutching a test tube. "With Azacca I could just be a woman," she said, her voice ragged.

Aimée could almost touch the light switch on the wall above her. If she could just inch closer and switch the light off, she could make a break for the other door. Her foot struck a cobweb-covered bottle near the bleach container.

"Maybe you didn't mean to kill him," Aimée said, her tone soothing. "But after he was dead, you recalled that Benoît had survived Duvalier's rule; he had spoken of the terror the tonton macoutes spread through the countryside and in his village. So you tried to make his death look like a tonton macoute reprisal. For you, it was easy: you're an anatomy expert. But with that circle of salt, you made a mistake."

"Do you think I got to my position by making mistakes?" Her eyes flashed. The woman's moods seesawed from moment to moment. "I don't make mistakes," she insisted.

But she had. Frantically, Aimée's fingers traveled higher on the cracked wall.

"He hurt you to the core, I understand," Aimée said. "You'd believed him. But he'd lied to you."

"It took all my savings to buy the apartment and furnish it with the things he liked," she said. "Then I took out a loan to pay for our honeymoon cruise. But he pulled away —"

"You couldn't have that, could you?" Aimée agreed. "Yet the guard, why kill him?"

"That meddling fool saw me leave the gatehouse!" Dr. Severat exclaimed. She sighed. "And Huby, who couldn't get a grant to save his life, hid Azacca's work."

Aimée remembered Severat's damp hair, her dripping raincoat when they met in the ENS lobby not twenty minutes after she'd found Huby's body. "So you shoved him from the window —"

"I couldn't have him discovering Benoît's results."

"It would raise questions?" Aimée asked. "Eyes might focus on the lab. Or you."

"I located these tubes myself," she said as if Aimée hadn't spoken. Another little sigh.

"You know the saying: give a job to a busy person if you want it to get done."

The muffled honk of a horn came from the back of the building. The lab workers, at last. Aimée hit the light switch, plunging the storeroom into darkness. Aimed for the door and kicked it open. And ran out.

The dim gallery shone in ghost-like light. Dissection instruments and bones littered the long tables. Sprinting forward, her heel caught in a wood slat. And she was falling.

Not now . . . she couldn't . . . she had to reach the. . . .

She stumbled into the glass-fronted wooden cabinets, knocked down the mounted human skeleton. The cabinet crashed, shattering glass. Yellowed bones cracked and skittered across the floor. She reached to pull herself up, but she was wedged between the fallen cabinet and the wall. A ripping sound filled her ears. And then her ankles were grabbed and duct tape wrapped around them, tight.

Dr. Severat shook her head. Shrugged. "Whenever people agree with me, I feel I must be wrong." Her voice sounded removed, vacant. "Oscar Wilde said that, but don't you agree?"

Aimée had been caught and trussed like a pig. Her hands scrabbled over the floor. Her fingers came back bleeding, gripping shards of glass and bone slivers.

"What are you doing? The lab workers —"

"Never enter this area at night," Dr. Severat interrupted. "Let's see." Dr. Severat tapped her finger on her chin, glancing over the long table as if checking out items in a store display. "I think I'll use these surgical bone-cutting pliers first." She pointed to a pair of long steel pliers glinting in the light. "I can render you unconscious later."

"Stop . . . you're crazy!"

"Shhh!" Dr. Severat knelt, holding the pliers mere centimeters from Aimée's bound ankles.

So close, she could have spit in her face.

"Don't move, please. Just cooperate. Otherwise, if I make a jagged cut through tendons, muscles, and bone, the pain will be excruciating."

"Cooperate?"

Aimée jabbed the pointed glass shards she held straight into Severat's palm. Severat gasped in pain, her grip loosened, and she fell sideways. Aimée sawed at the duct tape lacing her ankles, frantically trying to break free.

Then hands, sticky with blood, gripped her throat, choking her from behind. She couldn't breathe.

Summoning her last bit of strength, she dropped the glass pieces and jabbed her elbows back as hard as she could.

Severat sprawled against the lab counter, moaning, clutching her ribs.

Aimée struggled to pull herself up with her ankles bound. She grabbed the wires of Severat's hearing aid and knotted them around Severat's wrists. For the moment it would do.

Severat struggled, her eyes wild. "I can't hear!"

"You're big on cooperation. Try it," Aimée said. With the bone pliers she cut through the duct tape around her ankles. She bit her lip as she tore the tape from her skin. Ripping part of Dr. Severat's apron into strips, she staunched the wound in Severat's hand, then passed them around Severat's ankles and tied them across her quivering mouth. That done, Aimée applied a strip to her own fingers to stop their bleeding.

She took the test tube and the cell phone from her pocket.

"What's the matter with Dr. Severat?" A worker in a blue workcoat stood open-mouthed at the door. The sound of the van's diesel engine came from outside.

Aimée's legs shook. Blood trickled from her fingers.

"Didn't you hear the intercom?"

The man ran to the prone woman. "Dr. Severat's bleeding."

"She's probably broken a rib, maybe two."

"I don't understand." The man's breath stank of beer. He reached for the wall-mounted phone. "Who are you?"

Her hands shaking, she tried to punch in Morbier's number on her cell phone. But her fingers didn't work, her legs buckled, and the floor kept sliding until it came up to meet her face.

The quai's streetlamps were reflected by the dark Seine below. A lighted barge passed under the Pont Saint Michel. Aimée blinked, light-headed, as she looked out the ambulance window. The yawning entrance of the Hôtel Dieu's emergency entrance appeared.

"Park at the elevator. Log this in for me, eh? I'll take her to the sixth floor, the police medical facility," said the attendant beside her.

Fluorescent light illuminated the barred windows, the scuffed metal benches, the worn linoleum. Stale air laced with antiseptic filled the long hallway. Like any medical facility, Aimée thought; the police wing was no better.

An hour later, after a medical examination, she sat in the *"dépôt"* by the holding cells. In the "temporary" prison, underground, she awaited interrogation, faced with a twenty-four-hour detention period while the magistrate assembled evidence, based on which he'd either charge her or release her.

Two uniformed *flics* had ushered Dr. Severat between them and turned her over to a nun, recognizable by the short blue veil pinned on her head and her blue smock and thick support hose. Since the nineteenth century, *les religeuses* had staffed the women's section of *"le dépôt."* Aimée waited a long while before the intake officer, a fortyish woman with short black hair under her blue cap, called her.

"ID?"

Aimée set Severat's hearing aid down in the revolving glass window.

"Some kind of joke?"

"That's all I have. My bag was stolen. But if you call Commissaire Morbier —"

"What's this?"

"Dr. Severat's deaf. It's her hearing aid."

"I can't accept personal property before she's processed," the officer said.

"She reads lips, but —"

"I'll request the sign language officer," she

interrupted. "Regulations, Mademoiselle. You're to proceed to interrogation at Quai des Orfévres."

A sinking feeling hit Aimée in the pit of her stomach.

"It's your lucky night," said the *flic* who escorted her. "We're taking the shortcut." The shortcut consisted of a long dank tunnel running under the Tribunal, a private passage reserved for the Préfecture de Police.

After being interrogated and giving a statement, Aimée still sat on a metal bench, waiting. It was an hour before the door of an interrogation room opened and Morbier emerged, rubbing his neck.

"Severat's pleading that Benoît's murder was a crime of passion," he said.

Alarmed, she shook her head. "Three murders — ?"

"Steal one egg and you end up robbing the henhouse, eh?" Morbier interrupted. "A unit's searching her apartment and office and the lab. You left a messy trail, Leduc."

"I tried to be neat, Morbier," she said, "but I forgot my gloves." She stood, glad of the painkillers she'd been given. "Then I can go?"

"I need to question Mireille," he said once more.

She'd hoped it wouldn't come to this. She tried to control the shaking of her bandaged hands, couldn't, and stuck them in her jean pockets.

"Dr. Severat confessed. What more do you need?"

"My Immigration contact is persistent, Leduc."

"He wants a feather in his cap, right?" she said. "Two traffickers were rounded up at the rue Saint Victor false fire alarm last night. The traffickers kept a nice collection of false passports, papers, the lot. They're the kind who talk to save their hide. Squeeze them and they'll give you info on the trafficking ring."

She couldn't save the illegals, but she could save Mireille.

"And you're just telling me now, Leduc?"

"Haven't had time, Morbier. It's simple; I'll explain it. But first may I use the fax in that office?"

"Why?"

"René's ready to send over the links to Hydrolis's system," she said. "Expect some interesting and incriminating reports."

"You don't give up, do you?"

"Just read the reports. Then decide."

Inside the nearest office, she jotted down the number, then punched in René's line.

"Okay, René. 01 44 76 09 39." She glanced at the overflowing ashtray, half-full cup of coffee, and the nameplate on the desk. Roloff. The Commandant who'd headed the inquiry into her father's police corruption case. For a moment her heart thudded.

"Mark it 'Attention Commissaire Morbier' and do a cover sheet," she said. *"Merci."*

She hung up.

"It won't work, Leduc."

She sat in the brown leather swivel chair behind the desk, exhausted.

"What won't work?"

"Mireille."

"Morbier, there's no proof of Mireille's arrival in France, no stamp on a passport, no entry logged in the Immigration computer. She's not here." Aimée rubbed her head. "She'll evaporate. Like smoke. Belgium has room in their quotas for Haitian asylum-seekers. I checked."

Morbier loosened his tie. "Do you count on help from Edouard Brasseur?"

"A fellow Haitian employed in a large human-rights organization? He'll find her a job. She's a trained accountant."

"That's your deal, Leduc?"

"It works for everyone, Morbier," she said. "Think about it."

Morbier stared at her with a look she couldn't fathom. Then a grin erupted on his tired face.

"You look at home in that chair, Leduc," Morbier said. "Like you belong here."

She stiffened. The memory of her father's hearing that had taken place on the second floor had never gone away. The false stink of corruption still assailed her nostrils, the odor that had tainted his career and forced him to resign from the Force he loved.

"Not me," Aimée said, standing. "You know I don't like taking orders, Morbier."

She paused at the door. Sheets of paper had begun to emerge from the fax machine. "You'll see that those go to the right person, won't you? And this."

She placed Benoît's test tubes on the desk. "Don't worry. Others were messengered to the IMF *chargé d'affaires* and to Léonie Obin at the Haiti Trade Delegation."

"You think this will do any good? I want to help, but word came down from the top."

"And let Benoît's work count for nothing?" she said. "Read tomorrow's *Libération*. A half-page exposé of Hydrolis and its World Bank funding application, with facts and figures. I don't bet, but I'll wager you a franc it opens eyes."

"And knocks Diana off the front page?"

"It's only third page. Plus an editorial."

Morbier sat on the edge of the desk. He scraped a wooden match on the desk leg, lit an unfiltered Gitane, and blew a plume of smoke. "I'm getting too old for this, Leduc."

"Me too," she said. Taking the cigarette from him, she took a long drag.

Morbier stared at her hands. "You okay, Leduc?"

"My head hurts and I miss my dog." She handed him back the cigarette. "And I hate wearing tank tops."

Morbier stared at her. His red-lidded eyes drooped.

"Are you going to tell her?"

"You mean tell Mireille who her father was?" Tired, she paused at the doorframe in thought, then shrugged.

Saturday Noon

Aimée read the DNA result from the Laboratoires Sytel, DNA *specialistes.* Then she read it again. Light slanted over the mail piled on her office desk. The smell of sawdust and fresh-cut lumber hovered in the air.

"We framed the wall and installed support beams," Cloutier said, shouldering his tool bag. "On Monday we'll sheetrock and paint. Then we're all finished."

He seemed to be in a hurry.

"Have a good rest of the weekend, Cloutier," she said. "And thanks for coming in on Saturday."

"You, too," Cloutier replied. Then he suddenly halted his progress through the doorway. "Pardon, Mademoiselle. I mean 'Sister.' I didn't see you."

Aimée looked up. A tall nun stood in the doorway, a canvas travel bag in her hand.

"I wanted to say good-bye, Aimée," Mireille said.

Aimée's heart skipped. Mireille walked into the office. Her long black habit trailed on the floor, the stiff white wimple framing her honey-colored face. "Edouard's waiting in the car. Impossible to park — the traffic, you know — but if you'll come down. . . ."

"*Non,* it's all right," she said. "Please tell him thank you for me."

"Cloutier's done marvels here in the back room — *Merde!*" René, just coming through the door, stopped in his tracks. "Oh! *Excusez-moi.*" His face reddened. "Sister, I didn't know. . . ."

Mireille smiled. "I'm only dressed this way."

"Aren't you going to introduce us, Aimée?"

"Mireille, meet René, my partner."

471

René blinked and stared.

Mireille took a step forward. "I think you were right, Aimée."

"What do you mean?"

Mireille set down a copy of *Libération* on Aimée's desk opened to an article headlined "Hydrolis CEO Jérôme Castaing implicated in World Bank funding proposal scandal."

"That maybe I was in the wrong place." She gripped Aimée's hand in her warm ones. "Family takes time, *non?* This Castaing contacted me, but I don't feel ready. He says we're related."

Aimée looked down. And when she looked up Mireille had gone. Her footsteps echoed on the staircase.

"So that's . . . your half-sister?" René asked.

She stared at the DNA results. "Not according to this."

René rocked back on his heels. "Are you all right?"

"Fine." But she didn't feel fine.

René closed the folder on his desk, glancing at his watch. "I've got an appointment. We'll talk later. Dinner?"

And burden him more? "Go celebrate landing the Aèrospatiale contract with Saj."

He smiled. "You mean, order in and then put our feet up?"

She saw him rubbing his hip.

"Don't tell me, René!"

"Eh?"

"You're finally going to see that doctor," she said.

"You could say that," René answered, his eyes evading hers.

"About time, René."

She noticed what looked like a package half-covered by plastic sheeting under René's desk.

"Did Cloutier forget something?"

René was taking his linen jacket from the coat rack. "What?"

"I'll call him and check." She bent and lifted the plastic, revealing a brown metal box. "What's this?"

"That?" René fingered his goatee. "Something he found in the wall."

"You mean from before my grandfather's time?" She shook her head. "Open up a wall in Paris and who knows what you'll find."

She looked closer.

"But it's not very old," she said. "It's a safe, looks like from the seventies."

"Forget it for now, Aimée." René leaned down. "I meant to store it in the back. We can go through this clutter later."

Curious, she leaned closer. "René, the door to this safe is broken."

"Cloutier said he didn't mean to damage it," René told her. "He had no idea it was there until his sledgehammer cracked it open."

A breeze ruffled the papers on her desk.

"Then why didn't he tell me himself?"

Inside the safe she saw a bundle of envelopes rubber-banded together.

"You're a bad liar, René. You read them, didn't you?" Angry, she took them out.

"Aimée, I meant to tell you, but with all that's happened. . . ."

"If they concern Mireille, you should have!"

"Not Mireille," René said.

She saw a canceled American stamp on an envelope addressed to Mademoiselle Aimée Leduc in a childish scrawl.

A frisson raced through her. "From my mother?"

René stared at her. "Your brother."

ACKNOWLEDGMENTS

Many, many thanks go to Rico; Lillian; Grace; Diane; Marion Nowak, *la magnifique;* Dot; Barbara; Jan; and Max; Don Cannon; Susanna von Leuwen; Elaine Taylor; Leonard Pitt; Lauren Haney and the ever knowledgeable Dr. Terri Haddix.

The opinions here in no way reflect on the wonderful philanthropic work or the political stance of those working for equality, justice, democracy, and literacy in Haiti. On the Haitian front, gratitude goes to the very generous Margaret Trost; journalist Wadner Pierre; Pierre Labossiere; Louissant Bellot and Camille Christian; and Ben Terrall. Also, Michael Geller; Mellen Candage and *les anonymes* at the World Bank.

In Paris, many thanks to Vassili Silovic for that late afternoon espresso, the fossils and inspiration; Diane Cribbs; Elise Munoz, *une vrai amie* in the rain; Laura Sumser; Donna and Earl Evleth *toujours;* Pierre-Olivier *encore toujours;* Anne-Françoise; *la petite* Zouzou; Sarah Tarille, *la extraordinaire;* attorneys Pierre and Leila Djebrouni; Carla Bach; Monsieur Fernand of the café on rue Feuillantines who keeps the stories alive; Gilles Thomas for the underground explorations; Jean-Claude Mulés — Retired Commissaire Brigade Criminelle and Cathy Etile — Police Judiciare.

And nothing would happen without James N. Frey; Linda Allen; Laura Hruska; my son Tate, and Jun.

ABOUT THE AUTHOR

Cara Black lives with her husband, a bookseller, and their son in San Francisco. She frequently travels to France. This is her ninth mystery in the Aimeé Leduc series, for which she has twice been nominated for an Anthony Award.

We hope you have enjoyed this Large Print book. Other Thorndike, Wheeler, Kennebec, and Chivers Press Large Print books are available at your library or directly from the publishers.

For information about current and upcoming titles, please call or write, without obligation, to:

Publisher
Thorndike Press
295 Kennedy Memorial Drive
Waterville, ME 04901
Tel. (800) 223-1244

or visit our Web site at:

http://gale.cengage.com/thorndike

OR

Chivers Large Print
published by BBC Audiobooks Ltd
St James House, The Square
Lower Bristol Road
Bath BA2 3SB
England
Tel. +44(0) 800 136919
email: bbcaudiobooks@bbc.co.uk
www.bbcaudiobooks.co.uk

All our Large Print titles are designed for easy reading, and all our books are made to last.